CW00540149

At the close of the Old 1 ancient Hittite Empire is in has been assassinated in H: Assassin's Guild. Muwas blames the two sons of the p........ he insists he be the successor. The two sons of Huzziyas insist the next king be Tudhaliyas, son of Himuili. Neither side is prepared to give way, and the scene is set for civil war. Tagrama, the High Priest of the temple of the Storm God Taru, tries to broker a peace, but is up against outright stubbornness.

Muwas then hires Harep, of the Assassin's Guild, to kill Tudhaliyas. Only Mokhat, the former priest to the Assassin's Guild, knows what Harep looks like, and he's had enough of the Guild's murdering ways.

Muwas calls upon his Mittani allies, who send Artatama with an army to Muwas' aid. The Kizzuwatna King Shunashura changes allegiance and sends an army to help Tudhaliyas. The Pharaoh Amenhotep II threatens to invade Mittani unless they pull their army out of Hatti. King Saustatar of the Mittani refuses.

When Tudhaliyas meets Nikal, he falls for this daughter of the Kizzuwatna king. They announce their engagement. Harep, the hired assassin, makes a number of attempts on Tudhaliyas' life, but is foiled. The major Battle of the Wide Plateau settles the civil war but in the mean time, Harap manages to kidnap Nikal.

Murder in Hattusas is the 1st Volume of the Hittite Trilogy. The protagonist, Mokhat, is in search of himself after his sordid ministrations to a bunch of murderers. It is a bronze-age thriller, which includes a romp through the Hittite landscape, a civil war, and chariots in battle. This is a tale of love and adventure set in the most fascinating recently discovered culture of the ancient world. Volume 2 is due for publication in February 2011.

A must for all fans of the Hittite civilisation.

𒉿𒐊𒈠𒐊𒉿𒐊𒐊 𒐊𒌁𒐊 𒐊𒐊𒐊𒉿𒐊𒐊𒌁𒐊

Murder in Hattusas

Sasha Garrydeb

London

2011

First published in Britain in 2010
by ABC Publishers
24 Treadgold Street London W11 4BP
e-mail: abcpublishers@ntlworld.com

Printed in GB by ABC Publishers

A CIP catalogue record for this book is available from the British Library.

ISBN 978-0-9548144-6-5

ABC Publishers,
Notting Dale,
London W11 4BP

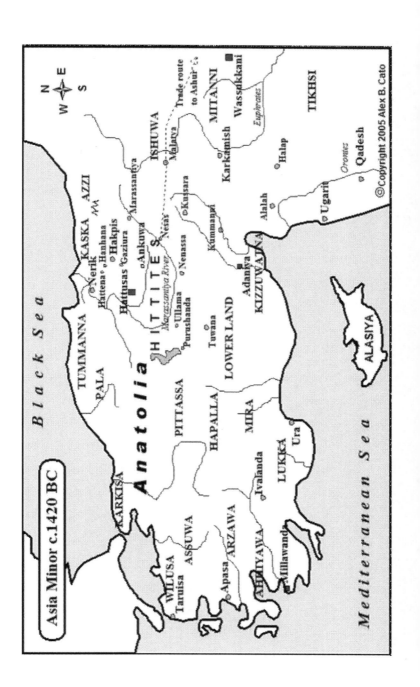

Asia Minor c.1420 BC

CHARACTER LIST (main characters in bold)

Muwatallis I (c.1422-1420 BC): elderly king assassinated

Muwas: brother/heir—the Gal Měsedi—contender for the black bull throne

General Ammuna: right hand to Muwas and commander of his army

Saustatar: king of Mittani and ally of Muwatallis

Artatama: son of Saustatar, a spitting image of his father.

General Satukani: commander of Artatama's Mittani army.

Huzziyas II (c.1444-1422 BC): king prior to Muwatallis.

Kantuzzili: elder son of Huzziyas and brother of Himuili

Himuili: younger brother of Kantuzzili

Tudhaliyas: 20, son of Himuili, contender for the throne.

General Zidanta: commander of Tudhaliyas' army

Tagrama: High Priest at the Great Temple.

Mokhat: priest, brother of Kasalliwa, spiritual advisot to Assassins' Guild.

Kasalliwa: king of the Kaska, and Mokhat's brother.

Palaiyas: Ahhiyawan mercenary. Son of the King of Tiryns.

Shunashura: king of Kizzuwatna and ally of Tudhaliyas.

Talshura: 17, twin brother of Nikal and son of Shunashura.

Nikal: daughter of the king of Kizzuwatna, in love with Tudhaliyas.

General Kirruwaiya: commander of the Kizzuwatna army.

Harep: third head of the order, hired by Muwas to assassinate Tudhaliyas.

Parap: impetuous younger brother of Rewa and Harep's nephew.

Rewa: Harep's bright nephew.

Pharaoh Amenhotep II: needs alliance with Tudhaliyas against the Mittani.

Merit-Amon: Queen Consort to pharaoh.

Tuthmosis: son of pharaoh

Prince Hapu, pharaoh's ambassador to Tudhaliyas bearing gifts.

Karaindash: King of Babylon

Ashurbelnisheshu: King of Assyria

Glossary

Cubit = 0.46m or 18 in. League = 5 km or 3 miles
The shekel was the state currency (named after the
Babylonian shekel)
> 40 mina = 1 shekel usually in copper or silver
> 2 weight mina = 1 Kg

Gal Mešedi = Chief of the King's Bodyguards

Ahhiyawa = Mycenae
Ahhiyawans = Mycenaeans
Alasiya = Cyprus

Keftiu = Crete

Millawanda = Miletus
Taruisa = Troy

karum is an Assyrian merchant's quarters
manes = spirits of the dead

Pharaoh Amenhotep II (1424-1401 BC)
Djat = First Minister to Pharaoh
Waset = Thebes
Mennufer = Memphis

Part of the Hittite King List

Old Kingdom
Huzziyas II (c.1444-1422 BC)
Muwatallis I (c.1422-1420 BC)

New Kingdom
Tudhaliyas I (1420-1400 BC)

Palaiyas **and** **Mokhat**

The Battle of the Wide Plateau

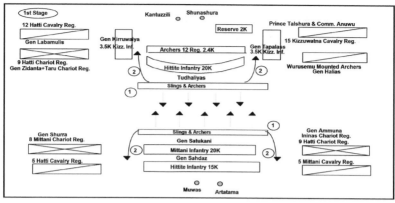

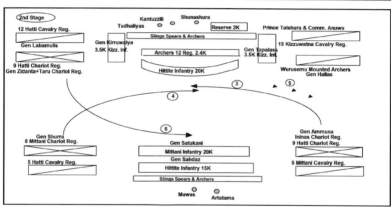

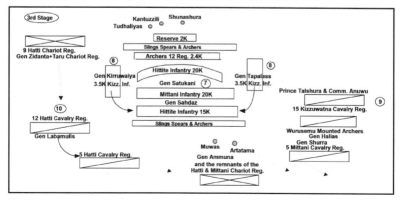

BACKGROUND

The story is set in the tumultuous period of the Hittite Empire, 1420 BC, in what is now Turkey, at the end of the Middle Kingdom and the beginning of the New. The events occur over a period commencing in close proximity to the spring equinox and conclude just after the midsummer solstice. The kings are real.

Chapter One

In the still time before dawn when the crispness of the cold squeezed the last dew drops from the night air, a figure enveloped in a thick dark cloak huddled tightly against the bottom of the grey fortifications. He remained silent, waiting for the sentry atop the lofty wall to complete his patrol and retreat back into the warmth of the watchtower. The Great Palace towering above the old city of Hattusas was protected by sheer granite cliffs to the east and north, while south and west, massive tall stonewalls topped by crenulations kept unwelcome interlopers at bay.

The intruder felt protected by the crisp moonless night, chosen specially for the task at hand. From beneath his rough woollen cloak bony fingers snatched a long stout rope wound in loops. A bronze hook swaddled in cloth swung on the end. Swiftly he moved from the wall and swung the hook rapidly in a circular motion with his outstretched right hand a number of times before propelling it powerfully upwards towards the top. The hook lodged amongst the crenulations and he scrambled up with an adeptness of a mountaineer.

Determined steely eyes looked around at the empty parapets, and he thanked the stars few of the guards braved the piercing winds of early spring—most had retreated into the warmth, waiting for daybreak. A deep pinkish purple in the eastern sky suggested this was nearer than he would have liked. Keeping low, he crept cat-like along the wall until he reached the watchtower, and then silently hurried down the spiral stone staircase to the bottom. Standing momentarily with his back to the base of the inner wall, he caught his breath, staring at the immense shadowy building housing the royal archive. The stillness felt deceptive, the darkness tangible. The day was soon to creep over the horizon and he, an uninvited visitor, had to be finished before then. He slid along the inner wall until he reached the door—slightly ajar. As promised.

He glanced to the far left where portal sculptures flanked the narrow corbelled arches of the citadel gates. They opened up into the lower paved courtyard holding stables, an armoury, various guardrooms and the official access to the upper palace proper. However, *he* intended using the unofficial access to the palace.

* * *

'How is his majesty this morning?' the tall chamberlain nodded to the bronze helmeted stern-faced bodyguards at the door. The two bodyguards, dressed in light green tunics, stood rigidly at attention, holding unsheathed long bronze scimitars at the ready.

'He's late getting up,' the larger of the two responded crisply. 'I've not heard a sound in there yet. It's a bit unusual for this time of morning.'

The chamberlain in his long sleeved amber shirt, pushed one of the servants, 'Go on—open the door—be *quick*!' Four other servants carried enormous trays laden with morning food. The door swung open and the chamberlain marched in—full of self importance. Servants hurried to open the heavy blue curtains and cedarwood shutters. The sun streamed into the room chasing away the night's shadows. The trays were set down and the breakfast table laid. Others made to light tinder in the fireplace. The anteroom to the bedroom bustled with activity while the chamberlain made for the bedroom door. Knocking on the cedar wood panel— he entered, as he did every morning. He froze in the doorway and his face drained of blood. '*Guards! Guards!*' he screamed in a high pitched voice. '*GUARDS!*'

The servants in the anteroom froze, ceasing their activity—fear spread through them. The chamberlain never raised his voice—*never*! The two Mešedi came in running, scimitars at the ready. The chamberlain pointed—to a dark cobra curled on the king's bed. The king lay with eyes open, staring into the afterlife. The queen was by his side and her face was petrified in fear—she had joined the king in the afterlife.

One of the bodyguards groaned in horror. They had failed to protect their king. The other bodyguard moved his long scimitar towards the snake. The ribs on the cobra's neck stretched into a narrow hood—the snake's head rose, alarmed and deadly. The menacing hiss preceded the spit—narrowly missing the guard's face. The guard brought his long scimitar down, managing to pin the four cubit snake against the white linen. His fear stricken partner quickly regained his composure, wielded his sharp scimitar and took its head off with one swift downward slash.

'Go get the Gal Mešedi—*NOW*!' the chamberlain commanded the bodyguards. 'And not a word to anyone. *Go*!'

The soldiers ran from the anteroom, footsteps echoing on the stone flags down the long grey corridor.

'No one leaves this room,' the chamberlain told terrified servants. He sat at the table his head in his hands, gently shaking with misery. The tension in the room was such that even a slight cough was all that was needed to make it explode.

A short while later more commotion was heard in the corridor and a stern faced Muwas, Chief of the Royal Bodyguards, the Gal Mešedi, came rushing in. 'What are my men babbling about? Who's dead?' he demanded angrily of the chamberlain.

'My Lord, I'm so sorry,' the chamberlain moaned. 'Your brother, King Muwatalli—is—dead.'

'*What*? How? Show me!' Fear, grief, followed by more anger flittered across the Gal Mešedi's face in quick succession. Both crossed to the bedroom. The Gal Mešedi brusquely pushed past the chamberlain and stared in horror at the scene confronting him. '*That...that...*,' he thundered pointing at the headless cobra, '*that is...ASSASSINATION!*' he shouted. 'I know the cowards behind this, may Taru curse their evil names!' The sight of his brother's open eyes, the pain of death still clearly visible, brought Muwas to silent tears. He walked to the old man's side and gently closed his eyelids. He then leaned over and closed queen Walanni's fear laden eyes. He simply couldn't comprehend how the assassin had managed to slip a cobra past his bodyguards. How could they do such a thing? His features hardened and his eyes took on a cruel glint. 'Where are the two Mešedi who were supposedly guarding the king?' Muwas' tone was menacing.

The older of the two bodyguards spoke, terror on his face, 'I...I...I was... mmm...with him,' he pointed at his nearby fellow bodyguard.

Muwas walked over to the man, his hand resting on his dagger. 'How *did* the assassin get a cobra past you if you were *guarding* him?' Muwas stared hard at the man's face.

'Nobody came past us...*nobody*...I *swear* your highness!'

'What! This is all an *illusion*? How dare you lie to me?' Muwas' fury exploded and he pulled his dagger and pushed it in hard below the man's ribcage, twisting the blade cruelly. The bodyguard's mouth opened but no sound came from it. He crumpled to the floor. A couple of steps and he used the same blade on the other bodyguard. 'This,' he announced loudly, 'is the way I deal with such lapses of duty —*and with LIARS*!' he shouted. Muwas turned away from the corpses and faced his brother, 'I call upon the Sun-goddess of Arinna, Wurusemu,' he vowed arms raised to heaven, long green sleeves hanging, 'Queen of the Land of Hatti, Queen of Heaven and Earth, mistress of the kings and queens of the Land of Hatti, to witness my curse. I shall not rest until those two sons of Huzziyas disappear from this land and their names are erased from all records. They shall be as "non-people." Never born—never *lived*!'

Somewhat late the chamberlain intervened, 'My Lord! No! You mustn't do this.'

'Quiet cur! Your work is finished. Leave me!'

'My Lord. This will mean civil war. Think again. I implore you!'

'I told you to leave! Are you deaf? The king is dead— he has no more need of a chamberlain.' Muwas glanced at his soldiers, then moved his eyes over the tall chamberlain. Without hesitation, they seized the indignant old man. 'Get rid of them as well,' he pointed at the cowering servants. 'Send for the physician—I want the king's death officially pronounced—*murder!*' He spoke to no one in particular, but his soldiers obeyed his every command. All were similarly dressed in light green tunics with kilt. Two evicted the seething chamberlain into the corridor. More removed the corpses of the two bodyguards. Some hustled out the terrified servants, others rushed to fetch the court physician. The anteroom slowly filled with Mešedi as rumours multiplied.

*   *   *

News spread fast throughout the palace. "The king is dead...the king is dead—*murdered*!" Along the grey corridors the whispers went—alarm spread to the kitchens... out into the brown earth courtyards. Officers changed sides. Oaths were sworn. Alliances furiously made. Soldiers looked at each other with suspicion. *Which side has he taken?*

Those taking Muwas' side, filtered through towards the part of the palace where the king lay, where the green clad Mešedi were congregating. Those against, were leaving the palace, heading south for the Yellow stronghold outside the city walls.

The news reached the marketplace—and the bustle increased. People began panic buying. These were unstable times. Sellers seized the opportunity. Prices escalated. As prices became too high to afford, people simply grabbed what they could from the stalls and ran. The market police were unable to cope. The mob—for that's what it was—went on the rampage, looting and settling scores. The market police sent for reinforcements. Troops arrived promptly from the palace and restored order brutally. Looters hanged on the spot. Others executed without recourse.

*   *   *

A young man's piercing eyes focused nervously at those assembled below, long dark hair falling over his cheeks. The long sleeves of his yellow shirt draped over the balcony. He could stand it no longer and began pacing like a caged tiger up and down the dark wooden gallery above the great hall of the Yellow Castle. Tudhaliyas was having his fate decided by the intrigues his father and uncle were forging amongst the army high council—but only with those who had chosen to attended his summons.

Junior clean shaven Generals reported to the grand hall and stood milling around talking in whispers. Prominent citizens in their everyday clothing, waited to offer advice and discover what fate lay in store for them. Merchants, ornately attired, sought reassurance that business would go on as usual. By mid morning, a steady stream of officers and soldiers made their way down towards the Yellow Castle. This citadel stood on a prominence outside the city walls of Hattusas, a thousand cubits south-west of the royal palace. The hereditary stronghold of the royal brothers, Kantuzzili and Himuili.

Tudhaliyas' father, Himuili, shorter than his brother, was working hard to have his son acknowledged as the next king of Hatti. To this end, he and his brother invited all those opposed to Muwas to come and swear allegiance to his son. Himuili raised his stout frame and insisted into the ear of one senior general, 'We are the legitimate heirs to the black bull throne—not that upstart Muwas.'

The seated general nodded, 'That's why I'm here, your highness. That's why I'm here.'

Kantuzzili and Himuili were royal princes in their own right, sons of the previous king, Huzziyas II, the one prior to Muwatalli I. Both sons were convinced Muwatalli had their father, Huzziyas, assassinated. But both would strenuously deny they had a hand in the death of Muwatalli. Kantuzzili, medium height and build, had invited the bald high priest of the Great Temple of the Storm God Taru, the weather god of heaven, situated one and a half thousand cubits west of the royal palace in the Lower Town, to endorse his nephew as the next king. But Tagrama had commanded both Muwas and the Kantuzzili faction to come to the Great Temple instead, to settle their dispute.

*   *   *

'A priest at the gates, your majesty, requesting your presence at the Great Temple,' the Watch Captain informed Muwas.

Muwas had also been summoned and he and his party emerged from the royal citadel and solemnly progressed west, through the streets and lanes of the Lower Town, watched by the townspeople, whilst another procession wound its way up from the Yellow Castle, along the wild stony path, towards the southern city gate. On a warm evening at sunset, two torchlight processions made their way towards the Great Temple of the Storm God Taru, situated to the west inside the walls of the Lower city. Both processions were heavily guarded by partisan lines of scimitar carrying soldiers. Tagrama's priests led both processions to the Great Temple under strict orders from the high priest to converge from different directions to avoid an early conflict.

The elderly cleric leading Muwas' green clad column guided it towards the eastern Temple entrance. The priest leading the Kantuzzili faction carefully guided his yellow clad charges to the southern Temple entrance. On reaching their destinations, soldiers of both factions remained outside. A group of priests interspersed themselves between the hostile soldiery, ensuring they stayed apart. Once through the elaborate rectangular central gateway, more of both parties remained behind and waited amongst the square piers supporting the roof. Standing with open arms under the stars in the main inner courtyard, waiting, the balding Tagrama watched the antagonists approach. Muwas striding out front led his senior general, Ammuna; followed by the two princes, Kantuzzili and Himuili.

'I greet you in the name of the Queen of the Land of Hatti, Queen of Heaven and Earth, mistress of the kings and queens of the Land of Hatti, directing the government of the King and Queen of Hatti,' Tagrama intoned.

Muwas waved away the greeting. 'Why delay?' he demanded, being in no mood for prolonged ceremonials.

'We must observe due ritual to the Gods,' the high priest replied in his altar voice. Tagrama knew if he wanted to have any chance of resolving this without bloodshed, he

8

would have to cool their tempers. Ritual always calmed people's passions, so he would drag the initial ceremony out as long as the divines allowed.

Muwas bit his tongue and let the skinny tall high priest attired in long white robes, continue.

Kantuzzili, clean shaven, auburn neck length hair falling on the collar of his long sleeved yellow shirt, smiled at the altercation and wished there was a way of prolonging it. Tagrama was irascible and unpredictable. This discord could only work to his faction's advantage.

'You must cleanse yourselves from all bloody deeds.' The old man led the way to the opposite end of the courtyard where a small freestanding shrine stood in one corner housing an underground pool used for ritual ablutions. He snapped his fingers and priests came forward to help them disrobe at the entrance.

Muwas surreptitiously removed something from his green robe and hid it in the palm of his hand.

One by one, the supplicants went down the stairs into the underground cleansing pool. As they emerged back up the steps, dripping holy water, priests held out white cloths so they could dry themselves. The same priests offered clean white robes for them to wear. They had little option but to accept. Thus, Tagrama managed to disarm all concerned without asking them for their weapons and dressed them in neutral priestly white. Kantuzzili's piercing intelligent eyes noticed the manoeuvre and added "wily" to "irascible."

'Now your *manes* will be more comfortable with what we are about to do.'

Muwas glared at the old priest with his dark eyes. 'This was found on my brother's breast!' He shoved a small cartouche bearing the sign of a black dragon in front of the old man's face.

Tagrama turned on Muwas, booming, '*You will wait until we have finished with the observances!*' Then more quietly, 'Even if you have no respect for the death of your king, try to show some respect for your Gods.' He scowled at Muwas with disgust.

The scowl had the desired effect stopping Muwas in his tracks. He reluctantly put the cartouche back into his white robes and followed the high priest through the square piers supporting the roof, into the innermost part of the temple, a structure built in granite rather than the usual limestone. Inside were the shrines of the deities of the temple. On approaching, they found before them on a low dais—the personification of the Weather God Taru, a black life-sized bull with precious metals adorning polished granite. On the left podium stood a gold-encrusted life-sized marble lion— the embodiment of the Sun Goddess of Arinna, Wurusemu.

Tagrama prostrated himself on the marble floor before the black bull, and lay silently for some time—then he began murmuring incantations. Muwas grimaced impatiently and shuffled his sandals to show annoyance. If Tagrama heard, he gave no hint of it. Finally after Muwas ceased his footwork, the priest arose. He motioned the party to follow him to a brightly coloured side room where a low wooden table had been set with food. Low couches surrounded the walls and all five settled themselves, the two factions facing; expressions grim.

'Now, may I have a look at that cartouche?' Tagrama asked Muwas, seating himself between the two factions.

Silently Muwas removed the dark brown piece of pottery and handed it to the high priest.

'Hmm! Illuyankas, if I'm not mistaken. And where did you say you found it?'

'Placed under his bed shirt, on the king's chest.' Muwas glowered at Kantuzzili—and the two brothers glowered daggers back at him.

The priest turned it over in his hands, scrutinising it. 'I wish we weren't—but I think we're all familiar with the misuse this image has been put to.' He held the oval piece of pottery up for all to see.

'As part of the *purulli* annual spring festival in the holy city of Nerik, our priests used to recite the tale of the Storm god's fight with the dragon Illuyankas. It's part of the New Year celebration for us where the victorious Storm God vanquishes evil. Yet the unholy Kaska have used,' he shook the piece of pottery, 'this symbol of evil to decorate the members of the Assassins' Guild.'

All those present tried to look suitably outraged—but failed.

Muwas interrupted, 'And that is proof—if it were *needed*—that my brother was assassinated!' He stared cold-bloodedly at Kantuzzili. 'In fact,' he decided to take the plunge, voice rising, '*I accuse THEM,*' he pointed at Kantuzzili and Himu ili, '*of hiring the assassins!*'

That was too much for Kantuzzili. He jumped up and shouted, 'And I accuse your brother, Muwatalli, of doing the same to our father, Huzziyas. If your brother was assassinated —then he harvested what he sowed.'

Muwas jumped up, dark shoulder-length hair flying and mindlessly grabbed for his sword—which of course was missing. He made to leap at Kantuzzili, but Tagrama quickly intervened, imposing his arms in between the two.

'*Is this why you were called here?*' he shouted. '*So you could FIGHT on holy ground?*' He looked as if he would strike them. 'You damned hot-heads! You would plunge the country into civil war at the flick of a horse's whip. You don't care how many die over your silly feuds. This has got to stop! You're on holy ground—in the temple of your Gods. How dare you behave like squabbling children?' Tagrama stared at both sides—forcing them back into their seats. 'Now here is what I propose,' Tagrama boomed at them. 'Neither faction is willing to step aside, I presume...?' he glared at the opponents as though the Storm God was within him.

Muwas shook his head, 'As the brother of my brother,' he stated defiantly, 'I intend to succeed him and thwart their plans to usurp the throne.'

'We do not intend the throne for ourselves,' Kantuzzili pronounced with false modesty, 'but will do all in our power to restore rightful descent, broken by the usurper Muwatalli. We, the sons of Huzziyas, step aside and propose Tudhaliyas as the rightful heir to the black bull throne.'

'*But he's the son of HIMUILI*,' shouted Muwas, 'and no different to themselves!'

'We will not, *cannot*, accept Muwas as successor! How can we think of rewarding assassination?'

'*I say this without proof*,' Tagrama raised his voice again, 'but *both* parties have employed unlawful means to seize power. If I had my way, *neither* would hold office. As it is, the kingdom is polarised. One of you will undoubtedly rule. I find it sad but inevitable. As an old man, devoted to the Gods, I wish for peace. To avert civil strife, I propose we consult the nobles.'

At the latter suggestion, a sharp intake of breath occurred by all those present.

Tagrama ignored this and continued, 'Let *them* decide who they wish for king. What say you? Do I have your word you will abide by a vote of the noble families of Hatti?' This solution was unacceptable to either side, having already decided to resolve the dispute on the field of battle. Yet they needed to show good will and pretend to make an effort to resolve matters without resorting to armed conflict.

Reluctantly, Muwas nodded his head in agreement and said deceitfully, 'Because of you, holy one, I will abide by the vote of the nobles.'

Voicing similar platitudes, Kantuzzili spoke for his side. 'Your words are wise and the will of Taru speaks through you. We also accept the will of the nobles.'

Tagrama was in no doubt that all he had achieved was a postponement of war. He blessed both sides for their wisdom in allowing a ballot. Then escorted the two belligerents to their respective exits. Sadly he watched both processions snaking their torch-lit ways back to their strongholds. He stood long under the stars, thinking, shaking his head, looking over the flat roofs of Hattusas. Covering his bald pate with the cowl of his priestly cloak he went back inside. He ordered his priests to start collecting all valuables from the temple precincts. They needed their precious artefacts taking somewhere safe until after the conflict to come. He expected the worst.

Chapter Two

'**W**e found him lying on his bed—rigid.' A sinewy Walhape told his companion.

'What? You mean poisoned?'

'It would seem so. Although how they managed to get it in him is beyond me.' Walhape poured a little more water onto the red hot coals. They were seated comfortably on wooden benches in a rough wood-panelled sauna. White steam rose in a sizzling gush, engulfing them with heat.

'That's a good one, "beyond even you," eh?' his mean faced companion laughed.

'Harep! It's no joking matter. We've not only lost the Head of our Order—but he was the best of us, or do you disagree?'

The two members of the Assassins' Guild were relaxing in the steam room deep inside the guild's grey fortress, a league outside the holy city of Nerik. After strenuous training, they looked forward to this meagre pleasure once a week.

'At least you're right there—he *was* the best!' The black dragon tattoo on Harep's medium build chest rippled as he belly laughed.

'Shush fool! Someone will hear you!' Walhape's bony features frowned worriedly. 'You never know who's listening outside.'

It did not do to make personal comments within earshot of others. The need for secrecy obsessed the assassins.

'D'you think it had anything to do with his last job?' Harep asked, still amused.

'How d'you mean? What last job? How d'you know who hired him? What d'you know I don't?' A crafty twinkle developed in Walhape's dark eyes.

The sly gleam did not escape Harep. He kept quiet. Another splash of water on the coals. More hissing. Both men looked at the wooden flooring, gauging what to say next. Should Walhape confide in his old comrade, the rumour going round the nearby town? Could he be trusted to keep his mouth tight? These assassins had only one thing in common, the tattoos on their chests. They bantered amongst themselves, but exceedingly carefully.

'Well? You gonna tell me?' Harep finally asked.

Walhape made a decision. 'You got to promise to keep your mouth buttoned. Promise?'

Harep's heavy brow furrowed expectantly. 'I promise!'

'The rumour is—the king and queen of the Hattite's been murdered. I think Molut's last job, was just that.' Walhape sat staring at his companion quizzically. Would Harep give himself away—did he kill Molut?

* * *

Some days went by and another death occurred in the Assassin's Guild. The second in such a short time. Walhape, the new head of the Order lay rigid on his bed. A sense of panic began to take hold of the remaining members of the guild. The unthinkable was happening. Somehow someone was killing the much feared assassins. This was simply unheard of. How could this be? Everybody was under suspicion. The lingering members avoided each other, keeping to their cells.

Only the tall lone priest of the Order ventured out to minister to their spiritual needs. Mokhat's sharp face was solemn and he fingered a pottery pendant round his neck depicting the dark dragon Lord Illuyankas. His tall frame ambled along the dim corridor of the guild fortress, then

15

stopped outside Harep's cell and listened a while before knocking on the thick door.

'Who's there?' came the cautious response from inside.

'Your spiritual advisor,' Mokhat called back loudly.

'Mokhat! Is that *really* you?'

'I said it was, didn't I?' Mokhat growled. 'Come on, open up!'

He heard the bolt withdrawn and an eye appeared in the crack. When Harep satisfied himself his visitor was who he said he was, the door opened and Mokhat was quickly pulled inside. Harep slammed the door shut and bolted it in a hurry.

'Really, Harep, there's no call for all this,' Mokhat brushed down his cloak with his hands.

'Is Walhape *alive*? Are you telling me you know who killed him? Do we have that person locked up in the dungeon? No? Then there *is* a call for all this!' He indicated menacingly at the door.

Mokhat smiled and then couldn't help chuckling.

'And what do you find so entertaining?' Harep demanded.

'You must admit, it is just a little comical. The feared assassin's guild cowering in their cells, afraid someone's going to do to *them*, what *they* usually do to others.'

'And that's funny, is it?' Harep pulled out a dagger and stuck it under Mokhat's chin, drawing a speck of red. 'I'll show you what's amusing,' he snarled. 'You lying in a pool of blood.'

'Now, now, there's no need for this.' Mokhat put his hand over the razor-sharp blade and gently forced Harep to lower it. 'Now put it away...and I'll forget you did that.'

Still grim faced, Harep replaced the dagger in his belt. 'I'm in no mood for your banter. Someone is picking us off one by one. Not just any one, but the *Head* of the Order. I would've sworn to high heaven, if you'll pardon the allusion, no one could have got to Walhape after what happened to Molut. But they did. Now what? Where's it going to end?'

'That's none of my business.' Mokhat forced a serious face back on. 'I've been doing the rounds, going to all the cells. They've all agreed—and nominated you as new Head of the Order. Aren't you pleased?'

'Are you mad? I wouldn't touch the job for all the gold in the world. Haven't you been listening? Someone's *killing* the Head—as soon as he's appointed.' A crafty look suddenly appeared on Harep's features. 'I'll tell you what—why don't *you* become the new chief? They wouldn't dare kill a priest.'

'That's very flattering, but there are two problems with that idea. One, I'm not really qualified to be the chief of the assassins—am I? Two, I'm a priest—not an assassin. No! I'm afraid you're stuck with it. You were Walhape's deputy. His right hand. It's natural for the deputy to move up into the boss's sandals. You're it. I wish you all the best in your new job. Now I've wasted enough time. I've got other people to see.' Mokhat turned, long dark hair whishing, and went to the door waiting for Harep to open it.

Grim faced, Harep pulled back the bolt and opened the thick wooden door to a crack, peeked out, then quickly opened it wide and pushed Mokhat out, re-closing the door with a bang.

Mokhat turned in the corridor, shook his head and began chuckling once more.

* * *

A sunny morning a few days later, one of the cleaning servants rushed into Mokhat's cell with out knocking, crying, '*They've all gone*!'

'Calm yourself!' Mokhat had been contemplating and wanted a few moments to collect his wits. 'What d'you mean? "They've all gone!" Who's gone?'

'The cells are empty—they've all gone,' the servant repeated.

'You're not serious! Have you checked every cell?' Mokhat had suddenly understood, but found it hard to believe.

'Every cell! I've checked! Not a soul in the fortress. I was afraid your cell would also be empty. I'm glad it's not.'

Mokhat went into the grey corridor and began a search of the cells. He simply couldn't credit that all the assassins might have fled. The fortress was the safest place, their home for many years. Yet at the end of a thorough and fruitless hunt, he had to admit the servant was telling the truth. He stood in the empty hall, closely followed by the terrified man, scratching his bald pate. This was surely the end of the assassins' guild. Without assassins, how could there be a guild? His emotions now tottered between tears and laughter. The tragedy of it all. All those deaths caused by their murders. Then in his mind he pictured assassins fleeing for their lives. Mokhat's watery eyes closed and a deep belly chuckle made the servant even more nervous. The priest gave the impression, to his observer; he was falling to pieces mentally. 'Don't worry, I'm all right,' Mokhat reassured the poor man, who was beginning to back away in fright. 'Do you live here, or in town?' he asked, trying to placate the man.

'In town, your reverence,' the man replied cautiously, looking over his shoulder.

'Go get your belongings or whatever you have and I'll escort you back to town.'

This seemed to have the desired result and the servant relaxed. Orders from the priest suggested he was his old self again.

Mokhat waited at the gate, looking with affection at the imposing fortress secreted amongst green trees. He had been there for nigh on four years serving the assassins' spiritual needs. Hearing that they had assassinated not only the king in

Hattusas, but also his consort, had been the last straw for Mokhat. But even now, he was sad to leave; although on the bright side, the guild as it had been, was finished. In his mind, he felt moral values had won a small victory. Everywhere he looked, the vibrancy of rebirth was making itself felt at this time of year. The birds were in full song. The wind rustled gently through the branches on this sunny morning. He perked up and straightened his shoulders thinking it appropriate that this year the rebirth of spring would be minus the assassins.

Soon the servant reappeared and both strolled through the main gate, along the pot-filled dirt road lined with vital trees, all of a leisurely league down to Nerik.

Some time ago in a previous battle, the Hittite Empire had lost Nerik to the Kaska tribes. Now the Kaska king claimed Nerik as his capital and lived in his castle there. The marketplace of Nerik was on the fringes of town and crowded with noontime shoppers when Mokhat led the dejected servant down the road. Both were thirsty from the long walk and Mokhat looked for a stall selling beer. 'I'm sure you could do with a drink.' Mokhat made his way to the makeshift tavern.

The servant's dark eyes looked eager, but his demeanour was diffident. Poorly dressed and close to penury, he wet his lips with his tongue. 'It's true your reverence, all that walking makes for a dry mouth.'

'Two jugs of your finest,' Mokhat ordered from the stall owner.

The stall owner gave Mokhat a startled look and stared at him dumbfounded.

'Did you hear what I said?' Mokhat asked quietly.

'Yes, your highness. Immediately your highness,' and he rushed to comply.

The jugs were filled with frothy beer from a pitcher and set on a makeshift counter before them.

'Your reverence will do,' Mokhat told the owner.

The stall owner touched his forelock and refilled the pitcher from an amphora behind him on his handcart, all the time giving Mokhat surreptitious side glances.

Mokhat dug a couple of *mina* from his purse and put them by the jugs. 'Well, drink up,' he told the servant.

The man needed no further encouragement and greedily put the jug to his lips. 'Ahh! I needed that,' he told Mokhat after taking a long swig. 'Your reverence is very generous.'

'You deserve it. All the other servants left without saying a word. At least you came and told me what happened. This is my thanks.' Mokhat took a few more *mina* out of his purse and gave it to the poor man. He knew it would probably be the last money this man would get for a while. 'Why don't you wander off home now? I'm sure your family will be waiting.'

'Thank you, your reverence.' The man put the empty jug down on the counter, looked around, took a few steps backwards and was soon lost to view, mingling into the crowd.

Mokhat was on the point of making his way to his brother's castle, when he spied a familiar face in the distance. At least he thought he did. Was that Harep? He was gone in a flash. Had he seen him? Mokhat pushed his way through the crowd, trying to follow the assassin. He wasn't sure he had actually seen him, it all happened so fast. He ran in between the stalls, mantle flying, through a patch where goods were piled, stepping over benches, pushing past startled shoppers. 'Excuse me, can I get past—mind there—*sorry*!'

'*Mind the goods*,' one irate stallholder yelled after him.

Again he spied Harep. This time he was sure. There were two other assassins with him. '*Harep*!' he called out. '*Wait, stop*!'

If they had heard, they took no heed and even seemed to put on speed. Soon all three were lost in the crowd of shoppers.

Mokhat stopped. *Why are they trying to avoid me? This is no good. I can't outrun them—I'll have to try and outthink them. They seem to be heading in the direction of the river.* Mokhat pulled up the long cloak and made a dash down a side street, parallel to the one he thought they had taken. Steep and stony, the street come-alley led to the river shore, but when he came out onto the narrow highway running along the river, there was no sign of the three assassins. 'Damn!' he muttered under his breath. 'Could have sworn I was right. Ah! To the dust with them, let them burn in torment. I can't waste the rest of the day chasing shadows.' He turned in disgust and slowly trudged his way up to his brother's castle.

*   *   *

Harep had holed up in a room above a tavern on the other side of the river to the main town. After he had evaded Mokhat, he had crossed the river. There he shared his lodgings with two other assassins, the one's he had been seen with when Mokhat spotted him. 'That damned priest nearly caught up with us, yesterday. Nice work, Rewa, retracing our footsteps,' Harep commended his nephew.

Rewa's thin limbs were stretched out overflowing his bunk; he touched his finger to his forehead in acknowledgement.

'You know the blighter's the king's brother? He'll report everything. Until we know who the killer in our midst is, we best lie low,' Harep reminded.

Parap, shorter than his brother, was lying on the other bunk, scratching himself, trying to get at the itch in the middle of his back. 'Can only trust family now,' Parap agreed voice straining.

Harep's two nephews considered assassination a family business. All the male members joined the guild on reaching puberty. Unfortunately, the casualty rate was quite high and only the three members present of the family were left. From the tavern below, a loud cheer reached up at them through the flooring.

'Someone's having a party, eh?' Rewa threw at Parap. 'Fancy joining them?'

'Don't you start!' Harep intervened. 'You know who's down there, do you? Could be anyone. Want to end up like Walhape? Best keep your head down. Once we've taken care of the killer, then we can relax.' The grim faces of his nephews told him they did not think much of his nannying. Harep still had no idea who had killed the last head of the order and he was taking no chances.

'All this laying around is getting on my nerves,' Parap exploded. 'When are we going to do something?'

'Yeah, how're we supposed to survive? The money's running out!' added Rewa.

'As to that, I may have us a job.' Harep smiled slyly.

Both his thin nephews perked their ears up. 'Come on Unc. Tell us! What's the job?' Parap demanded.

'Yeah, go on. Let us in on it,' Rewa added.

'As I said, I'm not sure yet. But this afternoon I'm going across to meet someone on the other side. I'll know more then. So you want a piece of the action, do you?' Harep teased.

'Is it...you know...?' Parap asked.

'That's what we're good at. They don't want us to help them look after goats!'

'Anyone we know?' Rewa enquired.

'I told you, I don't know the full score yet. When I find out, you'll be the first to know,' Harep replied grim faced.

Chapter Three

The city of Karkamish had double thick sandstone walls defending it with strong towered gates. In the centre of town stood a high citadel overlooking the middle of the Euphrates River. A rider now pushed his horse hard across the town towards the citadel. Townspeople jumped out of the way as the horse, snorting hard and near to collapse, galloped past them raising a cloud of dust. The rider urged the steed on for the final run through the citadel gateway before pulling up sharp on the brown earth. He jumped off and thrust the reins at the sentry, then ran up the stairs and was about to go through the main doors, when he stopped and looked back. His beautiful white horse had collapsed and lay quite still in the courtyard. 'Shame!' he muttered to himself. 'It was a good horse. Faithful. Can't be helped!'

Muwas' rider wore a Hatti Officer's uniform, distinguished by a tapering bronze helmet and went unchallenged. He came across a Karkamish officer and called out, 'I must see the king. Urgent message from King Muwas of Hatti.'

That got the bearded Karkamish's attention.

Muwas' courier added, 'Make sure you have a messenger ready to ride to Wassukkani. Your life may depend on it.' The implied threat was unnecessary but the courier was exhausted.

'Come, I will take you to the king. He's in the Temple performing his morning homage.'

They went into the courtyard where servants had gathered round the dead horse, wondering who was responsible. On seeing the Hatti uniform, they became quiet. Both officers ignored the staring servants. They continued on towards the Temple of Kubaba and hurried through the portico. A low murmur resounded within, coming from the chanting priests. At the end of the naos stood the celestial gold encrusted statue to the Goddess of Karkamish, Kubaba, a dignified figure draped in a long golden robe, seated and holding symbols of magic and fertility, a mirror in her right hand and a pomegranate in her left.

The substantial king stood before the enormous statue, head bowed, flanked by chanting shaven haired priests in white robes. He peeked at the intruders behind and quickly nudged the priests to finish their ceremonials. Then in a low voice he summarily dismissed all the holy men. 'Well? What intelligence from Muwas?' The king was expecting a report from Hattusas. News travelled fast, especially bad news and this had preceded the courier. The Mittani had spies everywhere, ready to put pigeons to flight.

The courier knelt on one knee. 'Your majesty, King Muwas sends these sealed writing boards for urgent transit to Great King Saustatar.'

'Am I not to know what's in the message?' the vassal king calmly inquired.

Pleadingly, 'Sire, I have my orders.' The Hittite handed over to the king the folded wooden boards each covered on the inside with coloured wax with classified text written in wedge shapes.

The king called to a waiting officer, 'Make sure this goes to Wassukkani at once, along the courier route. Wait! Better still; take it yourself to the first station. Ride hard and make sure the other messengers know of its urgency. Go now!'

*   *   *

Thirty leagues due east of Karkamish was Wassukkani, the capital of the Hurrian kingdom of Mittani, situated a hundred and twenty leagues south-east of Hatti. An Indo-European aristocracy ruled, yet the majority of the population were Semite. An empire centred on northern Mesopotamia with its heartland in the Khabur River region, where Wassukkani was located.

Since the arrival of the messenger from Karkamish, the colourful court of the Great King Saustatar was busily organising an expeditionary force to rush to the aid of King Muwas, the self proclaimed successor to his brother King Muwatalli. The unwritten secret treaty between King Saustatar, King Muwatalli and the then Gal Mešedi Muwas, called for immediate aid to be dispatched in the event of the untimely death of the current King of Hatti. Clearly, Muwatalli had feared assassination, especially considering the manner in which he himself had attained the throne.

'I want you to lead the army north yourself,' Saustatar was telling his son, Artatama, in the dazzling audience chamber. 'This is important. If we support the winning side and cement the alliance with a marriage of your sister to the Hatti king, we could concentrate on fending off the Pharaoh's attacks. Last year, Amenhotep crossed the Orontes River and captured Qadesh. This year he may intend to march towards Wassukkani. We need Hatti as our allies so we can take on Egypt. Do you understand?'

His son, a spitting image of his father, was well schooled by the priests and aware of the regional political situation. He winked conspiratorially at the tall queen sitting in all her finery on the king's left. Almost irritably he responded, 'Yes father! I know the danger Egypt poses. We *will* overwhelm Muwas' foes. Half the Hatti army is on our side—how can they hope to win?'

'Never underestimate your opponent,' Saustatar warned, dark eyes flashing, long raven-locks swinging. 'That way lies overconfidence and disaster!'

A bearded Mittani General marched into the impressive marble audience hall. He bowed. 'Your most gracious majesty, your army will be ready to march by tomorrow. We're conscripting the farmers and the allotted peasantry. The armourers are just finishing. The horse masters are collecting the herds. Chariots are harnessed and waiting. The baggage train is loaded with provisions. If we force-march we'll be outside Hattusas within twelve days.' The general looked satisfied with his report.

'Let's hope the intelligence we received is still trustworthy by then,' Artatama enunciated, looking at the general, but talking to his father.

Saustatar sighed, stroking his curly dark beard, 'We have little choice. Either we go or we don't. No half-way. If we don't, Muwas will never forgive us—and we can't get up there faster than twelve days. So that's that. Well done General Satukani.' With a wave of his hand, the king dismissed the general, who backed out of the marble audience chamber. The king clapped his enormous hands and a scanty clad dancing girl emerged onto the white marble floor, to the sound of flutes, sistrums and drums, discretely emanating from behind yellow marble columns. Tall bronze braziers threw enchanting flickering lights onto the captivating scene.

The king's tall consort, Kiluhepa, sitting in all her finery on his left, back erect, flashed kohl-painted eyes on the unfolding show, letting her rival from the harem know of the consequences that would befall her if she gave too brazen a performance. The dancer noted the flashed hostility and gave her hip an extra jerk in the queen's direction as the king turned to his son. She managed a seductive wiggle when she again had the king's attention, brazenly flouting the queen's unspoken ultimatum. The queen's high cheekbones reddened and she stuck her aquiline nose in the air, clenching her teeth. She could wait. She would deal with that slut later.

'Now, come, let's relax. Here, Artatama, sit by me. She's putting on a good show, eh!' The king patted the chair to his right and with his other hand indicated the seductive movements of the dancing girl. 'We'll let tomorrow be taken care of by Teshub, may he protect us all in these trying times.'

26

Chapter Four

Back in Hattusas in the Yellow Castle, preparations went ahead to move the household to Ankuwa, fourteen leagues south-east on this side of the minor branch of the Marassantiya River. Ankuwa was an ancient trading post and the designated gathering point for the regiments swearing loyalty to Tudhaliyas. Since the murder of the old king, a week had passed and a stand-off had developed between the Grand Castle and the Yellow Castle. King Shunashura of Kizzuwatna had broken with Mittani, although he still had not informed them and wished to ally himself with Hatti—if given a chance.

Kantuzzili welcomed the alliance. Coming at an opportune moment, the news swung a number of hesitant generals, together with their regiments, to his cause. A council of war was in progress in the main grand hall of the castle. All the members of the Kantuzzili "faction" were present. Even their wives watched from the high wooden gallery. Seated at a long polished cedar wood table were a large number of strapping Hittite Generals, lengthy hair covering their necks, each commanding infantry, cavalry, or chariot regiments. The former chamberlain of the royal household sat deep in thought, adding his cautionary voice to the proceedings. He had taken up his old duties with the young king in waiting. Kantuzzili coughed a few times to draw their attention. 'As you know, we have gained an important new ally in King Shunashura of Kizzuwatna,' he said in an unnecessarily loud voice. 'And Shunashura has sent his only son, here, as emissary and hostage.'

The hush in the long hall persisted but all eyes turned on the young Kizzuwatna prince, Talshura, the unfamiliar face sitting at the table; the face beamed at them ingratiatingly.

Kantuzzili paused for effect. 'Shunashura's spies in Karkamish and Wassukkani inform us the son of Saustatar is leading an army towards Hattusas to assist Muwas. I expected nothing less.' Another pause. 'This makes the moving of our forces to Ankuwa imperative. I've already sent out messengers to inform all our allies—those who could not be with us.'

One of the Generals interrupted. 'I still can't see why we simply don't take the Grand Castle. Surround it and storm it.'

'I've explained already,' Kantuzzili's voice was full of irritation. 'The Castle can withstand a long siege. It's impregnable. Muwas holes up in there and waits. How are we going to look when Artatama arrives in a week's time and catches us with our kilts up? Can you guarantee, General Labamulis, you will take the Castle before the Mittani rabble turn up? Eh?'

'Well…no-o. You know there are no guarantees in a siege. It just seems a pity—I mean he's so close.'

'I feel the frustration as well, General. Let me deal with strategy and you deal with tactics. I promise you I won't interfere when we go into battle.' Kantuzzili lifted his piercing dark eyes to the wooden ceiling in mock exasperation.

'I suppose…you may be right,' the General fell silent.

Kantuzzili continued his original train of thought, 'At the same time, I would like to express my gratitude to the chamberlain for having the foresight to bring with him some valuable objects from the royal treasury and even certain items of royal regalia—that is, with the help of a particular captain of the guard and his soldiers. Much appreciated!'

The tall chamberlain smiled. 'Muwas would have given the treasury away to the Mittani. That I couldn't tolerate.'

'I want us to be clear,' Kantuzzili continued, 'before we leave, I want…no, I *need* all here present to swear an oath of allegiance to our new sovereign king. In fact we should do it now—before we go further.'

All heads turned to look at the young man with the strong jaw, sitting at the top of the table. Tudhaliyas, dressed in his best light yellow tunic with kilt, stared determinedly to the front, trying to look regal. Kantuzzili had advised him to do this.

Kantuzzili stood and raised his goblet and waited. He carefully scrutinised each person as they got to their feet. All lifted their goblets in anticipation of the toast to fidelity. None hesitated and for this Kantuzzili was grateful, although he had expected some vacillation. 'I give you the next king of Hatti. Tudhaliyas the First,' He drained his goblet in one.

Those round the table repeated, '*Tudhaliyas the First,*' and drained their goblets with gusto.

Tudhaliyas smiled and gave a regal wave in acknowledgement.

Kantuzzili sat, as did the others. 'In the last report. I estimated we had the backing of two thirds of the army. We control the forces in the west, south and some of the north. Muwas has the eastern forces and the Mittani rushing up from the south-east. Do you agree Generals?'

Around the table the generals nodded.

'Our problem is we must draw Muwas out into the open where we can force him to do battle in a place of *our* choosing.'

The chamberlain intruded with his quiet voice, 'Am I to understand the vote being organised by the priests is to be ignored?'

'My dear chamberlain,' Kantuzzili answered, 'we have already had the vote. Those who voted for us are here amongst us—those who voted for Muwas are with him in the Castle. What other vote is required? It was always going to turn out thus. We knew Muwas wouldn't abide by a majority vote if it went against him. Tagrama was living in a land of wishful thinking when he thought he could resolve this struggle without combat. I admire the sentiments, but *I* must deal with reality.'

Chapter Five

Sitting in his own quiet contemplation room in the Great Temple of Hattusas, Tagrama listened with a pained expression to the information coming in. 'But why are they so intent on war?' he demanded angrily of his dark and skinny deputy. Why won't Muwas step aside?'

'Your Eminence, his brother's just been murdered—how can he not seek revenge? Add to that, he was the Gal Mešedi, the Chief of the Bodyguards. They assassinated the king under his very nose. He must avenge such an outrage—can you not see?' The deputy's dark face seemed to be sucking on dried honey—fixed in a mock reverential air.

'If he's so blind to others' fate, maybe it is best it goes this way. My big worry is—Muwas might win the black bull throne by force of arms. Then the slaughter will really begin.'

'I doubt he'll win,' the deputy tried to sound convincing. 'He has less than half of the army. Only a miracle would give him victory.'

'Are we not in the business of miracles?' Tagrama asked. A change had come over him as he realised the inevitable. He calmed and smiled benignly at his deputy. 'From the way the nobles are reacting, it would seem we have a new king. Tudhaliyas the First. Himuili's son. I hope he has a wise head on his young shoulders. Have you talked to his tutor?'

'Yes, eminence.'

'Amulas, wasn't it?'

'Yes, your eminence.'

'Well, what did you gain from your talk?'

'Amulas tells me he has a sharp mind, studied well. Asked intelligent questions; is still a bit shy and watches people carefully. From Amulas' observations, he agrees he would make a good king.' The deputy looked pleased with his briefing.

'I'm delighted to hear that—there may yet be hope. Have all the valuables been taken to the holy caverns?'

'Yes, eminence.'

'Then we are now in the lap of the Storm God of Hatti, may he preserve us. It would seem the tempest is soon to be upon us. Let us go and ask the Storm God to be merciful in his anger.'

Both priests made their way into the inner temple, to the idols of the deities, where they burnt incense and pleaded for mercy on behalf of the innocent victims of the coming war.

Chapter Six

Soldiers and provisions were still coming into the Great Palace by the western causeway. 'That's it, keep it coming!' a quartermaster was guiding the provisions to where he wanted his workers to stack them. 'Over there, against the far wall!'

Muwas was thoroughly convinced Kantuzzili would soon lay siege to the citadel. For him, it clearly seemed the logical military move. Take the palace before the Mittani arrive. He assumed Kantuzzili knew of the Mittani army hurrying through the Taurus Mountains towards Hattusas. In fact he was puzzled as to why the siege hadn't begun on the day of his brother's murder. 'That sly hyena's up to something,' Muwas confided in the strapping General sitting next to him. Both deep in their cups. 'Why doesn't he attack? What's he waiting for—an invitation?' Muwas sat dressed in a green Hurrian shirt tied with an ornamental belt, long sleeves hanging over the armrests.

The General burped loudly—lifted his goblet and took another long swig, spilling some on his tunic. 'We'll be wielding a sword soon enough, sire, what's the hurry?'

They had been killing boredom, exasperated at being pent-up in the castle all week. Muwas was itching to get the conflict started. Many of the nobles had refused to attend Muwatalli' funeral pyre and that galled, for it made too evident the size of his support. He had made a note of each absence—and would deal with them when the time came to settling scores.

The new chief officer of the royal household entered, fear showing on his face. 'Your majesty, my predecessor seems to have mislaid the royal golden crook.'

Muwas glowered at the small man. He had been understudy to the previous chamberlain and now felt all alone.

'Have you looked everywhere?'

'Yes sire. I fear he may have hidden it, or even taken it with him.'

'Look again! Make sure you turn the palace upside down—but *find* it.'

'I'm sorry, your majesty, but I also have to inform you, during the inventory of the Treasury, we found many items missing. I fear they may have gone the same way, I mean taken by my predecessor.'

Face crimson and ready to explode, '*Get out of my sight,*' Muwas dismissed the man with a contemptuous wave.

The new chamberlain backed out hastily, fearing for his life.

Muwas was rapidly gaining a reputation for cruelty. After he had calmed, taken more drink, Muwas finished by muttering more threats at Kantuzzili. A captain hurriedly arrived into the hall to distract Muwas but the Mešedi prevented him from approaching. 'Let him pass,' shouted Muwas.

The captain rushed forward and knelt one knee on the white marble floor. 'Sire, two more messages of support. One from the Ininas Regiment…'

'*Hah*! That's one of the top chariot regiments,' Muwas interrupted the captain, immensely pleased.

'…and from the Varama Regiment.' The captain got to his feet, gestured up by Muwas.

'You see,' Muwas patted the General's brawny arm, 'we're still getting stronger. One chariot, one infantry. Better late than never. The others will regret siding with that upstart. I'll see to it. Good work captain. If there's more news, bring it at once. On your way out, send those dubious spies in. You may go.'

The captain marched out smartly and informed the scruffy looking spies lurking at the door, 'The king wants to see you!'

Dirty torn robes, dusty beards, and high with the whiff of body odours. The two spies strode out strongly, belying their looks. Both knelt before the unanointed king. 'Your majesty, we have a bad report, but we know you ought to hear this,' the taller of the two declared.

Muwas waved his goblet at them, 'Well, out with it.'

'The king of Kizzuwatna has thrown in with your enemy. We can't confirm this yet, but we saw a Kizzuwatna high born ride into the Yellow Castle.'

The General's dark eyes flashed and he sat up, a frown on his face.

Muwas' good news of the new regiments faded and he burst out, 'Are you sure? I mean it could be just a visit.'

'Then he would have come up here to the castle,' the General voiced. 'No! Your spies have it right. Shunashura has thrown in with the rabble. Why he should do so is another matter.'

'You're probably right. Damned fish bellies. That makes it even more puzzling.' Muwas pointed coercively at the spies. 'I want to know why they still haven't attacked. I don't want guess work. Find out exactly—do you hear?'

'Yes, majesty.'

Muwas gestured them away and the two spies retreated backwards to the doorway. He snapped his fingers and a Mešedi rushed forward.

'Find a dispatch rider, send him to me.'

'Immediately, sire.'

The courier arrived followed by a Mešedi.

'You don't need to do that, he's quite safe,' Muwas assured the Mešedi.

'As you wish, your majesty,' and the guard backed away.

Muwas scrutinised his courier. He stood expectant, dressed in a light green tunic with a kilt, standard military issue. 'Are you familiar with the route to Mittani?'

'Yes, majesty.'

'A Mittani army is coming to help me, led by Prince Artatama. I estimate about this time they should be crossing the Taurus Mountains. Do you think you can find them?' Muwas scrutinised his courier.

'Sire, I will not fail. It must be a large body and it would be hard not to find them.' The courier was confident.

'You will inform the prince he must push his men hard. The balance is changing and we must have him here earlier than expected. You're to request he send his horse squadrons ahead of his main force and all the chariots at his command. Are you clear what you must do?'

'Yes, majesty.'

'Get the scribe to write the order and put my seal on it so the prince knows he should comply.'

'Right away, majesty.'

'Now, General Ammuna,' Muwas felt he had done all he could. 'I invite you to come and visit my harem. Take your pick and we'll get down to some serious relaxation. What d'you say?' Muwas knew he would have to keep his generals sweetened if they were to continue to remain loyal.

Chapter Seven

$\mathbf{A}$ squadron of Mittani was hard on the heels of a dozen Kizzuwatna cavalry, chasing them into a side gorge of the Taurus Mountains. Kizzuwatna scouts up in the hills watched the ruse working. One of the scouts rose and waved a red flag. That was the signal for a Kizzuwatna squadron to ride out of a small ravine and come in behind the Mittani. Too late, the Mittani realised they had ridden into an ambush. They wheeled about and tried to fight their way through back the way they had come. The fleeing dozen now joined the fight from the opposite end. The deep blue tunics of the Mittani were intermingled and outnumbered three to two, by the scarlet of the Kizzuwatna. The struggle was ferocious and going against the Mittani. The Mittani strenuously sought to disengage but the Kizzuwatna horse prevented them.

A conch horn sounded near the entrance of the gorge and the commander of the Kizzuwatna squadron bellowed to his men, '*RETREAT!*' Reluctantly his men obeyed, only finishing off their current opponent. In the distance another Mittani squadron was hurrying to the aid of their embattled comrades.

Back in the hills, General Kirruwaiya had his officers round him, staring at a skin-map on the table in his tent. 'I can't believe you actually engaged the squadron and after all I told you,' the strong voice exploded. He dressed down the dust encrusted commander of the recent ambush.

The man hung his head in contrition.

'It's sheer luck you bested them. It so easily could have gone the other way. Had you not broken off before the second squadron arrived, you would have been finished—and left me with a squadron short. I'm the one who has to tell your families. Only engage when the odds are at least two to one—not otherwise.'

They knew their commander was right, yet the twinkle in his eyes suggested he was proud of them. They had been harassing the Mittani army for days. A pin prick here, a hammer blow there. Each blow helped to slow the extended convoy. At one point it seemed the Mittani were getting ready to detach and send their cavalry and chariots ahead, but the General soon put a stop to that. He increased the raids making nonsense of the Mittani plan. Now he continued the scolding, 'I've told you, we're not here to take them head on. Our orders are to harass and delay. If we can fire their baggage train, all the better.' Then as an afterthought he added, 'But no looting. We haven't the time!'

A groan went up round the table, but all were smiling even while pretending to complain.

Chapter Eight

Kantuzzili rode alongside the spectacular looking general standing on his steady legs in the decorated chariot pulled by two white horses and shouted, 'General Zidanta, I am charged by his majesty to offer you overall command of our forces.'

If the tall, dark, powerfully built general had any inkling this was to happen, he gave no indication. He smiled through the yellow dust, nodded benignly and simply said, 'I accept.' General Zidanta, the commander of the famous Taru Chariot Regiment set his jaw and pushed out a broad clean shaven face. His legendary victories in the Kaska battles had his troops doting on him. Kantuzzili knew of his formidable reputation and as a result, had recommended his appointment. The commander of an army required competence, and the general had this in plenty. But he also needed popular support from his soldiers. This was a civil war and the "big game" required might as well as subtlety.

Time had moved on—it being the end of the second week after the murder of Muwatalli. Reports were coming in to Ankuwa that the Mittani, despite heavy harassment, were only two days march from Hattusas. To counterbalance this, the Kizzuwatna were making haste up to the valley to join Kantuzzili in his opposition to Muwas. Prince Talshura was looking forward to seeing General Kirruwaiya. He wanted to rejoin his own people, be among his own troops, to feel less of a hostage.

The journey from the Yellow Castle down to Ankuwa had been arduous and had taken four gruelling days, the mountainous terrain making the going difficult. People were tired and the animals exhausted. If it were just soldiers, they could have made it in half the time, but the baggage train included wives, children and spare equipment to forge weaponry and build more chariots. At every rest stop, more disenchanted soldiers had joined their ranks. Situated in a lush valley, Ankuwa was an ancient Assyrian *karum* trading post. Kantuzzili had chosen it as the gathering point for the regiments swearing loyalty to Tudhaliyas. He hoped the flat wide river valley would hold the forty thousand expected.

The merchants of the valley welcomed the invasion with one hand, looking forward to the prospect of more trade, supplying fodder and food to the growing army, but seemed uneasy with the loss of their normal trade. Only the nobles, priests, and high ranking officers were billeted in the town, the rest were bivouacked in hide tents out in the open on the valley floor. Chariot regiments and cavalry away at the north-eastern end where the river left the valley so the effluent problem could be contained.

*   *   *

Tagrama and his priests had taken over the local temple at Ankuwa and now the chief priest was pacing up and down the main isle making plans for his first service. 'I'm going to insist we sacrifice a pure white goat to Taru in the presence of the new king,' Tagrama was telling one of his young priests. 'I want to do the auguries on the liver. People need to know the Gods are on our side.'

'Yes your reverence!' the young man eagerly responded, flattered he was being consulted.

The Generals in the meantime took over the local taverns—adamant the local merchants supply huge quantities of wine for the officers and barrels of beer for the soldiers. They felt it made for a balance. The priests did their thing in the temple, whilst the soldiers did theirs where they felt most comfortable.

At dawn, following the day of their arrival, the king, all his nobles and generals, gathered in the temple situated on a terracotta hill outside of town. In the marble temple down the long naos at the altar, stood the black bull from the Great Temple at Hattusas, transported reverently by priests in a wagon of the baggage train. To have the Gods denied him would make Muwas less in the eyes of the people and Tagrama, having wholeheartedly lent his support to the young Tudhaliyas, would deny Muwas the blessing of Taru.

The temple atmosphere was heady with incense whilst Tagrama chanted before the statue of the Storm God. Deep long windows on either side illuminated the naos, throwing a brilliant light on the statue standing at its head. The pure white sacrificial goat paused docile, quietened with a poppy concoction. Tudhaliyas wore his regal attire, a long white garment reaching the ankles. An elaborately embroidered shawl over both shoulders and left arm, tucked under the right, the end hanging down freely over the front of the body. He wore a close-fitting white cap as head-dress. His long black hair hung over the neck and shoulders. In his right hand, he trailed the thick golden crook of office. This was the costume of the Sun God of Hatti. He represented the epitome of imperial elegance so apt as an image for a Hittite king.

Kantuzzili and Himuili were behind the king. Their respective wives, Gassulawiya and Tawana, watched from the sides among the square piers supporting the roof with other high born ladies, as was the custom. Behind Kantuzzili and Himuili stood the nobles and generals.

A priest led the white goat over to Tagrama, two priests lifted and laid it on the altar on its side. Another priest handed him a sacrificial knife and Tagrama cut the jugular with a practised jerk of his wrist. Using the same knife, Tagrama thrust it in and ripped the liver out. Tagrama examined the steaming dark red organ carefully, then turned to the king and said loudly, 'I pronounce it pure and without blemish. The auguries are propitious for the undertaking.'

As a closing act, a priest handed Tagrama a goblet of red wine and the high priest poured some of the drink-offering on the temple floor, passing the goblet to Tudhaliyas, who also poured a small libation on the marble floor in honour of the Sun God of Hatti. Most of the congregation smiled with relief at the good news from the auguries and all felt reassured the first sacrifice before the king had gone so well.

*　　*　　*

Later the same day, General Zidanta ordered practice manoeuvres and was watching his beloved Taru Regiment putting their magnificently decorated chariots through their paces. The flattest part of the green valley had been cleared for the purpose. Following the sacrifice at the temple, the king and all the Kantuzzili faction had come to watch the display. The vast area all around, contained soldiers eager to witness the premier regiment of their army showing what would happen to the opposition once the conflict was under way.

'I wish they'd be more careful. We're gonna have to repair the bloomin things when they wreck 'em. And they will, mark my words.' It was the chief of the army carpenters who built and maintained the chariots. He was complaining to his gruff deputy on the edge of the cleared exercise area. A small workshop encampment set to one side where they would bring the broken chariots for repair. A number of apprentices milled about listening and smiled at their boss's comments. Most knew he was right; there would be breakages the way the Taru Regiment threw the vehicles about.

'You remember—I told you last week. If they weren't so heavy, they wouldn't tumble over so easily,' his deputy reminded.

'We've had all that out. And you're wrong. It's the other way round. On this rocky terrain, we can't have the light Egyptian style chariot. It'd break up in no time. I keep telling you,' his chief insisted. 'Heavy means stability, got that.'

The Hittites thought of the heavy war chariot as the spearhead of a weighty assault formation that swept through and demolished infantry lines in a frontal or flanking charge. For such fierce movements they had to be robust. The heavy Hittite war chariot had a wooden frame covered by leather, with spoked wooden wheels mounted on a wide axle. The shaft pole ran from the underside to which a pair of horses was harnessed. The chariot held three occupants. The driver, the warrior with a stabbing spear and a soldier holding a protective shield for all three. On the flat an experienced charioteer might even control his chariot by reins tied to the waist leaving his hands free, whilst keeping it steady enough to fight with a scimitar.

The Taru simulated a flanking manoeuvre involving a sharp veer to the left round a line of thick tree trunks sticking up from the ground, as if they were coming round their own line of infantry. This managed to snag a couple of chariots, which needed repair. Next, they simulated a frontal charge, swinging round at the last moment, presenting wheels mowing down the implied oncoming enemy infantry. After each charge, the observers clapped and cheered encouragement. Teams of horses were then sent to pick up the broken chariots. Each time a chariot came to grief, the chief of the carpenters groaned.

'What d'you think?' General Zidanta asked of his majesty, pride bursting from his chest.

The king spoke all the right words. 'Splendid manoeuvres. I'm proud to watch such a distinguished regiment.'

The general's chest seemed to protrude even further on hearing the praise.

'We mustn't forget the rest of the army,' Kantuzzili reminded them.

The notables reviewing the parade were escorted to an area where more regiments were lined up. Of the fifty-four regimental commanders in the group, two generals on the outer fringes were in a heated discussion.

'I don't care what the Egyptians have come up with; we've always had groups of tens. Each regiment is in multiples of ten, a warrant officer in charge of ten, then a more senior officer in charge of a hundred and an even more senior officer in charge of a thousand. That's our system. An increasing hierarchy of responsibility. It's worked fine ever since the time of Labarnas. An infantry regiment of five thousand men commanded by a general.'

'But it lacks mobility,' argued the other general.

The first would have none of it. 'We've chariot and cavalry regiments grouped into squadrons of two hundred, still grouped in the tens. That gives us mobility. I don't care what some damned foreign general comes up with in Egypt. It's not for us Hittites.'

He refused to listen to anymore fancy new ideas and went to find someone less argumentative to talk to.

Arrayed on the brown parade ground stood four regiments of infantry, ten chariot and twelve cavalry regiments, two regiments of horse archers, twelve regiments of archers, eight regiments of sling throwers, six spear throwing regiments, all ready for inspection by King Tudhaliyas the First. With the Taru, a formidable army of thirty thousand men. 'Looking at them,' the king swept his hand over the parade, 'I'm fairly confident we will vanquish Muwas' forces. What do you think General Zidanta?'

'I'm cautiously optimistic, sire,' the general answered.

'The Wurusemu Archer Regiment over there.' General Zidanta pointed to the centre. 'They're equipped with the new composite wood and horn glued bow. And I've even put some archers onto horses. What d'you think of that idea your majesty?'

The king nodded sagely, belying his youth.

The general took a liking to this new young king and quietly thought to himself, *he'll do.* 'All the soldiers have new dress,' Zidanta continued, 'thanks to the merchants here. Wrap round belted kilts, deep yellow regimental shirts, helmets with earpiece and plume. The army forgers have been hard at work supplying each soldier with the standard short bronze scimitar and a hand axe.'

'It sounds like we're ready. Is that what you're telling me?'

'Yes, majesty.'

Chapter Nine

'Any news from the prince?' King Shunashura demanded of his advisor. He hadn't heard from his son for too long a time, not since he had left for Hattusas.

His chief advisor's worried face showed he was just as concerned as the king with the lack of intelligence regarding Prince Talshura. 'No your majesty, not a word.'

Adaniya castle faced the river and backed onto sheer cliffs for protection. The sizable town below spread lazily along the riverside and was a conduit for trade with other merchants operating their trading network on the big blue sea, as the Mediterranean was then known. Kizzuwatna had vigorous trade links with the Lukka at Ura; when they weren't causing chaos with their piracy; with the Ahhiyawa north along the coast at Milawata and in the other direction with Alasiya and Ugarit. When they were allied to the Mittani, trade with Hatti had suffered. Now it was expected to pick up. The Hittites traded mainly with the Assyrians to the east, with its capital at Ashur, whilst Kizzuwatna traded mainly with the coastal cities along the Mediterranean.

'What about General Kirruwaiya?' the dark lanky king persisted. 'Any more from him?'

'Not since he reported he was heading to Ankuwa to join Tudhaliyas, sire and that's where the prince will be. So the next communication from Kirruwaiya will include news of the prince.'

'And how are preparations going with the army? Is it almost ready to leave? We can't delay much longer.'

'Are you still determined to lead it north yourself, your majesty? I strongly advise against it.'

'I know. But I want to see my son, make sure he's all right.' The king was fond of his only son and heir, sometimes over protectively fond. Sending him north as a hostage was the hardest thing he had done in his life. He felt it was a way of helping his son to grow up, but it was also a heart-wrenching act deliberately designed to wean himself off of his own overindulgence.

'Your daughter's been pestering the wagon master to find her a place in the baggage train. I thought you should know.'

'Where is she? Where's Nikal? Find her and send her to me.' He shook his head and with it, his long black hair. His daughter's antics were a constant worry to him.

'As you will, your majesty.' The advisor backed out of the king's sight and went to find the king's missing daughter.

*　　*　　*

With a dark shawl obscuring her long brown hair and aquiline face, Nikal was browsing among the merchant's fine multicoloured cloth in the marketplace, like any common person, with only her bosomy maid for company.

The merchant ever eager to sell sidled over deferentially. 'You won't find better, milady. The finest cloth anywhere on the coast. All the way from Ugarit.' He unrolled the shimmering yellow cloth, delicately embroidered with gold thread.

'Yes, yes. Thank you,' she brushed him off and made to go.

'Milady, I have more…' he called, '…anything your heart desires.'

'Not today, thank you,' her maid told the merchant brusquely.

Nikal left the shop, watched by a disappointed shopkeeper. Cooped up in the royal castle, she felt the need to break out of her confinement for a short while, or, she insisted, she would go mad. Overprotect all her life, she sometimes slummed in the marketplace or along the dockside and dreamed of going on a long sea voyage to all the exotic places her father kept mentioning. Her father knew of her restlessness and cast around for a husband, but always found fault with every candidate. Deep down he was reluctant to part with her. She had come as a welcome bonus, being twin to her brother, and now that her brother was away up north, she brooded. Down the narrow winding alleyways of Adaniya, Nikal made her way to the dockside where the incoming ships were berthed. All along the wharf, the only other businesses were the many taverns catering for the incoming and departing sailors.

Her maid glanced around nervously, worried of the dangers lurking in such a rough neighbourhood.

'Look, Talarra, a beautiful ship from Ugarit. See the prow painted with the all-seeing-eye and the large sail with alternating stripes. See how striking it is.' Nikal could see herself on its deck, out on the open sea. The quay side was replete with two wheeled vehicles being pulled by donkeys or bullocks. Ships were being loaded and unloaded. Stevedores ran to and fro lugging heavy beige sacks of grain or such.

'Milady, your hood is slipping. People will recognise you.' The maid was afraid of the rough men on the docks.

The princess pulled the hood back over her head. 'Talarra, you worry so. See,' she waved her hand at the ships, 'all the magnificent ships. Can't you smell the sea air? Don't take on so. We're quite safe. Everybody's too busy to take notice of a couple of women out for a stroll.' Nikal may have deliberately ignored, or simply not noticed the common stares their passing provoked. Men undressed them with their eyes, made obscene remarks to each other of what they would like to do and in general behaved like rough men behave anywhere, especially men on the docks. Eventually a couple were emboldened enough to block the path of Nikal and Talarra. They were showing off to their workmates.

'Step aside, let us pass,' Talarra shouted.

'Now that's not very friendly,' one of the thugs cajoled.

'I command you to step aside,' Nikal joined in.

'Well of course, if you command, your highness, that's different,' the other said mockingly.

He had used the proper title, but for him, only as a sick joke.

'You don't know who you're talking to,' Talarra threatened.

The men moved to grab the women, but were rooted by the sound of a conch to the rear. It was the king's advisor looking for Nikal where he thought he might find her, leading a body of soldiers from the castle. The squad came rushing out of an alley behind the rogues, further along the wharf. He had correctly assessed the situation from a distance and ordered the conch to be blown.

The two stevedores, surprised, were quickly surrounded and led away, puzzled as to why soldiers had suddenly appeared from nowhere.

'Your highness ought to know better,' the king's advisor scolded. 'You might have been hurt. This is no place for you to go wandering about in. I don't know what your father will say of you roaming around the dockside. It's unseemly behaviour for a princess of the realm.' The advisor was shaken with the near catastrophe and was working the fear out in admonishing the cause.

*   *   *

Headed by their king the Kizzuwatna army column had been on the road for many days; it was making its way up to Ankuwa to join Kantuzzili. A long drawn out procession of chariots, followed by infantry, each regiment followed by its baggage train with the cavalry bringing up the rear. They had been on the road for three days and were approaching the famous Marassantiya River.

'Do we know who they are, general?' the king inquired.

'White tunics, no colouring,' the general looked annoyed. 'Spies, or at best, uncommitted soldiers. Could be just rabble. The hills are full of renegades in time of civil war.'

The king trusted the general to deal with this minor matter. His main worry was the bridge across the mighty Marassantiya. Was it still intact? The scouts reported it was, but that was a day ago. 'Are they a threat to us? What about the bridge?'

'I don't think they pose any risk, but they might try and pick off any stragglers,' the general advised. 'As for the bridge, we'll cross that when we come to it—if it's still standing.'

King Shunashura had been forced to take his daughter with him to Ankuwa, not trusting what she might get up to while he was away. The king's advisor had told of finding her on the dockside, being confronted by the two stevedores and it had shocked the king. The stevedores were not at fault. She should not have been there. He felt he had little choice but to keep her close. That she should prowl the docks was beyond him. He simply couldn't understand such reckless behaviour on her part. Not for the first time he wished he could find a suitable husband and marry her off.

Nikal, ensconced with her maid, was now content being driven in the royal four wheeled carriage. The ride was bumpy with all the pot holes, but the adventure compensated for all the discomfort. Although surrounded by lots of cushions, the jostling was still painful. She had got her way and was even now a little surprised her father had given in so easily. The twins were just on seventeen and seeking to expand their horizons. She thought of this as going on an exciting journey to a strange land. She would see her brother. And of course, she had heard of Hatti, but to actually be going there was a dream come true.

From somewhere in the distant hills, a deep rumble of an avalanche resounded on the wind. 'What the...!' the king exclaimed, alarmed it might be an attack. 'What was that?' he demanded of his general.

'I think a rock fall caused by that rabble we went after. Clever really. Using rocks.'

'For a moment...well anyway, it's not serious, is it?'

'No, your majesty.'

After a while, the scarlet tunics of the Kizzuwatna squadron came tearing back to rejoin the column. The captain in charge reported to the general, all the time nervously glancing at the king. 'Sir, the rabble we chased ended by throwing stones at us when we tried to close. Caused an avalanche. They've retreated onto a mountain and there's no way we can force them off.'

'Very good, captain. Rejoin your regiment. Better luck next time.'

The captain saluted the king and the general and rode to join his squadron.

The general looked at the king. 'You've heard the report, sire? Just as I suspected. Best to ignore them.'

Irritated, the king snorted his agreement. 'I'm afraid you're right.'

'It's kind of them to have left us half the bridge,' the king joked. 'We really have to find out why they've done this, don't you think, general?' The scouts had reported the bridge destroyed, but the scale of the damage only became evident when Shunashura came over the rise and saw it for himself. The Marassantiya was a fast flowing river and at this time of the year, spring, un-crossable without a bridge. Someone had taken the bridge apart, bricks by brick, from the middle right to the shoreline at the far side.

General Tapalass was looking beyond the bridge. 'I can just make out some of the marauders on the other side, inland from the river.'

'The bridge is more important, general,' the king snapped.

'Yes sire, but I agree with you. If we don't want more trouble, we have to find out who they are and what they want?' the general insisted. 'In the mean time I'll get my men started cutting trees. We'll need them to bridge the gap.' The general called over an officer and relayed his orders.

The slope down to the river was covered with green broad-leafed hillside trees and the Kizzuwatna soldiers soon had enough logs to begin repairs. They dragged the lumber to the riverbank for the army carpenters to clean. Troops brought the timber to where the gap was and with difficulty constructed a deck to the next pier. It took ropes, pulleys, and lots of precarious climbing, but with such a lot of manpower, the work progressed well. From a distance, it had looked worse than it actually was. It had been a sloppy demolition job carried out by desperate amateurs. They had left the two stone piers standing in the river and only smashed the interconnecting decking, making reconstruction easier than envisaged.

'How long?' the king wanted to know.

'I judge we'll begin to across well before dark.' The general sounded confident. 'It's not as big a job as I thought. We'll have the next gap bridged soon enough. The river's at its narrowest here, about ninety cubits wide. We're having to span roughly forty cubits, twenty to each pier. The delay is minimal.'

The army to the rear, travelling ten abreast, was spread out for a couple of leagues along the trail. It now had come to a halt. The animals were thirsty and could smell water, making them impatient and eager to quench their thirst. The troops were no different. They had been on the road since dawn with little rest and were looking forward to having a break. The command came for the army column to split left and right, each making its way down to the riverbank. Watering the animals, horses, asses, donkeys and bullocks, was made more problematic due to the swiftness of the river. The troops were careful to keep hold of their precious charges in case they wandered in too far and were carried away.

The king decided to camp on this side for the night, it being more secure. In the morning a couple of squadrons of cavalry would be sent across to talk to, or capture, some of the rabble causing trouble and find out why they were making a nuisance of themselves. The bivouac announcement was received with surprised satisfaction by most. The troops had been pushed hard for nigh on four full days and were close to exhaustion. That they could rest and eat hot food came as a longed-for welcome.

In the morning, the bridge had been completed and squadrons brought back prisoners from the other side of the river. 'It would seem, your majesty, they thought we were invading. All they were doing was defending Hatti. I'm sorry, but I find no fault in that. Misguided, yes, but clearly they were doing their duty.' The general thought it amusing.

'As simple as that, eh? Have you set them straight?' Shunashura was equally pleased they had sorted the problem.

'We're doing it now. The prisoners have been released with the message we're allies coming to aid their King. We're inviting them, if they wish, to join us on the road to Ankuwa.

* * *

An almighty roar resounded from the Hittite soldiers as the ten thousand strong Kizzuwatna force entered the Ankuwa valley—followed by two thousand Hittite soldiers in white tunics. They were led to the same parade ground that earlier held the Taru regimental manoeuvres and in deference to their long journey, were immediately invited to set up camp. They were to be fed and feasted by the Hittite cooks. The official inspection parade for the Hatti king could wait.

On their meeting, Tudhaliyas embraced Shunashura, 'I welcome you in the name of the people of Hatti and name you ally and friend, King Shunashura of Kizzuwatna. May our relationship be warm and long.'

Shunashura responded equally regally, 'We come not as a vassal, but as a friend and ally.' Those present understood the reference to "vassal," for Kizzuwatna had fought hard for its independence and its offer of alliance was to be an alliance of equals. Without further ado, the Kizzuwatna king was escorted with his retinue to the vacated mansion of a rich Assyrian merchant so he could rest and recuperate.

They entered through a decorative gateway with square piers on either side, into a spacious lush green courtyard with a central water feature and when they stopped, Shunashura ushered Nikal forward from behind him. 'May I present my only daughter, Princess Nikal.'

At the outset, she behaved demurely, whilst Tudhaliyas seemed enraptured by her good looks. But then she lifted her eyes and gave a lingering stare, far longer than would be deemed proper for a lady. Tudhaliyas was surprised by this. She lowered her eyes when she noticed her father's disapproving look. But in that fleeting instant, imperceptibly, a spark of attraction passed like lightning between them, reaching into their core. Hope had kindled a deep curiosity. 'I'm enchanted. I had no idea Kizzuwatna held such striking maidens,' Tudhaliyas responded with charm, returning the earlier stare with a piercing stare of his own, 'or I would have insisted we become allies much sooner.' He smiled.

Nikal's head went down, hiding a blush.

Shunashura couldn't help noticing and it reawakened a glimmer of optimism for his daughter's future. Nikal hurriedly stepped back and rejoined her brother.

'We'll let you settle in and then later we can have a discussion.' Tudhaliyas went through the gateway and stopped, waiting for Kantuzzili.

Kantuzzili made to follow Tudhaliyas, bur lingered. 'Before I go, I'm intrigued as to why you have Hatti soldiers with you?'

Shunashura was only too happy to clarify why he had two thousand Hatti soldiers in his army. 'After we explained to them we were coming as allies to help in your campaign, they came out of the mountains in large numbers, wanting to come and join you.'

'I'm gratified you're here and doubly pleased to have you return some of our soldiers. By the by, I've been looking after your son as if he were part of my family. I must congratulate you on having such a fine boy.' Kantuzzili felt the need to reassure his ally and glanced fondly at Talshura. 'He's comported himself like a true heir.'

Shunashura beamed with pride at such praise. 'I'm pleased to hear this. I've been looking forward to seeing him again. His sister even more so than I.'

'King Tudhaliyas looks forward to a private talk with you later,' Kantuzzili added, leaving, joining the Hatti king.

Talshura was in deep conversation with his twin sister, Nikal. They had missed each other as only twins do. A small apple orchard stood in the far right of the courtyard and they lingered under a tree, looking up at the pink apple blossoms.

'What's he like?' Nikal queried.

'What's who like?' Talshura teased.

'Oh don't play the dull-wit.' She pretended anger. 'You know very well who I mean. Their king, what's he like? You've been here more than two weeks; you must have got to know him.'

He furrowed his brow. 'He's been thrust into all this by events out of his control and he feels it. The sudden death of the old king. His father and uncle plunging into intrigues designed to make him king.' Talshura took his sister's hand and they walked slowly towards the house. 'I don't think he's comfortable with the title yet. He's only twenty, but expected to act twice his age. I'm amazed he's coping!'

Nikal shook her head, 'That's not what I mean. I want to know, is he kind? Does he dream?' She was gazing into the distance with a faraway look.

'You've got that wool-gathering look again. I don't know if he dreams. How could I know of such a thing?' He let go of her hand and went inside the house. She followed.

The rich merchant had an extensive mansion. Kizzuwatna royal servants were bustling about, bringing in chests laden with all sorts of personal items. Taking them upstairs to the wooden upper storey. Talshura, followed by Nikal, crossed the flagstone entrance into a square porch-room with a wide opening supported on wooden posts. Nikal snagged a nearby servant and both went in search of the bathroom down one of the corridors leading off to the right and left. Shunashura was beyond in the inner room, seated on a couch, eyes closed. Talshura did not want to wake his father and was tiptoeing past, intent on looking for the kitchen.

'My boy, I'm not asleep. I've missed you. How've you been? Did they treat you well?'

'Father! —I'm sorry; I didn't want to disturb you.' He sat down on the couch beside his father. 'I've missed you too. I've missed Nikal most.'

'You've always been too close. I sent you up here to wean you two off of each other.' Shunashura patted his son's knee. 'Both of you will have to be married soon and it must be the parting of your ways. I know you find it hard, but I also know you understand why I sent you here.'

'I do father.' A lengthy pause while each composed their bubbly emotions. 'They're good people, father...the Kantuzzili clan. He's been very good to me. Understanding. Only...I missed my own people. It's silly, really. By the way...you mentioned marrying us off. Did you notice how Nikal looked at their king?'

'Sharp of you! So you noticed as well, eh? It could be her chance...' The old king sat musing for a while. '...and

Tudhaliyas seemed interested in her. I think I'll have a word with Kantuzzili. See if he's interested in a family alliance to cement the political one.'

Talshura looked sideways and smiled at his father's machinations. 'Always looking for a chance to marry her off....I hope it works this time. She couldn't do better.'

'Talk to her my boy; ask her to be less pushy. I think she likes him...' The Kizzuwatna monarch and his son sat quietly on the couch, musing on the future.

Chapter Ten

The scout galloped up to the prince astride his black horse and reported, 'Your highness, Hattusas is over the next range ahead. We're almost there,'

'Well done!' Artatama told the scout. He turned to his companion, 'And about time! General, I'm exhausted. I need a bath, a massage, and some female company. Twelve days on a horse is more than a man should have to endure.' Prince Artatama rode side by side at the head of the column with General Satukani, both thoroughly dirty with their beards covered in dust. The Mittani army was finally nearing its destination. 'Look, there, coming over the ridge. What d'you make of them, general?' Artatama voiced uneasily.

'I think it's a welcoming party. They have their standard raised. They don't seem hostile and they're wearing Hittite green tunics.'

'You sure?' Artatama was edgy after the long journey.

They had been under constant attack from the time they had reached the Taurus Mountains. Everybody was jumpy and watchful. Every gorge or ravine, every valley, they had expected an ambush or open attack.

'They're not the scarlet of Kizzuwatna. This is the green of Muwas. I'm sure of it,' the general reassured.

The welcoming squadron of green clad cavalry made a rapid advance towards the approaching Mittani army column, wheeling about to join it abreast. The enormous Hittite general Muwas sent, rode up to Artatama and saluted clenched fist raised at right angle. 'King Muwas sends his compliments and welcomes his Mittani allies.'

'We're delighted to be here, general. How fares King Muwas?' asked Artatama.

'He's impatient for your appearance, your highness. I'm General Ammuna, right hand to the king. We have quarters ready near the city for you and your men.'

'I hope you can provide a bath and some company,' Artatama winked at the general. 'By the way, this is General Satukani—my right hand.' Artatama gestured at his dusty companion.

'General!' Ammuna nodded his acknowledged at the bearded Mittani officer. 'As for the bath and relaxation, your highness, I'm sure that can be arranged.'

'When do you estimate we'll arrive?' General Satukani asked his opposite number.

'It's mid morning now—sometime mid afternoon should see us there. It's about six more leagues.'

Artatama heard the exchange and encouraged his horse forward. 'I'm eager to see the Hittite capital. I've heard many stories. Tell me; is it really as impregnable as they claim?'

'You may judge for yourself soon, your highness,' Ammuna answered cautiously.

*   *   *

Long horns sounded from the ramparts of the city wall heralding a fanfare to welcome the Mittani allies to Hattusas. The Mittani column divided and the main body swung left to fill the area south of the city wall while the large royal group went on through the city gates up to the Great Palace. A guard of honour mounted in the lower courtyard of the citadel indicated a deep respect for this particular visiting royalty. Hatti soldiers in green tunics stood at attention on either side of the passages all the way to the Audience Hall.

Artatama marched proudly into the vast Audience Hall, with a bearing befitting a prince and heir to the throne of Mittani, followed by his generals. On either side of the walls stood lines of tall bronze torch holders brightly lighting up the enormous murals illustrating great events from Hittite history all the way back to Labarnas. Muwas sat regally attired on the granite black bull throne. Artatama halted before the throne and bowed his respect as a prince to a king.

The Chancellor announced, 'Your majesty, may I present Prince Artatama, prince of Mittani, son of King Saustatar king of Mittani, heir to the royal throne of Mittani.'

'We welcome you Prince Artatama,' Muwas boomed, his voice carrying to every part of the hall. 'What news do you bring of your father?'

'Your majesty, my father greets the king of the Hittites...King Muwas.' He paused so that all those listening would understand. 'We bring many soldiers, friends and allies, to aid in the annihilation of your enemies.'

The protocol was a necessary formality, mainly intended for other ears. The bit about "King Muwas," and "friends and allies," would reach the intended ears in Ankuwa.

'We thank you for being such good allies of the Hatti royal house and invite you, after your long journey, to withdraw to quarters so you may refresh yourselves.' Muwas beamed good naturedly at the Mittani prince, letting him know the welcome wasn't just protocol.

The Chancellor escorted Artatama and his party to the top right-hand corner of the Audience Hall, through a small doorway which led to a private room behind the throne room. Muwas merely got to his feet and walked behind the throne and through a heavy drape covering a discreet opening in the back wall and was already waiting for the Mittani prince when he was led into the room. Both king and prince, now out of sight of the many courtiers, clasped forearms in sincere and open greeting. 'It's good to see you again Artatama,' Muwas looked closely at his long time friend.

'And you, Muwas. Sorry, I should now be particular; "King Muwas." Both my father and I were deeply saddened to hear King Muwatallis was no longer with us.'

Muwas hung his head for a moment, the smile extinguished. 'I still can't believe he's gone. Murdered by those damned sons of Huzziyas!' He gently shook his head again.

'I regret we had to invoke this part of the treaty between us, but Muwatallis was always afraid something like this might happen,' Artatama commiserated.

'Yes. Well, anyway, I'm pleased you finally got here. Was it difficult? My courier said something about you being attacked.'

Anger leapt to Artatama's face. 'Kizzuwatna, damn them! As soon as we reached the Taurus Mountains, they started being bothersome, nipping at our heels. They kept it up almost to Hattusas. We've been free of them only this last day. It slowed us up. I got your message about sending the cavalry ahead, but I couldn't comply because of them.'

'Never mind, you're here now Artatama and it's good to see a friendly face. How many men did you bring?'

'Five cavalry, ten chariot and four infantry regiments. Five regiments of sling throwers, two spear throwing regiments and five regiments of archers. Twenty five thousand all together.'

'As much and even more than I'd hoped.' A big smile spread over Muwas' face. 'I'm giving you the Yellow Castle for as long as you're here. Treat it as your home. The surrounding area will hold all your soldiers. You brought hide-tents I presume? Settle in there. Best keep your soldiers away from the town for the moment. Might antagonise our locals.'

'Gracious of you.' Artatama looked tired.

'Go down there. Rest, settle in and we'll talk more later. But I tell you once more, you're doubly welcome. With my regiments and yours, we have now gained the upper hand.'

Chapter Eleven

A clash was inevitable sooner or later, yet both sides of the civil divide were under strict orders not to engage. The two sides had cautiously settled that one mighty battle agreed in advance, would be less complicated. But the gods have always had different thoughts than men and they would have a clash sooner than later. A joint patrol in strength of two squadrons of Mittani dark blue and two squadrons of Muwas' green, ventured further south than ordered, leaving clouds of brown dust in their wake.

'I advise against this!' General Sahdaz shouted at his Mittani counterpart.

The Mittani wanted to impress the Hatti with their forceful nature. 'Oh come on—we're just out for a ride. You know there's nobody down here,' General Shurra teased.

'We've crossed into enemy territory, that's for certain. Our orders are not to provoke. You're in breach of standing orders.' Muwas' general was incensed. 'I hold you responsible if anything goes wrong!'

'Fine! I'll take responsibility. It's the least I can do for you.' The note of sarcasm was intended and wasn't missed by his counterpart. 'For goodness sake, we've eight hundred men with us. More than enough to take care of any problems.' General Shurra felt sure there weren't many yellow shirts this far north. His scouts reported the opposition had fled far to the south. The Mittani commander wanted to push the limits and see if he couldn't provoke the opposition into a skirmish. The quicker the war was started the sooner it would be over.

As luck would have it, aided by the gods, Zidanta's cavalry were out on a reconnaissance mission of their own to determine how far south Muwas might have pushed. 'The scouts tell me there's enemy activity ahead, coming this way. I'll take my squadron left and you take yours right. We'll see if we can't teach this foreign affliction a lesson,' Commander Halias told his deputy. Deep yellow shirts veered left down a sunken ravine, whilst the second squadron swung right behind a terracotta hillock. Both squadrons waited for the enemy. It was noon on the third day of the third week after the death of the former king. The sun was blinding, aiding those arranging the trap.

Those setting the ambush were warned by the brown cloud of dust thrown up by the oncoming horses. When Muwas' four squadrons were in range, Commander Halias' men loosed volley after volley of arrows into the midst of the enemy. They made no attempt to break cover but rained arrows upon the exposed cavalry. Zidanta's innovative idea was to teach the archers to ride horses. This came as a shock to the Mittani whose cavalry had no bows or arrows. They were used to fighting at close quarters.

'*I told you*!' screamed General Sahdaz at his Mittani counterpart.

'*Sound the retreat*!' yelled General Shurra at his bugler.

The horn blew loud and those who could, wheeled about and galloped in haste the way they had come, followed by their commanders. Some of the wounded who had managed to stay mounted, pursued their comrades, but many wounded were left behind with their dead, to be taken prisoner. Heads would roll for this debacle, there was little doubt of that.

* * *

In the Audience Hall of the Great Palace an outwardly penitent General Shurra stood before Artatama and Muwas. Muwas was sitting on his throne and Artatama stood by his side. The bearded Mittani commander of the earlier ambushed cavalry squadrons was being brought to account for the disaster. The clean-shaven Hatti commander, General Sahdaz, stood ten paces behind, due to be called as witness.

'You lost me over a hundred good men,' Artatama was berating the ostensibly contrite general. 'Not to speak of the shame you brought down on Mittani arms. What were you thinking?'

Muwas whispered, 'I know it's a bit late, but might it not be best to do this in private.'

'It's on everybody's lips. Far too late for secrecy,' Artatama whispered back. Artatama returned to the general. 'Well? I'm waiting! What have you to say for yourself?'

'Your highness, my scouts reported the area free of the enemy,' the general wasn't as contrite as he made out.

'And was the report correct? No!' Artatama raised his voice. 'Those watching can now say we lost the first battle, thanks to your incompetence.'

'For that I *am* sorry. For the humiliation I have caused your highness.' This time the general seemed truly remorseful.

'General Shurra, when we go into battle, I promise to assign you to the worst job I can find. It's that, or demotion. Choose!'

'I desire the former. I am yours to command.'

'Dismissed!'

The general backed out to the far end. A low murmur rippled through the courtiers present in the hall. Muwas waited for silence. 'General Sahdaz, step forward.' It was Muwas' turn to resolve *his* general's role.

The general came smartly forward and saluted clenched fist raised at right angle. For the Hatti, there was none of the bowing and scraping the Mittani military went in for.

'General Sahdaz, you warned your co-commander of the risk?' Muwas boomed, more theatrical for those observers.

'I did, majesty. Twice.'

'And he ignored your advice not to go further?'

'He did, sire.'

'What I want to know is why *you* didn't turn back?'

'I thought it imprudent to split the force. We were too far into enemy territory. We would have won the encounter but for the cowardly use of mounted archers. That I didn't foresee.'

'As co-commander, you are stripped of privileges for a year. You should have made your presence felt. Dismissed!'

The general saluted again and retired.

The whole charade had already been played out in private, of course. Muwas had previously had a quite word with Sahdaz and congratulated him on his part in the affair. Publicly, he was forced to follow his ally's condemnation.

Artatama had tut-tooted his general when Muwas wasn't present. The general had carried out his private orders to engage the enemy. That it hadn't gone as planned was down to the fortunes of war. Publicly he had no choice but to be severe. It was expected. A tension had already sprung up between Muwas and Artatama as to how to conduct the war. Artatama couldn't, wouldn't understand why they did not head south with their combined army and finish the insurrectionists off. Their joint forces outnumbered the rebels.

On the other hand, Muwas needed the support of the Hittite nobles in order to win the population round to his view—to this end he was meticulous in following the rules of engagement agreed privately, if somewhat antagonistically, with Kantuzzili. Both wanted to keep the casualties to a minimum for the same reason. No matter who won, they would still need to defend the country from their predatory neighbours. They needed the Hatti army to survive.

Chapter Twelve

"**U**nc, can we come with you?"....."Unc, can we come with you?" still reverberated in his ears from his bored nephews.

Might just do the job myself, Harep brooded. *Bloody nuisance those two.* He sat in the boat, hood above his eyes, staring at the oarsman rowing hard across the fast flowing river to the main part of Nerik. He needed his nephews...yet he could quite happily do without their incessant chatter. Anything dangerous, he vowed, he would push them into it. 'Can't you row any faster?' Harep glared at the sweating oarsman.

The oarsman ignored his passenger and kept to a steady pace. This early in the morning called for a balanced tempo. He had the whole day to go yet.

Harep trailed his hand in the water, deep in thought. He still had no idea who was killing off the assassins. As the new head of the Order, he knew he was next. But who could get close enough to do such a thing? It had to be an inside job. In whose interest was it to get rid of the assassins? Who was out to do away with the Order? Who had they upset that they would do such a thing? If he was being realistic; all their past victim's friends and families would have been suspects. He really needed more information to sort this out. The oars splashed water on his arms. 'Watch out, you're soaking me, you fool,' Harep glared at the oarsman.

'Sorry guv,' the man apologised.

'I'll give you sorry!' Harep turned his attention to the reason for his current trip. He got to wondering who wanted to hire him. What the job was—and most of all—who the intended victim was to be? Finally the boat bumped the jetty and Harep disembarked. Without a backward glance he made for the nearest alley and began the steep climb to the main thorough-way running through Nerik. He found *The Sheaf*, a tavern adjoining the main bakery, squeezed in between a leather shop and a textile merchant.

The town stirred early and people were already bustling about, buying, selling. Stalls were set up on any available space. The Kaska market patrol was busily moving those who hadn't paid a bribe or who simply blocked pedestrian traffic. The tavern kept bakery hours and any spare emmer-wheat was used to make beer.

Harep entered and sat in a far corner, back to the wall, where he could keep an eye out for any danger. Incoming customers were few, but continuous. Workers downed a jug of beer instead of breakfast, then hurriedly left. One customer caught his eye, sitting in the opposite corner, dark cloak and dim light hiding his size and dress. He nursed a jug without making much effort to drink from it. The two cloaked men remained in their respective seats in opposite corners for some time, cautiously eyeing each other. Then Harep felt he had had enough, gulped the last of his drink, got to his feet and made to leave—as did the other man. That was the contact. Harep came over and sat at the other's table. 'You looking for me?'

'Might be,' the bulky man responded.

Even the cloak could not hide his considerable size, now Harep was up close.

'Did you send a message, or not. I'm in no mood for games.' Harep was getting fed up.

'You got any proof?'

Harep felt in the inside pocket of the cloak and pulled out a dragon cartouche. He flashed it at the stranger.

'Right! That's the one. Now we can get to business. Yes, I sent the message. If you're interested, I got a job for you?'

'What's the job?'

'The usual—and a bonus for speed.'

'Who's the target?'

'An upstart who needs to be dealt with. Your lot's done this before.' A whisper already, went even lower. 'We want you to do Tudhaliyas.'

If Harep was surprised, he did not show it. 'This isn't like the last one. Guards were lax. No one expected the last one just then. This time, it's exactly what they'll expect. I'll bet he's guarded day and night. I need to think about this.' He sat there, pondering.

'If you can't, then I'll have to find someone who can.' That was designed to get at Harep's professional pride. It worked.

'I didn't say I couldn't. I just said it would be more difficult.'

'If it was easy, why would we need to hire you?' The other was sounding irritable and shifted his bulk around on the stool. The stool protested.

'Let me see. I get rid of Tudhaliyas and he's replaced by Kantuzzili…or his brother. Have you thought of that.' Harep felt smug.

'Y—e—s, we know! So what do you suggest?'

'Why not get rid of…all three?'

'Can you do that?' Cautiously, the big man eyed Harep.

'I can try. But whoever's pulling the purse-strings better make it worth my while. I mean big. This is a one-off job. Then I'm gone—retire.'

'Fine, fine. Retire. As long as you get the job done.'

'I'm going to have to talk with my people. Meet me here in a couple of days and I'll give you my answer.'

* * *

A couple of days after the first meeting, Harep again made the steep climb up the narrow alleyway to the main thoroughfare running through Nerik. *The Sheaf* tavern doors were open and the babble of voices announced a crowd had gathered, enjoying a lunchtime break. The adjoining bakery was doing good business, as was the leather shop next door. The noonday sun beat down steadily. Harep was forced to produce a lot of doubletalk trying to dissuade his nephews from accompanying him to the arranged meeting with Muwas' agent. He implied the agent wouldn't approach them if others were present, or they may not be given the mission with strangers present or even the pay would have to be increased or somehow reduced with three assassins on the job. Doubletalk. Harep intended he should be the main beneficiary for any work done.

Inside the tavern, he spotted the same bulky agent sitting in the same corner, at the same table, the dark cloak still unable to disguise his considerable bulk.

'You're late,' came the gruff angry voice. 'I've been waiting all morning.'

Harep sat heavily. 'No ferryman,' he lied.

The anger lingered in his voice, 'Huh! Well if you pull this off, you can buy a fleet of boats.'

'I'll buy what *I* like, not what *you* suggest. Let's get to business. What's your offer, *if* I take the job?'

'I'm authorised to offer you thirty thousand shekels upon completion.'

'Fifty thousand! Not a *mina* less. In gold. Let's not cheapen the price of a throne.' Harep sat stony faced. Harep could hear the sharp intake of breath at his counter proposal. The agent stared hard at the assassin. Was he going to budge? He decided the assassin wouldn't.

'Right! Done! They said you'd drive a hard bargain.'

'I haven't finished. Five thousand up front—expenses. The balance to be held for me with the town treasury of Hakpis. I know you'll find the town. I don't get the rest until the job's done, but you must deposit the money in advance so I know it's there. When the Town Treasurer informs me he's got the deposit, I'll begin making my moves.' Harep felt smug for having come up with this method, but his face showed no emotion.

All the agent could say was, 'You're a sly one and no mistake. Hope you stay alive to complete the job.'

'What d'you mean by that?' Harep's hackles rose.

'Don't get touchy. It's my business to know what happens. We hear someone's having a go at your lot—you know what I mean.'

'I know what you mean. You'd better not have anything to do with it—or the deal's off.'

'It's in our interest to keep you alive, not to kill you. No! You'd better look closer to home for that culprit.'

'I don't need *your* advice. Stick to the business at hand. I told you before, if you think it's so easy to do this job, *you* do it. Otherwise, those are my conditions.' Harep kept his voice low, but with an icy tinge to it. He was intent on making the agent believe him.

'Reluctantly, I have little choice but to agree to your terms. I'm ordered to employ the guild. Personally, I would be only too happy to thrash you. My Lord Muwas, however, insists you be given the task. It is agreed. Wait here and I will go get you the five thousand.' The big man got up and left.

Harep sat at the table with a broad grin. So! The agent had brought five thousand in gold, had he? *I wonder where he's stashed it? Might be with some of his pals outside town.* It suggested he might have asked for a lot more. *Well, the deal's done. Too late now.* He intended to offer ten thousand each to his nephews to help. Anything dangerous and he would have them do it. He would tell them the job paid thirty thousand and he was being generous—and willing to split it three ways. Nothing about the advance. That would allow thirty thousand for himself. And he thought his nephews ought to consider themselves lucky he had let them have that much—if they survived. After what seemed a long time, the agent returned, empty-handed. Harep was furious. So it was all a stupid game. What did they take him for? A fool! He reached for his dagger.

'I have the gold outside,' the agent told Harep, sitting in his old seat. 'In some saddle-bags on a donkey. What? You thought I was going to diddle you, did you?' He had noticed the furry on Harep's face.

'The thought had crossed my mind,' Harep acknowledged. He quickly regained his composure. 'Let's go have a look.' Both left the table and went to see the laden donkey, a thin mangy animal, undernourished and maltreated. 'Is this the best you could do?' Harep accused.

'Do you want everyone to know what you're carrying? That's what animals look like around here, don't they? Why advertise?' The agent was amused at Harep's reaction. 'When you go back across the river, just leave her. She'll find her own way home.'

'You been spying on me?' Harep demanded, checking the load.

'Don't be so touchy. You've got what you wanted. All we're doing is protecting our investment. If you're satisfied, then I'll be getting along?' The bulk made to go.

'I'm satisfied with this,' Harep motioned at the donkey. 'As for the rest, we'll see.' He took hold of the reins and without glancing back at the agent, led the animal down the narrow alleyway to the river.

*   *   *

'You haven't told anyone, have you, what we're doing, where we're going?' Harep demanded.

'Of course not, what do you take us for?' Rewa jumped in quickly.

A couple of days later Harep and his two nephews were on the road to Hakpis. He wanted to check with the Town Treasurer if the money had been deposited as agreed. And he wanted to renew his acquaintanceship with the wily old treasurer, with whom he had dealings before. Harep looked at thin Parap astride his horse.

'No! Stop your worrying.' Parap seemed uncomfortable with the question.

Harep shook his head. 'You young fool. Who did you tell? Out with it, or I'll drag you off that horse and beat it out of you with a whip.'

Parap flinched at the prospect. 'Honest, I didn't,' he tried to bluff.

Harep was an old hand at lying and catching out liars. He knew his nephews. Rewa probably hadn't blabbed, but Parap, three years younger than Rewa, couldn't resist telling anyone who would listen what an important person he was. That included boasting. A few tankards and the whole tavern would know what his business was. At least, that was Harep's opinion. Harep stopped his horse and made to get off.

Parap saw Harep was serious about pulling him off the horse. 'All right...all right. I met one of our lot in the tavern below our lodging.'

Harep nudged his horse closer to Parap.

Parap flinched. 'You know... from the fortress,' Parap continued. 'Tohor, you remember him, don't you. Back in the fortress, on the corridor below us. We got to talking about who was killing the assassins. You're the head of the Order now and I was trying to help you. Anyway, we had a few drinks and he asked me what I was doing. I saw no harm in telling him. I mean, he's one of us, isn't he?'

'You loud mouth. You just couldn't resist boasting, could you?' Harep was riding on Parap's left and without warning, Harep swung his right arm out and hit Parap full in the face with the back of his hand. Parap fell backwards off his horse.

Rewa was riding on Parap's right and grabbed the reins to stop Parap's horse from bolting. The ground was rocky and Parap landed awkwardly—and lay still. Rewa jumped down to examine his brother. '*You've killed him,*' he yelled in horror.

All Harep said was, 'Good riddance to bad rubbish.'

That shocked Rewa into silence. He stared down at his younger brother, not understanding what just happened. Anger mingled with grief, but he kept his sword sheathed. Instead, tears welled up and flowed freely down his cheeks, silently.

Harep got down to make sure Parap was really dead. He felt his neck pulse. Opened his eyes and peered closely into them. 'Yep! You're right. Neck broken. He's dead. Bigger share for you, Rewa. Better still, we'll split his share. What d'you say? Is it a deal?'

Rewa stared at his brother…then nodded. His tears dried up. Greed got the better of him. Death among assassins was a common event. He tried to put this personal tragedy into perspective—helped by the thought of five thousand shekels in gold.

'I didn't mean to kill him,' Harep cajoled. 'I just wanted to teach him a lesson. Hit his neck on a rock when he landed. Still, can't be helped. We got to get on.'

'We can't just leave him like this,' Rewa objected.

'You're right,' Harep agreed. 'We'll burry him. The ground's all rock here, so we can't dig. It'll have to be rocks.' They hurriedly built a cairn over the body, remounted and put some distance behind them—in silence.

Rewa was sullen, despite the promise of a share of Parap's loot.

Harep left Rewa to stew—letting him store up trouble for the future.

Chapter Thirteen

'*Collect me again tomorrow, same time*,' Kantuzzili
shouted in the driver's ear.

'*Yes, sir*,' the driver responded.

The chariot came to a halt in a cloud of dust outside his
mansion and he jumped off. Guards hurried to open the gates.
The chariot quickly pulled away, followed by the cavalry
escort and disappeared into the dusk. Back from a strategy
meeting, Kantuzzili stood for a moment, looking at the
looming twilight. He breathed deeply and went through the
ornate gateway, nodding his thanks to them. The flat-roof two
storey mansion had belonged to the top Assyrian merchant in
Ankuwa. He had been only too happy to vacate it for the
Hatti royal family, avaricious eyes seeing future privileges
accruing in return. The courtyard had a central fountain.
Green trees were flowering in the early spring. Multicoloured
flowers were laid out in a dazzling geometric display and the
garden scents filled the evening air. Assyrian gardens always
tended to be over cultivated, thought Kantuzzili while he
walked along the flagstone path to the main entrance. Sitting
outside on the porch with its colourful wall decorations, he
came across his brother. 'Taking in the evening breeze?'

'It's so beautiful out here. The war seems so far away.
Anyway, how did the meeting go?'

'All the generals want to do is get started. They're
itching to be killing. I asked them if they were itching to kill
Hittites. They stared back in embarrassed silence.'

'What can you expect! They're soldiers. Killing is all
they know.'

'This is exactly why I'm holding back. If it were a
foreign enemy, I'd immediately unleash the lot. But it isn't.
We'll be killing our own. Our neighbours are waiting,

watching. Will we come out of this civil war so weakened they might profit? How weak will we be at the end? The Mittani are already here, thanks to that fool Muwas. He can't see further than his nose.'

'Calm down, brother. Remember, I know the problem. We're in this together.'

'The one good feature that stood out at the conference was Zidanta—he sat silent throughout the meeting. He senses what I do. He knows we're tearing ourselves apart. You were right to suggest him. He senses why I only want one big battle. One big slaughter that decides the outcome.'

At that moment two women came out into the porch area, sturdy Gassulawiya, Kantuzzili's wife trailing Tawana, Himuili's slender wife. 'What are you two plotting this time?' Gassulawiya chided pleasantly. Both had light garments on, dresses trimmed with coloured embroidery and a cloth tie round their waists.

Kantuzzili approached her and embraced his wife, kissing her lightly on the cheek. 'We're not plotting. All the plotting's been done. We're beyond that. Are we eating soon? I'm famished.'

'The servants are bringing the food now, setting the table,' Tawana informed them.

'Where's Tudhaliyas?' Kantuzzili asked.

'He's talking to Shunashura in the sun-room,' Gassulawiya answered.

'And the twins are closeted upstairs. They can't seem to get enough of each other's company,' Tawana added.

'I'm going to wash and get changed before we eat,' Kantuzzili went inside and turned left into the corridor. At the far end there was a large washroom and toilet. In the corner stood a clay bath with a built-in seat. Two servants brought water and helped Kantuzzili disrobe. One poured water over him sitting, whilst the other used a sponge to rub him down. Another servant brought a towel and clean clothing. After freshening up, he went along to the dining room and found his family, wives, brother, nephew, and the Kizzuwatna king with his twins, sitting round a long cedarwood table laden with a variety of roast meats, bowls of peas and beans. Unleavened bread and plates of pancakes. Figs, apples, apricot, pomegranates and medlars. Wine was poured into goblets by the servants and everybody gave themselves to eating.

*   *   *

Tagrama had issued orders for work to commence on the temple of the Storm God in Ankuwa, restoring it back to its pristine condition. 'I simply can't understand how they let things get to this state,' he complained to his deputy to the background sound of bronze hammers on chisels. 'We had to use it for the sacrifice, but I was far from happy.' Outside it was mid-noon, and the sun was high in the sky. Inside, smoke from the torches rose in shimmering spirals towards the ceiling. Both priests stood talking at the back of the altar. Both craning their necks upwards, inspecting some cracks in the back of the building. Like all Hittite temples, it had a flat roof supported by enormous wooden crossbeams fashioned out of cedars from Ugarit.

'It's mostly Assyrians here, your eminence. They don't follow the same gods. They all worship the heathen Marduk in their houses,' his deputy tried to excuse the foreigners for the neglect.

'Respect for our gods was a requirement of allowing this trading post to be set up. They had a duty to upkeep the temple.'

His skinny deputy shrugged. Tagrama had always been fastidious. They were interrupted from the naos on the other side of the altar, the sound of heavy metal clanged as one of the workmen above, dropped his bronze chisel.

It startled Tagrama, but he persevered, 'Yes, yes, I know you think I'm an old fuss pot, but I ask you, how can we serve carelessly? Either we respect and worship the gods, or we just go through the motions.' Tagrama wondered again if he had made the right choice in appointing Loros as his deputy.

'The work is well in hand, your eminence.' His deputy changed the subject.

'I can hear. They seem to have the falling sickness in their hands. Look, I've been thinking. The ballot of the nobles might have worked—if all involved had given it a chance. I find I can't just stand by while we slaughter each other.' Tagrama became animated. 'There must be a way to resolve this without all the killing?' They walked round to the front of the altar and continued the discussion there, where Tagrama could keep an eye on the workmen.

'If you could get Muwas to agree to a truce, maybe propose an interim regency? Neither ascends to power for say two years. I'm not saying they'll go for it, but maybe we could encourage them to delay hostilities.' Loros was simply groping in the dark.

'It can't hurt to send out feelers. I'm going to try. Find a priest you can trust and I'll send a message to Muwas. In the mean time, I'll try and see what Kantuzzili thinks of a delay. Go now, find me a messenger.'

Loros left, going down the naos, to find a suitable priest as courier to take the message to Muwas.

*　　*　　*

Some days later, a distressed priest hurried round the square piers supporting the roof searching for Tagrama, finding him in the peristyle, berating one of the workmen.

'How many times do I have to tell you?' Tagrama was bawling, 'I don't want a gravel ramp out front, but a regal paved ramp. Why can't you understand? Paved not gravel. You *do* speak Hatti?'

The stubborn fellow looked back sullenly. 'We *all* speak Hatti. Even us poor workmen.'

Tagrama ignored the insolence.

The distressed priest with the message waited to one side patiently, as he had been trained, until the high priest was free.

'So why am I not getting through to you?' Tagrama demanded of the workman.

'Because we can't get hold of paving stone, that's why. The stone dressers have all joined the army. Promise of loot.'

'Are you saying we can't get paving stones because there's no one to dress the stones? They've left for the army? We'll see about that. By tomorrow, you'll have the stone dressers back. I promise you.' Tagrama dismissed the workman and beckoned the messenger, noticing for the first time the young priest was close to tears. 'What's the matter? What have you got for me?'

'Your reverence, I don't know how to tell you,' and he burst into tears. 'Muwas sent his head back,' he sobbed.

'Who's head?' Although deep down Tagrama knew.

'The poor courier you sent with the peace feelers to Muwas. That monster enclosed this,' the priest handed him a waxed board.

Tagrama stood quietly remembering the old priest he had sent to Hattusas. He had served the gods all his life and wished nothing but to end his life doing the same. 'I'm sorry for that kind old man. He did no one any harm. I was stupid to think Muwas' mind could be influenced.' In a whisper, more to himself, 'It's the arrogance of being a high priest, I suppose. I think people will really listen to me because I *am* the high priest. I delude myself.' He opened the tablet and read the wedge-shaped impressions.

"You've chosen sides but you still want to have it both ways. You want your side to win, but you also want to stay blameless. Had you not sent this priest, he would still be

alive. On your head is his death. I send you his head. See if you can still stay blameless?"

Muwas did not sign it. He did not need to. Tagrama *did* feel blame. Deep inside where it hurt. He embraced the sobbing young priest, wanting to comfort him and felt hot bitter tears run down his own cheeks.

Chapter Fourteen

Nikal, one morning, took an early walk in the vicinity where she gleaned from her servants Tudhaliyas sometimes exercised his combat skills. She, accompanied by Talarra; Tudhaliyas always accompanied by a host of his royal bodyguards. Talshura suggested he accompany her, but unusually, she declined his offer. This intrigued him and he easily deduced why. Dutifully, he informed his father, the king. At hearing the news, Shunashura responded with a twinkle in his eye and a broad smile. Nikal stood almost blatantly on the red clay hillock, her long brown hair lifted by the gentle breeze, overlooking the otherwise flat exercise ground, watching whilst the soldiers trained in mock combat. Tudhaliyas noticed the two women and guessed by the aquiline profile, who one of them was. He was pleased Nikal took the trouble. It would make a subsequent approach to her far simpler.

On the second day, a table with chairs and shade was set aside a little distance from the exercise ground, downwind from the dust and Tudhaliyas sent a servant to invite Nikal to come and watch their activities in comfort. She found this too forward and left embarrassed at being so obvious. Yet on the morning of the third day, the table and chairs were yet again provided and this time, Nikal went straight to the proffered chairs with Talarra and both sat. Tudhaliyas' servants brought a bowl of fruit and drinks and after the training, the king joined her, still perspiring freely. 'Your highness, may I welcome you. What did you think of the spectacle?'

'Your majesty, I used to watch my brother exercise and it always gave me a thrill. Your majesty takes it much more seriously than he did.'

'Although I thoroughly enjoy the sparring, make no mistake, I have a battle to win and it is coming soon. I need to be the fittest I've ever been in my life. I train with the best instructors the army can provide. Although we have fewer numbers, we must beat Muwas. The alternative is unthinkable. You can understand, can't you?'

'Yes...I can.' She paused as if she were mulling it over. 'You'll win, I'm sure of it. They say your uncle's a brilliant strategist. With you at the head of the army, I'm sure your soldiers will follow you to the gates of the netherworld, if you asked them to.' She thought she might have overdone the praise and lowered her eyes in embarrassment.

'For those kind words, I thank you from the bottom of my heart.' He paused, letting the reference to his "heart" sink in. 'Maybe your highness would care to join me in an early picnic. I know a spot at the head of the valley, where spring has taken over the world.'

She felt this was going too quickly. 'I promised to show Gassulawiya how to do Kizzuwatna embroidery. It would be rude of me not to turn up, wouldn't it.'

'If you made a promise to my aunt, you must keep it. Some other time perhaps?'

'Yes, I think I would like that.'

'By the way, "your majesty" is so formal. My close friends call me Tudhaliyas. I would look on it favourably if you consented to be my friend. And I will call you Nikal—with your permission?'

'You do me an honour, your maj.....Tudhaliyas. I must go now. Till we meet another time.' Both women left the table and made for the hillock.

He waved her goodbye and watched sympathetically while she climb the hillock towards her mansion. When she had disappeared, he returned with increased vigour to his combat exercises.

*　　*　　*

A day went by without Nikal visiting the exercise grounds, although Tudhaliyas had the shaded table and chairs set out just in case. The way she excused herself, he guessed he had pushed the idea of a picnic too soon. Tudhaliyas was self-possessed enough to realise that if he were to get closer to this Kizzuwatna princess, he would have to be gentle, be kind, like he would with a reluctant horse. Make all the right moves so as not to frighten her off. Back off when need be, give her enough space to accommodate her evident feelings for him. That penetrating look she gave the first time they had met lingered in his mind, his heart, his very essence. If he could, he intended to make her his queen, his partner for the rest of his life. On realising the depth of his feelings, he knew he was in love for the first time. It frightened him. The responsibility of it.

The day following, Nikal appeared as usual, accompanied by her handmaiden, Talarra. Tudhaliyas welcomed her with a smile and she demurely returned his smile. She sat at the sheltered table as if it were the most normal thing in the world for a young unmarried princess to come and watch men exercise. Drinks and fruit arrived and even at that time in the morning, the sun was already hot.

A couple of chariots from the elite Taru Regiment thundered up in a cloud of dust and came to a halt by Tudhaliyas. That morning was to be chariot training; driving; throwing spears and firing with a bow at targets. None other than General Zidanta himself was taking charge of instructing the king. 'General, I'm honoured you should take the time off to exercise with me,' Tudhaliyas observed.

The general was a tough soldier with many years of fighting behind him. Tudhaliyas knew he was in for a rigorous work out. Nothing less could be expected from the involvement of the chief of his army. It started well with Zidanta standing astride one of the dark coloured chariots whilst Tudhaliyas climbed aboard the other. As was usual, there were three soldiers per chariot. The driver, the shield bearer and the spear thrower. Zidanta had Tudhaliyas take the role of the spear thrower in the first charge.

Both chariots—well spaced apart—built up considerable speed on the straight before wheeling tightly to the left. It was at that point the spear was hurled at the stationary wooden-pole target where it was suggested the enemy infantry might be. Tudhaliyas hit the middle of the target. Zidanta also hit the target. A roar of approval came from those who had gathered to watch their king being put through his paces by their army commander.

Nikal's face was full of apprehension when the chariots charged, but when Tudhaliyas hit the mark, she jumped up and cheered with the rest. Talarra watched her mistress with quite disapproval and not for the first time, bit her tongue at the unladylike behaviour. Many times on the docks of Adaniya she had been unable to suppress her disapproval at what the princess managed to get up to, cautioning her with what her father would say if he were there to see her.

The two chariots repeated the manoeuvre a couple of times to eliminate the possibility of them being judged flukes. Then there followed the same charge but instead, using a bow and arrow. Again two similar charges were carried out. Zidanta pronounced himself exceedingly satisfied with his royal pupil. Tudhaliyas acknowledged the praise. Finally, General Zidanta proposed one more assignment for the king. They were to assume the driver and shield bearer had been somehow dislodged from the chariot and Tudhaliyas was to become the driver and to wield a spear at the same time. This called for some fancy work with the reins. The reins were tied round the waist and the swivel action of the torso was to guide the horses, leaving the hands free to hurl the spear. It was the ultimate test for a charioteer. Both richly decorated chariots were whipped into a full charge, then the reins tied round the waists, for Zidanta insisted on performing the same as the king and the spear was to be hurled at the target as before. All went well on the straight until the tight turn near the target. The horses were well exercised and having already done the run six times, were getting a little tired in the hot sun. Tudhaliyas' weaker left side horse stumbled as he wheeled left, pulling the other horse down, making the chariot jump upwards when the shaft pole bit into the earth. Tudhaliyas was thrown upwards; coming down—he hit the ground rolling.

An "*ahhhhhh*" escaped from the crowd watching fearing the worst.

Nikal jumped up and put a hand over her mouth in anticipation of disaster.

Tudhaliyas rolled like a log over flat ground, until the impetus left him and he came to a halt. Then he simply got up, brushing himself off as if he had done this stunt many times that day. The roar of relief and approval was deafening and likely to have been heard in the next valley, at least Talarra would claim it was the case the next day when she retold the story.

General Zidanta pulled his chariot up by the king and jumped off scratching his head. 'It's clear your majesty is protected by the gods. Either that or there is cat blood in the royal family.' Tudhaliyas smiled crookedly with nervous relief at the benign outcome of such a horrendous looking accident.

'Lion blood to be precise, my dear general,' Tudhaliyas managed. Officers and servants rushed towards the king. Tudhaliyas stood, brushing himself from dust, smarting with the scratches on his arms and legs and chortled in exultation at his close escape.

When it was clear the king wasn't hurt, Nikal expelled a sigh of anguished release and tears welled up inside her. She dabbed at them delicately so no one would notice. Talarra watched her mistress expressing her love for the king of Hatti.

Chapter Fifteen

Muwas sat proudly out front on a black charger, a scowl on his face. He was leading a squadron of his green-shirted Mešedi the short distance north-east to the outcrop of rock where a couple of small recessed ravines were venerated for their intrinsic natural beauty. A wall had been constructed many decades earlier closing off the entrance to the ravine. Muwas thought the scurrilous high priest might have hidden his temple treasures there. 'I'll find his damned holy loot and appropriate them for my treasury,' Muwas cursed under his breath. 'I swear I will!'

They arrived at the wall fronting the outcrop of two natural chambers where in pre-Hittite times a spring once flowed. A sacred place for many hundreds of years, a spring-sanctuary from older times. Muwas dismounted and led a large body of soldiers through the irregular wall shutting off the main chamber from the outside world. A lone old priest emerged from the chamber to bar his way. Both stood staring at each other, Muwas' scowl deepening. 'Who else is here?' Muwas demanded loudly.

'No one else.' Defiance was writ broad on the priest's face.

'No one else, *what*? You insolent old goat.' Muwas' anger climbed.

The priest shrugged.

That was too much for Muwas. He closed on the old priest in a few steps, drawing his dagger from his belt as he approached, holding it waist level, gently cupped his left hand round the priest's crinkled neck and pulled him onto the dagger.

The priest pushed against Muwas and staggered backwards, still with the impudent sneer. Blood gushed freely as the dagger sprang free. The old priest fell on his knees, smiled and lurched sideways, dead.

'No one else, *your majesty!*' Muwas shouted at the dead priest. 'Maybe they'll teach you respect for your king in the netherworld.' To his soldiers he commanded, 'Spread out. Search the place thoroughly. Tear it apart if you have to. You know what you're looking for.' Muwas went and sat on a marble bench by a sculpture of a stag standing against a wall, watching his Mešedi commit sacrilege, turning stones over, tearing at hangings. It was unnecessary wanton damage and Muwas enjoyed it. He felt he was getting at Tagrama with a long hand. After a while each report came back: nothing could be found. 'I know it's here,' he raged at his men. He picked out a captain, 'I want you to stay here with ten men and make a painstaking job of it. Demolish the place, if you have to, but find the treasure. Do I make myself clear?'

'Yes, sire.'

Muwas found his horse, remounted and left the despoiled sanctuary heading back to Hattusas for Tagrama's main temple. He had asked Artatama to provide a couple of his Mittani priests, worshipers of Teshub. Artatama had obliged, curious as to what a Hittite king would want with priests to an alien god. The short ride to the main temple, down through the North Gate, was memorable only to Muwas. He kept mulling over in his mind his recent perceived humiliation. Tagrama *should* have acknowledged him as king, not delayed with his ridiculous vote of the nobles. It galled that the high priest had the nerve to impede him. *Who the Yarris did he think he was*? Muwas was going to teach him what power a king could wield. The black charger's hooves clattered loud on the large stone cobbles outside the temple. Again he dismounted. He turned and called the priests of Teshub to him. He pointed at the temple and told them, 'This is your new home from now on. Hatti will no longer hold with Taru if their high priests turn traitor to their rightful king.'

The Mittani priests were utterly astonished at what they heard. Was it a joke of this strange king? For an instant they weren't sure he had actually said what he had. 'Your majesty, are we to worship Teshub here?' the elder asked.

Muwas nodded. 'Go into town, find some acolytes, train them to worship Teshub—for that is now the religion of Hatti.'

That was clear enough. The Mittani priests couldn't believe their luck.

Muwas led the way inside with his soldiers following. He drew his scimitar sword and prepared to slaughter any priest of the old religion he found in the temple. To his vexation the temple was empty. Not one priest did he find to sacrifice to his new religion. Leaving the temple in the hands of their new owners, he made his way through the town to the southern gate. The townspeople came out as the news spread. "The king is here." Half heartedly the meagre crowd waved and cheered the new incumbent of the royal castle. Muwas noted the lack of enthusiasm and became stern faced, taking his soldiers down through the South Gate to Artatama. Outside the gate, all around was a sea of hide-tents. Twenty-five thousand Mittani soldiers encamped round the Yellow Castle.

The citadel, Artatama's new residence, stood on the highest and most precipitous part of the prominence outside the city walls of Hattusas, a thousand cubits south-west of the royal palace surrounded by wilderness. The tower-like "keep" was approached by a tortuous path through an outer system of multiple defensive walls. It now stood vacated by Kantuzzili and was to be occupied by Artatama while the Mittani contingent remained in Hatti. Mittani blue shirts had control. On the castle ramparts, blue shirts noted the king's squadron and the massive gates between the towers were hurriedly thrown open.

Muwas' squadron cantered left down a double wall siege trap, right into a redoubt and then through a series of contravallations into the castle courtyard. The defences were formidable. Neither the previous king, nor Muwas had ever set foot in Kantuzzili's castle. This was now his, by right of kingship and conquest. He dismounted, gave the reins to a Mešedi and took the stairs two at a time through the main entrance. In the main hall he found Artatama with his senior officers sitting round a long cedarwood table, eating and discussing the coming campaign. All jumped up at the approach of the Hatti king.

'Welcome King Muwas. We would have greeted you with an honour guard had we been forewarned of your arrival.' Artatama came round the table to greet Muwas.

Although they both disagreed about when to begin the battle, Muwas and Artatama needed each other and so their previous disagreement was put aside, for now. Muwas was about to lower Artatama's guard by flattery. 'No need to be so formal. I just came to tell you I've left your priests up in the main temple. The one's you kindly supplied.'

Artatama's quizzical expression implied he had forgotten all about them. 'Yes, I remember. Are they to learn the ways of Taru?'

'Certainly not! I've given them the temple so they could teach us the ways of Teshub. He is to be our new deity. Hatti has a new religion in honour of its allies.'

Artatama's countenance spread into subtle amusement, as did all those standing round the table. But as one, they gave a loud cheer for the Hittite king.

Chapter Sixteen

The meal over, the tall queen stood and took her six months old baby boy, from the wet-nurse, holding, rocking him gently from side to side at her bosom. The chubby wet-nurse hovered nearby anxiously watching.

King Kasalliwa, dark and beefy, sat at one end of a long dining table, sipping wine, deep in conversation with his brother, Mokhat, who was also holding a goblet. 'We brought in one of the assassins last night,' the king was telling Mokhat. 'A patrol found him in a brothel near the river. He was refusing to pay and the old woman and she sent for the law enforcers. He resisted and had to be subdued. Wouldn't talk at first, so I went down to the dungeon and took off my shirt. Once he saw my Illuyankas tattoo, he opened up. He told me a story he got from Parap, a nephew of someone called Harep. Do you know them?'

'I do indeed. Harep's their new chief.' Mokhat rubbed his chin in recollection. 'The other day, before I came up to the castle, I saw him in town with two others. Tried to catch up with them but they gave me the slip. So what did he have to say for himself?'

The king took another sip and continued, 'Tells me Muwas has hired one of them to finish Tudhaliyas. Not only Tudhaliyas, but Kantuzzili *and* his brother. Harep's going down to Ankuwa to do the job. Taking his nephews with him for help...I'm not sure we ought to let him do this job. What d'you think?'

Mokhat's mouth was open. 'The stupid harebrained oaf,' he exploded. 'He simply can't leave things alone. I thought when they fled from the fortress, that would be the end of them. Now this!'

'Yes, yes. Calm yourself.' Kasalliwa put a hand on his brother's arm. 'The question is...should we stop them?'

'That you should ask is beyond me. Of course we should put an end to this trade. I mean the assassination industry. You should never have allowed it to continue in the first place.'

Kasalliwa, rubbing his full beard, would have none of that. 'I allowed them to continue to counter the Hittite expansion. On the field we were no match. This way I put the fear of Yarris in them. I admit it's got out of hand. But there were sound reasons for them at the time.'

'But that reason is long past—and Harep's a menace.' Mokhat's face was fierce.

'Why so?'

'He's good. Probably better than Molut. If Tudhaliyas can be assassinated, Harep's the man to do it.'

Kasalliwa banged his goblet down on the table. 'Then he must be stopped. Agreed?'

'Agreed!'

'It's time we tried to make peace with Hatti, I mean a solid neighbourly peace based on trade. This constant warring benefits neither side. We need to grab this opportunity of a change of king; Muwas is of the old mould, to establish a fresh relationship between our peoples. I think Tudhaliyas is the man to deal with—and so—we have to stop this assassination. You have to stop this Harep. The future of both nations is in your hands.' Kasalliwa had raised his voice for emphasis and was almost shouting.

'I will do my utmost to prevent Harep,' Mokhat reaffirmed, equally loudly.

The noise woke the baby and he began to exercise his lungs loudly. The queen took him further down the room, away from the discussion, followed by the wet-nurse.

'That settles it. Since you're the only one who knows what Harep looks like, I want you to take a message down to Tudhaliyas. Tell him he has our support. Make sure you get through to him his life's in danger. You must stop Harep, at all costs.' The king features grimaced into iron will and determination.

Chapter Seventeen

Nikal stood firmly, feet apart, knees bent, hands gripping the rail to her left, confident her guards would protect her. The chariot driver was under strict instructions not to go too fast. Opposite stood Talarra, also gripping the rail with white knuckles, face white, bosom heaving. Talarra was terrified at the prospect of riding the chariot, nevertheless she insisted on going where her mistress went. The chariot built for three now held four—the driver on the reins and a burly guard at the back preventing the women falling off.

Tudhaliyas was in another chariot abreast, watching them like a hawk. The slightest sign of trouble and he would intervene. He had finally managed to convince Nikal to go on the picnic, with the help of a little gentle coaxing from his mother and aunt. They reassured her it was quite proper, and anyway, they would chaperone her. So it was on a fine spring morning twenty chariots and a wagon set out to where the river entered the valley. The sun drenched the green scenery and the vegetation soaked up the life giving energy, becoming more vibrant in the process.

Nikal seemed extraordinarily exhilarated by her first chariot ride and if she had dared, would have urged the driver to persuade the horses into a gallop. As a young girl, she and her brother used to ride bareback and the feeling of speed was a rush she would never forget. As a young woman it was unseemly for her to ride bareback anymore and she turned to daydreaming. Now, suddenly there was the possibility of recapturing just a small measure of the excitement of her youth and she was thrilled by it.

The route to the head of the valley went along red earth paths, through blossoming trees and vibrant young foliage.

Flowers were out in full colour and the birds were commandeering their territories by an explosion of song. All of nature was proclaiming the rights of spring. The intense blue sky; the high mountains surrounding the valley. All colluded in the rebirth of nature. Nikal breathed all this in deeply, inhaling crisp fresh air. Feeling intensely the thrill of life through every fibre of her body, standing on a moving platform, watching the flora and fauna of the valley speed by her.

The picnic site was flat lush grass, with the river flowing rapidly nearby. The winter snows had almost entirely melted in the high mountain passes, adding impetus to the swell of the river. The convoy of chariots drew to a halt and parked in a semicircle by the riverbank, enclosing the large grassy space. The king's bodyguards did this protective manoeuvre automatically. The wagon was brought to a standstill in the middle and Tawana and Gassulawiya climbed down, gently rubbing their buttocks. 'A bumpy ride, all those potholes,' Tawana complained.

'And it'll be just as bumpy on the way back,' observed Gassulawiya.

Talarra alighted just after Nikal—and promptly fainted.

'Bring some water,' Nikal called to one of the guards, while she fanned Talarra's face with a piece of cloth.

Tudhaliyas rushed over and sat on his heels opposite Nikal. 'Is she all right?' an expression of concern on his face.

'She was terrified all the way. I think she just fainted with relief. She'll recover shortly. It's just fright.'

'Good! I'm pleased to hear that. For an instant I thought we might have to abandon the picnic. So now we continue.' Tudhaliyas rose and went to observe his majordomo supervising servants pulling out tables and chairs from the wagon. He nodded in satisfaction as they were setting up the sun covers over the tables and chairs.

Nikal left Talarra with Tawana and Gassulawiya and went down to the river to get the water she had ordered the guard to get. She couldn't understand what was taking so long—there was no sign of him. She came back in a hurry with the rag thoroughly soaked and wiped Talarra's brow and cheeks. Her maid gave a weak moan and opened her eyes.

'There, she's moving!' Tawana exclaimed.

'I'm sorry,' she managed to Nikal.

Nikal looked down on her sympathetically. 'Don't worry. You can go back in the wagon.'

'Lie still, you'll be better with a little rest, my dear,' Gassulawiya added.

Talarra would have none of it. She insisted on getting up. She struggled to her feet, dusted herself down. 'I'm terribly sorry, your highness. It won't happen again.' She breathed deeply and exhaled slowly, her heavy bosom going up and down.

'I'm delighted you're all right. Now, can we get on with why we came here,' Nikal suggested. Both went to stand by Tudhaliyas, Talarra more meekly than usual. They were followed by Gassulawiya and Tawana.

'Has your maid recovered?' the king spoke without looking round.

'Quite recovered, majesty,' Nikal reassured.

'Tudhaliyas, please.'

'I'm feeling a bit queasy,' Nikal told him. 'Can we wait a little while? Let's take a short walk, then we'll eat. A gentle walk will stimulate the appetite.'

The prospect of walking alone with her roused Tudhaliyas' enthusiasm. They walked down by the river, followed discreetly some paces behind by thin Tawana and sturdy Gassulawiya as chaperones. Twenty paces behind the party, four armed bodyguards. A few hundred strides in absolute silence, watching the sun sparkle off of the river, just feeling the nearness of each other made Nikal's and Tudhaliyas' hearts beat faster.

They walked by the river for a while and the king talked to Nikal of the valley and the surrounding countryside. It was chitchat with an undercurrent of something else—words unsaid. 'I'm not boring you, am I?' asked the king.

Nikal smiled and then turned away and winced. 'No, my lord.'

Tudhaliyas had noted Nikal was quiet, seeming preoccupied within. 'Shall we return and eat? The food must be laid out by now,' he suggested.

The party turned and approached the campsite noting the attendants stood ready to serve.

'My goodness,' she exclaimed suddenly, holding her stomach. '*Uhh*!'

'What's the matter?' Tudhaliyas turned to her, alarmed.

'*Ohh*!' unexpectedly she sat on the grass, still holding her stomach. 'I have a cramping pain.'

Gassulawiya quickly kneeled beside Nikal, worriedly looking into her face. Tawana called the bodyguards over and they hurried up. Gassulawiya was now holding Nikal's face by her bosom. 'She's burning up. We must get her back to the house and call for Tagrama.'

*   *   *

The temple precincts were quiet, the workmen departed, serenity re-established. But a raised voice from a side room, suddenly disrupted all that. '*How in Yarris does he think he can disestablish Taru from the people*?' Tagrama sat on a wall seat shouting at the priest who brought the news.

The poor priest stood quivering, unable to answer. How *could* he answer such a question?

'Who *told* you they'd installed Teshub in my temple in Hattusas?' Tagrama tried to control his temper.

'Some travellers and a number of deserters from Muwas' army, just arrived from the north,' your eminence.

'What proof did they bring? How do we know they're telling the truth?'

'Two of them say they've been to the temple. Forced to go, the say.' The priest's voice was unsteady.

'I'm not going to bite your head off. Calm yourself. So they claim to have seen these Mittani priests in my temple, do they?' Tagrama had real difficulty holding back his anger.

'Yes, eminence. They left because of the disruption caused by the Mittani soldiers to the food supply. They're commandeering all the food. The townspeople are going hungry. They say there's twenty-five thousand extra mouths to feed. That's on top of the twenty thousand Hatti soldiers billeted in the town.' Now Tagrama had stopped shouting, the priest was less frightened.

Tagrama subsided, 'Kantuzzili will need to know.' The idea these Mittani usurpers could simply set aside the Hittite gods like some dog discarding a bone, outraged Tagrama beyond what he thought he could bear. Just before this priest brought news of his temple, other reports reached him of Muwas' senseless butchery of the old priest in the rock-sanctuary. *He was no harm to anyone. Why kill an old man?* He had bemoaned. For one wild moment, he had actually contemplated heading back to Hattusas to reclaim the temple —taking all his priests with him. But it was a reckless impulse soon abandoned. Tagrama stared at the messenger. 'Look, what I want you to do is go up to Kantuzzili's house. D'you know where it is?'

The priest nodded, 'It's back closer to town, on the outskirts.'

'That's it. Tell him I sent you, then tell him about the twenty-five thousand Mittani soldiers. All you have to give him is the number and maybe who told you. Can you do that for me?' Tagrama now spoke with a soft encouraging voice.

'Yes, eminence.' The priest half smiled. The high priest wasn't going to shout at him anymore.

'Wait! Before you do, find Loros and send him to me. Now go.' Tagrama's face was grim. He had been right to abandon that monster, Muwas. Now it seems the good people of Hattusas were near to starvation due to those foreigners. How could he do this to his own people? He decided there and then, Muwas must never be allowed to ascend the black bull throne.

Loros came sauntering in, looking pleased but somehow just a little guilty and found Tagrama behind the altar, looking up at the rear wall.

'What have you been up to?' Looking at his deputy, Tagrama asked offhandedly, more of an opening to conversation than a desire to know.

'Oh! Nothing. Just teaching some of the novices the right way to perform a sacrifice.' Loros screwed up part of his face as if having to answer was an unpleasant intrusion in his private life.

'Then why so guilty? Oh, never mind. I haven't the time. Look, I want you to find a suitable pair of priests to go to Hattusas. I want them disguised as merchants of some kind. I leave the details to you. I want them to find out exactly what's happening at the temple, nothing more. Then report back as soon as they can.' Tagrama was watching his deputy carefully.

Loros smiled, nodded almost brusquely, turned and went as he came.

Tagrama stood looking at the receding back, puzzled as to what Loros was up to. That he was up to something was clear. Another elderly priest arrived just at that moment, walking up the naos to where Tagrama stood. Scratching his chin Tagrama began, 'Did I or didn't I ask you to check the work *before* you dismissed the workmen?'

'Your eminence, I did check the work, just as you ordered.' The priest looked alarmed.

'Come with me.' Tagrama led the way behind the altar and pointed high up on the rear wall. 'Can you see? Is that or is that not a crack?'

'But your eminence, it's so high up. I'm sorry, but I missed it. Even now I can hardly see it.' The priest seemed indignant at Tagrama's sharp eyesight.

'I want it finished properly.' Tagrama's expression brooked no dissent. 'In gods house we must strive for perfection. This is not! Please see to it. Bring the workmen back and finish the job properly.'

'Yes, eminence.'

'And don't to be so sloppy the next time.'

'Yes, your eminence.'

*　　*　　*

'Have you sent for Tagrama?' Gassulawiya dabbed at Nikal's forehead.

'Of course I have. He's on his way. We sent a chariot for him.' Tawana, Himuili's wife was more composed, but just as worried.

Gassulawiya motioned to one of the elderly female servants standing against the wall, 'We'll have to change the sheets again. Go tell the other servants.' Nikal moaned, eyes closed tight with stomach pains.

'My poor dear! What can it be? It's as if she's eaten something poisonous.' Gassulawiya frowned, her face working overtime.

'You're not suggesting someone's poisoned her, are you?' Tawana asked disdainfully.

'Of course not. All I'm saying is *it's as if* she'd eaten something which might have been poisonous.'

'Well it's not poison she's eaten but that river water. You heard her yourself—"river water".'

Nikal was soiling the bed often enough to keep the house servants dreadfully busy. Shunashura and Talshura were outside worriedly pacing up and down in the corridor. The diminutive Kizzuwatna chief physician was in the kitchen preparing a herb potion to ease her suffering. Kantuzzili and Himuili were in the garden with Tudhaliyas, trying to pacify the young king. 'It wasn't your fault. There's no way you could have known,' his father insisted.

'But how can the river be contaminated at the head of the valley? The other end, yes, but not where we were, surely?' Tudhaliyas was beside himself for fear of losing her.

The three royals were acting as if it were conclusive that river water was the cause of Nikal's illness.

'We've sent infantry and cavalry up into the hills beyond where you were to find the cause. If the water's infected, then there's someone up there doing the polluting. Stands to reason!' Kantuzzili had taken control of the situation. Because this incident affected a royal princess of a valued ally, Kantuzzili put General Zidanta in charge of clearing up the mystery.

The general immediately suspected the cause and was determined to surround the area so the culprits wouldn't escape. He sent a whole infantry regiment to surround the possible area. It occurred to him to take the opportunity to exercise his men, break their boredom. He pondered on sending another regiment but with that kind of overkill, he was afraid of appearing ridiculous. Nevertheless, he insisted on sending four squadrons of cavalry in after what he assumed was probably around ten men. He would look silly if they escaped.

The sound of a number of chariots came from the other side of the garden wall. Tagrama had arrived. Kantuzzili left Tudhaliyas with his father and hurried inside to meet the high priest. He was the most respected physician in the whole of Hatti.

'Where's the patient?' Tagrama almost running, came into the corridor.

'Through there,' Kantuzzili pointed at a door, as did Shunashura and Talshura.

Tagrama rushed through the doorway and waved the women aside. 'Let me have a look at her. Open the curtains, give me some light.'

'We thought keeping the room dark might help to keep her calm,' Tawana explained.

Gassulawiya pointed at the curtains and a servant rushed to draw them open. Sunlight burst into the room.

'That's more like it. Did she say how she came to be ill?' Tagrama enquired brusquely.

'She drank a little water from the river, while wetting a rag for her maid. Her maid had fainted, you see,' Tawana told him.

'Yes, yes. So we're dealing with fouled water. Tawana, can you go into the kitchen and put some sea salt into a goblet, then mix in some honey. Don't let the servants do it; do it yourself. And make sure it dissolves. Bring it to me.'

'Right away,' Tawana rushed out of the room.

She passed Kapiliwa, the short thin Kizzuwatna chief physician coming in with a herbal potion. He saw Tagrama and stopped in the doorway, not sure how to deal with the Hatti high priest.

'Don't just stand there, come, give me your opinion.' Tagrama was uneasy and hid it by being abrupt.

Kapiliwa approached the bed and showed Tagrama a decoction in an earthenware pot. 'I've brought a potion to reduce her cramps and change the balance in her stomach. It should ease her condition. Make her more comfortable.'

Tagrama sniffed the mix and nodded in agreement. 'Will you share the ingredients with me? I think I can smell sage?'

Kapiliwa nodded and smiled.

'Mint?'

Again, Kapiliwa nodded.

'Chamomile?'

'Yes.'

'And poppy petals, by the looks of the colour.'

Kapiliwa beamed as if his pupil had just passed a test. 'I would have expected no less from one of your reputation.'

'That's kind of you. I've just asked one of the ladies to make a mix of salt and honey. I've found for some unknown reason, it's extremely effective in such cases where diarrhoea is involved. Especially if children are the patients. It makes the difference in the balance of a patient's survival.'

'I've never come across this,' Kapiliwa raised his thick eyebrows.

The two physicians began talking cures as Kapiliwa gave Gassulawiya the potion to administer. 'I once watched a dog suffering from diarrhoea search for salt, as though by instinct. I've added something sweet to make it less bitter. I've also found honey settles the stomach,' Tagrama confided.

Tawana arrived with the dissolved salt and honey. After much effort and spillage, Gassulawiya managed to get Kapiliwa's potion down Nikal, then it was Tawana's turn to get Nikal to swallow Tagrama's remedy.

Tagrama told Gassulawiya, 'Make sure both remedies are repeated each day until I say stop. Do you agree?' he asked Kapiliwa.

'Most certainly!' the Kizzuwatna royal physician responded.

'Tomorrow,' Tagrama continued, 'I want to try a little willow bark decoction. That will bring the fever down. I think the stomach is too delicate at the moment.'

'I've never come across that either. I would deem it a kindness if we could swap remedies. I feel I could learn much from you,' Kapiliwa enthused.

The two men, one tall the other small, went out of the room, whilst servants arrived with new sheets and helped Tawana and Gassulawiya to lift the delirious Nikal from the bed. They placed animal skins on the bed, then put Nikal on them and began washing her down. This done, a new sheet replaced the skins and the patient was laid gently back while Gassulawiya returned to the task of mopping Nikal's brow.

Chapter Eighteen

Pharaoh Amenhotep II sat staring into the pool in his magnificent garden, contemplating the nature of the lotus flower; its beauty, its sacred property, its visionary quality. The lotus was the symbol of rebirth sacred to the god Nefertum, used in the temple rituals. Re's power and birth was celebrated in the *Lotus Offering*, a hymn sung on days of festivals glorifying Re' as the "Great Lotus," emerging from the primeval pool at the moment of creation. If he, pharaoh, the personification of Re', ate a couple of flower heads, he would "see" chimeras of ecstasy. Beside him sat his queen consort Merit-Amon, luxuriating in the various scents drifting in the garden, watching the approach of the Djat alongside the long pool at the far end. The Djat was in a hurry and soon arrived in the presence of the deified king of Egypt. The first minister to pharaoh waited patiently to be noticed by his majesty. Merit-Amon touched her husband's brawny arm, breaking his meditation.

'Speak up, what is it?' Amenhotep demanded.

'Your serene majesty, regarding the Hittite civil war. Another set of wax-boards have arrived, from you know who.'

Pharaoh nodded calmly, suggesting his Djat continue.

'Two further items. Our spies in Hatti report that after all this time, still no major battle between the contenders for the throne. Secondly, we've received a reply to our demand for Saustatar to remove his troops from Hatti. The Mittani king insists he's merely fulfilling his side of a long-standing bilateral treaty of mutual assistance between Mittani and Muwatallis. He contends the Egyptian borders are not threatened and there should be no reason why Egypt be concerned at what happens in so remote a kingdom. He thanks you for your suggestion but declines to follow your advice.'

'*Suggestion! Advice!*' shouted Amenhotep. 'I'll give him "suggestion." I want you to send an ultimatum. Either he pulls his troops back to Mittani, or I will encourage him to do so by another visit to his precious Mittani. Remind him of the fate of the seven Tikhsi princes which I sacrificed and hung on the enclosure wall of the temple at Waset. I smote them with my mace and I will smite any who oppose me. They were vassals to him and under his protection. How did he protect them? Wassukkani isn't much further than Tikhsi. My borders may be safe, but are his? Send it without delay.'

'Oh beloved of Horus. I hear and obey. I will have the scribes draw up the papyrus and it shall be sent today.'

'You are dismissed.' The Djat backed out ten paces, turned and hurried from the garden. 'The impertinent Hurrian upstart. If I didn't have to deal with the Nubian unrest, I'd march the army to Wassukkani tomorrow. The threat should suffice, don't you think?'

'I'm sure you're right. By and by—what were you thinking of, so deeply, before the Djat arrived?'

'Of the lotus flower: handed down to us from our ancestors, it has become a central symbol in my kingdom. It is indeed sacred and for good reason—on that, I was meditating. And you, my dear. What were your thoughts?'

'I was taking in the scents of the garden. *Shemu* is such a rich time of the year.'

Chapter Nineteen

Mokhat drew his horse to a halt and turned for a last glance at his brother's castle perched high atop of the hill. He was embarking on the most perilous task of his entire career and was loath to leave the security the castle provided. That said, he knew the assignment had to be pursued to wherever it eventually took him. It was onerous, but probably the most important mission he had ever undertaken. Future relations between Kaska and Hatti depended on its success. The normal route from Nerik to Hattusas was a road through Hattena and Hanhana to Hakpis where a series of fortified posts were embedded. The land, valleys and mountains aligned that way. The main road to the Hatti capital followed the lie of the land. But Mokhat decided to take the path as the crow flew. More difficult, but it only took two days to get to Hattusas, travelling through the lush greenery of the north, over rolling hills and into the rich fertile plain which supplied much of the capital's corn. During the day at this time of year, sowing would have been in full swing.

In the evening of the second day he finally rode upwards onto the granite-grey promontory Hattusas stood on. He passed by the sacred rock-sanctuary, revered by both Hatti and Kaska alike and was shocked to see the area in front of the wall littered with broken statues and debris as if a looting army had passed through. Near the town, he crossed the north stream and came upon the still open North Gate where he was stopped by green clad sentries. The arched gateway was flanked by huge irregular blocks of masonry extending from the outer to the inner side of the whole wall and through this ran a tunnel leading into the town. On either side of the tunnel entrance stood a number of sentries holding bronze scimitars, scrutinising anyone wishing to enter.

'State your business in the town.' A burly gruff sentry challenged.

'I need a bed and food for the night,' Mokhat explained to the sentry.

The sentries glared at his dark cloak suspiciously. 'Where d'you come from in this period of twilight?'

'I'm coming from Hakpis and it's a long road. Won't you let me pass? I'm so hungry I'm likely to eat this horse if you don't let me in.'

What passed for a wry smile appeared on the burly one's face. The added touch of humour made him relent. 'I ought to make you wait till morning, but you might die of hunger and I wouldn't want that on my conscience. Go on, you can go through.' He waved his hand and returned to whatever he was doing before Mokhat's arrival interrupted him.

Mokhat went down the tunnel and came out after a couple of cubits, north of the glowing Great Temple all lit up in the dusk. Once he passed by the main temple, from which strange chanting could be heard, he observed the sea of flat roofs before him as far as the distant Great Palace. 'It's a big city,' he mumbled under his breath. Unlike Nerik, he had heard sewers in the capital were run through fired earthenware pipes dug in under the surface, leaving the narrow streets clean and dry. All the walls were whitewashed and his first impression was exceedingly favourable. Along the main east-west thoroughfare he found a tavern with the sign of a black cat nailed near the door. Many voices clamoured above the faint music coming from inside and Mokhat felt his priestly robes might not stand out so much in such a large crowd.

Inside it proved even more crowded than the voices indicated. Near the bar two musicians and a male singer desperately tried to make themselves heard. A lyre and panpipes accompanied the singer, but he was losing the struggle with the background racket. At the moment while

Mokhat was watching the musician's efforts, a large bunch got up from a table against the right wall and made to leave. Mokhat hurried to occupy one of the vacated chairs and raised his hand to call over the roving waitress. 'A big tankard of ale and I need a meal. What d'you suggest?'

A large elderly woman arrived, probably the landlords wife, Mokhat ventured. 'I can do you some bread and cold mutton; might even do you some cheese. We've finished serving food this late. Is that all right, dear?'

'That'll do fine.' He would have preferred something hot, but she was right, it was late.

The people at the next table were in some kind of dispute. The well-built fellow with his back to Mokhat was dressed in an unrecognisable uniform and had a strong foreign accent. *Probably Mittani*, Mokhat guessed. The whole town must be crawling with them. His brother had informed him a huge contingent was camped outside Hattusas' walls, waiting to attack Kantuzzili's forces. The dispute was getting louder between the stranger and four other Hatti sitting round the table, the latter berating the foreigner.

'*You puffed up mercenaries are all alike. Big mouths, all of you,*' one of the Hatti voices was shouting. Others at the table vigorously nodded in agreement.

'*And I say, give me a thousand Ahhiyawan warriors and we'll settle this civil war of yours.*' The foreigner asserted, equally loudly.

'*So you're claiming the Hittite soldier's got no balls, are you?*' another man at the table joined in.

By now, all the voices in the tavern were quiet. Even the musicians had ceased their striving. They were all listening to the belittling of Hittite manhood and they did not take too kindly to the person doing the slandering. Many of those on their feet wore Hittite green uniforms from the twenty thousand soldiers billeted in the town. A big man at another table behind the foreigner stood, picked up a chair by its back and lifted it above his head, intending to bring it down on the foreigner's skull.

That was too much for Mokhat. He did not like backstabbers. He stood and grabbed a leg of the chair, preventing it coming down. For no reason, Mokhat noticed the mass of freckles on the burly man's arms, as if he were watching from a great distance. '*Watch out, behind you*,' Mokhat shouted a warning.

The stranger looked behind and rose to his feet, head butting the one with the chair in the stomach, lifting him off his feet with his head and over his shoulder onto the table he had been sitting at. The table collapsed and the others jumped at the foreigner trying to pull him down. The whole tavern heaved into uproar. People were jostling to get a better view, soldiers were pushing forward and another fight between excitable viewers started behind Mokhat. It was an opportune moment to leave, Mokhat decided. He would have to abandon the food and bed. The crowd was enjoying the spectacle and some even decided to join in.

Somewhere under a pile of bodies, a head thrust out. It was the foreigner. '*Quick, give me a hand*,' he yelled at Mokhat.

Mokhat grabbed the hand and pulled, extracting him halfway with considerable difficulty, then upwards and out of the melee. The tall foreigner kicked and stomped his way erect and then made a dash for the door, jumping over and pushing through the other fights. Mokhat did not wait for an invitation. He scramble over bodies and rushed after the retreating stranger who had already reached the exit and was disappearing through the door. Mokhat emerged a few paces behind and made directly for his horse.

The foreigner was rounding the far corner of the tavern, shouting, '*Go, I will follow, hurry*!'

Mokhat undid the bridle and jumped on the blanket, urging his horse into a canter. Figures were emerging from the tavern in hot pursuit of the stranger, angry he was getting away—shouting obscenities. Mokhat was already galloping down the road, heading into the dark—anywhere away from the fighting. He looked over his shoulder and glimpsed another figure on horseback, following. He panicked for a moment, thinking someone from the tavern was on his trail. Then as the other horse closed, he realised it was the stranger, the one who had started the whole mess.

Mokhat galloped in a blind panic until the stranger overtook and then he had no choice but to follow the other down to the South Gate. It wasn't long before the tunnel to the gate loomed up ahead. They went in without any thought as to what they would find, but as luck would have it, the gate stood open. Sentries milled about at the entrance, ears pricked at the sound of hooves echoing down the tunnel at this time of the night. They scattered as the two horses came tearing out past them, disappearing into the darkness.

*　　*　　*

It was just after dawn as Mokhat sat warming himself round a blazing fire. The stranger had volunteered to get some water from the nearby stream and seemed a long time away. They had spent what was left of the night huddled under the stranger's fur skins after their frantic escape from Hattusas.

'I'm fairly certain it's clean, but to be sure, we'd better boil it.' A heavy accented voice told Mokhat as the stranger hung the pot of water on a bent branch above the fire with strong-bronzed hands.

Mokhat was staring quizzically at this unfamiliar person who had disrupted his plans by his strident opinions. He had a solid fighter's build. Sharp dark eyes returned his stare. He wasn't Mittani as he had first assumed; in fact, Mokhat gave up. 'So tell me, whose skull did I save? Where are you from? What's your name?' Nothing about the man was familiar.

'I am from Ahhiyawa, to the far west. My name is Palaiyas.'

'Well Palaiyas, you know you asked for it last night?'

'I suppose I did. But since we're exchanging introductions; you're not a Hittite are you? Where are *you* from?' Curiosity had intruded on Palaiyas' sense of decorum.

'My name is Mokhat. I'm a Kaska from Nerik in the north. Almost on the coast.' Mokhat went cautiously until he knew a little more about his companion. 'Ahhiyawa! I've heard little of it and even then only rumours. Somewhere near Arzawa?'

'They're neighbours of ours. I'm a messenger for... was a messenger for...the Ahhiyawan king, Parmodius. I was sent to give a message to King Muwatallis. Then got involved with a Hatti woman in Hattusas.' Palaiyas sat for an instant, musing. 'I've been here too long. Should have been back in Milawata months ago. What about you?'

'I'm on a mission for the Kaska king. I stopped in Hattusas to get some food and a bed for the night.' Mokhat shook his head gently at the memory. His stomach grumbled. 'Some hope! I suppose you've nothing to eat?'

'Some dried meat. Probably some dried bread, if it's still edible. Want some?'

Mokhat's interest increased appreciably. 'Most certainly I would. My stomach thinks my chewing teeth have a grudge against it.'

Palaiyas searched around in his belongings, finding a sack. Strong arms threw the sack at Mokhat. 'All yours! Part payment for saving my life. You did you know! When I turned, I saw you preventing the chair from crashing on my head. My mother thanks you for your intervention, my father thanks you, but most of all, *I* thank you.'

'You have an interesting turn of phrase, Palaiyas. Are they all like that where you come from?'

'Pretty much. Gruff, rough and all experts at being mean.' Palaiyas laughed. 'I'm taking to you, my friend. It's

not just that you went out of your way to save my life…
although it helps.' He laughed some more.

'And what do you do, apart from being a courier?'
Mokhat was tearing into the dried meat, chewing with gusto.

'I hire myself out—I'm a mercenary.' He looked every
bit a soldier. 'Was just about to offer my services to
Muwatallis before he got murdered. That idea was Mahera's
—the woman I told you about, the one I was staying with.
She was hoping I would stick around. I think she had plans
for me. Pretty little woman.'

'Aren't you going back?'

'Not sure. Got to think it over. Last night she told me
she was with child. That's why I was in the tavern,
celebrating, and trying to think it through. Should I settle
with this little woman or head back to Milawata? Then those
baggage hands joined me at the table. Started exercising their
wit on me. I gave as good as I got. That's when the fellow
with the chair joined in.'

'I presume you mean Millawanda when you say
Milawata?' Enquired Mokhat.

Palaiyas nodded. 'We call it Milawata—but you're
right.'

'In the middle of the Hatti capital,' Continued Mokhat,
'With all those soldiers, you decide to pour scorn on Hittite
prowess. Whatever possessed you?' Mokhat actually wanted
to know if Palaiyas had a death wish.

'Oh, I know it was foolish. I was thinking of Mahera
and got angry at being interrupted. I'm usually more careful.
First fight I've been involved in Hattusas.' Palaiyas was
gazing at Mokhat's clothing, the dark long hooded cloak he
was wrapped in.

'You seem to have a shield, all your armour, spears
and sword with you. It's a strange combination to take to a
tavern with you—you even had furs with you. I mean you
haven't been home but you're fully armed. How is that, if you

don't mind me asking?' Mokhat felt the need to satisfy his curiosity.

'You're right. At the back of my mind, I think I'd decided not to go back to her but head for home—to Ahhiyawa. So I was fully packed.' A lengthy pause followed while they looked at the ground, each within their own thoughts. Then Palaiyas asked, 'Are you a priest of some kind? I mean that clothing looks priest-like.'

'You've just noticed, have you?' Mokhat was amused. 'Yes, I'm a priest. I serve Illuyankas, the black dragon god of the Kaska. You've no objections?'

'None whatsoever. Just struck me as peculiar. Me a mercenary...out here with a...priest,' and Palaiyas laughed loudly at what he thought was a joke.

'It's not that funny, surely? The water's boiled. Want some chamomile tea?' Mokhat was getting irritated at the laughter.

'*Ha, ha, ha.* Yes please. How come a priest...got involved in a brawl? *Ho, ho.*' Palaiyas seemed to find everything funny just then.

'Wouldn't have if it were just those at your table, but I can't stand backstabbers.' It struck Mokhat all his assassins were just that. Sneak thieves sneaking people's lives away. He grimaced at the thought.

Palaiyas calmed his fit of laughter and sipped tea gratefully from a copper mug. The spring morning was crisp and he was thankful for the heat rolling down his throat.

'What was the message?' Mokhat asked.

Palaiyas raised his eyebrows, 'What message?'

'The message you were carrying to Muwatallis.'

'No idea...*then*. It was sealed and I was told, if I opened it, I would be signing my death warrant. That was enough for me. My lot mean what they say.'

'You mean the Ahhiyawans?'

'They're a mean bunch and no mistake. I should know!' That made him grin again.

'So you came all this way without knowing why? Did you find out?' Mokhat was curious.

'Ahhiyawa wants a treaty with Hatti to curb the Arzawa to the north and the Lukka in the south. That's what I overheard the Chancellor telling a scribe in a reply letter.' Palaiyas felt more comfortable with a hot drink inside him and even began rubbing his stomach.

'Why didn't they send you back with it?' Mokhat wanted to tie up the loose ends.

'They didn't trust me. Not after me getting roaring drunk with some of their bodyguards. They sent one of their own. Made me redundant. Went on a bender in town, ended up with this nice young woman. Mahera she called herself. Pleasant face.' He sat quietly deep in thought.

Mokhat drank his tea and chewed more of the dried meat. Strange, but it was quite filling. Mokhat had an idea. 'So what d'you want to do now? I mean, where are you headed?'

'Don't know. Looks like I'll be heading home. Had enough of Hattusas, for the moment at least. Suppose I could go back and join the mercenaries in Muwas' lot.'

'Look, why don't you come along with me. We'll ride together. Give you time to think—sort things out. Use me as a sounding board. Unless you've got ideological reasons for joining Muwas?'

Palaiyas sat and scratched his chin. 'Didn't say where you were going, did you?'

'I'm going south. Down to Ankuwa. That a problem?'

'What? To join the other king? What's his name?'

'Tudhaliyas. I asked you if it was a problem.'

'Not really. One lot's just as bad as the other. Not a *mina* between them. Didn't take you for a fighter, though. Ah! Remember now. You're on a mission as well—for your king. All right, I'll come. I've a debt to settle.'

Mokhat knew what he meant. Saving a life had its own reward.

A goodly distance down past Hattusas, the terrain changed to a dryer more dusty red earth. Mokhat and Palaiyas were riding side-by-side, spreading small red clouds with the horse's hooves, exchanging personal backgrounds, when they felt raindrops falling from a cloudless blue sky. 'We'd better get under cover. Strange weather. How can it rain without clouds?' Palaiyas complained. They quickly galloped to the left for the shelter of a small wood of broad-leafed trees, managing to get under just as the heavens opened.

'That's better. It's only a brief shower. It'll clear soon,' Mokhat soothed. 'I hope you're not blaming me for this rain?' he bantered.

'Not yet but you're supposed to have connections up there. Anyway, as I was saying, before the rain interrupted. I was stationed on Keftiu, place called Phaistos, with the rest of my hometown contingent. I told you I was from Tiryns, didn't I?'

'Yes you did. Keftiu—that's what you call the big island in the big sea after Alasiya?'

'That's right. That was five years ago. The locals rebelled and we had to restore order. They wanted us out; we didn't want to go. They kept on about some King Minos or other. Anyway, I've seen fighting but this was pure butchery. It turned my stomach. Old men, women, children. All were put to the sword. At the end, I quit. Went back to Ellas. That's what we call Ahhiyawa. You call us Ahhiyawans; we call ourselves Ellinike. Same people, different name. My father was happy to see me, but the king in Mycenae, Tiryns being vassal to him, didn't like I'd quit and wanted me to go back to Keftiu. I said no. One thing led to another and I had to flee. I went first to Taruisa, stayed there a year, then went down to Milawata.'

'Why did you leave Taruisa?'

'A spot of woman trouble. I had a fling with a highborn woman; her husband didn't take to it. Had a horde of soldiers looking for me. Threatened to castrate me if he got his hands on me.'

'From the sounds of it, someday a husband is likely to catch up with you. I hope I'm not there when he does.'

'That makes both of us,' Palaiyas laughed.

'You might want to curb those inclinations.'

'I can't help it if the ladies find me attractive.'

'No! But you could try not reciprocating.' Mokhat was serious.

'Life would be a bore without them.' Palaiyas' features suggested *he* was serious.

'So you sold your arms to the king in Millawanda?'

'Yes! King Parmodius. That's about the size of it. The rest you know.' The shower spent itself and the rain stopped.

'Better be on our way. We could put another couple of leagues behind us before we have to stop for the night.'

The sky was still clear blue and Palaiyas eyed it suspiciously. 'Could have a snowstorm next.'

'Don't be silly. The rain hasn't finished with us yet. Then comes the snowstorm.' Mokhat was getting into the spirit of the teasing.

Back on the road, Palaiyas kept putting his hand out from time to time, wearing a quizzical expression, to check for rain.

'Tell me of your hometown, Palaiyas. What's it like? Are the people happy? Do you come from a good family?'

'Tiryns is located on a rocky hill in a vast plain only a quarter of league from the sea, surrounded by a good wall.' Palaiyas paused in reflection. 'D'you know, I haven't thought about the place in a long time.'

'You've been away too long. Maybe you should think of making a trip back. See how the family is. Got any brothers or sisters?' Mokhat was staring in front into the far distance.

'Only a brother. He's probably married by now. Could be you're right. I should go back for a visit. When this is over, I think I will. What are you staring at?' Palaiyas now saw Mokhat's attention was taken with something ahead.

Chapter Twenty

'I've had your order proclaimed, majesty. "No Mittani soldiers to enter Hattusas without Prince Artatama's special permission".' General Ammuna bowed his large head and was about to withdraw.

'Wait! Stay awhile. I want your opinion on a couple of matters. First, let me ask. How are the people taking to the new religion?' Muwas wasn't really concerned on that score, he just wanted to open the conversation.

'They're not!' Ammuna reported. 'Any other religion might have gone down indifferently, but not Mittani. They're already unhappy with their own soldiers eating them out of house and home. Now they're expected to feed the Mittani *and* adopt their foreign religion. Lots of grumbling.' Ammuna sat his heavy frame down where Muwas indicated.

'Let me try and explain something to you—and at the end, you can tell me what you think.' Muwas sat in a chair near the general. 'The point of the new religion—my intention is to lower Artatama's guard *and* to throw mud in the face of Tagrama and by implication, Kantuzzili and Tudhaliyas. I know it's a cheap move, but it really doesn't effect you or me. I tell you this because you have as much regard for the priestly dogma as I do.' The king watched the general carefully. Muwas did not believe in the gods, but made a great show of attending religious festivals. Muwas believed in Muwas. That was his religion. On the other hand, the dual manoeuvre of getting at Tagrama and Tudhaliyas had given him immense pleasure.

'A move of great astuteness, your majesty,' Ammuna said cautiously.

'To blunt the people's anger, I ordered you to announce that proclamation. It shows I'm controlling the

Mittani. Now, in confidence mind you,' he paused to let the "confidence" part sink in. 'I feel Artatama's too conceited, too boastful of Mittani prowess and I intended to cut him down a peg or ten.'

The general's mouth fell open in astonishment. But he made no comment.

Muwas felt the need to confide in someone, so he continued, 'I've known Artatama since my youth when I was sent to Mittani to broaden my horizons. In Wassukkani we did a lot of weapons practice with each other and you know yourself, that's when you get the measure of a man. Artatama is devious and cunning. And when we wrestled, I always won. Artatama was a bad loser. I'm expecting him to pull some kind of mischief. His father's all right, honourable, but his son's a bit wild.' Muwas paused, deep in thought.

The general coughed.

'You wish to say something?'

'Only...I'm not sure *what* you would like me to say.'

'Patience, general, I haven't finished.' An icy glint crept into Muwas' eyes. 'I've promised myself to deal with this upstart prince of Mittani. During the main battle, I want you to organise a couple of Mešedi to deal with him.'

'Deal with him? I'm not quite sure I follow. Am I to put an end to him?' The general was attentive on the outside, but absolutely flabbergasted inside.

'Make sure of the Mešedi you pick. They must be tight lipped. Pick only the best. They'll need to get past the princes bodyguards. Have them wear a Mittani blue tunic under their green. When the time comes, they can tear their green off and blend in with the prince's bodyguards. Get them to study the Mittani fighting style so they're familiar with it. Find a way to counter their style. This needs to be done with discretion. Are you with me?' Muwas needed the general if this was to succeed.

'I am yours to command, majesty. The only comment I can think of is—is it really necessary?' The general would carry his orders out to the full, but was aware of the consequences if it went wrong.

'Believe me, general, I would not consider it if I thought it unnecessary,' Muwas almost snarled back.

Chapter Twenty-One

King Saustatar was furious. 'Who does he think he is, sending *me* ultimatums! This won't do. I'm his equal, not his vassal. Egyptian lout!'

'Shhh! Calm yourself. I'm sure he's bluffing,' his consort wife consoled. 'He's got far too many problems with the Nubians to waste time sending forces up here. And of course you're his equal, dear.'

'I've a good mind to retake Qadesh. Teach him a lesson. I can do it you know. There's only a small garrison left there.'

'Don't do anything rash, dear. Take your time and think things out. Why not have a lie down? Might calm you. It's so hot today.'

The king of Mittani and his consort were in their private apartments with the morning audiences at an end. Petition after petition had arrived at Wassukkani from outlying areas of the kingdom. Some arrived in person, others sent twiddling lawyers. Each petition had to be heard. Spring was supposed to be fresh, but the morning had been stifling. He was tired. Saustatar had had enough on his mind. Then his chief minister had brought pharaoh's ultimatum. It really was too much for the poor royal head. The king was in a conundrum. Pharaoh threatened to send an army to Mittani unless Saustatar recalled his troops from Hatti. But if he did, there could be no alliance. Without an alliance he was at the mercy of that Egyptian lout. It went round in a circle. Telling him what to do. The idea of it!

Saustatar fumed on and on. He paced up and down the royal apartment, wringing his hands. His consort gave up trying to pacify him, settling down to one of her favourite pastimes, some intricate weaving. Eventually the king decided to call the pharaoh's bluff. At length he burst out, 'That's it. I've had it with this pharaoh. Let him come. Only if he arrives in person with his army, will I send for Artatama.'

'That's nice. I'm content you've made your decision.' His consort always encouraged Saustatar to reach his own decisions. 'Maybe now we can settle down to a relaxing afternoon. I'll send for some refreshments. What would you like?' She really had no inkling of what might happen if pharaoh decided to storm Wassukkani.

Chapter Twenty-two

They had been riding since dawn and Rewa hadn't said much for the past two days ever since Harep killed Parap. He rode quietly and kept his opinions to himself.

'Hakpis is just round that hill,' Harep informed his nephew.

Rewa rode on in silence, deep in a sulk.

'Did you hear what I said? We're almost there... Oh, please yourself!' Harep gave up trying to get through to his surviving nephew.

They rode in silence for a while and then entered a fertile valley with vivid colours to the landscape. The afternoon sun was hot and both travellers felt uncomfortable in the heat. 'You gonna be mute for the rest of journey?' Harep demanded, the tone of voice menacing.

It occurred to Rewa if he did not make conversation, he might end up like his poor younger brother. 'I'm speaking... I'm speaking. Only...I've little to say. Don't hold that against me. I'm quite happy to talk to you.' Rewa's tone was almost pleading.

'Right! Just wanted to hear from you. Can't stand surly people.' Rewa's answer seemed to satisfy Harep. 'When we get there, keep an eye out for anything unusual—anyone prying at us. I still haven't figured out who's out to destroy the assassins. Could be anyone. If they get me, they'll probably get you as well—and you know what that means. No shekels. Keep your eyes peeled!'

Rewa made no answer, but he did make an effort to be more alert and less sullen. Hakpis served as a Hittite provincial capital for the northern area. The governor was held in high regard in Hattusas and the post carried clout with the king. It was a town that had sided with Muwas. When they finally went through the town gates, they found a typical provincial town, a few streets, shops and a sizable market, all enclosed by a tall thick wall. Without dawdling, Harep made straight for the town centre, or what passed for a town centre. He had been to Hakpis before and knew where to find the Town Treasurer. It was an unimposing two storey building, situated near the citadel, nestling in amongst many flat roofed bungalows, meant to hold the tax collectors and other administrative financial people. Both Harep and Rewa slid off their horses and tied them round the side.

Harep told Rewa, 'Wait for me down here. Look after the horses, stay sharp, make sure no one steals them.' It wasn't a request. Harep went round the front and through the entrance. At the top of a flight of wooden stairs in a large room sat the self important treasurer. Harep did not knock but sneaked in like a thief. '*How are you*?' Harep suddenly shouted at the treasurer.

'*Wha*.....? Harep you rascal. You nearly scared me out of my skin. What are you doing down here? No, don't tell me! I remember. You have a fortune waiting for you. How…?'

Harep put his hand up to stop the treasurer. 'Whoa there! Hold on! Your running ahead of yourself. Slow down. Let me sit down for a while. Those stairs don't get any easier.' Harep needed to procrastinate a little if he did not want to give too much away. 'Look, I can't go into details about the money, you know. It's hush-hush, work in progress. All I needed to know from you was—had the money arrived?'

'Yes it has. Forty-five thousand shekels in gold. I'm ordered to release it to you when the upstart is no more.'

'Tudhaliyas. No need to use code, my friend. Hakpis is loyal to King Muwas which is why both parties feel safe in doing business here. You now know my mission. Keep it to yourself, or else.' Harep gave the bureaucrat a meaningful glare.

'I know when to keep my mouth shut, don't worry. You know that.'

'That's why I chose you. I've got my nephew downstairs. He's in a hurry to get on. So I'll see you when I finish doing what I'm doing. Must dash. Bye.' That was it. Harep was finished. He bounded down the stairs leaving an open mouthed treasurer. He found Rewa sitting propped up against the wall near the horses. 'Fine. Let's go. Anyone looking strange at us?'

'No! Nothing unusual.'

Harep mounted his horse. 'I don't feel much like sleeping in town right now. We'll get as far along the road as we can until dusk, then camp. How're we doing for food?'

'Got plenty. Remember we're one person light.'

Harep glared at Rewa. 'You gonna keep reminding me?'

'N-o-o! I just meant we have more food than we bargained for. Didn't mean anything by it, honest.' Rewa was now scared of Harep and did not think he would come out of this alive.

*   *   *

Although the lay of the land flowed in the direction of Hattusas from Hakpis, Harep and Rewa made the difficult crossing directly through the mountains to reach Ankuwa. By now Rewa was terrified of Harep that for some slight, he would do to him as he did to his younger brother. He desired to leave but was prevented from doing so by the fear of being caught. He wished he could crawl away from this monster, but remained in the hope that if he was able to hold on to his fear and do whatever it was Harep wanted of him, he might yet manage to collect his promised payment. He would then never have to worry about anything for the rest of his life. He could even hire someone to take care of Harep. The stakes were high. Greed and revenge. It was a power almost equal to religion. Indeed, some had made it their religion.

What Rewa did not notice was Harep's preoccupation with trying to work out who was always after the head of the assassin's order. He was next in line and it made the matter urgent. Thus far, after giving it much thought, he had no better idea of who was trying to kill him than he had before. Harep concealed himself with Rewa in the hills above the road leading into the valley in which Ankuwa stood. He had decided to wait for a large group travelling into the valley so he and Rewa could join them. He needed to be sure he did not stand out, that the guards did not especially notice the two of them coming in. Unobtrusiveness was the manner in which he worked.

A day passed and another cold night was spent up in the hills. The following morning, Rewa spotted two groups coming down the road. One group was with four carts pulled by bullocks; merchants bringing provisions to Ankuwa. He could see no way to blend in with them. The next group, twenty or so, seemed to be refugees by their bedraggled state. This was more to Harep's liking. Into this group, he and Rewa could easily blend, if they were allowed. They would have to ingratiate themselves. Quickly, the two assassins scrambled down the hill and sat by the roadside. Harep pulled out his dagger and made a shallow cut on his left upper arm. Lots of blood but little damage. Rewa watched fascinated. Harep smeared blood over his face and some on Rewa's right leg, the latter was to make it seem the long trek had taken its toll and left them damaged. As the refugees rounded the bend, Harep pretended helplessness. 'Ohhh my poor feet!' he moaned. 'My poor arm!'

The tired group reached where the two were sitting and stopped. A middle-aged woman immediately felt sorry for Harep. 'Look, he's injured. What happened? she asked.

'Attacked by bandits. Robbed. Took all we had. Ohhh, what am I to do?' As acting goes, Harep was just passable.

'You poor thing. Let me have a look at your arm.'

Harep held it up for her.

'I'll bandage it for you, least I can do.'

'Bless you, you're a kindly woman. May Taru be merciful with you.' The reference to the Hatti god went down well. The woman tore part of her dress to make a bandage. Although the woman was travelling alone, her companions were giving her disapproving looks. They did not like the look of Harep or his friend. The woman took no notice. 'Are you going to Ankuwa as well?'

'We were. Just had to stop for a short rest.'

'Yes, yes. You poor dears. Why don't you come along with us? I'm sure they won't mind,' she looked pointedly at her companions.

'Are you sure? We wouldn't want to intrude,' came from Harep's deceitful tongue.

'You come along with me dear, lean on me, it's not far now.' And so Harep and Rewa joined the refugees. When they came to a checkpoint guarding the entrance into the valley, soldiers looked them over carefully but found nothing amiss. They had had scores of refugees coming in seeking protection from Muwas' new religion, fleeing the sweeping hunger of Hattusas. This lot did not seem any different. They waved them through and Harep was one step closer to his intended victims.

Chapter Twenty-three

Zidanta's men, after a little searching, found the culprits who had fouled the river water. They were hiding half a league upriver—unaware they had exposed themselves. Three bedraggled foul smelling individuals, when spotted, had made a dash for horses stabled in a cave. With the tight ring of soldiers surrounding them, they had no hope of escape. Once they had realised the game was up, they came quietly.

Back in town, General Zidanta took charge of the interrogation. He was intrigued by their foul state and purpose. 'Out with it, how long you been up there? No lies, mind you. I've no time for them.' As an inducement to speech, he had brought in a pair of ferocious looking wolf-hounds. They sat watching the prisoners, a barely concealed snarl just audible. The prisoners kept their mouths tightly clenched, glancing nervously at the dogs, for all of the time it takes to boil a pot of water. The dogs got louder, the snarls more evident.

'Do you really want me to let these nice animals loose on your disgusting smelling flesh? They'll tear you apart, one by one. So whose going to be first?'

The prisoners twitched, struggled half heartedly against their bonds and finally the short one broke. 'We meant no harm, honestly. We're just simple goat hunters,' he pleaded. 'Just trying to make a living.'

'Do I seem stupid to you? Well don't say I didn't give you a chance.' The general gave a low whistle and both dogs went for the legs of the short "goat hunter."

'*Arghhhh...stop them......ouch...ouch...*I'll talk, I will!'

Zidanta called the dogs off and in an angry tone demanded, 'So talk! What were you doing up there?'

'We were spying on you. Orders from King Muwas.' His legs were bleeding, flesh torn.

'If I don't get your full cooperation, I'm walking out of this door and leaving you to them,' he pointed at the dogs. The rest had had enough. A sudden babble of raised voices were coming from the prisoners, eager to confess. '*O-n-e a-t a t-i-m-e. P-l-e-a-s-e!*' the general shouted at them. 'You there,' he pointed at the tallest. 'How long have you been up there?'

'Ever since you came down here,' the lanky fellow answered resentfully.

'Got any contacts in our camp?'

The tall one hesitated. The general made to go to the door, threatening to leave them with the dogs.

'A priest,' he said grimly. 'He visits from time to time, passes on information. What moral is like—numbers. What you're doing. You know the type of thing. If you're thinking of marching north.'

The general nodded coldly. 'This priest's name?'

Another hesitation, then, 'Loros.'

'What? You mean Tagrama's deputy? Are you serious? You'd better not be deceiving me or there'll be trouble.'

'Please yourself. You asked—I told. Now will you please get someone to see to his legs?'

'I need some kind of proof,' the general challenged.

'He keeps a record. Payments owed for such and such information. Always makes a note on wax tablets. Pompous fool. I told him it wasn't a good idea. He told me not to stick my nose in where he didn't want it. Find the tablets and you have him.' This time the spy seemed almost smug.

Zidanta called for his orderly. 'Get someone to fix his legs,' he pointed at the short snivelling spy. 'Then lock them up. Make sure they're well guarded. I'll hang the guards if they escape. Tell them that.' The general called for his chariot and went to see Tagrama. He found him teaching acolytes outside in the sun, in a semi circle, with him sitting against the temple wall. All of them were chanting some invocation to the Storm God of Hatti. Zidanta waited until they finished, then raised his hand to get Tagrama's attention.

'It's good to see you general. We don't see nearly enough of you. What can I do for you?'

'Bad news. Nikal's illness was caused by spies in the hills up the valley. But you'd guessed as much. Well I've caught the rascals—and they inform me someone's been feeding them information.'

'Well, well. Yes! I'm not really surprised. So, how does that effect me? Do you want my help to find this spy?'

'It's worse. I know who the spy is and you're not going to like it.'

Tagrama raised his eyebrows. 'Well don't keep me in suspense. Who is it?'

'One of your priests.'

'Nonsense! I'll vouch for *all* my priests. They're *all* loyal to me.' Tagrama did not want this. He knew it would cause him pain.

'I want you to help me search a priest's sleeping quarters. I'm looking for wax writing tablets. It's the proof both you and I need to put a stop to this traitor.'

'Who do you suspect?'

'Loros.'

'*Loros!* You're not serious?'

'Deadly serious! He's for the netherworld if the proof turns up, as I suspect it will. Where are his quarters?'

Tagrama and Zidanta discovered the incriminating wax tablets hidden in the outhouses attached to the temple. Loros' personal acolyte showed them where he went sometimes, after they explained why they needed to know the information. The young man was shocked. Loros, his teacher, was helping Muwas. The wax tablets had money owed, information supplied, and a lot more. It put his guilt beyond question.

Tagrama pleaded with Zidanta, to let him handle his deputy. 'I have to find out why he's done this to me. Why he's gone against my wishes. I need to know—surely you must see that?'

At first the general refused, insisting it was a treasonable offence and Loros would have to pay the ultimate price for treachery. At last, he relented, but on condition that when Loros was to be confronted, Zidanta would surround the temple with a tight cordon of soldiers, just in case something went wrong. They agreed. It was thus that Tagrama collected four of the burliest priests he could find, explained what was to happen and on no account must they let Loros escape. Then they went in search of Loros. All five priests removed their sandals and crept to the entrance of the room where Loros was located. They found Loros in a side room of a side room of the main temple, where he thought nobody would notice, standing in front of a sacred fire burning in a bronze bowl placed on a marble plinth. From there the five observed him at a strange ritual and watched quietly for a time.

Loros was standing with his back to them. He picked up a small wax figurine and a mutton-fat figurine both representing Tudhaliyas and cast them into the fire, chanting, 'As this wax has flattened, as this mutton-fat has perished, so shall Tudhaliyas be flattened and perish when he takes up arms against the true king of Hatti, King Muwas. May the curse of Yarris be upon all those who have joined Tudhaliyas in their treason against King Muwas, the rightful heir to the black bull throne of Hatti.'

That was too much for Tagrama and he ordered his four burly priests to move in and grab Loros. The deputy was shocked he had been discovered. He struggled ferociously, kicking and biting, but to no avail. The four burly priests had an iron grip.

'*Not only do I discover you are a traitor*,' Tagrama shouted at his former deputy, waiving the wax tablets in his face, '*but I now find you casting black magic spells against your rightful king—Tudhaliyas.*' He calmed and in a sinister voice, 'I've a mind to put an end to your miserable existence here and now, you wretch.'

Loros struggled one last time then ceased. The anger and shock of being caught left him. Suddenly he burst into tears. 'I'm sorry your eminence. I don't know what came over me.' Sobbing. 'I won't do it again, please believe me. I'll do anything you ask. Please—another chance.'

'Do you take me for a simpleton? Is that how you've seen me all this time? Someone who could be lied to, to…to be deceived like some befuddled fool? Yes, I've been a fool. A fool for having trusted you. Look at these! They condemn you out of your own mouth.' Tagrama was beside himself, punching the incriminating wax tablets in Loros' chest. He had long suspected he had made the wrong choice in appointing Loros as his deputy, but to be proved so wrong was simply beyond his own comprehension. How could he have been *so* wrong? Was he going to have to review all his decisions? What other errors of judgment had he made?

Loros, seeing this time he wasn't going to bluff his way out, began struggling again.

'Bring him!' Tagrama commanded.

They half dragged the cursing Loros down the naos and outside. When Loros saw the waiting soldiers and the furious general, he quietened. He suddenly realised what might be in store. Tagrama, he thought he could handle. But General Zidanta he knew was quite a different proposition. He had a vision of his own death waiting nearby in the wings. He had thought of this spying as merely a game to while away the boredom of his pitiable priestly existence. It was to be a route to riches and a new life. Now he knew with conviction spying was the most dangerous trade of them all.

Had he had this revelation earlier, he would never have kept the damning records now tucked under Tagrama's arm.

'Well, here he is, general. Thinks he can still pull the wool over my eyes,' Tagrama almost spat the words out. 'I'm handing him over to your custody. Do as you will.'

The general and the high priest had agreed Loros would be incarcerated in isolation in the military prison compound. Heavily guarded. Just in case he had any confederates who had any ideas of freeing him. But Tagrama was to decide his fate. The only stipulation the general had made was it had to be fatal. The general would have liked to have torn Loros to shreds in front of all, as a warning. Tagrama had his own punishment in mind.

Chapter Twenty-Four

The tall muscular pharaoh made a point of daily combat training to keep fit for the coming battles in Nubia. The Egyptian soldiers respected this pharaoh for putting himself at risk just as they did. The Djat found his majesty in the exercise yard in close quarter hand-to-hand fighting with his instructor. Pharaoh insisted on wearing his blue electrum war crown, even in training. He waited until the pharaoh had vanquished his opponent then coughed noisily for attention.

Pharaoh Amenhotep II, dressed in battle leathers, sweating profusely came across, followed by servants trying to dry him off. 'Well, what have you got for me, my dear minister?'

'Another set of wax-boards from you know who in Hatti; just come in by sea.'

'I'll read them later. What about that Mittani upstart? Has he complied? Did he understand my message?'

'I'm sure he understood, your majesty. I made it quite plain in my communication. Withdraw or else. He's declined,' the Djat explained.

'So this refusal then is a direct challenge?' Amenhotep had hoped it wouldn't come to this.

'It would seem so, beloved of Horus. He thinks your majesty is bluffing. He must know our attention is focused on the unrest in Nubia. Saustatar is gambling we will deal with Nubia first and by then he expects the civil war will have been resolved.'

'He leaves me no choice. D'you agree? I have to send at least two divisions to Mittani and compel him to withdraw his forces to defend Wassukkani. If I can prevent the Mittani allying with Muwas, then it's in the interests of Egypt. Tudhaliyas might not win, but it would be irresponsible of me not to help him. If he wins, the Mittani and Hatti will be enemies. That's in Egypt's interest. Is that how you read it?'

'Exactly so, majesty. I will organise the sending of the Ptah and Amun divisions north. They're the premier divisions. If they have to fight, they will acquit themselves with distinction. Who shall lead them?' The first minister waited.

'It's time my son made his mark with the army. Make sure Tuthmosis understands the purpose. He is to fight only as a last resort. The point of this sortie is to make them withdraw their forces from Hatti. If they do, then he is simply to return to Egypt with the divisions intact. Is that clear?'

'Yes, majesty.'

'I shall lead the army myself south to the first cataract. We shall see if the Nubians are as rebellious when they feel the might of Egypt on their doorstep.'

'You are wise without parallel, majesty.'

'If we are extra clever, we could make it look like the army I intend for Nubia, is in fact readying to follow Tuthmosis north. Can you make it seem so?'

'I will have loud noises made to that effect. The Mittani spies are bound to report this. Unobtrusively, the senior officers will be told the truth. They will keep it secret until you are well on the way.'

'You are a most diligent Djat and I will have to find some way of honouring you. Now as a bonus, would you care to wrestle me my fine first minister?'

'Everlasting are the manifestations of Re'. Majesty, you're too kind. Unfortunately my prowess is with words not brawn and my meagre effort would give you no satisfaction. I fear I would be an appetiser without substance. If you insist, of course, I will do as you command, but I beg you not to waste your time on such a scrawny meal.'

'Fear not, my good Djat. I had no intention of forcing you to go against your inclination. I value you too much as

134

my close adviser. Go! Inform Tuthmosis of my wishes. He is to start up north as soon as possible.'

The Djat breathed a sigh of relief. Fighting with weapons of war was not something he was any good at. Words—that was another matter. He could use words as a soldier wielded a weapon. He was thankful for the pharaoh's wisdom and backed away, leaving the pharaoh to his training.

Chapter Twenty-Five

'*This can't be!*' exclaimed King Saustatar as he was being carried on the royal palanquin to the temple of Teshub. He had been handed a communication by a royal courier half way enroute to the temple to celebrate the Spring Festival of Sowing. 'Turn round,' he ordered the palanquin supervisor, 'back to the palace. This can't wait.' The festival would be postponed till the next day. Pharaoh would have to be dealt with immediately. The king sat frowning at the papyrus and then half smiled. *So that king of rogues has called my bluff. So be it! I half expected as much* Egypt had many years of ancient diplomatic history to call upon. Saustatar remembered a saying his father was fond of. "Bluffs only work on the weak minded." The Egyptian king had just proved he wasn't weak minded. It would seem he would have to recall the army from Hattusas. He could see no other option. If only the Libyans weren't so weak. A threat from the other side of Egypt would put a stop to the pharaoh's game. On reaching the palace, he alighted and stretched. His shock and frustration was fading as the need for action reasserted itself. 'Where's the Chancellor? I expected him to be here, waiting.'

Kiluhepa, Saustatar's consort remained in the palanquin waiting to continue on to the temple.

'Come down from there, my dear,' the king commanded. 'Can't you understand. The festival is postponed.'

'Oh! I'm sorry. Aren't we having it this year?' She was off somewhere else in her mind and unaware of what was taking place.

'Go and lie down in your bedroom. I haven't time to indulge you at the moment. Serious business to attend to.' He was feeling exasperated. 'Where's that minister of mine?'

The Chancellor came hurrying in with another official through the main entrance. 'I'm sorry your majesty, I was collecting the Master of Birds as a precaution. I thought he might be needed.'

The king stopped and stared at his minister. 'As ever, you're one step ahead. I should have known. Nothing slips by you. So you've heard! Pharaoh is sending his army.'

'Yes, majesty. And I fear we have little choice as to our next move.'

'Recalling Artatama! I know. Never mind, it can't be helped.' Saustatar took his minister by the arm and led him to a seat. The Master of Birds followed discreetly.

'So is this news verified? Is he really sending an army? What size, do we know?' Saustatar was beginning to feel miserable.

'My agents in Waset inform me two divisions have left for Mittani. They made no secret of it. They wanted us to know. The Ptah and Amun divisions led by pharaoh's son Tuthmosis. They then made it known to all who cared to listen they were readying more troops which were to follow his son, commanded by pharaoh himself. I fear a large force is being sent to admonish us.'

'Then my dear Chancellor, by all means send the pigeons recalling my son. He must hurry home to defend Wassukkani. Pray Teshub he makes it in time.'

Chapter Twenty-Six

$\mathbf{A}$ week had gone by since Tagrama ordered Tawana to make a salt and honey potion. Nikal was sitting in bed, impatient to get up. Tagrama was to visit that day and pronounce on her recovery. She was hoping he would finally allow her out of bed. She was getting bored, even with, or in spite of Talarra's games and ministrations. She could hear her father and brother out in the garden, deep in conversation and longed to join them.

Tawana came through the door. 'Hmm! My son wishes to come and pay his respects. Will you see him your highness?'

'Of course. How can I refuse the king?' She coloured and looked at the bed linen.

Tudhaliyas clearly heard from the corridor and quietly entered. 'Your highness—Nikal, you frightened all of us here with this illness. We were worried you might setback relations between Hatti and Kizzuwatna.' He smiled broadly to show it was merely a small joke. 'Are you better now?'

'Yes your maj...yes Tudhaliyas. Much better thank you. In fact, my physician is due and I'm hoping he'll let me out of this bed. Make him let me get up. Please! I can see through the curtains and it's so pleasant outside.' She was full of colour, the health back in her cheeks.

Tawana interrupted, 'I'll talk to the high priest and insist he let you up.'

'And I will command him. How can he refuse?' Tudhaliyas added still smiling.

He was elated to see how well she looked and Nikal was full of the joys of spring. Tudhaliyas had come especially to see her and with luck, she would be out of bed and into the garden this day.

Gassulawiya entered at that moment bearing a hot drink of honey. Smiling encouragingly, 'You're to drink this up, Tagrama's orders.'

Tawana whispered to Tudhaliyas, 'Do you think she's up to being told about Zidanta's success in catching the villains?'

'What are you two whispering about?' Nikal had noticed despite Talarra trying to distract her with fruit. She took a sip of the warm sweet liquid.

'I was agreeing with mother,' Tudhaliyas replied, 'that you're well enough to be told. General Zidanta has caught the culprits who contaminated the water in the river. It seems they were spying on us.'

'Oh! Spies!' Nikal did not care. She had Tudhaliyas here, her health was back and all was right with the world— her world. She took another sip.

He saw she was totally uninterested in the news and thought to himself, *Why should she be? Wars, spies, what had any of it to do with her? She was well and it was all that mattered. This girl was an innocent, caught up in troubles that were of no concern to her.* He understood her for the first time. He promised himself he would protect her from the world and its machinations. Try to cocoon her in her innocence for as long as it would last. It was the least he could do for his beloved.

Tudhaliyas walked Nikal out into the garden, the air hanging a little heavy in the late afternoon. She perched on a bench quietly, expectantly. He stood beneath an apple tree, smelling the blossoms, heart pounding. 'Don't you find this time of year full of vitality? Spring is for...' He paused, then took the plunge. 'You know, this is the first real chance I've had to be alone with you.'

She blushed a little, waiting, hoping. Talarra had been deliberately waylaid by Gassulawiya to do a chore that was of little consequence and could have waited. All in the household had conspired to contrive this moment for the young couple.

Tudhaliyas continued, full of trepidation, but trying to be casual, 'You must know how I feel about you. Have you guessed what's in my heart?'

'I...I think so,' she muttered hesitantly, nervously, her heart fluttering.

Reaching up he picked a blossom flower from the tree, gently bringing it to his nose, inhaling deeply. 'Ahh! Were I not the king, I would give free rein to my feelings; sweep you off your feet and carry you off.' He walked over to where she sat, bowed, and held the flower out to her.

She plucked the flower from his hand and looked at it longingly. 'Were I not a princess, I might be free to respond.'

'Nikal! This is an instant granted to us from above. We have known each other for only a short time, but in that short time, I have grown especially fond of you. Not "fond," that's not the right word, more, much more. I...I want...to spend my life with you. Do you know what I'm saying, what I'm implying?'

She looked up into his eyes, much in the same manner she had done the first day they met—so long ago now—a lifetime. The look was bold, innocent, yet strong and determined. It was a look of total commitment. If she were to give her heart, her eyes stated, it would be for always. She gave a hint of a smile, then nodded timidly. 'Ever since we met...I've been drawn to you. You have a quiet strength I find extremely attractive. You are kind, honest and I cannot spend a day without thinking about you. At night...I dream of you, of us being together.' She moved along and made room on the bench, patting the free space, inviting him to sit.

He accepted the invitation, sat and gently took her hand. 'I'm content you feel the same. I couldn't bear it any other way. If you were to ask it, for you, I would abandon the throne without the slightest hesitation.'

She looked shocked, 'I would not ask it of you. I want whatever you want. All I ask is to be at your side—for as long as you want me. You must complete the undertaking with Kantuzzili. Win this war. I will support you come what may—whether you win, or god forbid, should you lose. I would not feel happy if you didn't put all your energy into destroying that monster Muwas.'

He squeezed her hand in joy. It's what he wanted to hear.

'I'm full of joy to hear that,' he told her softly. 'Although I made the offer to abandon the throne, it would have broken my spirit to have done so. You must have guessed that. I have dedicated myself to putting an end to my family's humiliation.' He admired her encouraging sentiments, her strength of purpose, more so now than ever before. 'I promised to protect you from the harm in the world, to do all in my power to encourage your love for me.' He longed to hold her in his arms, touch his lips to hers, but that would have to wait. 'I promise we will be together. And I will prosecute the war until Muwas is vanquished. But now I want to ask my father to talk with your father. Nikal, do you give me permission to do that?'

'I do!'

Chapter Twenty-seven

A reluctant Artatama rode through the narrow corbelled arches flanked by portal sculptures of the citadel gate into the lower paved courtyard holding stables, an armoury, various guardrooms, and the official access to the upper palace proper. He and his escort dismounted, leaving the horses with those designated, whilst Artatama led the rest up the steps of the Great Palace. Sentries sprang to attention, others rushed to find the king and inform, the prince of Mittani was here.

King Muwas made his way to the throne room in readiness to receive his visitors, followed by his Chancellor. Artatama, feeling the solemnity of his purpose, strode imposingly into the Audience Hall, surreptitiously glancing left and right at the grand frescoes devoted to Hittite history. It reminded him something of a similar kind ought to be done in the Audience Chamber at Wassukkani. He stopped near the throne and bowed his head.

'Your majesty, I bring bad tidings.' Artatama was clearly uncomfortable.

'Prince Artatama, I'm sure it can't be that bad or I would have heard of it myself.' Muwas was being serious and a little sarcastic.

'It pains me to tell you I've received instructions from my father, King Saustatar, for the army to return to Mittani with the greatest of speed. My men are already decamping as we speak.'

This was an unexpected blow and Muwas face clearly showed it. 'But why? What has caused this sudden change? Is Mittani under attack?'

'I fear we may be soon. Pharaoh has sent an army to our borders and as much as I would personally like to remain, our borders take precedence. You must understand. I can do little else. I'm deeply sorry.' And it seemed Artatama was indeed regretful.

'May I speak with you in private, prince.' Muwas rose from the throne and led the way behind into the room at the back. 'Now, what's all this about, my friend?'

'It's as I stated. Two pigeons arrived with messages recalling the army. One word was given as the reason. "Pharaoh." That can mean only one thing. Pharaoh is to attack Mittani. I must hurry back home, or there will be no home to hurry back to.'

'This is the worst news to come my way. I can't face Kantuzzili with the forces I have. The latest figures sent to me are that he has about forty thousand. If you go it leaves me with twenty thousand and I can't join battle so badly outnumbered. I might as well abandon hope of the throne.' Muwas was speaking to himself as well as Artatama. He felt the need to talk the problem out loud, to try and get a perspective.

'What I can promise you, Muwas, is I will return with all speed as soon as I can. I owe you that much. I wish I didn't have to go but I know you understand. You would do the same in my sandals.'

Muwas looked closely into Artatama's eyes and found no guile. This Mittani prince was sincere. He would have to talk to General Ammuna. 'You're right. I would do the same. I wish you god speed, success in battle and a swift return. I hope to see you soon, my friend.' This time Muwas actually meant those sentiments.

Artatama turned about and strode hurriedly out of the room, picking up his waiting retinue. He was quickly out of the palace and down to where his men waited. 'General Satukani, I need you to take most of the cavalry and all the chariots, no baggage and return with all speed to support my father, your king. Push as hard as you can. No stopping. You must reach Mittani before the pharaoh. Is that clear?'

'Most clear, your highness. I will leave now.' The general made to go.

'I will follow as fast as we can travel. No stopping mind you!'

'Yes, your royal highness.'

Back up in the Grand Castle, Muwas was waiting at the back of the throne room for General Ammuna.

The general entered. 'You wished to see me your majesty?'

'How are the two Mešedi coming along? You know the ones I mean?'

'Yes, majesty. They're doing fine. Almost ready.' The general looked pleased with himself. He had done as he was required and more.

'I'm going to give you another order, general. I want you to cancel their task. Make sure they understand. No killing! Clear?'

The general's face registered surprise. 'Cancel it? If you say so, majesty. I will of course obey.'

'I may not like admitting it, but I was wrong about that man. I just found out. He is a friend, a good friend and I have no wish to do him harm. There you have it. Your king admits to being human.' Muwas winked at the general. 'Don't tell anyone.'

*   *   *

The following day riders rode the morning streets of Hattusas loudly proclaiming, 'On this day you are all commanded by his majesty King Muwas to attend an oath of loyalty at the Great Temple.'

That got the people all stirred up, both with indignation and fear. What oath of loyalty? They weren't in his army. Why should they attend a loyalty oath? Who was supposed to swear this loyalty? But in the end they all gathered where they were told to, clogging the surrounding streets, fearing the consequences of not attending.

Up in the palace, General Ammuna was counselling the king, 'Now the Mittani have gone, it will be difficult to maintain the new religion. The people won't stand for it. I've been told by my officers, people go by and spit in the direction of the temple. The Mittani priest dare not venture out for fear of attack.'

'This is why, my dear general, they must be made to swear loyalty to me *and* the new religion. I will stomp out any rebellion at its roots. Give orders—any who fail to swear the oath will be put to the sword. Make sure the soldiers encourage people to attend the oath taking. Close all the gates. Get them to herd the population towards the temple. That should put a stop to their nonsense.'

'As you command, sire.' The general would do as he was ordered.

'One other matter.' Muwas led the general to a couch. 'You pointed out just now the Mittani have gone. That leaves us with only twenty thousand troops. I want you to make arrangements to evacuated Hattusas. If Kantuzzili marches up here, as I expect him to, we will have to retreat to Hakpis until Artatama returns. Our strategy is to retreat until we are rejoined by our allies. Only then will we join battle and resolve this war.'

'That sire, is a wise move. In fact, I've already made such arrangements in anticipation of just such an order. I was hoping you would give it soon.'

'You sly old dog. It's good to know you're on top of things. Good work. I fully expect Artatama to keep his promise to me and return as soon as he can. We must endure until then. Now go and supervise the oath taking. I don't want to leave anything to chance.' Muwas dismissed Ammuna and the latter bowed out.

Up in the temple, crowds were beginning to gather, grumbling, and moaning at being forced to attend, at sword point, this new edict of their unanointed king. The priests had brought from the sanctuary, to be displayed, the personification of Teshub. A bearded deity holding a club and thunderbolt and wearing a horned headdress standing in his chariot drawn by white bulls. This effigy of Teshub was set up on a large flat boulder high enough for all to see. It made for a lot of tetchy comments, all done in whispers so the soldiers couldn't hear. 'How can he still call it the black bull throne?' one old man whispered to his crone of a wife, nodding in the direction of the displayed effigy. Many were of the same opinion.

When evening came and most of the oath taking almost over, not one person had refused to swear. Some did it with fingers crossed under their clothes. Others were entirely indifferent which god they were forced to pray to. Only when a few were left, did the soldiers come across a couple of die-hard stubborn refusals. Two merchants who were quite happy to swear loyalty to King Muwas, but bluntly refused to renounce Taru and swear to Teshub. They were cajoled and threatened but to no avail. Ammuna was called. He took one look at them and ordered them to be bound and taken into the temple. The general did not want to do what he intended to do in full sight of spectators. 'Strip them. I think you will find Taru's three-pronged thunderbolt symbol tattooed under their right arm.'

The officer supervising the stripping looked and shook his head. 'How did you know, sir? It's where you said it would be. Who are they?'

'Priests! Priests in disguise. Tagrama must have sent them. Can't think what kind of mischief they could get to up here. Never mind. I'm going to teach both Tagrama and these two priests a lesson they won't forget in a hurry.'

'What am I to do to them?' the officer wanted to know.

'I want you to remodel their skins right now. Flay them until they're raw. Use a horse's whip. Make sure every square measure of their skins feels the lashes. Then kick them out of the main gates. Let them walk back to Ankuwa.'

Chapter Twenty-eight

A day after Harep and Rewa entered Ankuwa, Mokhat and Palaiyas travelled down the same road towards the checkpoint. From their dress and overall appearance, there was no hope they would simply be let through. Palaiyas had a shield shaped in a subtle figure of eight, a helmet reinforced with boar's tusks, two thrusting spears and a sword on a baldric in a tasselled scabbard. That was about as alien to Hatti as it came. Mokhat was little better. A dark cloak with a hood but unlike any priest the soldiers had ever come across. Hittite priests wore white. Both were taken into custody, searched and disarmed, then taken further down to the next checkpoint that had an officer in charge. They did not resist.

'I don't know who you are or where you come from, but this is one decision I'm taking higher up,' the officer told them.

'That suits me. I came to see your king. I have a dispatch from King Kasalliwa of Kaska for King Tudhaliyas.' He held out the waxed boards. 'He must see them.' Mokhat insisted on retaining the waxed boards.

Palaiyas kept quiet, but seemed impressed by Mokhat's command of the situation. They were escorted right into the valley to where Ankuwa was situated. When they first saw the town, Palaiyas nudged Mokhat, 'There's no wall round the town. Can you believe it?'

Mokhat just shrugged his shoulders and tilted his head at the surrounding mountains as if to say, there are your walls.

The two strangers were shepherded into Ankuwa under strong guard and taken to see General Zidanta. The general was on the parade ground, or what passed for one, watching his favourite regiment practicing manoeuvres. The officer dismounted and marched up to the general, saluted, then pointed at his prisoners, 'Sir, we caught these two trying to get into the valley. One of them is a Kaska and says he's got a dispatch for our king. I thought I'd better bring them to you.'

Zidanta looked the two strangers over, sitting on their horses and paused on Palaiyas. 'Ahhiyawan?' he asked.

'Yes.' Palaiyas agreed.

'Hmmm! And you?' he turned his attention to Mokhat. 'You're a Kaska.'

'Yes, general. I have a dispatch from my king for King Tudhaliyas.' Mokhat showed him the waxed boards.

The general held his hand out to take the boards.

'General,' Mokhat held the boards to his chest. 'I'm ordered by my king to place these in the hands of either his majesty King Tudhaliyas, or Prince Kantuzzili. No other. Would you have me fail my mission?'

Zidanta eyed Mokhat, then smiled. 'No, of course not. Come, I will take you to Prince Kantuzzili. Let him decide what to do.' He hailed one of the chariots and jumped on, inviting Mokhat and Palaiyas to board with him.

Mokhat declined, 'I think I'll ride this horse, if you don't mind.'

Palaiyas jumped off his, giving Mokhat the reins. 'I'd like to join you general, if you've no objections.'

Zidanta looked pleased. 'Jump on!' Two more chariots followed as escort. They arrived at the interim royal residence amid a cloud of red dust. Zidanta jumped down as did Mokhat and Palaiyas. The general led the way past the Mešedi, through the gateway into the garden, up the path to the house. They found both brothers relaxing on the patio.

'General,' Kantuzzili called out. 'Welcome, welcome. Come sit. Have some refreshment.' Kantuzzili peered at the strangers with the general and waited.

'Highness, one is an Ahhiyawan and the other, a Kaska,' Zidanta motioned at the two following him. 'The Kaska says he has a dispatch from his king for our king. Won't tell me what it is. Says he's to hand it to the king or to you, personally.'

Mokhat strode forward. 'I'm Mokhat, brother to King Kasalliwa. If you are Prince Kantuzzili, then I have a communication for you of vital importance.'

At hearing Mokhat was the brother of a king, Palaiyas rolled his eyes in surprise.

'I am Kantuzzili,' and the seated man rose and held out his hand.

Mokhat handed the wax boards over. Kantuzzili scrutinised the boards before breaking the seal. 'Well I never! Come priest, sit with us—and you,' he motioned to Palaiyas.

'So all is well?' the general asked.

'Oh yes, quite well. Thank you for bringing them here.' He returned to reading the wedges on the boards.

'Well I must get back to my men. Good bye.' Zidanta turned.

'Won't you stay and have some refreshments?' Himuili called out after him.

'Thank you but no. I must get on.' Zidanta walked back the way he came.

'Good bye, general,' Himuili called out after him.

'Do you trust your friend?' Kantuzzili asked Mokhat.

'With my life.'

'Then I can tell you the communication warns of danger to us all. Do you know what this contains?' Kantuzzili held the wax boards up to Mokhat.

'Yes I do. I helped write them. It tells that Muwas has hired the Assassin's Guild to kill Tudhaliyas, you Prince Kantuzzili and your brother here. What it doesn't say is who the killer is.'

Kantuzzili raised his eyebrows, 'And you know who he is?'

'I'm afraid I do. That is why I'm down here. I'm the only one who knows.'

'Apart from the question of how you know, will you tell us who it is?' Himuili bluntly asked.

'An assassin named Harep. He has two nephews with him. I think I know what the nephews look like, but Harep I can easily point out to you.'

'Good! That's a start. For the moment we won't ask the obvious question—how you know this Harep. We might come to that later.' Kantuzzili sat holding the wax boards, pondering. 'I must go tell the king. I'll bring him out here and introduce you.' Kantuzzili rose and went inside.

Himuili sat quietly observing these two incongruous strangers. He couldn't contain his curiosity. 'What may I ask is a Kaska priest doing consorting with an Ahhiyawan soldier? For that matter, what *is* an Ahhiyawan soldier doing here?' The question was directed at Mokhat.

'It's a long story. It might be better if we delay the account till after I see the king.' It wasn't a rebuff; Mokhat just wanted to concentrate on one thing at a time.

*   *   *

After the meeting with Tudhaliyas in the dining room, Mokhat sat quietly at the table, sipping a goblet of wine, whilst the king read the wax boards from Kasalliwa. Kantuzzili and Himuili had entered quietly and joined them. After Tudhaliyas finished reading, all four walked back through the house towards the entrance to where they had left Palaiyas. At the entrance, Mokhat asked to see the high priest of the Hatti.

'Why do you want to see Tagrama?' Himuili asked.

'I am here to uncover an assassin. To do that, I need to disappear from view. If he's to accomplish his mission, Harep will be watching the royal household. If he sees me we'll lose the advantage. I must try to get behind him in such a manner I don't tip my hand. Remember, I'm the only one who knows what he looks like. Your royal bodyguards protect you, but a sneak thief knows that. I must become unobtrusive. I'm a priest and I need the disguise of a temple. I'm hoping your high priest will provide that.'

'I'm giving you full authority to stop this assassin,' the king told Mokhat. 'If you should need anything, go anywhere, you are free to do so without hindrance. I will instruct my people to give you all the assistance you require. You should know we have news of Muwas. His Mittani allies have abandoned him and as a result, we march north in a couple of days. You should prepare to deal with the assassin here, or on the road, and most likely in Hattusas.'

'You are gracious, sire. I will make preparations. Palaiyas, here, is my personal bodyguard. You should trust him as you trust me.'

'I will let it be known,' the king told him.

Mokhat added, 'I strongly advise you to double your bodyguards until this assassin is caught and dealt with.'

'Yes, that will be done. In the meantime, there is a chariot outside waiting, at your disposal. It will take you to the temple. May you uncover this assassin with all speed. We cannot relax until you do. Farewell. May Taru guide you!'

'Thank you, sire.'

Mokhat never liked chariots and outside, insisted on riding his own horse, but Palaiyas handed the reins of his horse to Mokhat and eagerly jumped on the chariot. He grabbed the reins from the chariot's driver and encouraged the horses to a high speed gallop that had the driver grabbing for the rails. Mokhat expected the whole thing to end in a pile-up yet to his surprise, Palaiyas was an outstanding charioteer. Mokhat could only follow the dust trail left by the two-wheeled horse-drawn vehicle. Their arrival at the temple was an equally dusty affair. Mokhat made a show of pompously dismounting, tied his horse at a rail and then began very obviously dusting himself down, watched by an amused Palaiyas. The driver of the chariot was eager to have his reins back and hastened away as though from a madman.

'It's good honest dirt,' Palaiyas said.

'Yes, but why must *I* wear it?' Mokhat smiled back.

'Come, let us find this high priest of yours.'

Tagrama was still fretting about his imprisoned deputy, pacing up and down in the same room Loros had been found making his blasphemous incantations. A priest led Mokhat and Palaiyas to Tagrama. The priest stopped and politely coughed to draw his attention.

'Eh, yes. What is it you want?' he said brusquely, looking at the strangers.

'King Tudhaliyas sent us to see you in the hope you might save his life,' Mokhat wanted this priest's attention.

Tagrama couldn't believe what he had just heard. 'I beg your pardon? What did you just say?'

'It's true! I swear it! We are here to save the king,' Mokhat repeated.

'And how do I fit into this? Who are you? I've never seen you before.' Tagrama's attention was now between them and Loros.

'We recently arrived from Hattusas. Can we find a place to sit and then I will tell you our story.'

The mention of Hattusas finally broke the link with Loros. 'Come, we'll use a side room with seating.' Tagrama led, they followed. When they were seated Tagrama ordered the priest who had brought them, 'Find some fruit and bring some goblets and wine.'

'Yes eminence.' The priest hurried away.

'Now, what is all this about saving the king?' Tagrama gave them his full attention.

'My name is Mokhat and this is my friend and bodyguard, Palaiyas.' It was the explanation they had agreed to. 'I'm from Kaska where my brother is king. Muwas has hired the Assassin's Guild to kill the king, Kantuzzili and his brother Himuili.'

Tagrama's ears perked up. 'That foul stench has risen again.'

'I am the only one who knows what the assassin looks like. The king has assured me his full cooperation. Now I and my friend here, need to blend in. I'm a Kaska priest and I thought my natural attire might be of a Hatti priest.' Mokhat stopped to see how the proposal might go down.

'I see. The king has given you his full support, eh? Then you have mine. I suppose we could manage to find a priest's outfit for you. What about your Ahhiyawan friend? How is he to "blend" in?' Tagrama's eyes twinkled. He was enjoying this.

'I thought we might inveigle him into the same costume. I think he'd make a fine priest.' Now it was Mokhat's turn to grin.

'Now wait just a shake of a horse's tail,' Palaiyas exploded among amused chuckles. 'If you think you're going to pass me off as a priest, you've got to be out of you collective minds. Me a priest? Are you joking?' Palaiyas made a lot of noise, but knew he was caught.

When the transformation was completed, both Mokhat and Palaiyas stood before Tagrama for a final inspection. 'Well, will we do?' Mokhat felt little different. The dark grey was simply changed for white.

Palaiyas on the other hand fidgeted, seemed uncomfortable and his face registered distaste. 'Make sure you look after my weapons and tunic. There's not another like it for two hundred leagues. I'm serious, I need to have them back. If we're going back to Hattusas, pack them well and tell me where they are.' His face was dour.

Tagrama said with a grin, 'Don't worry! We'll look after them. Just make sure you're able to collect them.'

*   *   *

154

Tagrama arose with a heavy heart, although when he opened his eyes, the day was glorious. This day was the day for Loros' execution. He still couldn't understand how he had made such a monumental blunder. How could he have appointed such a man as his deputy? Tagrama made his way to Loros' cell in the prison compound where he was being held. In reality, Tagrama had come to find out if Loros believed in the gods. Had *that* all been a deceitful sham as well? The guard opened the cell and stood back. 'Well my ex deputy, today's the day when all your hard work is to be repaid. Admittedly not in the way you expected.' The guard slammed the cell door shut. He waited outside. Tagrama found Loros sitting on the floor, head bowed. 'I've come to say good bye.'

'Hmph! Needn't of bothered!' Loros was clearly in a bad mood, as indeed he had every right to be.

'No bother,' Tagrama responded cheerfully. 'No point in sulking now. You brought all this upon yourself.'

'I can do without your gloating. Why don't you go and play with your statues?'

At that instant Tagrama had his answer. Loros' piety *was* a sham. He had never believed. Tagrama was rooted speechless, shocked. He had almost put the Great Temple in this charlatans hands. If he had been somehow incapacitated himself, this…this disgusting man sitting before him, would have become high priest. Suddenly he couldn't stand being in the same room. '*Guard!…Guard*! Come let me out. The air in here is fouled by the stench of Yarris.' The cell door was quickly opened and Tagrama rushed out. He breathed deep in the corridor and pondered the deceit. On his way out, he was questioning if he should remain as high priest. In the open he found General Zidanta's chariot outside the compound commandant's shelter. He needed to talk to someone he could trust and he hurried over to find the general.

Inside the shelter two officers sat quietly drinking goblets of wine. 'Ah! Tagrama. We are honoured. Come, sit, have some wine.' General Zidanta welcomed him enthusiastically.

'I see you've come to oversee the execution,' Tagrama noted.

'I'm a man of my word. This is one of the worst cases of treachery I have ever witnessed and believe me I've witnesses a few. The *deputy* of the high temple? Whatever next?' Zidanta looked disgusted.

Tagrama looked at the other officer and decided he looked sensible enough to keep his opinions to himself. 'You look only at treachery; but I have to decide, in the light of the fact I appointed him my deputy, whether I should remain high priest any longer.'

'Oh, come now!' the general consoled. 'I've seen this rascal and you've nothing to reprove yourself with. The man's a fraud through and through. Honey wouldn't melt in his mouth. It would be a double tragedy if on top of all this, we were to lose you. Put this out of your mind.'

'If only I could.'

'We're about to carry out the sentence passed by the king. I'm sure it would help you rid your doubts if you were to witness his demise.' The general was trying to be encouraging.

'I *was* intending to stay and witness my shame. The question I ask myself is, what other decisions of mine will have such disastrous consequences?'

'Look Tagrama, in the past, I've made my share of mistakes. We all have. If I resigned every time, I would still be an ordinary soldier. Then I would have little or no influence on anything that matters. If you were not the high priest, then someone much worse would be doing your job and you would be the first to complain.' The general intended to make sure Tagrama did not leave his responsibilities to someone else. He was fond of Tagrama and thought he did excellent work.

'I thank you for those kind words of comfort and I assure you, I'll think about it,' Tagrama promised.

'Let's get this over with,' the general led the way out of the shelter. At the back of the prison compound, a wooden block had been set up. A burly warrant officer had volunteered to perform the execution and had an outsized scimitar at the ready. He did not like priests, although Tagrama was not to know this.

Loros was being frog-marched out of the barrack between two burly soldiers, struggling—to the place where his end awaited him. '*I don't want to die…I don't want to die*,' he kept blubbering. They half dragged him to the block and forced his head down, holding it fast while the scimitar was raised above his head.

'*Stop!*' Tagrama suddenly shouted. 'I told you I'd deal with him.' He rushed to the startled executioner and snatched the scimitar from the warrant officer's hands. Eyeing Loros' neck, Tagrama raised the scimitar and angrily brought it down in one mighty blow. Loros' head shot forward, blood spouting from the big veins in his neck. Tagrama leaned on the sword and silent tears flowed down his cheeks. 'I had to do that, don't you see?' he said softly.

Soldiers quickly collected the head and placed it in a sack, still dripping.

'Congratulations,' General Zidanta approached and placed an arm round Tagrama's shoulder, trying to comfort him. 'I didn't know you had it in you.'

'I said I would deal with him,' Tagrama repeated sadly.

'And you did, well done.' The general paused in thought, then made his mind up. 'I think you may have more important matters to deal with shortly. Maybe I shouldn't be telling you this, but we'll be back in Hattusas soon. Make sure you keep this to yourself for the moment. I've seen dispatches saying the Mittani have left Muwas. If that's the case, then in a day or so we'll be leaving here. You'll have your temple to purify back in the capital. That'll keep you busy cleansing it of the Mittani contamination.'

Chapter Twenty-Nine

Returning scouts reported the southern army led by General Zidanta was on the march, heading up to Hattusas. Muwas quickly ordered General Ammuna to implement plans for the retreat to Hakpis. No other choice was available.

'We have to be out by morning,' the general was advising Muwas. 'It would be unfortunate if we were to be hemmed in here. The city might not survive the encounter. That would make all our enemies happy.'

'Yes, we must keep the capital intact, no matter who wins. Can we withdraw at night? I mean can we depart so the residents don't even know we've gone. This might be a chance to assess the discipline of our troops.'

'Hmm! That's a splendid idea, your majesty. Hooves wrapped, horses muzzled, wagon and chariot wheels muffled, axles greased, all metal blackened and silenced. We sneak out as an exercise in ambush. I'll tell the officers.' *Like thieves in the night,* thought Ammuna.

'Yes, yes. See to it! I have a splitting headache, I'm going to lie down.' Muwas dismissed the general.

That evening the people who were forced to billet the troops in the city were told all the soldiers were moving to a hide-tent encampment where the Mittani had been, outside the city gates. All the citizens were only too pleased to see the back of them, even though they were Hatti troops. No one likes strangers in their homes, winking at wives and daughters, making as if they owned the place. When the troops left the city that night, it raised no suspicions. The city assumed they were moving to the new encampment; all had been well prepared in advance. But instead of pitching tents, they kept going, ever so slowly, ever so quietly. By the middle of a moonless night, Muwas was out front with his staff, leading his army to Hakpis. They travelled all night and only finally rested in the morning after dawn. All the muffling was being slowly removed. They had hardly built their campfires when a detachment came riding in hard.

The officer in charge jumped off his horse and reported to General Ammuna. 'Sir, we're being watched. Kaska I think. They're growing in numbers, more arriving all the time. My guess sir, is they're gathering for an attack.'

'Very well captain. Let your men get some food. Do the horses first. Rest up.' Ammuna shook his head.

Muwas was in his pavilion, stretched out, asleep. The Mešedi opened the flap for the general, who quickly walked in and gently shook Muwas' shoulder. 'Heh! What's up? Where are we?' Muwas woke startled.

'We've got company. Kaska! I think they may be gathering in force. Some time today I would guess they're going to attack. Scouts just reported in.'

'Damn them! How far would you say are we from Hakpis?'

'Another day, if we hurry. Might be an idea if we make this a forced-march instead of this easy going pace.'

'I agree. Give the order. Let them finish this food, then make sure everyone knows the Kaska want to have a go at us. They're reputation for viciousness ought to get the troops moving. We don't stop till we're in Hakpis.'

'I will go and give the command, sire.' The general threw orders at his officers.

By late afternoon, squadrons had been sent a number of times to engage the Kaska, but each time they refused to fight. When the Hatti cavalry approached, the Kaska melted away.

'It's no good, sire, we'll have to make a fortified camp for the night.' General Ammuna was irritated. 'They'll cut us to ribbons in the dark unless we stop and erect defences.'

'Why won't they fight? Why all this running?' Muwas was equally angered.

160

'I'm not sure, but it might be they're way of warning us not to go too far north.' The general shrugged. 'You know how they are, these Kaska. Unpredictable. They've always fought unconventionally.'

*   *   *

Kasalliwa was in the middle of a forest, sitting round a campfire in the twilight, in a circle with his officers.

'We have them worried, sire. They're trying to engage us, but as per your instructions, we're avoiding a fight. Strange people though, they shout insults at us as if they were weapons,' a tribal commander observed.

'It's frustration!' Kasalliwa explained. 'They always try to provoke, like children. Thinking we might get angry and make mistakes. First, I want to get all the tribes together before we attack. The main point at the moment is to slow them down. If we can tire them, we weaken them, while keeping our losses to a minimum. When we engage, we'll have done Tudhaliyas a good service.'

'Sire, more men are arriving all the time. By morning, I estimate, we'll have most of the tribes gathered here,' another tribal commander reported.

'Good! Mind you, keep your men provoking them all night. Let's make sure Muwas doesn't get any sleep.' Lots of nods from the chieftains. 'You tell me they've dug in behind a palisade. I want archers, sling throwers and spearmen lobbing volley after volley into the enclosure. Everyone we disable is one less to worry about in the morning. All night, mind you!' Kasalliwa sat back and looked please with his men's efforts. He had been planning this move ever since he had been told the Mittani had departed. Only for him it was all intellectual and he quite overlooked the need to send out a call for the tribes. He knew Tudhaliyas would move to retake Hattusas and predicted Muwas would be forced to retreat to Hakpis. Only when he had decided to harass Muwas' withdrawal did he send out couriers for a gathering of the tribes. He could kick himself for treating it all as simply an intellectual game. Had he moved sooner, he could have attacked by now. As it was, he would lose a day.

* * *

Behind the enormous palisade, General Ammuna was doing the rounds, inspecting the men's handiwork. '*Keep your heads down, that's an order!*' he shouted into the night. The beleaguered soldiers did not need to be told this. Arrows, stones from sling-shots and spears arrived with horrendous regularity. Many of the men were wounded and a number killed. That night there was a full spring moon and it did not help. It threw light on the possible targets and the Kaska made full use of it.

The general had rejoined Muwas in his dugout, strengthened by a solid wooden roof. It kept the missiles out. 'Damned barbarians!' Muwas ranted. 'Why are they doing this? We weren't attacking them, just trying to get to Hakpis. Anyway, how did they know we were here? We were moving so quietly. The whole point of all the muffling was to prevent this happening.'

'Do they ever need a reason to attack us?' Ammuna asked. 'We've always been at logger-heads with them, sire. Ever since we lost Nerik to them, they've been pressing us further.'

'Once the succession is settled, I'm going to deal with the scum. For starters, I want you to draw up plans to retake Nerik. Do you hear me general?'

'Yes, your majesty.'

Dawn tiptoed over the clearing within the palisade, throwing light on an exhausted twenty thousand strong army of Hittites. Most were simply pleased to be alive and uninjured. General Ammuna was up and determined, addressing his tired officers, 'I want you to organise the column into a mobile battle formation. We're breaking out of this palisade as soon as you've done that. I have every intention of getting us to Hakpis today, in one piece. Remind your soldiers the Kaska are cowards. Stay together, stay disciplined and we'll win through. Strength on the outside, the weak in the middle. Put the baggage train in the middle with the cooks and the medical people. That's how we're organising the order of march. Get the cavalry to fan out and keep the Kaska at a distance. Good hunting.'

'*Y-e-s s-i-r!*' they replied loudly in unison.

* * *

Kasalliwa was urging his troops to engage the enemy. He led sortie after sortie, but was somewhat reluctant to join outright battle. He was still weaker than the Hatti and would have to commit all his men to do so.

'Get closer, man. This is much too far away,' a tribal commander was urging his men. He commanded a body of soldiers using slings. The Hatti horse were desperately defending the elongated speeding column, chasing off the Kaska attacks. The slings were still too far to do effective damage. All day they had harried the Hatti but had failed to halt Muwas' army. Kasalliwa was expecting the enemy to stop and form a protective circle but the general in charge had a different agenda and pressed his men forward, urging and cajoling them to make haste. In this manner the protagonists and antagonists confronted each other until they were only a league away from the gates of Hakpis.

In a desperate attempt to halt the convoy, more of the Kaska hurled themselves at the racing army column making for the city gates, encouraged by the tribal leaders. Each time they were driven back by an equally desperate cavalry or chariot counter charge. 'See if you can do more damage to those Hatti archers. They're creating havoc in our ranks,' Kasalliwa ordered the commander of his archers.

Yet cubit by cubit the Hatti moved towards the safety of Hakpis. Before long, fresh troops were sent by the governor of the city to sally forth to help the king's soldiers. At that point Kasalliwa began to falter and began to call off the attacks. His men were suffering further losses and he took pity on their suffering. He sat on his horse with his tribal commanders, watching the last of the Hatti army disappear into the safety of Hakpis and wondered if the cost had been worth the price in lives. A thought flitted through his mind, 'I wonder—could we take this town?' He stared hard at the closed gate through which Muwas had disappeared.

'Not with so many soldiers inside,' the tribal commander answered.

'Maybe we could try if and when they leave...' Kasalliwa mused.

Chapter Thirty

Tuthmosis was encamped on the eastern side of Halap with his two divisions, waiting for news of Artatama. He had sent scouts to this side of the Taurus Mountains, waiting for Artatama to appear. To encourage him, he led sorties towards Wassukkani to stir things up with Saustatar, pillaging the Mittani countryside, burning and looting where he could. Saustatar in response, sent forces to intercept the Egyptians but by the time his troops arrived, Tuthmosis was well away. A cat and mouse game was being played. Tuthmosis obeyed his father's instructions and avoided battle. Saustatar was waiting for the main Egyptian army to arrive and feared pushing Tuthmosis too far until his son brought the extra troops back home to support him.

Although the king of the walled city of Halap had invited Tuthmosis to his palace, built on a man-made central mound, he was far from happy at this Egyptian invasion. He would be forced to feed the two divisions, ten thousand troops. It stretched the resources of his city almost beyond what the ruler thought he could endure. Halap, only twenty leagues from the sea, began for the first time to import food. It's main industries, cotton printing, the manufacture of dyes and the preparation of hides, wool, dried fruit and nuts, were used to pay for the food imports. Tuthmosis made no effort to assist the ruler. He considered him vassal to Egypt and feeding his troops was part of its tribute. Worse was to come for the king. Tuthmosis demanded he supply a contingent of troops to add to his two divisions. More raids into Mittani country followed.

The Tikhsi remembered Amehotep's last visit and vowed to avenge the dead princes by allying themselves with the Mittani. They did not announce it publicly but were active in disrupting Tuthmosis' logistics. Couriers vanished, caravans were ambushed. Revenge, was a double edged sword and the Tikhsi knew Tuthmosis would pay them a visit.

*　　*　　*

King Saustatar worried and waited for the main body of pharaoh's army to appear and couldn't understand the delay.

'Sire, we've just received news of the Egyptian army. They're down in Nubia, led by the pharaoh himself,' the chief minister informed Saustatar as differentially as he could whilst the king conferred with his generals.

'*What*?' exclaimed the king. 'Are you certain? How can this be?' The space was large and the words echoed round the room.

'It seems we've been duped. The army left Waset and headed north to Mittani, then changed direction in the desert, returning to a quiet spot on the river and embarked onto ships going up the Nile to Nubia. I've only just found out. They couldn't hide the army on the Nile, so our spies spotted them.' His chief minister knew someone's head would roll for this blunder.

'Let me understand this correctly. What you're saying is, the only Egyptians up here are those…those hooligans pillaging the land—the two divisions—and that's all. We'll soon see about them! Get all the forces ready,' Saustatar told his nearby generals. 'We're going to pay pharaoh's son a visit. One he will remember till his dying breath.'

'Immediately, sire!' The chief of the army indicated to the other generals they should leave.

Within a short time fifteen thousand Mittani cavalry, chariots and infantry were rushing at top speed from Wassukkani towards Halap. Saustatar led the force himself. He was furious at falling for such a simple trick. In fact he

166

was so angry he pushed his force across the Euphrates River within the space of one day. After he calmed down, he turned left so he could approach Halap from the south, attempting to cut the retreat of the two Egyptian divisions. He wanted to completely annihilate Tuthmosis. Wipe the smile off of pharaoh's face. He would teach him to play games with the Mittani.

Then he remembered one incredibly important omission. Pharaoh had played this trick to compel him to bring Artatama home. To forestall the latter, he sent a number of couriers to intercept Artatama and redirect him back to Hattusas, without delay. That ought to upset pharaoh's plans. At a rest stop he concocted retribution. 'I'm going to play pharaoh at his own game.' He confided to his chief of staff. 'The Kizzuwatna are Tudhaliyas' allies, are they not?'

'I believe so, sire.'

'And the Lukka pirates are almost next door, eh? Let me see...' and the king fell to contemplation.

Two and a half days later, he neared Halap without coming across any Egyptians and he felt a premonition. He sent scouts ahead to Halap and when they returned, his worst fears were confirmed. The Egyptians had left the previous day. He had missed them by a whisker. He took it out on the king of Halap. After a three day siege, Saustatar entered the city and had the king publicly executed for helping his Egyptian enemies.

The king of Halap was a prisoner of his location and the power politics of the day. Both the Mittani and the Egyptians lay claim to Halap. Even Hatti lay claim to Halap, although being so far away it made it difficult to enforce.

Chapter Thirty-one

General Zidanta rode at the head of the Taru Regiment with King Tudhaliyas standing by his side in his chariot. Forty thousand troops had been on the move from daybreak, stretched out in a line four leagues long coming out of the Ankuwa valley. The king looked back at the column extending into the far distance and felt proud. 'Don't they look just fine, heh general?'

'Picturesque, sire. Yes indeed!' The general had seen it all before.

In the middle of the procession was a wagon containing the black bull deity beside which Mokhat and Palaiyas sat quietly pretending to be invisible in their priestly outfits. Their horses were tied to the rear of the wagon. Tagrama sat opposite with a few burly priests, silently praying not too much damage had been done to the Great Temple in the capital.

The Kizzuwatna allies, led by King Shunashura, brought up the rear of the Hatti army. Nikal thought it best she travel with her brother and maid in the special royal coach with all the pillows. It would be more seemly and suitable for a princess of Kizzuwatna. Tudhaliyas would send for her and seal his commitment once Himuili had talked with her father. Both families needed to announce the engagement in an ostentatious manner befitting the union of two royal houses.

Harep and Rewa were somewhere at the rear of the Kizzuwatna with the rest of the stragglers and other refugee civilians. Harep had not yet come up with a plan to carry out his assignment and it troubled him. He simply hadn't found a way of getting past the bodyguards. On top of this, he was busy keeping alert for that murdering bastard who was out to kill all the chiefs of the assassins. To this end he had to keep out of sight. Security had been tightened round the royal family, almost as if they were expecting some kind of attempt. Had they been informed? Were they expecting him? That damned blabbermouth Parap may have spoilt any easy chance he may have had. Now it would be doubly difficult. He assumed the worst. They were expecting an assassination attempt. Couldn't be helped. He would have to *earn* his money. What he needed was to create an opportunity—but how?

Kantuzzili sat astride a splendid white horse at the head of a cavalry regiment. He was in deep conversation with his brother Himuili, asking worriedly, 'What do you think? Have they left our castle intact? Remember...some deserters informed us the place had been given over to the Mittani by Muwas.'

'Don't worry!' Himuili pacified. 'That's what happens in war. Whatever damage they might have done, there's nothing can't be fixed. This is the biggest gamble of our lives, trying to restore our family's name. We must be expected to make some sacrifices.'

'Yes, I suppose you're right.'

It was a ride in reverse of the time not long ago when they had fled from the Yellow Castle, down to Ankuwa. Now they were on their way to reclaim the capital of the Hittite Empire. Late afternoon on the second day, scouts returned with a tale for General Zidanta.

'Sir, there's a farmer ahead who says he has two priests, one dead, the other scarcely alive. He pleads for us to take them with us.'

'Priests, you say? Better get Tagrama,' Zidanta ordered his adjutant. 'It's his province more than mine. Oh! And you'd better help the farmer fetch the priests to us.'

Tagrama arrived on Mokhat's horse, more curious than concerned. The soldiers helped the farmer bring the priests on a cart. One look at them and Tagrama burst out in anger, 'Oh

Great Taru, is this how you look after the priests who serve you?' Immediately as he said the words he felt ashamed. These two priests were his responsibility. It was he who had sent them to Hattusas disguised as "merchants," to be thus flayed alive. 'I'm sorry,' he mumbled as an apology to his god.

The farmer had done his best but could not save the elder of the two. The other's wounds were infested and he was delirious. 'Bring them,' Tagrama ordered the soldiers. They made their way back to the wagons and loaded the dying priests inside. Frantically Tagrama did his best to make the one still alive more comfortable. He gave him herbs to ease his pain and rubbed ointment into the wounds to ease the inflammation. Tagrama sat, prayed and worried, but to no avail. The second priest died during the night. Tagrama intoned over the bodies. He pulled the wagon out of the line and had the bodies removed and cremated. More words of supplication and atonement were said as the flames consumed the departed priests. Then the funeral party had to catch up with the moving convoy.

On the third day after an arduous ride, they spied the Yellow Castle sitting on its promontory and a little further on the tall grey granite walls of the city. The gates were wide open and people emerged to cheer the encroaching army. They had not been sure what to expect, but were happy the people chose to come out and greet them. Zidanta was relieved at the people's behaviour. 'What did I tell you, sire! They choose *you* as their king. You needn't have worried so. How can anyone in their right mind prefer Muwas?' Frankly, he had hoped this would be the outcome, but he had had his doubts. No one ever asked what the ordinary citizens wanted simply because no one in power ever thought to ask. It was an alien notion. The common folk did as they were told and if they did not like, they could lump it.

Kantuzzili, purely out of reminiscence, looked over the Yellow Castle, his former home. He and his brother found to their surprise, the Mittani had taken good care of it. Then Kantuzzili offered the residence to Shunashura for as long as he wanted it. Tudhaliyas and the Kantuzzili clan would sleep that night in the Great Royal Palace towering above the old city of Hattusas. Kantuzzili knew an immense battle was yet to come, that Muwas had simply retreated, not given up. He felt pleased his own ruse had recalled the Mittani troops back home, but this was not the end of it. They would be back and the two contending forces for the black bull throne would nevertheless have to meet and settle their dispute on a field of battle.

* * *

The four wagons carrying Tagrama's party and his deity wound up to the Great Temple and a large group of priests got out. They walked quietly through the temple entrance and down the naos to the spot where they met a thin line of Teshub followers. The three Mittani priests arrogantly barred their way, standing ahead of their acolytes. Behind them stood Teshub's empty war chariot drawn by the two white bull gods Seris ("Day") and Hurris ("Night"). No sign of the statue of Teshub himself. Tagrama walked forward, pointed at the chariot and boomed, '*Get that abomination out of my temple!*'

The Mittani, dressed in dark blue robes, stood their ground. The same burly priests who had detained Loros now came forward. They grabbed the Mittani and ripped their robes from them. The Mittani did not struggle. Their acolytes backed away, trembling and suddenly fell to their knees, begging to be spared. Mokhat and Palaiyas stood in the background and watched the high priest deal with the defilers of his temple.

'What have they done with the statue of their filthy god?' Tagrama demanded of the fickle acolytes. 'Speak up or the same fate waits all of you.'

One of the acolytes was bold enough to answer. 'He's lying behind the altar. They're trying to hide him,' he pointed to the back.

Tagrama struggling to maintain his temper, turned on the Mittani, 'You're walking back home, that is your punishment for desecrating my temple. If you *ever* come back I will sacrifice you to Taru; make no mistake.'

The cowering acolytes were required to remove the chariot and the statue, carry both outside into the encroaching dusk. The Mittani were forced to watch as both were laboriously broken into small pieces by their former acolytes using large stones. Then the Mittani priests were stripped naked and hounded through the city streets by the burly priests, while people came out of their houses and watched, jeering, laughing and sometimes throwing rubbish at them. They were chased through one of the southern postern gates and out into open country, then the gate was symbolically slammed behind them.

*　　*　　*

'I simply can't understand why we can't find three miserable wretches amongst these people. They should stand out like three wedding guests at a funeral. I'm tired of looking.' Mokhat was fed up and moaned to Palaiyas. When they were in Ankuwa, he and Palaiyas prowled for days among the refugees coming into the valley. Not a sign of the three assassins, yet he knew Harep. He would be somewhere near and probably even watching as he searched. The priestly camouflage was their only disguise, but Mokhat thought it sufficient. He did not think Harep knew he was being hunted.

'The way you describe them, I can't argue. I agree, they should stick out.' Palaiyas was trying to look serene in his outfit.

Both had been provided with a single cell inside a building attached to the temple grounds. After eating in the hall with the other priests, they had retired to the cell and plotted how to find Harep and his nephews. Late that night Mokhat decided the next day they would search the taverns and the usual lodgings—and they must have a guide, because frankly, they did not know Hattusas that well—Palaiyas might, but Mokhat doubted it.

The next morning they ate with the priests in the eating hall and afterwards went to see Tagrama. They found him down the naos with the other priests, burning incense before the altar in preparation for the purification ritual.

'Good morning to you,' Mokhat opened with a greeting. 'We need to ask a favour. We need someone who knows Hattusas like the back of his hand.'

Tagrama stopped what he was doing. Eyebrows raised, 'Has this to do with finding these assassins?'

'It has! We can't stop until they're uncovered. We're need to search all the taverns and lodgings and neither my friend Palaiyas here, nor I know all the nooks and crannies of this town. We need someone to show us.'

'I have just the man. He's a bit of a know-all but no one knows this town like he does. I think he's probable still in his cell. Would you mind showing our friends where Amulas sleeps,' he asked one of the priests standing nearby. The priest led the way, Mokhat followed, trailed by Palaiyas. They found Amulas where Tagrama said he was, asleep after partaking of a little too much beer. 'What, this early in the morning?' Mokhat grinned. They woke him gently, gave him water to dilute his overindulgence and waited till he had a semblance of awareness. Mokhat explained their dilemma and found an enthusiast for their mission. It turned out Amulas was a jovial old priest with a penchant for a jug of beer. He knew all the taverns and some of the seedier places people congregated for various reasons.

While they waited in the corridor for Amulas to dress and join them, Palaiyas agreed, 'He seems just the fellow, but we'd better watch his drinking.'

'We'd have missed the seedy spots, that's for sure. As for his drink, I'll keep a watch on him if you watch our backs.'

Out of the building and into the courtyard, Amulas led them down to the lower town where the main street had a number of taverns conveniently situated. 'You're from Ahhiyawa,' Amulas told Palaiyas.

It startled Palaiyas. 'Why yes! How did you know?'

Mokhat listened with curiosity.

'I've been to Millawanda. I recognised your accent. It was many years ago, mind you. So what're you doing here?'

'I came as a messenger for my king, then stayed for a while. You're the first person I've met here who's actually been to Milawata. Mostly people say, "Where's that?" when I tell them where I came from.' Palaiyas' face played with a smile.

'I even learnt a few words of Ahhiyawan while I was there.' Amulas told him.

'I'm actually from Tiryns, not Milawata, but it's still Ahhiyawa, or as we call it, Ellas. But you knew that, didn't you?'

Amulas nodded. 'Here's the first place we should look in. Some of the priests use it.'

They came to a large tavern and since it was early, few customers were inside. Because of the two foreign accents, Mokhat suggested Amulas do the talking. Three priests of Taru walked to the counter and Amulas asked the owner, 'Have three Kaska been in drinking or looking for lodgings? Two young ones and an older fellow in charge—medium build, dark with a mean face.'

'Sorry, nobody by that description's been here in the last three days.'

They thanked the barman and turned to leave. Amulas raised his hand, 'Look, while we're here, why don't I buy you a nice cool drink.'

'We'll have a drink when we're half way done, not before,' Mokhat told a disappointed Amulas. 'I promise we will have a drink, but later.' The next seven taverns proved to be equally disappointing, but the eighth one gave them what Mokhat treated as negative information. It was closer to the main palace. The burly owner was too enthusiastic about his denials and it was supported by his buxom wife. The owner treated them to a round of drinks and this made Mokhat extremely suspicious. Back outside Mokhat whispered to Palaiyas, 'I think Harep was in there. The owner was trying too hard. He kept giving his wife meaningful glances when he denied he'd ever seen them. I wonder why?'

'Maybe Harep paid him to keep quiet,' Palaiyas suggested.

'But that would only draw attention to himself. I don't think he'd do that. Remember, I know a little of how he works, how he thinks.'

'Why are you whispering?' Amulas asked. He had downed a couple of jugs.

'You want everyone to know our business?' Palaiyas scowled.

Chapter Thirty-two

Harep stood outside the tavern, watching some naked bald men being chased by priests, at the same time cautiously eyeing the people near him. Rewa stood wearing a serious face and watched Harep. That's all he ever did now. He wanted to be ready if Harep ever swung his arm out at him. Someone in the tavern had yelled they were clearing the city of refuse and invited the drinkers outside to watch the spectacle. They had been lucky to find a room for the night. Many people had arrived from the south causing overcrowding in the capital. To ease matters, all the troops were ordered to sleep outside the city walls in their hide-tents. This more than anything proved to the people their king was thinking of them.

Back in the tavern, Harep ordered food for both Rewa and himself, but in the meantime they sat nursing drinks. Harep wasn't a big drinker, whilst Rewa did not dare let himself get inebriated, not with Harep nearby. Harep brooded on who the assassin's killer was. It was forever on his mind since his safety depended on discovering the person's identity.

The buxom middle-aged waitress came with the food. 'Here you are gents. Hot mutton and nice dark bread. I hope you enjoy it!'

She was about to go when Harep suggested to her almost absent mindedly, 'I'd enjoy it better if you kept us company and sat here,' he patted his knee.

She looked outraged. 'Keep your bloody hands to yourself or I'll have my man over there teach you some manners.' She pointed at the bar.

'Now there! No need to take on like that. I meant no harm. Just being friendly,' Harep laughed. His smutty joke hadn't been appreciated.

'Well I don't like it. So there! What'd ye take me for, a common trollop?'

A big man ambled up to their table while others in the tavern watched. 'You messing with my missus?' He glared at Harep menacingly.

'Of course not. Just paid her a compliment, that's all.' Harep thought, *this is getting out of hand.*

Two other men from a corner table stood and joined the big man. 'He giving you trouble, Lewa?' One of them said gruffly. Harep made to reach for his dagger and the big man walloped him full in the face, knocking him off his stool. The others came round and began kicking Harep as he lay, while Rewa jumped up and backed away from the fight.

'Wise move,' the big man commented through clenched teeth.

By the time the three had finished, Harep was lying in a pool of blood, unconscious. The two from the corner table lifted Harep by the armpits, dragged him to the door and threw the limp body headlong out into the street. Harep bounced a couple of times. Rewa quickly and meekly followed. He stooped over Harep and saw he was badly injured. He half lifted half dragged him across the street, down an alleyway, right up to the dead end. Puffing from the exertion, he propped him up against a house wall and sat beside him. Rewa kept shaking his head. 'Well I never,' he muttered to himself. 'How strange! Now what? What the Yarris am I to do?' He noticed blood was coming from Harep's mouth and nose. 'If he dies on me, how am I to get the money?' He decided he had better find lodgings. He left Harep propped up where he was and went looking on the main street.

Some time later he returned with a young woman leading a donkey. They found Harep slumped sideways on the ground. Rewa bent to check. 'He's still breathing, but only just. It's good of your mother to let us stay in her spare room. You'll see, I'll make it worth her while,' Rewa told her while they loaded Harep, face down, across the back of the donkey. The young woman led the donkey back along the main street, then down a series of alleys to the lodgings. Rewa followed her into the poorest part of town. At the door an elderly woman waited and the young woman led the animal through the house to the room where they off-loaded Harep onto a prepared bed. Three oil-wick lights burned in the room, throwing a sinister glow on the proceedings.

The old woman began to undress Harep helped by her daughter, 'Remember what we agreed. A hundred shekels in gold! A quarter up front?' she stood with her hand out.

Rewa had been prepared for this. He had stabled their horses before looking for accommodation, then removed what was left of the five thousand he had found—some hidden on Harep when he had searched him—some in a leather pouch in the horse blanket. He had separated a hundred and fifty out, hidden the rest among their combined belongings, then counted two lots of twenty-five ready to pay for any accommodation—in this case the woman. Their belongings with the money he had earlier carelessly tossed into the corner of the room. He reached inside his shirt and pulled out the amount and handed it to her. 'Twenty-five each time there's a big improvement. The next twenty-five when he opens his eyes and is comfortable, right?'

She nodded her agreement to the terms. Until he put the gold in her hand, she had not believed in any of it. Now she looked inside and checked. Her eyes widened. 'Oohh-er!' she crooned, then coming to a decision, put the bag away inside her bodice. She had agreed to fix up the injuries when her daughter had led Rewa to her without knowing what she was letting herself in for—but in her poverty, she was forced to take chances. She had been a poor country girl who had settled in the city when her farm had been razed to the ground by bandits. That was a long time ago. 'Get some water Raiysa,' she ordered her daughter, then returned to undressing Harep. 'His ribs are broken. There might be other bones broken as well.'

When she saw his state, she drew in her breath. Harep was black and blue all over. Her daughter stood shocked at the injuries. Blood still trickled from Harep's ears, nose and mouth and mercifully he was still unconscious. She looked worried. 'He's bad. I don't know if he'll survive.'

'If he doesn't, you don't get paid,' Rewa reminded her.

Twenty-five shekel in gold was a fortune to her beyond her wildest dreams. She never thought she would see such a sum in her whole life. Now, three more lots waited for her if she could only pull this stranger through. 'I know,' she said irritably. 'Raiysa, I told you to get a bowl of water, some rags, bring them to me, *now*.'

Her daughter went to do her bidding.

'How did this happen?' she asked.

'We were set upon by a gang of hooligans, robbers. My friend didn't run fast enough—that's all.'

She glanced suspiciously at Rewa. Frankly, there was something fishy about these two strangers. For starters, they weren't Hatti. She couldn't think straight—the money kept getting in the way. She would be set for life if she could get her hands on all hundred gold shekels.

*　　*　　*

Harep moaned as the old woman bathed his forehead. She kept a cold wet cloth covering his head to bring his temperature down. She had bandaged his ribs and the broken arm as best she could. She had given him herbal medicines leant in her youth from the old crones in her village. If it could, the old woman knew the body would heal itself, given rest, peace, and quiet. Harep had kept fit and otherwise seemed strong. Three days had gone by since his encounter in the tavern, he had woken for a little while, then relapsed and gone back into a coma. He had been badly concussed by the kicking and was struggling to stay alive.

Rewa insisted on hiring out another room from the old woman, closeting himself in there and then took to drink. Wine and lots of it. He could afford it. He sent the daughter out to buy the wine. She, in her turn eyed Rewa with interest when she handed him the jug, both for his wealth and his youth. If...only...she could... Rewa was elated Harep was near death, sad his brother *was* dead, unhappy at the prospect of losing ten thousand shekels. He knew he would never manage the assassination alone. He wanted Harep to die, but he also needed Harep to live. So many contradictions competed for dominance in his head, he felt overwhelmed. Unwilling, or unable, to sort the problems out, he took to drink to soften the impact. On the third day, the long suppressed bereavement burst forth and he began to cry. Under the influence of too much wine, he finally gave vent to a catharsis and began fully to grieve for his little brother. He had badly missed Parap but Harep's presence had made it impossible to express his wretchedness, his sense of loss. The old woman heard her young lodger wail and guessed from snatches of blabbering someone had died. She left him alone to his grief, knowing time would even heal this wound as it was healing the young man's companion in another room. It was thus Rewa began to recover his sense of himself, to see the accident of his brother's death as just an accident. He had blamed Harep and he still thought he was a mean son-of-a-bitch, but he no longer wanted to kill him. Harep was Harep. "Unc" had always been mean, it was his nature. He stopped drinking and went to see how Harep was coming along.

The old woman was delighted to see him and put before him a bowl of soup with dark bread. After he had eaten, she showed him the room where Harep lay. Harep was snoring, fast asleep—asleep, not dead. He had woken that day and she had explained where he was. He had accepted the explanation. She told Rewa it would be five weeks before Harep would be well enough to get out of bed, but she assured Rewa he was on the mend.

The daughter watched Rewa carefully, predatorily, looking for a chance to get a part of the gold she knew her mother would deny her. *Patience*, she told herself.

When Rewa returned to his room, the daughter followed. She knocked almost inaudibly on the door— without waiting for an answer, opened it and slipped quietly inside.

Chapter Thirty-three

Tudhaliyas was closely examining the murals decorating the Grand Audience Hall illustrating the two hundred year old Hittite history from as far back as Labarnas. 'Aren't they magnificent?' he told Kantuzzili and Zidanta. 'Something to inspire, not disgrace as Muwas seems intent on doing.'

At the entrance, Himuili proceeded to walk down the hall followed by Talshura and a strangely dressed lord. Himuili had been appointed Chancellor by his son. The king returned to his throne, hurriedly but regally. 'Your majesty, pharaoh has sent a letter and many wondrous gifts to King Tudhaliyas.' Father bowed to his son as protocol demanded of the Chancellor. 'An Egyptian ship has berthed at Adaniya. This Egyptian lord is sent as ambassador to our court by pharaoh.'

'Bid him approach,' Tudhaliyas commanded.

The Egyptian lord walked forward with a stately bearing. Tall, sunburned and dressed in lavish finery. He stood before Tudhaliyas and then fell to his knees, prostrating himself before the king as he would before pharaoh. In Hatti they did not go in for that and the performance took everyone by surprise.

Tudhaliyas smiled, 'Please rise. How are we to call you, ambassador?'

The Egyptian rose to his feet, 'I am named Hapu, a son of pharaoh by a minor wife. Pharaoh Amenhotep, ruler of Iunu, beloved of Horus, lord of the Upper and Lower lands of Egypt, sends greetings to the king of the Hittites, King Tudhaliyas.' He bowed deeply.

'Prince Hapu, we are delighted pharaoh honours us with so important a personage, however, pharaoh must realise we are in the middle of a war of succession. If I lose...'

'Pharaoh knows of your war. It is why I was sent as ambassador to you and not to the pretender Muwas.' A sigh of approval reverberated gently through the hall. This remarkable scenario revealed the relationship between an internal struggle and the far-off outside world. Egypt had decided it had an interest in the outcome of the civil war and had opted for this king. Prince Hapu continued, 'I have a papyrus from pharaoh I'm to place in your hands.' He drew the papyrus from within his costume and approached the Chancellor's outstretched hand.

The Chancellor looked closely, broke the seal and then glanced at the contents. He drew near to his son and handed him the document. 'It's in Akkadian,' he whispered.

Tudhaliyas knew a number of languages as part of his regal education. Amulas had been thorough. The papyrus was in the lingua franca of diplomacy, Akkadian, and the wedge-shapes spoke of the desire of pharaoh to strengthen relations with the Hatti royal house. With this in mind pharaoh was sending his ambassador bearing gifts to King Tudhaliyas and pharaoh hoped he would be successful in prosecuting his rightful succession to the black bull throne. He, pharaoh, warned of the threat posed by the expansionist policies of Mittani to both Egypt and Hatti alike.

Ahh! So that was it. Tudhaliyas now understood. 'We thank pharaoh for his kind wishes and gifts and accept his interpretation of the situation. It seems we have a common enemy in Mittani. You may assure pharaoh, we will do our utmost to prosecute our opponents with the utmost ruthlessness, and that invader of Hatti Muwas calls his ally. At the same time convey our thanks and our intentions to pharaoh.'

Kantuzzili stepped forward and directed the Egyptian ambassador to the side where he proceeded to engage him in a deep conversation. 'I want to send an urgent message to pharaoh. Have you a route?'

'Yes, of course. I suppose it's confidential?' the ambassador asked.

'It is with regard to a possible attack on Kizzuwatna by our mutual enemies.'

*   *   *

'I still can't get over it; *you* the brother of a king.' Palaiyas was teasing Mokhat as next day they continued their search for the assassins. 'It puts my poor father to shame.'

'What's your father got to do with it?' Mokhat inquired.

'Did I forget to mention it. He's the king of Tiryns. I'm the son of a king. I don't want you to feel like you're consorting with riff-raff.'

'I thought you were part of the disreputable rabble occupying Keftiu? Isn't that what you told me?'

'I was *commanding* the contingent from Tiryns. That's why, when I quit, the king of Mycenae took it so hard. He thought he'd a vassal in revolt, whereas all he had was a fed up commander.'

They had arrived at a part of town where quite a few seedy drinking establishments were situated. Amulas led the way and he knew them all. The previous night after they had stopped searching and gone for a bite to eat, Amulas had been allowed to let go and fill his thirst. They couldn't believe how much he put down his throat. Yet at the end of it, Amulas had helped Palaiyas carry Mokhat back to the temple.

One story they had bribed out of a tavern keeper was that if he was looking for an unsavoury character such as the priests described, then that person would most likely try to blend in amongst those in the seedy drinking quarters of town. He would be wise as not too drink in them if they had any sense as they were unregulated, warned the tavern keeper. They sometimes spiced the beer with herbs that rendered the drinker unconscious. It was easier that way when it came to rob them. Mokhat urged Amulas, 'You lead the way, you're the expert.'

The one storey building they came to had tall walls enclosing a courtyard. Two burly men guarded the double gate. As soon as they saw Amulas, they opened the gate and nodded him in. One of them said, 'Any friends of Amulas are welcome here.' Inside, the courtyard was small with oblong tables containing rough looking quarry men, baggage hands and other assorted disreputable people. When the three priests entered the courtyard, all ceased talking. The dim lighting inside the house looked forbidding.

Just then the most extraordinary trembling of the ground occurred. It shook and wobbled like a waking nightmare. People ran out of the house in panic, standing in the open looking bewildered. The tall walls surrounding the courtyard collapsed. Tables tipped over, jugs smashed on the stone flags. '*Earthquake*,' yelled Mokhat and sat on the ground. Palaiyas copied him. Amulas' eyes seemed to go round in their sockets. He grabbed his chest and keeled over.

Palaiyas leaned over Amulas and saw pain in open staring eyes. The ground stopped moving just as suddenly as it had started. The stillness was as disturbing as the earlier motion. '*He's dead*!' Palaiyas announced loudly in surprise.

Mokhat crawled to where Amulas lay. 'Hmm! I'm afraid you're right. Poor sod! At least the quake has stopped.'

The house with the drinking den lay in ruins. People escaped just as soon as it was safe to stand. The two remaining "priests" found someone outside trying to steady a kicking donkey, scared by the tremor and after it was quietened, they hired him to carry Amulas' body back to the temple. It seemed the fat priest was well thought of at the temple. Tagrama dropped everything and came hurrying to supervise the rights of passage.

All afternoon the body lay in front of the altar surrounded by chanting priests wafting incense at it. That night the funeral pyre was built high in the courtyard of the main temple. The king insisted he come and pay his respects after being informed, as did a large number of high born Hatti. The whole Kantuzzili faction was present when they lit Amulas' pyre. The fire soared high into the night sky and the chanting from his fellow priests resounded loud around the temple precincts. Mokhat stood quietly with Palaiyas at the back and said their own farewells in their own way.

When the ritual was over, Tagrama sought out Mokhat and said quietly, 'He was tutor to the king, you know. Did he tell you? One of the cleverest men among us. But of course in the short time you knew him, all you saw was a bit of a soak. That was his only outlet. It really did no harm.'

Chapter Thirty-Four

'*Keep them moving...keep them moving*,' Artatama shouted to General Satukani. The Mittani cavalry, infantry and chariot regiments were rapidly retracing their trail back to Muwas. Artatama was fearful he might not be in time. One of the couriers from Saustatar found General Satukani on the Asian side of the Taurus Mountains with all the horse and chariot regiments racing for Wassukkani. After being informed of pharaoh's game, Satukani wheeled about retracing his route, finding Artatama only halfway through the mountains at the front of marching infantry. Another couple of couriers confirmed the orders to return to Hattusas as swiftly as possible.

The communication from King Saustatar said, "Do not to come back to Mittani but return immediately back to Muwas. There was no Egyptian threat." At that point, Artatama left his infantry behind and rushed back north with only the horse and chariots, incensed at the Egyptian ruse. The couriers had explained all, how only two Egyptian divisions had arrived at the Mittani borders.

As Artatama rode deeper into Hatti, he gleaned from the local population that Muwas had been forced to retreat from Hattusas and was currently entrenched in Hakpis, possibly surrounded by the Kaska. On discovering Muwas' predicament, Artatama swung his horse units towards Hakpis and sent back orders for the infantry to go straight on towards Hattusas. He rightly concluded that when Kantuzzili got wind of the return of the Mittani forces, he would as swiftly abandon Hattusas as he had taken it.

When the Mittani force was only one day away from Hakpis, Muwas sent out cavalry to meet and greet them, for he had received intelligence of Artatama's imminent arrival.

To no one's surprise, the Kaska blockade melted away as if they had never been. The gates of Hakpis were thrown open and Muwas rode out to greet his Mittani brothers-in-arms. 'I'm overjoyed at your return,' Muwas told Artatama when they met in a forest not far from Hakpis.

'Remember—I gave my promise to you when I was forced to leave—that I would return as speedily as I could.' Artatama rode side by side with Muwas.

'Yes, I remember. "Artatama, whose abode is justice".' Muwas quoted the literal meaning of the Mittani prince's name. 'And you have kept your word. On behalf of all my men, I express my sincere gratitude to you and your father.' The worry lifted as his numerical superiority was re-established.

'I feared you might have been forced to engage the enemy while I was away.'

'That would have been imprudent. Their Kizzuwatna allies would have given them the advantage and I would have certainly lost my throne. No! I knew you would not fail me. I waited.' They rode chatting in the spring sunshine, the luxuriant greenery burst out all around them. On approaching the high grey walls of Hakpis, the town's population came out to cheer both Muwas and Artatama. They lined the highway and the ramparts and cheered themselves hoarse.

'General Satukani, quarter the troops outside, usual precautions. Then join me in the citadel,' ordered Artatama.

'Yes, your highness.'

General Ammuna ordered the trumpet fanfare as both king and prince rode through the town gates with their retinues.

'I like this town,' Artatama told Muwas. 'They're much friendlier than the capital.'

'I fear you're right. I've even thought of moving the capital here when we've dealt with Kantuzzili.' Muwas seemed serious. 'It would then be easier to retake Nerik and deal with the damned Kaska.'

'Now our forces are once more joined, I would recommend we retake Hattusas first. Was that also in your mind?'

'It was. Rest here tonight and we'll set out for the capital in the morning. Are the infantry following?'

'I gave orders for them to march directly on Hattusas. They should have arrived by the time we get there.'

'That was first-class tactics. I commend you for your foresight.'

The citadel of Hakpis stood on a small hill in the centre of town and was usually occupied by the governor, but he had quickly relinquished it to his king. The two royals rode through the narrow streets, through the citadel gates and up to the steps leading to the entrance, dismounted and went inside. 'I've had quarters made ready for you and your generals. I'm sure you'd like to clean up and have a bath.' Muwas was delighted Artatama was here.

'I'm hungry, thirsty and dirty, in that order,' Artatama replied.

'Through here to the food hall.' Muwas led the way. 'Servants are waiting to serve you. Food and drink is on the table.' The festivity went on well into the night. It finally broke up in the early hours of the morning with many having to be helped to their beds by tired servants.

The following morning, heads throbbing, the senior officers mustered their men and the combined force headed off into the blossoming countryside, back towards Hattusas. A long convoy of Mittani horse and chariot and the twenty thousand Hatti who had thrown in with Muwas. The latter had a bounce in their steps having regained the upper hand, as they saw it.

When Artatama left to return to Mittani, some of Muwa's soldiers thought good riddance to these foreigners, until they realised victory for Muwas would be impossible without them. It was only then they missed the Mittani.

*   *   *

Kasalliwa watched the last of Muwas' soldiers leave Hakpis from a distance and vowed, 'I'll make them pay for their lack of foresight. The arrogant stupidity of Muwas; that pompous so-called king of theirs. How dare they leave the town undefended? They think we are as nothing, of no consequence? He's taken the town's military to bolster his own forces. I'm going to teach him a lesson in tactics.' That evening the Kaska gathered, surrounding the town, for contrary to reports, they hadn't scattered and gone back home. They had waited patiently until the balance tipped in their favour, a manoeuvre long employed by the Kaska. Then they struck. Firstly, fire arrows were sent over the town wall, volley after volley. Although the town was mostly built of stone, there was still a lot of timber that could be set ablaze. This lit up the town like a beacon, anyone on the walls was a silhouette and a target. Next, a battering ram was brought to bear on the gates. A huge log mounted on wheels, covered by a hide roof, pushed and pulled by many, whilst others used shields to protect the sides. This was charged at the solid gate.

Defenders poured boiling fat on to it, setting it alight, but by then it had done its damage and the gate was burning—and after a short time it was breeched. This was when the lack of town soldiers to defend them became most evident. The townspeople fought for their lives in the streets and alleyways but were no match for the ferocious Kaska warriors. The town treasurer hurriedly buried Harep's gold and the rest of the treasury in the citadel dungeon. Only he and a few of his department knew where. By morning the slaughter was nearly over and the town in flames. Looting and raping was widespread as part of the spoils of war. Bodies littered the town, including all those of the treasury, leaving a heavy stench of death hanging in the air.

Chapter Thirty-Five

Palaiyas spotted Mokhat sitting on a bench in the shade at the far end of the temple courtyard. 'A priest is looking for you,' Palaiyas informed as he came and sat by him. 'He's got a message from your friends.'

Mokhat was engrossed, reading some wax tablets and did not look at Palaiyas. 'Huh? What message?'

'I don't know. He wouldn't give it to me. Told me it was for you only.'

Mokhat put down the reading material and glanced at his unusual companion. Forced to dress like a priest, but he simply couldn't carry himself like a priest, did not walk like one and to Mokhat, did not look like one. They made a strange combination. 'Come on, let's go find this priest of yours,' Mokhat tucked the tablets under his armpit and took Palaiyas by the arm—they went in search of the messenger. They found the old man out in front of the temple, in the peristyle, pacing up and down, looking outwards. Mokhat and Palaiyas approached quietly and Mokhat tapped him on the shoulder.

He jumped and turned. 'Ah!...Found you! Some friends of yours left you this.' He handed Mokhat a cartouche with a dragon on it.

'And the message?' prompted Mokhat.

'The message...ah, yes, ehm...they...ehm...want you to meet them tonight at sunset...ehm...outside the North Gate. Ehm, that's it. They said it was extremely important. Yes, that's it.' Having passed the message on, the priest nimbly disappeared through the temple entrance into the pronaos, belying his age.

'What's all this about?' asked Palaiyas.

'I sent a message to my brother suggesting he come and meet Tudhaliyas, here in Hattusas. I assume this is something to do with it.'

'Well, we've got a little time to kill. It's mid afternoon now, so what d'you want to do?' Palaiyas asked.

'Come and sit with me on the steps here.' Mokhat motioned to the stylobate and eased his buttocks on the top step. 'Tell me a little of Tiryns. How big is it? What's your house like?'

'You sure you want to hear this?' Palaiyas wanted Mokhat to ask him twice.

'I'm sure. Unless you're ashamed of your origins?' goaded Mokhat.

That got to Palaiyas. He settled and began, 'Tiryns itself stands on a big terraced hill and it wouldn't surprise you to find our house stands on the summit of that hill. All around the town there's a wall, but there was talk of pulling it down and of building a new bigger, thicker, stronger wall before I left, of enclosing more of the area. Some of the Hatti building methods would work well and I might use them, if I ever get back.

'The house is really a palace full of beautiful frescos. My favourite scene is of a boar hunt with spearmen and spotted hounds in pursuit of a wounded beast. Other rooms have dolphins leaping, octopuses, ships sailing. Most of the ideas for the frescos come from Keftiu; then there are scenes from our religious beliefs.'

The last bit raised Mokhat's interest. 'What exactly *are* your beliefs?' Mokhat interrupted.

'Are you really certain you want to know?'

Mokhat nodded.

Palaiyas wet his lips and began, 'Our chief god is Diwo, the ruler and protector of Ellas and all Ellinike wherever we are. When angry, he strikes with thunder and lightening, sends rain and winds. In his right hand he carries his traditional weapon, the thunderbolt. On his left hand sits an eagle. He is the great Lord of the sky and all weather.' Palaiyas stopped for an instant thinking of home.

Bemused, Mokhat said, 'I don't want to worry you, but did you say Diwo or Taru? Because what you've just described is the Storm and Weather God of Hatti. You must know that, surely.'

'No I didn't. I described Diwo, God of the Ellinike. I can't help it if the Hatti have appropriated and misnamed him Taru.' Palaiyas refused to acknowledge any similarity. 'If I may be permitted to continue,' he said tetchily.

'I'm sorry, yes, do go on.' Mokhat gave up.

'As ruler of heaven, Diwo led the Gods to victory against the Giants and successfully crushed several revolts against him by his fellow gods....'

'Yes, yes, I see,' Mokhat interrupted the flow, feeling somewhat uncomfortable at this description of another religion. As a priest himself, Mokhat saw other beliefs as curiosities, which is why he had asked Palaiyas to describe his belief, but as he listened, his inner priestly being felt the profanity of the description. He had to hold himself back from crying out loud, "Stop!"

Palaiyas continued looking into the distance without noticing Mokhat's discomfort. 'Diwia is queen of heaven and consort to Diwo ....' Suddenly Palaiyas stopped having finally noticed the pained expression on Mokhat's face. He asked, 'What's the matter?'

'I know I asked about your beliefs, but can you say less about religion and more of your home. Enough on the gods!'

Puzzled, because he did not understand Mokhat's distaste for other's doctrines, Palaiyas complied with his wishes. 'Our palace is well built but small, approached through a patio. The great megaron is a noble hall entered through a court and the inner court contains an altar and a colonnade. I've not seen anything like it here. Our piers are round supporting the roof, not square as here. Our construction has been greatly influenced by the buildings on

Keftiu. We've occupied that island for about a hundred and fifty years and even before, their customs were admired and copied.' They had been sitting, chatting, watching priests of Taru come and go, whilst the afternoon wore on. 'Tiryns is near the sea. When I was a boy, I went diving with my friends, using a tube device allowing us swimmers to breathe while just below the surface of the water. We spent many days just floating, watching the sea life going on below.'

Mokhat held his hand up. 'I'm sorry, Palaiyas, it's time to go. I must be at the North Gate, remember.' They rose and walked round the temple, west towards the agreed meeting place. The North Gate was at the back of the Great Temple by the quarters of the old Assyrian merchant colony. They reached the gate and went through the tunnel, nodding a greeting to the yellow tunic sentries on guard and then loitered outside the gate until the sun began to set. After a while they noticed a small band of strange warriors appear on horses and stop a distance from the gate. The leader dismounted and waited for Mokhat to approach.

Mokhat seemed to know the leader and they greeted each other warmly, hugging. Then they got down to a serious conversation. Palaiyas hung back and gave Mokhat the room he needed, so as not to alarm the strange warriors. After a while, the leader remounted his horse and the small group disappeared the way they had come. Mokhat rejoined Palaiyas, deep in thought.

They made their way back up through the gate in silence. Something important was going through Mokhat's mind and Palaiyas decided to wait. Mokhat would tell him when he felt it was time.

'By the way, those were a group of scouts from my people,' Mokhat finally said. 'They have critical news for the Hatti king. Muwas is on his way back here, to the capital. He's got the Mittani with him again.'

That last part startled Palaiyas. 'That *is* bad news. What are they doing back here? We must go to the palace immediately. The king in must be told.'

'Quite right! We have to go to the palace. Let's go and tell Tagrama first, it effects him too. He's going to have to get his people together.'

'Do you think they'll fight now? You know, defend the capital? Good thick walls surround this city. If it were my people this would be finished by now. They must surly bring an end to this standoff. Or are we to run again?'

'That's not our concern. I'm here to find Harep and his nephews and put a stop to them. It's true, I'd prefer a King Tudhaliyas to this King Muwas, but it's not for me to decide. They must settle this amongst themselves.'

'I suppose you're right. We should stay out of it. We have a saying back home in Tiryns: "get in the middle of a family quarrel and both sides will turn on you".'

'We have the same sort of saying up in Kaska.'

* * *

'Careful, there, your pulling too hard...go gently,' Nikal rebuked. Talarra was brushing Nikal's hair in readiness for her visit to Tudhaliyas up in the Great Palace.

'I'm sorry your highness, I'm so excited for you. You, a queen—a queen of Hatti. Goodness gracious! I'm so pleased for you.' Talarra was bubbling over.

She was going to wear the most wonderful dress Gassulawiya had especially made for her, with ruby red trimming, gold thread embroidery and scarlet flowers. It was emphasised by a gold embroidered cloth tie round the waist.

Now he was in possession of it, Tudhaliyas had invited the Kizzuwatna king and his family up to the Great Palace for a splendid feast. A state reception which combined their homecoming and a surprise engagement. The banquet was to be the moment when the formal announcement of the engagement between King Tudhaliyas of Hatti and Princess Nikal of Kizzuwatna was to be made. Himuili had talked with King Shunashura and was pleasantly surprised when the king showed enthusiasm for the match. Was the princess in agreement to pursue the match? Her father and brother seemed to think she was as wholehearted as her father. They two young people had known each other for only a short time but in an arranged marriage, that was of no concern. It was for the families to decide. It was purely fortuitous the couple were also in love.

The town was abuzz with the leaked news. Kantuzzili had let it "slip" to a courtier, who he was certain would spread it through the capital. He wanted the townspeople to have something to celebrate, somehow to become personally involved in the affairs of the royal family. He even paid the tavern-keepers to supply the first two drinks for free as long as they mentioned who had stood the drinks. They were to toast the royal couple and drink to their health. The free drinks did more positive work on behalf of the Kantuzzili faction than any promulgations or bulletin boards could ever do. The people lined the streets, cheering the Kizzuwatna princess as the carriage paraded through the town to the palace. In the palace courtyard, Tudhaliyas himself came down to escort his bride-to-be. Tudhaliyas wore a kilt embroidered with roundels in the shape of Lion's heads, his yellow cloak bore diamond shaped silver platelets in the same design. An imprinted gold crown kept his hair in place. He looked every inch the king. 'Welcome to the palace,' he told King Shunashura and a special welcome to Princess Nikal.' He hugged her regally, then turned his attention to Talshura and greeted him.

Tudhaliyas took Nikal's arm and they ascended the steps, through the entrance and into the magnificently decorated banqueting hall situated on the ground floor. Kantuzzili and Himuili walked Shunashura to the tables. Once all were seated, the servants became busy fetching in dish after dish. The eating went on for a long time and finally Himuili could wait no longer and banged the table with his goblet. A hush descended and he rose to his feet. 'Your majesties, highnesses, honoured guests, I had prepared a long speech regarding the benefits that would naturally be the result of a joining of the two houses of Hatti and Kizzuwatna, but I see we're all well and truly "relaxed," so I'll make this brief.' He raised his goblet, 'I give you King Tudhaliyas, my son and his bride to be, Princess Nikal of Kizzuwatna. May they have a wonderful engagement and wedding.' He swigged his goblet to the last.

All the guests raised their goblets and drained them. Servants hurried to refill them. Then King Shunashura rose, 'And I'll make mine just as brief. I support Prince Himuili's sentiments.' He raised his goblet and drained it. The guests followed his example. Servants again refilled the goblets.

Kantuzzili stood, a little shakily, 'And may this division in our society be healed as soon as possible.' Again he drained the wine, spilling some on his tunic.

The guests were well into their cups by now and musicians struck-up to accompany the overindulgence. A senior servant came from the entrance and whispered in Tudhaliyas' ear. Suddenly the king became exceedingly solemn. He banged his goblet on the table for an announcement. 'Friends, may I have your attention—*please*!' A silence come over the hall. 'We have important news. I'm going let the messenger give it to you first hand. Call forth the priests.' He sat.

Mokhat and Palaiyas stood in the entrance of the banqueting hall, sombre faced. They walked into the middle of the hall and bowed to the king and guests. Mokhat spoke, 'We are sorry to interrupt this festive occasion but we are the bearers of bad tidings. News has just been brought to us the Mittani are back and they are heading towards Hattusas with Muwas' army. They're expected to reach the capital by evening tomorrow. Considering the timing, we thought it best you should know this as soon as possible.'

'Thank you,' Tudhaliyas told them.

The two priests, having relayed their message, turned and went out the way they had come. Inside the banqueting hall everyone began talking loudly. Drunken comments, shouts and an air of building hysteria slowly crept into the large room. Tudhaliyas banged for order and kept banging until he got their attention. 'This party is at an end! Please leave and return to your homes.'

Kantuzzili had immediately sobered at the news and a hurried council of war was being organised in a smaller room.

Chapter Thirty-six

Tagrama woke up early just before dawn and lay for a few moments with his eyes closed, pondering on events. Civil war; the succession; assassinations; death. A streak of light crept through the cracks of the covering on his window and he opened his eyes. *Think positive!* he ordered himself.

Swinging his legs out of the cot bed he went over to a dresser. From a pitcher, he poured water into a bowl and washed. His cloak was neatly folded over the back of the bed and despite warranting a personal aid to help him, he had always dressed himself. He insisted on doing everything for himself. Now he was ready to carry out the morning devotional.

Once down in the temple he made his way to the naos and stopped, stupefied, utterly shocked at what he saw—or rather *did not* see. The black bull of Taru was gone. Where the statue had stood, now there was only an empty space. He choked back a cry of alarm, looked around frantically and found a young priest cleaning in a side room. '*Where's the Lord Taru*?' he shouted.

The poor young priest was startled and looked back questioningly. 'Your eminence, why…whatever's the matter?'

Tagrama stabbed at the space where the bull had stood. '*Where is the statue?*' he repeated, hardly able to contain his voice.

'But eminence, you know where it is. Your priests have taken it back to Ankuwa.' The young priest was surprised he asked.

'*Who told them to? Answer me!*' Tagrama shouted.

'But eminence…you gave them the order.'

'Are you out of your mind? When did I give that order?' he was quietening.

'Eminence...they said it was at your orders.' The priest was adamant.

'Who said? Who were these priests?' Tagrama's eyebrows shot up in surprise.

'Priests from Ankuwa...they said they were from Ankuwa...special detail...to carry the statue back...they came during the night. They said Muwas was coming and they had to transfer the statue back to Ankuwa.' Alarm was showing on the young priest's face. He knew something was wrong.

'I gave *no* such order. Quick, go raise the alarm. The statue of Lord Taru has been stolen. *Hurry*!' Tagrama was beginning to see a sinister hand at work. Someone had come in the night, clothed as priests and removed the precious statue. Likely the work of Muwas. Dressed as priests, eh? Could be Mittani priests disguised as Hatti priests? Various speculations ran around in his skull. Priests came running to the naos to see for themselves. Was the deity really missing? Had someone the nerve to steal the holy statue? A crowd gathered around him and Tagrama waited until a semblance of calm had settled. He stood angrily in front and told them, 'As you can see,' he pointed a shaking finger, 'the blessed statue of Lord Taru is missing. Someone suggested *I* gave the order for it to be moved. I gave *no* such order!' That caused a stir and much whispering. Tagrama waited till they subsided. 'Those who took the sacred effigy implied I gave the order and *that* should speak for itself. I must take it for granted Muwas was somehow involve in this. It's the only thing that makes any sense. All of you here, I want you to think back. Any who can answer any of the following questions, please stay behind. I would like to talk with you.' He paused and then presented the questions: 'Were you present when the statue was removed? Did you see those who took it? Did any of you talk to the thieves? Maybe you saw which way they went? Have you any scrap of information that can help us to retrieve our beloved deity. Those who have no information, please, go about your daily tasks. Later I will tell you what has happened—when I find out.' Tagrama grabbed one of the departing priests and asked him to go and find Mokhat. The young priest went off on the errand. Of those remaining, about seven priests, he told them, 'Please follow me and we'll see if we can't get to the bottom of this.' He led them off to a side room where they sat uncomfortably and looked at each other with a bemused air of expectation. Tagrama waited until Mokhat appeared, trailed by Palaiyas.

'The young man who came to fetch us,' Mokhat sat himself discreetly just apart from the priests, 'said something about your god being stolen.' Palaiyas sat next to him. 'We passed the altar and I can't see your black bull statue. Is that what your messenger is referring to?'

'Yes! I'm sad to say he was telling the truth. Sometime last night thieves carried off the statue. They claimed I'd given the order for it to be transferred to Ankuwa. What brazen audacity!' Tagrama was getting angry again.

'May I suggest something?' Mokhat saw the anger rising and wanted to divert it.

Tagrama calmed, 'But of course.'

'Have you informed his majesty? Kantuzzili? They have scouts out on patrol all the time. If anybody is on the roads out of the capital, they could report it—but only if they knew.'

Tagrama struck his forehead with the palm of his hand, 'How stupid of me!' He turned to one of the sitting priests, 'Go and find a messenger, someone reliable. Tell them to go to the Great Palace and inform the king and Kantuzzili the statue is missing. Ask them to have their patrols on the look out for anyone trying to sneak it out of the city. Ask them to ask the sentries on the gates if any saw a wagon leaving during the night or if the patrols saw a wagon on the roads.' The young priest rushed off, eager to be doing something—and be away from the questioning. Tagrama turned back to Mokhat, 'I'm gratified you're here. In all the confusion I'd lost sight of the larger picture; the need to inform the king and to enlist all the soldiers at our disposal. Thank you for reminding me.'

'It's frightful what they've done. Even unthinkable.' Mokhat thought how he would react if the statue of the Lord Illuyankas went missing. 'I know we already have the task of catching the assassins, but I'd like to see if I can help. I feel your outrage as if it were mine at this sacrilege.'

Tagrama could see the sincerity in Mokhat and was appreciative. 'If you think you can spare the time I would be grateful.'

'We'll make time, won't we, Palaiyas?'

Palaiyas was startled to be included and half shrugged, but then nodded in agreement.

*   *   *

'I think it's time to bring this to a conclusion,' Himuili was telling his brother, Kantuzzili. 'This has gone on long enough. We must stay and defend the capital.'

'You're wrong, brother of mine. We must pack up and leave—go back to Ankuwa. I know how it looks, but while we're not killing each other, there's hope of resolving this without bloodshed.' Kantuzzili was adamant.

'*Without bloodshed*? Out of the question! The sooner we join battle, the quicker it's all over and the healing can begin.' They were pacing up and down in a smaller room of the Great Castle, arguing without resolution for some time.

'What if I showed you how to resolve this without bloodshed? Will you then follow my advice?'

'Show me first, then we'll see.'

'Did you know I was responsible for the Mittani being withdrawn—for making them leave Muwas?'

'You say that now, but how could you have been? Did you ask Saustatar to order Artatama back home?' The sarcasm bit hard.

Kantuzzili firmly told his brother, 'Next best thing. I forced Saustatar to order Artatama back home. Did you know I've been in contact with the pharaoh ever since this confrontation began? That it was at my suggestion pharaoh sent his forces to the Mittani border. I thought if I could separate the Mittani from Muwas, there would be no way he could fight—not so badly outnumbered.'

Himuili's mouth opened in astonishment. 'You cunning old fox. You've been in contact with pharaoh, eh? Why didn't you tell me? I had no idea.'

Kantuzzili continued, 'Even now, if I can get rid of his allies, the civil war is over. Our problem isn't so much Muwas but Artatama. If there was a way of causing a threat to Saustatar, he might still pull his forces back. I'm working on it right now. I didn't tell you because the fewer people who know about this, the better. If *I* can stir up Mittani's enemies, *they* might be able to stir up some for me, like the Arzawa or the Lukka. What if the Mittani pay the Lukka pirates to attack Adaniya? Our Kizzuwatna allies would have to leave to protect their capital, wouldn't they? I don't want that idea to surface. Keep this very tight, nobody must get to know what I'm up to or they'll do to us what I'm planning for them.'

Himuili knew his brother was devious, which is why he was the strategist, but these manoeuvres were outstanding, at least Himuili thought so and he swore to his brother, 'I pledge you my word, it stays with me. Not even my son will know, not until it's all over.'

'So now we agree. Tomorrow we go back to Ankuwa. If they call us cowards for refusing to stand and fight, remember that a few words are preferable to a lot of dead Hatti soldiers. In the mean time I'm talking to the Egyptian Ambassador, trying to work out a scheme which might force Saustatar to pull out his forces.'

Himuili was smiling with quiet admiration at his brother strategic skills. He would no longer question his wisdom, but follow his orders to the letter. He could see now, his brother had the best interests of all Hatti at heart. 'On a different subject,' Himuili continued, 'I've just learnt that the statue of Taru has been stolen from the Great Temple. A priest was sent by Tagrama to ask us to tell our scouts to keep a lookout for a wagonload of false priests. This is Muwas' work, I can feel it. Him and his damned Teshub. The Mittani have conditioned him to take up all their Hurrian ideas. The fool can't think for himself.'

Kantuzzili was not interested. 'I'm sorry for the high priest, but I have bigger problems to think about than a statue. It'll sort itself out. Let the priests take care of it. We must find Zidanta and tell him to get everyone ready for tomorrow. We've done it once—so we know the drill. However, I make you one promise— within a week or two at the most, we will have resolved this issue. If I can't get the Mittani to retreat, we will join battle with Muwas. I've already picked a battleground halfway between Ankuwa and Hattusas. This move to Ankuwa is the last time we avoid battle.'

'I trust you, brother. I'm pleased you told me of the other, you know.'

Kantuzzili came and put his arm round Himuili and they both went to find their wives.

Chapter Thirty-seven

'Have you heard, King Karaindash of Babylon has concluded a treaty with King Ashurbelnisheshu of Assyria?' the pharaoh asked his Djat. Pharaoh lay relaxing in Waset on a magnificent couch, being fanned by slaves, holding audience with his first minister. Once he had dealt with the Nubians, taken a number of princes prisoner, hung others from the bow of his warship and subdued all sign of revolt, he had hurried back to Waset to establish how Tuthmosis had fared on the Mittani border.

'Beloved of Horus, but why would they want to antagonise the Mittani. Saustatar has already threatened to lay siege to the Assyrian capital of Ashur again.'

'Be reasonable, First Minister, how can he with a large part of his army up in Hatti. If there was ever a time for Assyria to throw off the Mittani yoke, surely this is it. The only question is how to persuade them both to menace the eastern Mittani sub-kingdom at Arrapkha simultaneously. If King Ashurbelnisheshu encouraged the cities of Arbil and Nineveh to assert themselves, even rebel, aided by Babylon, it would greatly discomfort Saustatar. Despite the many Mittani military units stationed there, he may feel they're not enough.'

'Sire, he won't fall for the same ruse twice. The only way we can force him to pull Artatama back to Wassukkani is to create a *credible* threat. Assyria, even with Babylon, is no threat to Saustatar. Begging your majesties pardon, but we and Hatti are the only force the Mittani respect. That's why Saustatar is so keen to make an alliance with Hatti. It leaves him free then to turn his attention on to us.'

Upon his return from Nubia, pharaoh discovered his son had carried out the Mittani raid according to his wishes. That it did not entirely have the desired effect was not his fault. Artatama was still in Hatti. Amenhotep was forced to leave a sizable garrison in Nubia to keep the rebellion from erupting again, so it was to the new Babylon-Assyrian axis he now turned to stir up the Mittani.

'Assyria's weakness is for ever expanding trade and this always drives its foreign policy. Sire, what can we offer Ashurbelnisheshu? Trade concessions, gold?'

'Let me think on it. What of Prince Hapu? Have we heard from our new ambassador to Tudhaliyas?'

'Yes, sire. The first dispatch from the Hatti court arrived by sea the day before you returned. Prince Hapu's made contact with the person who's been sending the wax tablets to your majesty. From now the ambassador will pass along any requests.'

'Good! You have a think on how we can help Assyria free itself of the Mittani. Six generations as a vassal kingdom is more than enough. I'll do the same. Maybe we can come up with a plan that will yet discomfort the Mittani. That will be all. You may go! We'll meet again tomorrow. Be sure you have a plan for me by then.'

'Oh beloved of Horus, I hear and obey.' The Djat bowed all the way out.

Chapter Thirty-eight

Saustatar stood admiring the huge silver and gold door he had looted from Ashur a few years earlier. 'Beautiful, isn't it. I couldn't resist bringing it back here. It'll remind the Assyrians who's in charge. Vassals, nothing more,' he told his chief minister dismissively. Saustatar had removed the main door leading to the Assyrian king's Audience Hall and installed it as the main entranceway to his harem. A calculated insult to the greatness that *was* Assyria. 'Pharaoh's up to his tricks again. We've just received news of grumblings and rebellion from the governors of Arrapkha, Arbil and Nineveh. Ashur is even demanding we pull our forces out of Assyria entirely.' Saustatar was dismissive of the news. 'I thought I'd show you what happened the last time Ashur made demands.' He swept his hand at the silver and gold door. 'Tell the governors to suppress any rebellion with all the forces at his command. Make examples of those he sees fit. I want that area quiet.'

'Yes sire. Regarding the matter of King Karaindash of Babylon—he is reported to have concluded a treaty with our Assyrian vassal, Ashurbelnisheshu. We should demand an explanation.'

'Yes, yes. We'll get round to that. But first, can't you feel pharaoh's hand in all this?' Saustatar was furious at these tricks. 'He's again trying to get me to pull Artatama back, but not this time. I won't do it. If I don't see pharaoh himself at the head of a great army outside the gates of Wassukkani, Artatama stays where he is. Assyrian rebellion, huh! He must think I was born yesterday.'

His chief minister could only stand and listen to the angry outburst. Although he agreed with the king, he treated these "tricks" as part and parcel of normal diplomatic chicanery. Were the roles reversed, he would be advising his king to do something similar.

'Now to Babylon. Send a strongly worded demand to that Kassite upstart Karaindash, he must explain this treaty he's concluded with our vassal, Ashurbelnisheshu. If he wants a treaty he should have turned to us, not to our puppet. Remind him that Babylon is not much further than Ashur and that my reach is long and strong. Make sure he understands my meaning.'

'I will have the tablet imprinted and sent off today, sire.'

'What's the latest from Artatama? Have they joined battle with the opposition?'

'Not yet, sire. They've retaken the capital and when all is secure, intend to follow the enemy down to their base camp in Ankuwa. Artatama reports he's fed up of this hide and seek nonsense. All that seems to be holding back an outcome is Muwas seeming reluctance to attack. Earlier he didn't want to fight, hoping somehow Tudhaliyas would fade away. I think he's firm now.'

'I'm beginning to wonder about our Hatti ally. Is he really the resolute friend we are looking for?'

Chapter Thirty-Nine

General Ammuna slipped out of the palace late that night without the king's knowledge. He left the capital by the north gate at the head of a tough looking bunch of men, all thirty riding dark horses. He led his own bodyguards to the rock sanctuary to take charge of the stolen statue. Ammuna was the conduit to the king, the chief of the army, answerable only to his majesty. He rightly assumed nobody would challenge his authority to take a course of action, taking for granted the deed had been commanded by the king. Only if Artatama, for unknown reasons, brought it to the king's attention, would he have to find an answer as to why he disobeyed a direct order.

The troop crossed the northern stream running by the capital and was soon on the processional path to the grotto. They rode the short distance, a league north-east to the outcrop of rock and arrived at the wall fronting the two natural chambers where a group of Mittani stood sentry duty. A sacred place for many hundreds of years, a spring-sanctuary from olden times. The Mittani officer in charge came smartly to attention as he recognised the chief of the Hatti army.

Ammuna dismounted, 'Cold night captain. I've come to take over your burden. Gather your men and go back to Hattusas. We'll take over from here on.'

The Mittani captain seemed mightily relieved to be rid of the duty. 'Thank you sir. I can't say we enjoyed this. The place gives me the creeps.'

The captain led the way through the irregular wall shutting off the chamber from the outside world. Ammuna followed.

'There it is,' he said pointing out the black bull statue standing in front of the main chamber. Ammuna's Hatti bodyguard cautiously kept their distance, overawed by being so close to their deity.

'I formally hand this over to you, sir. Come lads,' he called out to his soldiers, 'our job's done here. Back to the capital.' He led his Mittani soldiers out leaving Ammuna staring at the statue he had come to rescue.

'You're clear what you have to do?' Ammuna asked the captain in charge of his bodyguards.

'Yes sir, load the effigy back into the wagon, take it up to Gaziura.'

'Very good, captain. I have to be back in the palace before I'm missed. You're to guard it as if it were me—with your life. I will send orders as to what to do with it once you're in Gaziura.'

'Yes sir.'

'Carry on!' The general went to the soldier holding his reins and remounted his horse. As a parting shot, he told the commander, 'I'm relaying on you to take good care of the effigy. Good night captain.'

'You can count on me. Good night, sir.'

Chapter Forty

'*Ouch*! A curse on these pot-holes. I'm going to be black and blue by the time we reach Ankuwa.' Tagrama was in a wagon with Mokhat and Palaiyas back on the road south.

'I've noticed, the more you complain, the more pot-holes we hit,' joked Palaiyas.

'You've a hard rump and a sharp tongue my Ahhiyawan friend,' chided Tagrama, rubbing his lower spine with the back of his hand.

'He means no harm, your eminence,' Mokhat interrupted. 'But the wagon is a lot lighter without the statue.'

'That brings us to the matter of the missing deity. What have you found out?' Tagrama was still rubbing his lower back.

'We asked around at the gates,' Mokhat told him. 'The sentries at the south gate reported a wagon passing through just before dawn. Thirteen priests taking the statue down to Ankuwa and they claimed you'd authorised the move.'

'It's the same with my priests. They spoke of "thirteen" priests. This compels me to conclude it is the work of the Mittani.'

'How so, your eminence?' Mokhat was curious at the deduction.

'The sacred number for our Storm God is twelve and in this we follow the Babylonian system. But the followers of Teshub consider thirteen as a sacred number. If it had been Muwas he would have known that thirteen is an unlucky number for the followers of Taru and would not have had thirteen priests. It could only have been Mittani—probably led by those Mittani priests we had earlier hounded out of the temple at Hattusas.'

'I see. Yes, I can go along with that. It makes sense,' Mokhat agreed. Just at that moment the wagon keeled to the left barely staying upright, throwing all inside onto the wagon floor. Priest's white robes lay in a pile, arms and legs fighting to free themselves.

'Mind where you're sticking your leg.' One voice was heard to say.

'Hey! Watch your elbow,' another voice complained.

'That's my robe you're pulling,' came a third voice.

The driver turned in his seat and shouted to the back, 'Sorry, your eminence, couldn't help that. Didn't see the hole.' After a while everyone was again sitting, fumbling with and straightening their attire.

'Where were we?' Tagrama asked a little blustery.

'You'd just demonstrated it was Mittani priests who stole the statue,' Palaiyas reminded him.

'Ah, yes. So now you say they managed to get it out of the south gate, eh? Any idea where they took it from there?' Tagrama said, brushing dirt off his robe.

'We think they may have doubled back up north and taken it to the rock sanctuary. Muwas will have to pass that way, probably there already,' Mokhat suggested.

'But why do they want it? We destroyed their Teshub so it must be revenge,' Tagrama answered himself.

'Could be. Or they might want to ransom it. Could they be trying to curse our path using the statue?' Mokhat was just throwing out ideas.

'Black magic, eh? Not the first time someone's tried that.' Tagrama tried not to look embarrassed.

214

'Either way, you would do well to begin making a new one.' It was a pessimistic assessment by Mokhat.

'I can't do that.' Tagrama was emphatic. 'All the craftsmen are in Hattusas. Anyhow, I want to see the pieces before I commission another statue. We've sanctified it, blessed it and sacrificed in front of it for many years. I can't just let it go like that. It took a lot of effort and hard work, not to mention the cost, to produce that effigy of Lord Taru. I'm not abandoning the present carving without a lot more endeavour. We might try a raid on the rock sanctuary tonight—or the next night. What d'you think?'

'Interesting! A raid eh? Might work.' Mokhat began pondering the possibility.

*   *   *

The muffled neighing of horses came from the picket line. The whole camp was asleep and only sentries patrolled the perimeter. Palaiyas followed closely by Mokhat crept out of camp, leading their horses quietly so no one would see them go. A troop of twenty of Zidanta's best men silently followed the Kaska priest and the Mycenaean mercenary out of the camp into open country. They mounted well away from camp and headed back up north, speedily but carefully galloping in the moonless night back towards the capital they had only just left a couple of days ago. By dawn, they had made good progress but the horses needed rest. They stopped for a short meal, both for themselves and the animals.

'When d'you suppose we'll reach the capital?' Mokhat asked Palaiyas. As a soldier, he would be better able to make an estimate.

'I think we ought to make it there by evening. It might be better to wait for darkness and then skirt the Mittani camp.'

'Yes, that was my assumption as well,' Mokhat replied.

'I hope your guess is right about the rock sanctuary. Coming all this way for nothing would be a letdown.'

'Not as much of a letdown as it would be for Tagrama if we don't recover it,' Mokhat parried.

'Right lads, we've rested enough. Let's get a move on,' Palaiyas encouraged all those present. 'We've a long way to go yet.' He had taken command of the little band of raiders. They remounted and continued their journey. The late spring sunshine beat down strongly, adding to their problems and the heat soon became oppressive. Horse and rider suffered, both perspiring freely. Around noon, Palaiyas ordered another rest, a little longer this time, but they had eaten up the leagues towards the capital and felt much closer to their destination. 'I'm sure the capital is over that next range there,' Palaiyas shouted to Mokhat in the late afternoon.

'Ask one of the Hatti, they should know,' Mokhat shouted back.

Palaiyas called a halt and confided in the nearest Hittite soldier. 'Tell me trooper, is Hattusas over those hills?'

'Yes sir. Another couple of leagues should see us in sight of the capital.'

'Thanks, soldier.' Palaiyas raised his voice so the others could hear, 'Right, another short rest, make sure the animals get some water. We'll wait here a while till it begins to get dark. Then we'll move on.'

As darkness crept in, the band of twenty raiders doused the fire, gathered their stuff and repacked their gear on the back of the horses, then made ready to continue. 'Before we start, can you take off the yellow and change into your white tunics. That way, we keep them guessing,' Palaiyas told his listeners. 'Then we'll swing wide to the west and that way we should avoid Hattusas. I'm still worried about patrols, both Mittani and Muwas'. If we're spotted, I suggest we ride directly west to throw them off the scent.'

Tunics changed, Mokhat rode side by side with Palaiyas. 'I'm glad you had the wit to think of using a disguise,' Mokhat declared.

'That's your fault. I'm beginning to think like you,' he told Mokhat. 'You forcing me into a priests outfit gave me the idea. Wearing a white tunic makes what we do ambiguous. They don't know who we are or what we're doing.'

They rode through the evening dusk, around the capital and on to the rock-sanctuary. As they neared the grotto, Palaiyas dismounted and went ahead to determine whether there were any guards. He soon returned and yelled from a distance, 'No one's there! Come on in!'

Mokhat led the group through the irregular wall to the main chamber where Palaiyas waited. 'What's happened? Where's the statue?' Mokhat couldn't contain himself.

'It's been here but it's gone. We're going to have work out to where. Look!' Palaiyas pointed at horse manure, 'A large group's been here until dusk, then they left. See, that's where the wagon stood,' he led the way over to a wall where wheel tracks were still visible. 'A heavily laden wagon,' he added.

'But where have they moved it to? Back to the capital?' Mokhat was puzzled.

'I don't think so, not if he's serious about changing the religion. I've been inside, had a look, no sign of anything else. The Mittani have been here, one left a cloak. Sloppy fellow.' Palaiyas led the way.

'There, that's where the statue stood,' Mokhat looked closely at the ground near the entrance to the main chamber. 'See, the four hoof marks left by the effigy. Remember, it's extremely heavy.'

'I think we should try to follow the wagon tracks, see where they lead. Might give us a direction. Look, my Kaska friend,' Palaiyas faced Mokhat, 'how far do you want to follow this?'

'I want to cast my eyes on the statue—that's how far. Then when we do, we decide if we can take it or we're forced to leave it. If there's too many of them, we'll have to back off. I want to tell Tagrama I've seen it. It looks like it's still in one piece.'

'Right! So let's follow the wagon tracks, see where they leads us,' Palaiyas agreed.

*   *   *

The statue of the Storm God of Hatti had almost reached Gaziura when the officer in charge stopped and sent a scout forward to determine the lay of the land. 'I hope the Kaska haven't taken Gaziura as well,' he voiced his concern to his second in command. To the surprise and consternation of the thirty green clad Hatti soldiers, archers came out of the undergrowth pointing arrows at them, from behind trees and in such numbers that it was pointless to resist. Hundreds of men with swords, spears and on horseback surrounded them, indicating they should lower their arms.

The commander of the Kaska ambush raised his hand to stay his men, 'Don't harm them yet. I'm far more interested in what's in your wagon. You've been nursing it so carefully that I had to have a look.' He smiled with menace. When the Kaska commander looked inside, he gasped. 'Explain yourself,' he turned to the

Hatti captain. 'What are you doing with this?' he gestured at the wagon.

'I'm under orders to take it to Gaziura,' the Hatti captain replied gruffly.

'But why? And how is it you have it at all? Why isn't it in the temple in Hattusas?'

The captain shrugged and set his mouth.

'I suppose you do know what you've got there, do you?'

Again, the Hatti captain shrugged his big shoulders. Why should he explain anything to these barbarians. More to the point, how could he explain why he was in charge of the holiest relic in the whole kingdom. The general had told him what to do and he was doing it. He did not explain why.

The Kaska commander shook his head. He used his sword in a swift slashing movement and cut down the second in command. He fell of his horse dead.

It clearly shook the captain. 'I can't tell you what I don't know,' he protested. 'My general told me to take this wagon to Gaziura and wait there for further orders. That's what I'm doing.'

'Where from?' threatened the Kaska.

'From the rock sanctuary. I'm telling you this honestly. You don't need to kill any more of my men. Ask your questions and I'll answer as best as I can.' He stared back defiantly.

'How did it get to the rock sanctuary? Why isn't it in the temple in your capital?'

'We took charge of the statue from a squad of Mittani. My guess is they stole it from the temple. I think King Muwas wanted the statue destroyed. He's installed the Mittani Teshub in the temple instead of...' he tilted his head at the wagon. 'General Ammuna is trying to save it. We're part of his personal bodyguard.'

'There, you see, it didn't hurt a bit to answer my questions. Had you cooperated immediately, he'd still be alive.' He indicated at the dead soldier lying in a pool of blood.

Although they had no intention of fighting, all the Hatti stood their ground and acted defiantly. They were old foes and neither side liked to lose.

The Kaska commander got off his horse and so did the Hatti captain. They faced each other and squared their shoulders. 'I'm feeling generous today, so I'm taking this wagon and sending you back to the capital. I don't want any argument from you or any protests. If your general wants it back, he'll have to pay handsomely. Are you clear with what I'm saying to you?'

'Yes! You're holding the statue for ransom. Any idea how much you want?'

'Not yet. The statue is going to Nerik. That's where your general can contact us. Now *go* before I change my mind.'

The twenty nine Hatti picked up their dead comrade and slowly retraced their steps from whence they came, leading their horses behind them.

Chapter Forty-one

The evening of the first day on the road back to Ankuwa, Tudhaliyas got into arguing with his father, Himuili. They had stopped at the side of the road and waited while the column came to a halt. Camp would be a long drawn out affair stretching alongside the road for leagues. The Kizzuwatna royal family would join the Hatti royals for the evening meal, whilst the senior officers would join General Zidanta for their evening meal. One was a social affair, the other a military analysis of the planning to date.

'I can't understand you, father. One minute you agree with me, the next you side with Kantuzzili. Even at this point, I'm still for turning and holding our ground. I've had enough of this running. It makes me out to be nothing but a weakling. How can people have any respect for a king that refuses to fight for his kingdom?'

Himuili again patiently began explaining, 'Before I talked with your uncle, I was in the same mind as you, but now I see I was wrong. He made clear to me and I must now agree with his analysis of the situation, that another week or two might make all the difference between a bloodless victory and a useless slaughter.' At that moment, the Kizzuwatna royals approached with Nikal looking forward to seeing her husband to be.

'I don't care,' Tudhaliyas did not want to listen to his father. 'I want you to order General Zidanta to turn and fight.' He looked defiantly at his father.

His father returned the same look. A clash of wills began to raise the temperature between father and son. It was more than merely to do with the timing of the battle. It was a son asserting his right to be treated as a king.

To demand the respect due from his subjects—even if one of the subjects was his own father. He had given a command and Himuili was arguing with his authority. Both dismounted their steeds and stared at each other in anger. Tudhaliyas' mount felt the antagonism and reared, at which point Tudhaliyas took his rage out on the horse, whipping him with such force that all around were shocked. The more he whipped, the more the horse reared and tried to break free. The more it defied him, the more he brought his whip down on its flanks.

Nikal was shocked to witness such behaviour from her beloved and cried out, '*No! Your majesty. ... Tudhaliyas...please stop...!*' but he was in a deaf rage and no one dared to interrupt the king. Nikal couldn't stay and watch such cruelty. She was riding beside her brother and she turned her horse in distress, galloping off into the night the way she came. Her brother followed.

The Egyptian ambassador, Prince Hapu, watched from the side as the king of the Hittites took his rage out on a horse. He understood such a performance better than others since pharaoh sometimes took his rage out on his servants. Just human behaviour. Zidanta on the other hand watched with disgust at the lack of restraint. He did not like mistreatment of any kind, soldiers, animals, or women. It pointed to an encroaching chaos and a situation that might be out of control; out of his control. He wouldn't, couldn't tolerate such indiscipline. The soldiers all around watched flabbergasted at their king's outburst. But smiled at the same time for it showed their king was only human.

Finally, Kantuzzili rushed over and grabbed the whip as Tudhaliyas was bringing it down for the umpteenth time. The king turned to strike the impertinent individual who had dared hinder him—and stopped himself. The horse jerked free and galloped off into the night with soldiers running after it, trying to catch it.

Tudhaliyas looked at the blood soaked whip and the anger faded. He suddenly realised what he had done and stood ashamed at his own behaviour. He shook his head, 'I...I didn't mean to...I lost...control. Forgive me.' He looked into the face of Kantuzzili. He saw only love and forgiveness reflected in his uncle's face. The older man understood the frustrations facing the younger person. He had heard the argument and what it was about and identified with it. Who was he to criticise his nephew! So much responsibility had been laid upon his shoulders, so quickly, that he had wondered how Tudhaliyas managed to stay so calm. Now he had let go and a poor horse had got the brunt of the explosion, whereas his father also stood looking sheepish at having caused his son to go off the deep end.

'I'm sorry son, I should have been calmer.' Himuili turned to his brother, 'It's all my fault. I was tired after all the day's riding. I should have waited until we were eating.'

Tudhaliyas was still apologising, 'I'm sorry; I don't know what came over me.'

'*We* accept your remorse and absolve, but I fear your princess may not be as forgiving. She's rushed off and I think she was extremely distressed and angry at what she witnessed,' Kantuzzili told him.

'Oh, no! Why didn't somebody stop her? She must know I didn't mean to hurt the horse. It just got out of hand.'

'You'd better explain yourself,' his father advised.

'Father, please...find the horse and get one of our physicians to treat his injuries. I'm going to find Nikal now.' And so with a heavy heart, Tudhaliyas set out to find Nikal where the Kizzuwatna were encamped, followed by his bodyguards. Near the rear of the linear camp, he found Talshura, but there was no sign of Nikal. 'Where can I find your sister, prince?' the king asked.

'I have a message for you,' her brother countered. 'She doesn't wish to talk to you. She's dreadfully upset at what happened to your horse. You must give her time to recover. She's still young and says things she doesn't mean. At the moment, she says the engagement is off. She cannot marry someone who can be so cruel. Her words not mine. I'm sure she'll get over it, but she needs time. She's sulking in her carriage, but sire, please, let her be. I will work on her and so will father. She really does care for you deeply, which is why she's taken this so badly.'

'Tell her I called. Tell her how sorry I am. The pressure just got to me. I'm having the horse's injuries treated as we speak. Ask her to forgive me. I didn't mean to do what I did.'

'I'll tell her—and later you can tell her yourself.'

Tudhaliyas rode back to his part of the camp with a heart that was on the verge of breaking. He couldn't lose her now, not now, not on top of everything.

*   *   *

Tudhaliyas was in a bad mood, verging on depression. He wanted, needed to talk to Nikal—but she stubbornly refused to see him. Coupled with the rift, was his nagging desire to end the stalemate with Muwas. Himuili made no further attempt to explain and Tudhaliyas did not ask. Father and son were polite but somehow strained. The son was embarrassed at his own behaviour with flogging an innocent animal and the father did not want to push reconciliation until his son put out feelers telling him he was ready. In the mean time, Tudhaliyas moped. The lengthy convoy had now reached a point half a day away from Ankuwa and all the horse and chariot regiments had been sent ahead to occupy the same corner of the valley from where they had decamped. The rest of the convoy took its time with baggage trains following their regiments, various wagons, infantry, and camp followers following them.

A priest brought news they would be in Ankuwa by nightfall and Tagrama asked him, 'Any word from Mokhat?'

'No eminence. No sign of them.'

'I hope nothing's happened to them. They've been away for two whole days now. I was hoping they'd be back with some news of the statue,' he told his neighbour sitting on the bench next to him in the wagon.

'I passed the king on the way here,' the bringer of news announced. 'He's gone to try to talk to his princess again. You know she won't see him?'

'Watch your tongue, there,' Tagrama warned. 'You're talking of your king. Show some respect.'

'But eminence, it's all over the convoy, what happened. I'm not really gossiping,' he tried to justify himself.

'That's no excuse for adding to the tittle-tattle,' Tagrama admonished.

Tudhaliyas met Talshura a little way from his destination. They both sat on their horses and talked. 'How's your sister?' the king asked tersely trying to assume a veneer of calm he did not feel.

'I'm sorry your majesty, she shows no sign of changing her mind. She still insists the engagement is off. I've talked to her at length and so has father. I think she must be deeply in love with you. She's often stubborn but this is an exceptional obstinacy that I've never seen. On the positive side, she's just as likely to suddenly change her mind as when she decided on this course. I believe she simply needs time.'

'I hope you're right. I would hate to have to be bereaved so quickly of someone I care for so deeply.'

'Maybe the aftermath of battle will be more appropriate. I'm led to suppose we will engage the enemy soon?'

'I'm trying my best to make this happen. I too am weary of this deadlock. We exist in a never land of false peace. I can't take it any longer. That's what caused my rage and loss of control with the horse.'

'How is the animal? I want to be able to tell Nikal.'

'He's fine. The physicians put balm on his skin and it's healing nicely. He's being pampered.'

'She'll be pleased to hear that. Sire, I beg, give her some time and I'm sure she'll come round. She was simply shocked by what she saw. The battle casualties will put that in perspective. I'll see to that.'

'You seem to be older than your years with such advice. Tell her I'm thinking of her.' Tudhaliyas swung the horse around and made to depart. 'We will have the battle soon, I promise. Give her my love and farewell,' he called back.

Chapter Forty-two

'**I** want you to send people round all the informers and get them to tell you who's been helping my rival. They were here for two weeks and I know they were cheered. I want the names of all those that cheered.' Muwas was back in the Great Castle, in a rage at all his supposed enemies.

'But that can't be done, your majesty,' General Ammuna was explaining. 'We'd have to include at least half the city. It's not reasonable to antagonise so many people.'

'Find them! At least find the main supporters of Tudhaliyas. You can do that much can't you?'

'Yes sire, that we can do.'

'And it's time we sorted that lot out.' He meant Tudhaliyas of course. 'Artatama is getting on my nerves, almost calling me spineless for not attacking Ankuwa. Hasn't had the nerve to say it outright to my face, but hinted at it many times in the last three days.'

'The circumstances are still the same. I agree we need to sort this out but if we tear each other to bits, who benefits? Sire, Mittani's just waiting to take us over. I know you don't like me saying that, but it's true. Their occupying Assyria and that's just one example. They claim Halap and even Ugarit as vassals.'

'Enough! I told you, I don't want to hear anything against the Mittani. Let's deal with one problem at a time. The Mittani are my allies and here to help me.' He paused at a thought. 'Hmm! So let them help me. When we plan the order of battle, we might put the Mittani where we expect the biggest slaughter—in the centre, out front. Either they'll acquit themselves well and survive, or perish on Hittite spears and swords.'

'Now I like the sound of that. They'll do all our work and get slaughtered in the process. We must goad their prowess so they don't suspect.' General Ammuna looked pleased.

'What about the other matter? Did we succeed?'

The general smiled, 'Everything went smoothly— like taking money from a drunk. We have it up in the rock sanctuary. They're just waiting for your order. What do I tell them?'

Muwas' face became grim. 'Tell them to destroy the statue. Break it up into little pieces. I want no sign it ever existed.'

'To *destroy it*? I thought you might want to use it.' Ammuna was clearly unhappy.

'You heard me. Tell them to break it up.' Muwas stared hard at his general for questioning his command.

'Yes, majesty! I'll tell them!' In secret Ammuna intended to disobey the order to smash the statue of Taru. He wasn't a great believer but he wanted no part of the outrage, the sacrilege to his own people.

'Make sure you do it! Artatama tells me they're sending another carving of Teshub up from Wassukkani but it won't be here for some time. I'd liked to have seen the high priest's face when he found it missing. That would have been something. Make no mistake; I'm determined to remove the old religion. When this is over, I intend to hang Tagrama from the temple. I'll teach him to snub me.'

As Muwas was ranting, Ammuna was trying to think of a way of saving the statue without causing himself trouble. He had to get the statue away from the Mittani squadron guarding it—and give a plausible explanation as to why he was doing it. But then why should he? He was the chief of the army and why should

228

he have to explain? He finally decided to use his dedicated troop, soldiers loyal only to him personally. Men he had specially picked as his own bodyguards. In a fight, they watched his back, in peace they did his bidding whatever, no questions asked. A select group of fifty who answered only to their general. They had been useful in the past and now would do as he bid.

'General! Are you listening to me? You seem to have drifted off somewhere.' Muwas had noticed Ammuna's inattention.

'Sire, I was contemplating the coming battle, the disposition of our forces—the enemies disposition—not a moment goes by without me trying to find some kind of advantage.'

Muwas looked impressed. 'I must commend you on your diligence. Well all right, don't let me detain you any longer. You can go back to your planning. Despite having superior numbers, that Kantuzzili has a reputation for outwitting the odds. We must try to stay ahead of him. If we could only get hold of *his* battle plans that would be a coup.'

'I have people working on it, sire. We might be able to do just that.' Ammuna saluted and backed out of the room.

Chapter Forty-three

'**S**hush! I think there's someone at the door,' Rewa whispered to the young woman lying in bed next to him.

'I didn't hear anything,' she answered.

'I'm sure I heard scraping. It might be your mother. Do you think she suspects?'

Whoever it was on the other side of the door tried opening it. The wooden barrier across the door held. 'I know you're in there you young trollop,' the old woman's voice came from the other side. 'Come out at once,' she demanded.

'Keep quiet, she's only guessing,' Rewa told his companion softly.

'Raiysa, you come out of there or I'll knock the door down,' the old woman threatened. This was followed by something heavy hitting the door. '*Argh*! How dare you! *Ouch*! Get away from me.' The noises came from the corridor, from the old woman. 'Don't you come at me with that...*argh*...*you*... you...you've done...for me....' A thud came as of a body falling.

Rewa rushed to the door, lifted the cross-bar and pulled it open. He saw Harep bending over the old woman, using her dirty skirt to wipe his dagger clean. '*What have you done*? *You've killed her*! *Why*?' Rewa was dumbfounded.

'Just before she came bothering and spying on you, she came to see me. Wanted more money—or she'd go to the authorities. Greedy old bitch! Don't waste your time feeling sorry for her. She got what she deserved.' Harep looked at Rewa, standing there with no clothes on. 'Better get dressed. We've got a job to do. We've been here long enough. I'll wait in the kitchen.' Harep turned and went.

Rewa blundered back into his room, to the old woman's daughter lying on the bed, eyes closed.

'Who was it?' she asked lazily.

'Your dead mother,' Rewa told her callously.

He had no illusions about Raiysa. She was after the money she thought he had, he knew that, but did not care. Everybody he had ever met was after money. Why should she be any different? Only for Rewa it grew different. At first he simply enjoyed her body, knowing she was out to trap him. But as the two weeks went, Rewa found he began to care for the girl. They had to be careful the old woman did not find out, but lately they did not even care if they were discovered. Now it did not matter. Harep had seen to that. Raiysa did not react to her mother's death. She had had a difficult life and seen death at close hand. Her mother hadn't been very motherly, beat her at every opportunity. Now she was free, free to go with Rewa.

When the young couple had donned their clothes, they went to the kitchen where Harep was digging into a lamb broth, slurping spoonfuls into his mouth, shovelling chunks of bread on top. 'You're not fit for travelling yet,' Rewa suggested timidly. In the last three days Harep had been walking around, almost his nasty old self. Doing exercises, using the near-mended arm. His ribs were still bandaged but otherwise no one would know that a couple of weeks ago he had been close to death.

'I'm as fit as I need to be. There's a job to be done, or had you forgotten?' Harep looked lewdly at Raiysa.

She looked away awkwardly, eyes on the floor.

'No I hadn't forgotten.' Rewa moved in between Harep and the girl, shielding her from his gaze.

'We'll stay here the night, then head down to Ankuwa in the morning—if that's all right with you?' Harep kept shovelling the spoons to his mouth, dribbling some down his shirt.

'It's fine by me. Only one thing. She's coming with me.' He pointed at Raiysa.

'Please yourself!' is all Harep said.

But he said it in such a way as to make it menacing. Rewa took her hand and they went back to their room, firmly putting the cross-bar back in its place.

*   *   *

'Now don't get jumpy but I need to know.' Harep was riding just ahead of Rewa and Raiysa and turned on his horse to look at them. 'While I was laid up, you didn't tell anybody our business?'

'What d'you take me for? Course I didn't! I knew you'd kill me if I did.' Rewa's answer had no hint of fear and Harep found that intriguing. Was it the girl that made him so bold?

'That's all I wanted to know. Anything else been happening that I should know?'

'As a matter of fact, there has. The Kaska have taken Hakpis. Oh yea and the black bull's been stolen from the temple, right from under the nose of the high priest.' Rewa did not notice the shock on Harep's face, he just waffled on. 'It was all over town just before that lot fled south. You know, Muwas is back in control of the capital? Well of course you do, all the sentries are back in green uniform. We passed them on our way out.'

'When?' Harep was grim.

'When what?' Rewa asked.

'When did they take Hakpis?'

'Just before Muwas regained the capital. Must be what...three, four days ago. Something like that.'

232

They rode on silently, Harep deep in thought at the implications. Was his money safe? Did the treasurer manage to hide it? Was the treasurer still alive? Who was going to pay him if he did the job? 'Any more news from the town? Hakpis I mean.'

'No! Refugees arrived, said the town was burned and looted. Some got away, but most were massacred.'

All the time Raiysa rode quietly, keeping Rewa in between her and Harep, not looking at the older man. She saw Rewa was always weary of his uncle, always ready to defend himself, as if the old man was about to attack. They were a day out from Hattusas, on their way down to Ankuwa, a place she had never been to. So many recent changes had occurred in her life that she was finding it difficult to adjust to them. She had now linked her life to this young Kaska man and although he seemed to have money; she was unsure of her future. Mother dead; they had buried her under the earthen bedroom floor, in the manner of the olden days. No home to speak of. What was to become of her?

Harep ignored the two young love birds. He wanted to get in to Ankuwa in the company of others, to again misdirect anyone watching for him. But this time he did not use any tricks, camping near the road south, he just waited until travellers going in that direction came past. Then he joined them discreetly, following not far behind. He gauged that sooner or later over the period of a day or so, he would end up in their company, travelling with them. In the evening, he went over to one of the four campfires, wanting to buy some salt, offering a rabbit or two in return; they got to talking and as casually as he could, he moved his camp closer to them. They were an assorted bunch and he was able to fit in nicely. The obvious devotion of Rewa for Raiysa and her for him, made for a talking point.

'Look at them!' one woman commented. 'Reminds me of when I was young.' She looked at her husband and tried to coo.

He scowled back at his elderly wife and tore off another piece of mutton from the spit-roast, waving it at her, before putting it in his mouth.

'They wed yet?' the woman asked Harep.

Rewa and Raiysa sat on the other side of the fire from Harep, keeping close. She cut the meat off for Rewa and tried to feed him playfully.

'Not yet! Soon though. I'm hoping to get one of the priests in Ankuwa to tie the knot,' Harep answered amiably. It was in this genial company that Harep reached Ankuwa the following day.

Chapter Forty-Four

The wheel marks of the wagon hauling the statue took Mokhat and Palaiyas north-east towards the spot of the Kaska ambush. Thanks to Palaiyas' tracking skills, he was able to tell how old the tracks were, how heavy the load was, how many were in the escort and even if they were Hatti or not. Mokhat could only marvel at such tracking talent. Palaiyas went out front a good hundred cubits so the following twenty soldiers would not interfere with his tracking.

This was the morning of the fourth day of their trek and Mokhat was uneasy they had been gone so long. Who was keeping an eye out for Harep and his nephews? At this rate, Tudhaliyas could be killed and he could do little to stop it. On the plus side, he was coming closer to home. It was a puzzle as to *why* the black bull statue was being taken up here. What was in the thinking of those taking it north? It should have been on its way back to the capital, yet here they were not far from a Hittite town called Gaziura.

'Look, there,' Palaiyas pointed at a lot of broken soil, letting the rest of the group catch up. 'Blood on the ground. Someone's been killed or injured here. See, the hoof marks change. I'm not familiar with those but they considerably outnumber the Hatti. Mokhat, this is your area, can you recognise them?'

Mokhat came and looked at the spot Palaiyas was pointing at. 'Hmm! Seems like my lot. Could be they've taken them prisoner. Just the sort of thing they'd do.'

'No!' Palaiyas told him. 'The Hatti have been released and sent back the way they came. The wagon's been taken. If this is your lot, then they've got the black bull. This is getting most peculiar.'

'Most! What on this earth do they want with the statue of Taru?' Mokhat was baffled.

'The tracks veer off in that direction,' Palaiyas swung his hand towards north-west. What's there?'

'Only...Nerik...they're taking it to Nerik! That's the only explanation. This is easier than I thought. My brother will hand it over to us and we can take it back down to Ankuwa—he'll even provide an escort.' Mokhat was certain of it. The following day around noon, having spent an uneasy night under the stars, Mokhat spied a wagon being driven at high speed towards the Kaska capital.

'*The bull will never survive that bashing, what a waste*,' Palaiyas shouted at Mokhat.

They watched the wagon jumping over boulders, speeding over hillocks, wobbling from side to side with the high speed and Mokhat urged his horse to go faster, hoping to catch up with the hundred or so riders. All were throwing up dust in their wake as they hurried to get to their destination. Then some of them noticed they were being pursued and they attempted to increase their speed. Some twenty riders peeled back to intercept their followers. Mokhat, out front, met up with the twenty rearguard and they stopped. Palaiyas rode up with his twenty Hatti and found Mokhat deep in conversation with the leader. Suddenly one of the Kaska went charging after the wagon.

'I've explained who we are and sent one of the men after the wagon to halt it,' Mokhat informed Palaiyas.

Palaiyas noticed all the Kaska glancing deferentially at Mokhat as if he were due respect. 'Do they know who you are?' he asked.

'Yes. They'll do as I tell them. Most of my people know me. They're surprised to see me, but that's to be expected. Now we've to choose whether to go on to my brother's capital, or turn round at once. Palaiyas, we can go and say hallo to my brother, or go straight back and hand over the bull to Tagrama. I'm going to let you decide.'

Palaiyas couldn't resist going to Nerik to meet Mokhat's brother. They were so close to the Kaska capital that he made the choice to delay returning the bull. 'It'll only be one day's delay, won't it?' he excused his decision.

'Only one day,' Mokhat agreed.

'And it would be such a shame for you not to see your brother again, wouldn't it?'

'Yes, I suppose so,' Mokhat went along with the teasing. Mokhat was riding ahead with the Kaska leader on one side and Palaiyas on the other. The twenty rather nervous Hatti soldiers tried to keep close to the wagon carrying the black bull deity of Hatti, surrounded by a large Kaska escort. They had cushioned the statue with lots of leaves against further damage. Shortly, they reached the shallow valley with the river running through it and caught sight of Nerik in the far distance nestling against the hill on this side of the river.

'Beautiful but foolish,' Palaiyas commented. 'I've noticed this is the second town that seems not to care about its protection. Do they know something I don't?'

'You mean the lack of a town wall,' Mokhat affirmed. 'It doesn't need one. A wall on the side of a hill is virtually useless as a defence. The castle has a wall, but it stands against the cliffs. If the town's attacked, the people leave. Used to be a Hatti religious centre, now it's our capital. You'll like my brother, down to earth; a no nonsense sort—and I think he'll take to you.'

'I hope you're right.'

They entered the town and the white Hatti uniforms drew a crowd. The townspeople hadn't seen Hatti uniforms in its precincts for a long time and the anachronism reminded the older folk of the bitter struggle that had taken place for the town all those years ago. They rode down the main street and up through the castle gates. The sentries had been forewarned the king's brother was coming and all stood at attention.

King Kasalliwa, dark features beaming, was on the steps waiting to receive his brother, but that he was waiting surprised Palaiyas. 'Welcome brother, doubly welcome...but tell me...oh it can wait.' Kasalliwa embraced Mokhat.

'Brother, may I introduce a friend of mine, Palaiyas. Our roads crossed and our paths are now as one.' Palaiyas came forward and knelt on one knee before the Kaska king.

'Please, any friend of my brother doesn't need to kneel. You are welcome! Come let us go up and have some refreshments. I can see you've come a long way.' The king led the way inside. When they were seated at a table in the grand hall, wine and food in front of them, Kasalliwa turned to his brother, 'You know I'm always glad to see you, but what are you doing up here? Have you dealt with...you know who?'

'Palaiyas knows all about our friend Harep—and no—I still haven't found him. Tudhaliyas is on the lookout and has doubled his bodyguard, as have the other two targets. No, we are here because of what's in the wagon which came with us.'

Kasalliwa was confused. Although he had had word brought to him that his ambush band had taken charge of the Hittite deity, he was at a loss as to what the statue was doing so far north away from the Hatti capital. 'I need someone to explain the background to me. Well?' He looked to Mokhat for the explanation.

'I'll start with the Mittani stealing the statue of Taru.....'

The lengthy explanation had Kasalliwa smiling and then chuckling at the bizarre goings on. 'So Muwas wants to change to the Mittani religion, does he? I think he must be unbalanced. I've never taken to the man, nor his father before him.'

'So you see dear brother, we have to take the statue back to Tagrama. It strengthens the cause we are supporting. Don't you agree?'

'Yes. Pity! We could have got a sizeable ransom for its return.'

'Not from Muwas.' Mokhat was adamant.

'No!' But Kasalliwa continued counting shekels in a daydream.

'And we wouldn't want to ask for ransom from Tudhaliyas, would we?' Mokhat looked quizzically at his brother.

'Well, all right! Take it back to Ankuwa. But tonight we feast and make merry. You can go in the morning. We shall show our hospitality...by the way... where's your friend from?'

'He's an Ahhiyawan...far to the west. I've taken a liking to him and him to me. So for the duration of this assignment, we will work together to stop Harep. All I ask from you is an escort of say fifty warriors to accompany us down to Ankuwa. I think the Hittite deity warrants such an escort.'

'You have it! Now—*MUSIC!*' Kasalliwa shouted down the hall at the top of his voice.

*　　*　　*

239

Mokhat and Palaiyas rode in silence, each nursing a hangover from the festivities. Each jolt of the wagon, each stamp of the hooves seemed to be a hammer blow in their heads. Even the late spring bird song overwhelmed their senses.

'I liked your brother,' Palaiyas whispered to Mokhat as they rode side by side.

Mokhat offered his water skin to Palaiyas. 'And he took to you. He thinks you complement me. He hopes you'll be an effective bodyguard.'

Palaiyas took the water skin and gulped the liquid trying to dilute the contents of his sour stomach. 'It'll take us roughly three to four days to get back to Ankuwa. Tagrama must be worried out of his wits.'

'At least we'll return his statue. My big concern is Harep.' Mokhat was really worried. He knew some of the tricks the assassins used and people simply did not expect anyone would be so underhand as to use such outlandish methods. 'He'll be sneaking around trying to get past the guard—I hope they're good enough.'

'It's no use worrying at this distance. You can't do anything,' Palaiyas soothed.

'Maybe I can. I've had a thought. What's slowing us down—is this blasted wagon. If we left the wagon and raced ahead to the valley, we'd be there in half the time. Then we'd be there if Harep tried anything.'

'What, leave them to find their own way?' Palaiyas wasn't sure.

'Yes, the Hatti soldiers know the way. We'll take ten of the Hatti with us just in case and leave the other ten with my Kaska. What d'you think?'

'I wish it was some other day than today,' Palaiyas was thinking of his hangover. 'Well if we must, we must. You go tell your Kaska leader the plan. Make sure they stay on friendly terms with the Hatti. I'd hate to find a wagon full of dead bodies coming down to us.'

Mokhat gave Palaiyas a meaningful look, as if to say that couldn't happen. But he still told the Kaska commander to treat these Hatti as friends and allies.

'Make sure the Hatti soldiers replace their white tunics with yellow ones when you get past Hattusas,' Mokhat advised his Kaska leader.

They checked their water and rations, made sure those to go with them did the same, then picked out fresh horses and all twelve made a dash for Ankuwa.

Chapter Forty-Five

'**K**ing Shunashura of Kizzuwatna and his son, Prince Talshura and daughter, Princess Nikal,' announced the Hittite Chamberlain. It was the first night back in Ankuwa and Kantuzzili had invited the Kizzuwatna royal family to join the Hatti king for dinner, to discuss the coming battle and the failing engagement. They seated themselves round the long cedarwood table, waiting for the food to be served. Tudhaliyas looked at Nikal, but she firmly avoided his eyes, determinately looking down at the table. He looked grim and sad at the same time.

Shunashura raised his hand, 'I've had a message from Adaniya. There's been an attempt made to attack our capital by Lukka pirates but they've been prevented by an Egyptian squadron protecting the river entrance. Not that I don't appreciate the Egyptian presence, but how is it they're there?' Shunashura looked at Kantuzzili and waited.

Kantuzzili's piercing eyes met Shunashura's and the former smiled. 'I might be able to enlighten you as to how the squadron came to be there. When Prince Hapu presented his credentials, I sent a message to pharaoh asking him to send a squadron. If I could try to outflank the Mittani, I saw no reason why they wouldn't try to do the same to us. Our ally is Kizzuwatna and so I assumed that was where the danger lay. Who could be induced to attack them? To me it seemed obvious, the Lukka pirates are the scourge of the eastern part of the great sea and I saw them as the natural danger. A little Mittani gold...well you know what happens...'

Shunashura smiled. 'I suspected as much and you have my people's gratitude for such a farsighted move. I see now that your reputation is well deserved.' Shunashura stood and went round the table to Kantuzzili, who also rose from his chair. The Kizzuwatna king embraced the master strategist in a show of real appreciation. Without a word Shunashura returned to his seat and lifted his goblet of wine. 'I propose a toast to our victory.'

All those round the table drained their goblets. The chamberlain appeared in the doorway and asked, 'Sire, is it a good time to serve the food?'

Tudhaliyas looked at Kantuzzili, who answered, 'Presently. Give me just a little more time.'

The chamberlain nodded and retreated. Servants refilled the wine goblets.

Kantuzzili continued, 'This is a night for announcements—so I give you another one. I've sent an invitation to Muwas to join battle with us in two weeks time at a place seven leagues south-east of Hattusas and eight leagues north-west of here. I should have asked you before I sent the invitation,' he looked at Tudhaliyas, 'but does that meet with your approval?'

'And about time, too,' retorted Tudhaliyas. 'I approve wholeheartedly.'

King Shunashura smiled at Kantuzzili. He said, 'We came to support you, not to dictate strategy. If our master strategist thinks it's time to settle matters, then I on behalf of my army also agree wholeheartedly.'

'Good! The decision was taken as a direct result of what happened with the king,' Kantuzzili lowered his voice, 'and the horse on the way down here. The pressure of inaction is getting to us all and we must settle this. It's dragged on long enough.'

Tudhaliyas looked embarrassed but Nikal looked interested.

'That's settled then,' Kantuzzili looked around the gathering and beamed at them. 'I've already warned General Zidanta to be ready. He says he knows of the area and isn't all that happy. It's still not flat enough for his chariot regiments to manoeuvre. He says he's going to send a thousand men to get rid of the stones and boulders littering the proposed battlefield. He wants to flatten the ground as much as possible. I think he's worried his much-loved Taru regiment isn't going to perform at its best.'

Everyone round the table smiled at such preparations. No one had ever heard of the like. It all felt a little like a game. Preparing the ground, inviting the enemy to join battle at a time and place of mutual consent. But then it was a civil war and the unusual was becoming commonplace. By mutual agreement the rivals for the throne had come to the conclusion that if they were to stave off foreign invasion from their neighbours, the army of the Hittites had to survive. One slaughter was to decide it all and the winner acquired all the opposition's armed forces without reprisals. After the battle only one Hittite army was to survive.

Kantuzzili continued, 'After dinner, I would like to discuss the hiccup in the engagement, if that's acceptable with everyone here?' He did not wait for an answer and said, 'But now we eat,' and he motioned to his chamberlain to begin serving.

Chapter Forty-six

A camp had been set up for all the many refugees that followed Tudhaliyas to Ankuwa. Harep occupied one of the numerous hide-tents allotted to the poor migrants and was mightily pleased to be so anonymous among them. He deliberately dressed poorly, as was Rewa and Raiysa, so as not to arouse attention. To date, Raiysa hadn't an inkling of what the two assassins were up to, why they were in Ankuwa and Harep warned Rewa not to blab to her—or else. On the second day of their arrival, Harep began to look for a way to get at the Hatti royal family. 'I think I have an idea,' he confided to Rewa when they were alone in the tent.

Raiysa had been sent out at noon to buy provisions from the bustling marketplace. The valley hadn't been so busy with merchandise in a long time. Forty-two thousand soldiers and then there were at least five thousand refugees living in the valley. It stretched the food supply and the ensuing sanitation to its limits.

'What? A way to finish the job?' Rewa looked furtive and lowered his voice.

'Even if we only get one of them, its one step nearer to finishing *and* being paid.' Harep told him.

'So what's the idea?'

'I've been scouting the villa they're staying in,' Harep informed him. 'There's another villa nearby. I want you to set fire to it—then leave the rest to me.'

Certain areas of the valley were off limits, places like the head of the valley so as not to contaminate the drinking water. Soldiers were stationed there after the Loros business. All the areas around the royal villas were guarded day and night by large contingents of bodyguards. Anyone approaching had to have an incredibly good reason to be there. Harep had watched carefully and made mental notes when they were there the previous time. No one got in or out of a tight ring round the villas.

'I acquired this,' Harep pulled a sack from the corner of the tent, 'the last time we were here. I was getting ready back then, but then we had to leave the valley and I buried it. Just been to collect it.' He emptied the sack and laid out the contents.

'It looks like a soldier's tunic, yellow for this lot,' Rewa commented. 'So, what're you going to do with it.'

'Stupid, its not just any tunic. I bought it from a bodyguard. The kilt is a little more fancy and there's a red braid round the bottom of the tunic. That's what distinguishes the bodyguard from the rest. I'm not going to tell you the rest of the plan—just in case. You don't need to know. Just set the villa on fire and I'll do the rest. Make sure there's lots of smoke. I want it seen from a long distance.'

Rewa nodded, implying he would do as he was told and knowing Harep, he did not ask any more questions. 'Just point out the villa and I'll do my best,' he answered.

'Your best had better be good,' Harep stared at Rewa with menace, 'because this is too good a chance to miss. We won't get another shot at them as easy as this. They'll be even more on guard if this succeeds.'

'I'll do what you want. It's in my interest as well as yours,' Rewa stared back grimly.

'I want to do it tonight, so in the afternoon we're going to go and scout the villa I want you to burn. It's just on the edge of the out-of-bounds area. We'll reach it from the blind side. That'll give us a chance to get inside. We'll probably have to deal with the owners and servants, no matter how many. Bring your sword. Once we clear the villa of people, you stay inside until the last quarter of the sun is just about to go below the horizon. Then make it blaze in the twilight. That should get their attention.'

Rewa listened to the plan and guessed that the fire was to be a distraction.

'As soon as you've set it ablaze, get out of there quickly. Head back here. Now listen—when your girl comes back, before we leave for the villa, I want you to give her this.' Harep pulled a small pouch from his robes and gave it to his nephew. 'Put her out for the night.'

Rewa undid the tie and smelt the contents.

'It's only a sleeping potion,' Harep told him. 'I don't want your woman to get nosy or be awake while we're doing this. With this she'll sleep till we get back. By then you'll be at her side as if nothing was amiss. No arguments—this has got to be done.'

Rewa saw the sense of the plan and reluctantly agreed.

* * *

The cordon of royal bodyguards faced the front of the villa—so Harep and Rewa climbed into the villa over the back wall from the far side of the out-of-bounds area. They crept through the garden until they reached the edge of the house. A servant was on his hands and knees fishing debris out of the pool in front of the portico. Harep crept up behind catlike and slit his throat, holding on to his mouth so he wouldn't cry out. Then both went through the house looking for any more inhabitants. An old woman in the kitchen was left in a pool of blood—Rewa's work. In another room, the elderly owner was dispatched by Harep. Three more servants died without remorse, one male, and two female. That cleared the villa of its inhabitants.

'I'm going to leave you now,' Harep told Rewa. 'If any more visitors arrive, you know what to do. Remember, when the last quarter of the sun is just about to go below the horizon—make it blaze in the twilight. Get all the cloth, soak it in oil—that should get their attention.'

'Right Unc, leave it to me.' He hadn't used the short "Unc" since Parap's death.

Harep noticed and seemed pleased. Then he disappeared back into the garden and slipped quietly over the back wall.

Chapter Forty-seven

Kantuzzili sat in quiet conversation with Himuili in the sun room, making adjustments to various plans on the coming battle. Tudhaliyas paced up and down like a caged lion, frowning. What was he to do about Nikal? How was he to approach her? She hadn't spoken to him since the horse incident. What could he do to bring her round—to explain? Nothing he tried seemed to help. '*What the Yarris am I to do*?' he exploded, feeling at the end of his tether. The coming battle combined with Nikal not speaking was driving him to desperation. What was he to do? He glanced at the garden through the open door and saw twilight fast approaching.

Himuili looked concerned at his son's anguish, but he felt powerless to help. The stubborn streak in the Kizzuwatna princess rebuffed every approach made to her. She wanted to forgive, but seemed unable to forget the incident. Holding on to it almost as a reason not to continue the engagement. Not for the first time, Himuili thought she was really afraid of the responsibility that went with growing up. The looming duty of a marriage was frightening her. She was using the incident merely as an excuse to delay and postpone.

A commotion from the front of the house began to intrude on the three men and Tudhaliyas went to investigate. He returned shortly to announce, 'There's a fire across in the other villa.'

Kantuzzili and Himuili leapt to their feet. They followed Tudhaliyas out into the portico. They could just see over the garden wall, a dim light visible in the dusk as the last vestiges of the sun began to set. Kantuzzili grabbed Tudhaliyas as he tried to go down the garden path to the front gate, but Himuili was already striding down it. The gate stood open and bodyguards milled around inside and outside. Some were across the road looking at the fire increasing as the villa was consumed by flames. It lit up the surrounding countryside. Himuili was so intrigued that he stuck his head out of the gate, then took a few paces to stand behind a bodyguard trailing a stick in his right hand. His ankle brushed the stick and he felt a small scratch. '*Mind what your doing with that*,' Himuili berated the guard.

'Sorry your honour,' the guard turned and apologised.

'Be more careful!' Himuili glared at him.

The guard moved away swiftly going towards the fire, then turned and walked off at right angles to the blaze. Himuili watched the guard thinking, *he's afraid of retribution and rightly so.* Then he frowned. *What the Yarris was he doing with that stick, clumsy clot?* He felt a twinge in the ankle and bent to rub it. Without meaning to, he keeled over and fell heavily. *My goodness, what's wrong with me?*

Guards saw the king's father fall and rushed to help. From inside the gate, Kantuzzili watched, horrified, but he held onto Tudhaliyas in a premonition, gripping his arm tightly as Tudhaliyas tried to pull away. Bodyguards carried Himuili into the garden and up the path and only then did Kantuzzili let the king's arm go. They took the already delirious Himuili into the house and laid him on the couch.

Tawana rushed through the doorway and shrieked, '*What's happened*?' She came to him and dropped on her knees by his side. '*Hurry, call Tagrama, now!*' she yelled. 'Can't you see he's very ill? My poor darling, what have they done to you? How did this happen?' she asked.

Kantuzzili ordered one of the bodyguards, 'Go fetch Tagrama, urgently. *Hurry man, hurry*!'

No one knew how had it had happened? One moment Himuili was standing watching a fire, the next instant he lay ailing. Tudhaliyas was kneeling by his mother, holding her, one hand round her shoulder, the other holding his father's arm. He could see the life force leaving his father's body, drained by some unseen spite of the gods.

During Himuili's funeral pyre, Tudhaliyas' grief was plain for all to see and although his eyes stayed dry, his heart was crushed by such a heavy blow. Nikal stared at him in open compassion, while the pyre burned, although Tudhaliyas was in no fit state to notice. 'There, there, mother, we all miss him. You knew this might happen,' he was attempting to calm his mother, who wailed in unison with Gassulawiya; one for the loss of her beloved husband, the other in overt empathy.

Kantuzzili silently wept for the loss of a close brother and his hunched shoulders seemed to indicate he had been trampled by such a cruel misfortune. General Zidanta's watery eyes glistened in the evening haze, while his features remained grim. The huge sombre gathering of all ranks from the army held downcast faces, all come to pay their last respects. The brightness of the pyre, high flames lighting up the night sky, was overshadowed by the dimness of spirit of those present.

After the funeral, Nikal wanted to go to the king but felt awkward and did not think it the right moment to initiate moves for reconciliation. But she so wanted to tell him she understood, that she felt for his loss, that she was sorry for her earlier stubbornness, that of course she wanted to be with him—always.

Chapter Forty-eight

Two days after leaving the wagon, Mokhat and Palaiyas accompanied by the ten Hittite soldiers finally reached Ankuwa. A sizable group of sentries were strung across the entrance to the valley, gruffly checking all incoming traffic. They stopped Mokhat and his party and demanded they all dismount. Dirty and tired they began to object to this treatment, especially their Hatti soldiers. However, it soon became clear to Palaiyas that some significant incident had changed their behaviour and produced this edginess. He nudged Mokhat to be quiet and waved down his accompanying soldier's objections. 'Don't get angry—something enormous has happened here while we've been away,' Palaiyas told Mokhat.

'Oh no!' Mokhat exclaimed, thinking the worst. He caught the attention of the senior officer in charge. 'Is the king all right? Please tell me he is.'

The Hatti officer looked at the dishevelled band seemingly led by a priest, 'The king's safe and sound. Who are you? Why d'you want to know?' he demanded.

'We're on a mission to bring back the statue of Lord Taru to Tagrama,' Mokhat explained. 'There's a wagon coming through here in a day or so with the statue. There'll be about fifty Kaska and ten more Hatti with them. Make sure they're taken straight to Tagrama.'

'Who authorised this "mission"? Who d'you answer to?' The officer wasn't convinced.

'We answer to the king. We are under his direct orders. Please escort us to General Zidanta—at once.' Mokhat was getting fed up of the obstruction.

At the mention of the name of the chief of the army, the officer's manner changed. He became cautious and less abrupt. 'Please remount and follow me. I'll take you to him.'

'First, tell me what's happened here? Why all these precautions?'

'Orders from above. After the murder of the king's father, we've been ordered to search all who come in and out of the valley. How long have you been away?'

The latter information forced a sharp intake of breath from Mokhat. 'I was afraid something like this might happen. I told you, didn't I?' He bemoaned to Palaiyas. To the officer he said, 'When did this murder happen?'

'Three days ago. The funeral pyre was two days ago.' The officer wouldn't go into details since he still wasn't sure who these people were. The party arrived at the heavily guarded royal villa escorted there by twenty aggressive looking sentries.

At the gate of the villa, the general was sent for and arrived with a big smile on his face. 'I'm pleased to see you. Mind you, it could have been under better circumstances. I gather you've heard the bad news. Come inside and I'll tell you what happened.' To the ten soldiers that had accompanied Mokhat and Palaiyas on their long journey, 'Rejoin your regiments. Good work!' To the officer of the escort, Zidanta nodded and ordered them back to their posts.

'I said to Palaiyas, I was afraid something like this might happen. I said Harep was good, didn't I?' All this was said in a sombre soft tone.

As they walked to the house, the general told them about the fire and the scratch Tagrama found on Himuili's ankle. 'Poisoned! And only with a small scratch. Who'd believe it?'

'I'm afraid I would,' said Mokhat. 'I can't emphasise this strongly enough. The assassins are not to be underestimated.'

'We haven't,' the general insisted. 'The bodyguards were alert and doubly strengthened. After a lot of questioning, they claim to have seen no one. How he managed to do this baffled us for a time.' They reached the house and stopped in the portico.

'Yet Harep did manage to do it,' Mokhat reminded him. 'You say the bodyguards were alert, but now I want you to make certain each bodyguard knows the guard next to him, by face and voice. Every so often they must check each other so no stranger slips in.'

'That last bit you just mentioned,' Zidanta affirmed, 'seems to link with the only conclusion I can draw; one of the bodyguards wasn't a bodyguard. No other stranger was seen in the vicinity, but if the killer was dressed as a guard, no one would notice. If that was the case, it would mean this Harep of yours infiltrated the area dressed as a bodyguard and carried out the deed. There's no other explanation I can come up with— and Tagrama seems to be of the same mind in my analysis. Now with what you've just said, you've virtually agreed with us.'

Mokhat shrugged and nodded.

'But now you're here, I want you to carry out your own assessment. Question all the bodyguards yourself. Get to the bottom of this.' The general's face was grim.

Mokhat though for a moment, 'I'd like to add one more process but I warn you its going to be laborious.'

'If it helps to find the killer, especially after this murder, we'll do it. What is it?'

Mokhat paced about a bit and then stood facing the general. 'I want to visually check every refugee in the valley—and I mean *everyone*.'

The general was startled, 'Are you sure? That *is* going to be a big job.'

At that moment, the king and Kantuzzili came out of the house to join the general, he nodded towards Mokhat and Palaiyas. They seated themselves in the portico and immediately servants came out with squeezed fruit drinks and bowls of fresh fruit. Tudhaliyas looked downcast and when he did glance at the Kaska priest, to Mokhat there seemed to be a hint of accusation in the stare.

'I'm unhappy your majesty for not being here when I was most needed. I'm also extremely sorry for your loss. Words are inadequate, but I do apologise for my absence.'

Palaiyas kept quiet—he tried to blend in with the background while all this was talked about. It was Mokhat's concern, Kaska king to Hatti king.

'Oh! It wasn't your fault,' Tudhaliyas said quietly. 'There were bound to be casualties in what we embarked upon. More of us may die as yet. The battle is not yet begun. It just seems a shame that my father went the way he did, taken like a sneak thief stealing valuables in the night. If I am to die, then let it be in battle facing the enemy with a sword in my hand. This way of poisons seems so sordid.'

*　　*　　*

The following day after Mokhat's return, Tudhaliyas' sorrow broke and transformed into outright anger—not at any particular person, but onto everything in general. Talshura had brought back news the king was shouting at his servants, his chamberlain, but especially at his bodyguards. At hearing this Nikal called for her chariot to be brought round and resolved to visit Tudhaliyas—no matter what the outcome. Talarra as always, insisted on coming on the white knuckle ride to the nearby royal villa. A servant met the Kizzuwatna princess in the portico and rushed to fetch Gassulawiya.

'I'm so pleased you've come. I wish you'd go and talk to him.' Gassulawiya said to her, without needing to say who she meant.

She directed Nikal to the sun room where Kantuzzili sat looking out into the garden, gazing at his nephew sitting with his back to him on a bench, staring up at the sky.

'I came to apologise and try to console him. I'm sorry I've been so obstinate.' Nikal was almost in tears.

'There, there. Hush now,' Gassulawiya comforted. 'He's out in the garden, ever so wretched and lost. Go to him. Soothe him—he needs you now more than ever. Only you can bring him out of this despair.'

Tawana sat miserably, head in her hands, softly shaking in anguish, missing her husband. Gassulawiya guided Nikal gently towards the garden and went to sit by Tawana.

Hesitantly, Nikal stepped through the portal towards her beloved, but even then she still held back. Seemingly coming to a definite decision, her steps became firm and her bearing more erect. She walked over to Tudhaliyas and put a hand on his left shoulder. 'I'm sorry,' she said softly.

At hearing her voice, he turned and for an instant frowned with no comprehension. His thoughts were so far away, that it took an effort to bring them back to earth. Then he jumped to his feet. '*Nikal*...my love. You've come at last. You've no idea how I've missed you.' He held out his arms—and she glided into them, resting her head on his shoulder.

'I've been such a fool,' she murmured, then sighed contentedly at being so close.

'And I,' he whispered. 'Now I might be able to bear the pain.' He did not need to explain, she knew he meant the pain of his recent loss.

'And I will help you, I promise,' she asserted under her breath.

'You know I didn't mean to hurt the horse.'

'Shush, my love. I know you didn't. Don't talk— just hold me.'

They stood for a long time holding each other— feeling each others closeness. Inside the sun room Gassulawiya held Tawana's hand and pointed at the young couple in the garden. For the first time since the death of her dear departed partner, Tudhaliyas' mother gazed at them and smiled.

*   *   *

When the wagon carrying the black bull statue pulled up outside the temple in Ankuwa, Tagrama and Mokhat was waiting with impatience to welcome the Lord Taru back to the arms of his believers. The Kaska leader of the convoy dismounted and ordered his fifty followers to dismount. The ten Hatti soldiers with him did as they wished; they were back with their army. Mokhat went to embrace the Kaska leader of the convoy, they spoke quietly for a short time and Mokhat came and told Tagrama, 'He's tired and hungry and I've suggested they rest up here outside the temple, if that's all right with you?'

'Why of course! I'll get some priests to bring food and since there's not that many, I'm sure we can find shelter for them.' Tagrama ordered a priest to get food for two hundred—he assumed they had be able to put it away.

Mokhat thanked the Hatti soldiers for their efforts and told them to rejoin their regiments. Then he helped

Tagrama, who was supervising the off-loading of the statue.

'I'm overjoyed at having our deity back. You don't know what it means to me.'

'I think I do, otherwise I wouldn't have made such an effort to retrieve it.'

'Yes, of course, thank you. Thoughtless of me really! Please be sure to thank your brother and the convoy leader for all their efforts. I won't forget this.' Tagrama watched a large group of his priests take the statue up the pristine regal paved ramp then down the naos to the dais, where it was carefully positioned back onto its devotional plinth. 'Now we'll have to ritually cleanse it,' he told Mokhat who had followed him inside.

'It's survived quite well, hasn't it?' Mokhat reflected.

'Yes! The Lord Taru protects his own. I would have expected nothing less.' It was the voice of conviction. 'The purification ritual will be held tonight,' Tagrama informed the priests surrounding him.

Mokhat took that as the cue to go find Palaiyas. Both were deeply involved in organising the check of the entire refugee population of the valley.

Mokhat made a suggestion to General Zidanta that all the refugees be herded to one end of the valley and then funnelled through a single channel to where Mokhat would check the entire refugee population one by one. It was the only way he knew of ensuring a thorough inspection of each face. Harep would not escape this time. If he was in the valley and Mokhat was pretty sure he was, this time he would be caught. Harep and both his nephews were now trapped, Mokhat felt quite certain. The hills were surrounded by soldiers, nothing could get in or out without scrutiny. One by one, the refugees were pushed and forced through a narrow passage enclosed by a fence constructed for the purpose. Each person was looked at, made to uncover their heads.

'Even if it takes all night and the next day,' Mokhat declared to Palaiyas, 'I'm taking a good look at each and every one of them.'

The senior Hatti officer in charge overheard the comment and scowled so his men could see. He did not like being part of the detail and would much rather have been training his troops for the coming battle. Mokhat noticed. 'What's the point of fighting for your king if these assassins manage to do away with him? Think on that while you're scowling.'

Suitably rebuked, the officer went to his work with extra gusto, pushing more refugees up to Mokhat for examination. Many reeked to high heaven, encrusted with dirt and crawling with fleas. Some even had festering wounds, others were ill with racking coughs. To Mokhat, some of those people looked dreadfully ill and he felt compassionate enough to send them to the group of priests he had asked Tagrama to supply for just this purpose. They would tend to their wounds or minister to their ills. The processing of so many took until the evening of the next day and by then all involved were exhausted. Yet Mokhat found no sign of Harep and his nephews.

*   *   *

As soon as Harep carried out the assassination of Himuili, both he and Rewa returned to their tent, grabbed all their belongings and collected a drowsy Raiysa, then fearing a morning curfew and blockade, they hurriedly left the valley during the night, climbing into the surrounding hills. The poor girl was half carried on Rewa's shoulders and had no idea why they had to travel in the dark, why they had left the tent, or where they were going. They made good their escape going high up into the hills and into the next valley, hiding high in a small cave, probably a bear's hibernation hole. The next day they watched from a vantage point, soldiers surrounding the Ankuwa valley, cutting it off from the outside world. Their foresight had put enough distance between them and that valley so they were outside the ring of steel ordered by Zidanta.

Harep guessed why the soldiers were ringing the valley. He knew they would screen everybody in the valley in an attempt to find the killers and Harep laughed in delight. 'One down, two to go,' he joked with Rewa.

By then, Raiysa had completely recovered from the drowsy potion, but on the advice of Rewa, she kept her mouth closed.

'The next scheme involves an even bolder move,' Harep continued. 'I want to see if we can ingratiate ourselves into King Shunashura's household, possibly as gardeners or something similar. We'll claim we've been sent by the Hatti king. I'll claim to have special skills in this type of soil, which the king thought might be useful. You'll be my helper.'

'But why the Kizzuwatna?' Rewa asked.

'The Hatti will be expecting another attack from us. Each deception succeeds only once per target—that's the rule. So if I want to go after another of the Hatti royals, I'm going to have to outflank them by getting them to come to me. The Kizzuwatna won't be expecting us.'

This had Rewa intrigued.

Chapter Forty-Nine

For once in all the recent troubles, Muwas was at a loss as to what to do. In a recent talk with Artatama, the Mittani prince brought news that the general he had put in overall charge of his army had seriously disobeyed his orders. Instead of destroying the statue of the old religion, he had absconded with it—to only he knew where. But why? What in the name of Yarris could he possibly want with a statue of a black bull? Muwas had little choice but to ask General Ammuna to explain himself, but he couldn't very well lambaste him in front of people without compromising the general's standing with the army. He did not have another general nearly half as competent as Ammuna and so with caution, Muwas invited the general to come and see him. Apart from being angry, he really was curious as to why the general had disobeyed his order.

The general knew by the summons that he had been discovered. And so with a heavy heart, he spruced himself up to look his best and went to face whatever the king was to dish out. The summons had been to the room behind the throne room, for which Ammuna was thankful. It wasn't to be a public humiliation. It gave him hope. He marched in and saluted. 'Your majesty wanted to see me?'

Muwas was sitting and bade the general sit. 'I think you know why I sent for you. I must say, I'm a bit disappointed to find my leading general disobeying a direct order.'

Ammuna kept his eyes front as if he were on a parade ground. His seated posture was at attention.

'I need to know—why? I *must* have an explanation. Well, general?'

'Sire, may I speak freely?'

'You have my permission.'

The general relaxed a little, 'I couldn't in all conscience follow an order which your father assuredly would not have given. You know how I feel about the Mittani presence and the danger I feel they pose to our very existence. You've turned on the Lord Taru in anger at Tagrama's betrayal of you, but our ancient religion is not to blame—only Tagrama is to blame. But the people won't understand and will see this as an abandonment of our long religious tradition.' The general saw Muwas was actually listening and seemed thoughtful. He saw a chance of talking sense and threw caution to the wind. 'I was hoping that you might eventually change your mind about switching to the Mittani religion. It isn't just the people of Hatti but the common soldier that I was thinking of. Our soldiers already feel as if they have little to fight for. A large Mittani army sits at Hattusas' gates. Their foreign religion has replaced ours in our main temple. To them it *is* an occupation. If that wasn't enough, they're expected to go and lay down their lives for this foreign ascendancy. Sire, I know we have to put up with the Mittani presence, or we lose this conflict, but why must we put up with their religion?' The general paused; he needed feedback to see if he were getting through to the king.

Muwas' brow creased and uncreased in a long silence. He spent an eternity sitting quietly, thinking while the general watched out of the corner of his eye. A messenger arrived at the entrance and Muwas waved for him to wait there until he had finished. Finally Muwas said, 'If you win this coming battle, General Ammuna, I will not only absolve you of this gross disobedience, but

I will restore the Lord Taru to his rightful position in Hatti's religion. Now go before I change my mind.'

The general's face beamed with the decision and he jumped up. 'Sire, I *will* win this battle for you. I will win it for the soldiers and people of Hatti. Thank you for making such a wise judgment. I will not fail.' He smartly exited.

Muwas noticed an extra spring to his general's step. He made a decision and then beckoned the waiting messenger. 'What have you for me?' the king demanded.

'Sire, I have mixed tidings.'

'Good news first,' Muwas ordered.

'One of the brothers is dead, I mean Himuili. Assassinated! It just came up from Ankuwa. It happened some days ago.'

'Huh! Finally! Now *that's* made my day. One less usurper to worry about. And the bad?'

'You gave orders to locate the black bull statue.'

'Yes....you've found it? Where is it?'

'Sire, it's been taken back to Ankuwa and the report has it—back in the temple there. Our spies have seen it.'

Muwas' whole demeanour changed to fury as he heard this. '*Go! You're dismissed. Get out*!' he shouted. To himself, Muwas angrily resolved that after the battle, he would deal with his general's disobedience once and for all.

* * *

Muwas made ready to join his troops and lead them down to the agreed battlefield. 'We've been over the deployment a number of times,' Muwas conferred with General Ammuna. 'One last time, are you confident this'll work? I don't want any slips. If I go down, you go down, make no mistake.'

'Your majesty, it will work. It's a classical manoeuvre. Strength in depth in the centre and we'll slice right through them. From what I gather, they're weak where we are strong. We outnumber them and with this deployment we stand a better chance in beating them.' Ammuna was quietly confident. 'We start with the standard barrage of archers and slings, then they retire to the back. This is followed by the chariot charges, first from the right flank, the Ininas Chariot Regiment led by me and then on the left flank the Mittani led by General Shurra. That will demolish the front ranks of their infantry. Then General Satukani charges his Mittani infantry into the enemy infantry and the spears are hurled at the right time. With our might we will overrun their infantry like an avalanche running through a forest and the field will be ours at the end of the day.'

Muwas looked meaningfully at his general, 'I hope you're right, for your sake.' Muwas had called General Sahdaz in, he of the disastrous skirmish, to give him his orders personally. 'General Sahdaz! Remember some time ago, I promised you a rotten job and now I intend to keep my promise. This day will be your chance to show your mettle. You are to lead the Hittite infantry in the centre of the field. You'll be behind the Mittani but I expect you to push the Mittani forward onto the enemy's swords. They will do the hard work and you will make sure they do.' They were all ensconced behind the throne room with General Ammuna making final arrangements for the coming encounter.

'Sire, I will do as you command. It is an honour to serve you,' General Sahdaz insisted. The general simply couldn't see how the enemy could withstand such a concentrated onslaught in the centre. Bearing in mind the deployment of the forces, he actually expected to come out of this alive. The infantry would slice through the enemy centre with its superior slashing power and end up chasing Tudhaliyas down to Ankuwa.

Muwas earlier had reminded Ammuna that he *needed* to win and Ammuna had understood the implied threat. The affair of the statue now strained relations between them. Muwas could no longer trust his senior general to unquestioningly carry out his orders.

'Sire, we must leave now. The Mittani prince is waiting,' Ammuna prompted the king.

Artatama was breaking camp, looking back at the tall grey walls of Hattusas, waiting for Muwas to join him, reforming his army into marching order near the Yellow Castle. Cavalry fanned out in front on the lookout for ambush. Each regiment followed by its baggage train. Infantry marching in open order five abreast. The rearguard following its baggage train. Artatama was to lead the lengthy convoy down south to the wide plateau whilst the Hittite forces would follow, since that was how they were to deploy when they got there. When Artatama was informed that Muwas had come through the South Gate he ordered his column to move forward. General Ammuna would follow the Mittani and Muwas rode ahead to join Artatama and ride at the front of the combined army.

Chapter Fifty

Standing in the dawning sun before Zidanta, spread in a fan shape, were fifty-four Hatti and twenty-six Kizzuwatna regimental commanders, waiting for him to give them their orders. 'Fellow countrymen…and assuredly—welcome allies… we are ready. Today we leave for the battlefield… and if the agreement holds, by tomorrow evening we will have decided who sits on the throne of Hatti. I for my part will do my utmost to see that the insignificant entity calling himself Muwas does not ascend it.' A roar came from the generals to support his sentiments. 'The time for strategy is at an end. Now we tacticians take over. Each of you have been given the plan of battle and the position your regiments are to take on the field. Make sure you secure that position. Know who's on the right of you and who is on your left. Listen to orders and above all—fight hard and make sure your men fight hard.'

From the pavilion tent behind Zidanta, King Tudhaliyas emerged. Faces swung in his direction and Zidanta guessed why. With the Hittite king came King Shunashura and Prince Talshura of Kizzuwatna, then Tagrama, the high priest of Hatti.

'*I give you King Tudhaliyas the First*,' Zidanta shouted.

The crowd responded, '*King Tudhaliyas the First!*'

Tudhaliyas joined Zidanta on the small rostrum.

'*My fellow soldiers*,' Tudhaliyas' voice seemed to thunder, 'I will join you on the battlefield and together we will restore the rightful line of descent to the Hatti throne. We have two murders to avenge, my grandfathers, King Huzziyas the Second and my fathers, Prince Himuili. I will not rest until that false king is with Yarris.'

Another prolonged cheer went up from the generals.

'Now I hand you over to our high priest to say a few words. Tagrama?' Tudhaliyas stood aside for the high priest.

Tagrama's thin tall frame lifted itself to its full height, 'I greet you in the name of the Queen of the Land of Hatti, Queen of Heaven and Earth, mistress of the kings and queens of the Land of Hatti, directing the government of the King and Queen of Hatti,' Tagrama intoned. 'In the name of the Great Storm God of Hatti, Lord Taru, I place his bolt of power into your arms and call on the god of war and victory to support your just cause. May you be victorious. *Tudhaliyas the First*!'

Another great roar of approval emanated from the regimental commanders. The crowd answered, '*Tudhaliyas the First*!'

'Now my fine comrades, to your regiments, we leave shortly,' boomed Zidanta.

As the generals dispersed to their regiments, the king led the way back into the pavilion. Tagrama quickly made his excuses and returned to the temple to perform a rite to victory, leaving only the king, Kantuzzili, Shunashura, Talshura and Zidanta having a goblet of wine. 'One last time, general,' Kantuzzili spoke, 'take me through the plan of battle. I want to make sure I didn't miss anything. Indulge a feeble old man,' he cajoled.

The general was only too happy to oblige. 'The way I see it developing is this way. I'm assuming Ammuna will follow his normal ploy—remember I know him well—and go for a huge overkill in the centre by deploying his numerical superiority in infantry there for a hammer blow. He will try to crush our centre line, trying to overwhelm my infantry and hope to rout us. This is after the initial slings, spears and archers have had their go. I've prepared for his central thrust and I hope he doesn't disappoint me by doing something different. As you are aware, this battle is a bit strange in that we've agreed the place of battle beforehand—the wide plateau almost halfway between Hattusas and Ankuwa. I'm letting him make the first move and that will be a charge by his chariot regiments. I've cooked up a little surprise for him there. I've often wondered how to stop a chariot charge mowing down so many infantry at the outset. Now I think I have a solution. Anyway, my intention is to put my infantry into a bow formation facing outwards towards Muwas and as his infantry forces mine back, the bow will buckle and reverse. We move back and pull him forward into the crescent. I have given our Kizzuwatna allies,' Zidanta bowed his head towards the Kizzuwatna royals, 'the job of securing our flanks. We will be on the outside of the crescent, with the enemy in the centre. My cavalry on either flank will force the envelopment and surround him—and hopefully that will be the end of Muwas and his Mittani allies.'

'What about their cavalry, won't they attack and disrupt your flanks?' Tudhaliyas asked.

'Sire, we are weak in infantry but have a superiority in cavalry and our cavalry have been given the task of protecting the flanking Kizzuwatna—and of suppressing their cavalry. There should be three battles going on. The envelopment of Muwas' centre; then separate left and right flanks struggling to turn each of their counterparts. If for some horrendous reason either of our flanks is compromised, we will be in deep trouble. Our two thousand infantry are to be kept in reserve for just that predicament. They of course will be supported by the archers, sling throwers and spearmen, who are then to fight with their swords.' Zidanta stopped and waited for the expected mauling. He was disappointed. No mauling ensued.

The master strategist smiled and nodded. 'I knew we'd picked the right man for the job. General Zidanta, I compliment you on a fine plan. If the enemy deploys as you expect, I see no reason why your plan should not succeed. Congratulations!'

The general looked pleased. 'I'm gratified it meets with your approval. Now if you'll excuse me, I must get ready.'

'Just one moment,' Tudhaliyas cut in. 'I have made my decision—I intend to position myself out front where all my soldiers can see me—where the leader is supposed to be.'

'*Sire, no! I cannot permit this*,' Zidanta exploded. 'I cannot be responsible for your safety if you lead in the centre. Even with the Mešedi protecting you. There will be horrendous slaughter there.'

'How can I expect my troops to fight for their king when he skulks at the back afraid to fight for his own cause?' Tudhaliyas said to Zidanta, but stared at Kantuzzili, who kept quiet.

'No one suggests, no one dare suggest you are afraid. The king always directs from the rear so he can have control of the reserves,' Zidanta pleaded.

'General, you know Kantuzzili will do that task. I'm superfluous at the back—but I can have a huge impact on moral out front. As the commander-in-chief of the army, I must insist. That is my wish and my command.'

Zidanta pleadingly looked at Kantuzzili in the hope he would intervene, but Kantuzzili knew his nephew. He had never seen him so determined and knew deep down the king would have his way.

'We must accept the king's command,' he said fatalistically and then winked at Zidanta so the king did not see.

*   *   *

The drawn out solemn cavalcade led by Tudhaliyas, Kantuzzili, riding with Zidanta, followed by Shunashura and his son, Talshura, slowly emptied out of the valley heading north to settle matters with their arch enemy Muwas. In a couple of weeks, Tudhaliyas was thinking, the great festival of the Summer Solstice would be celebrated, the mystical time when the day would be at its longest and the night at its shortest and he was determined to be in Hattusas standing with the high priest in the Great Temple rejoicing in his victory over his rival by then. In his mind there could be no alternative. Moving at a steady pace, the troops marched through the morning haze just after dawn when the dew was just rising from the ground in a sweet mist. Tagrama had prophesised clouds for the day of battle, but then he was on safe ground, since it had been unusually cloudy for the past couple of days. This was the third time they had travelled along this now well worn road. Some were thankful it was to be the last time. In the humid heat of the day, they spent the whole of the day getting to their destination.

It was late afternoon when they climbed onto the wide plateau via the southern route and found to their amazement that Muwas army was already encamped at the northern end. The apprehension level of the troops rose noticeably with minor arguments breaking out among the soldiers for the smallest of reasons.

A lone rider was seen approaching bearing a white pennant, signalling he wished a truce. When challenged he said he had a message from King Muwas for Tudhaliyas.

'Now what the Yarris does he want?' General Zidanta exclaimed. 'Pass on the order to bivouac here for the night,' he told his aide-de-camp. 'This is going to be the strangest night of my life—what with the enemy so close.' The rider with the white-flag was shown to General Zidanta. 'Well? What does your master wish to say?' he demanded.

'It is only for Tudhaliyas,' the enemy officer replied.

'It is *King* Tudhaliyas on this side of the plateau and if your man has anything to say, spit it out or get back to where you belong before I lose my patience with you.'

Muwas' messenger wavered but finally understood he would not be able to see the enemy king and blurted out, 'King Muwas gives you one last chance to renounce your false claim and save your lives. Leave by morning and he will spare you—stay and you will suffer the consequences.'

'Return and tell you master the same. Repeat what you have just said word for word. Add that if he likes the Mittani as much as he seems to, he may leave with them when they depart.' Zidanta waved his hand at the enemy officer in dismissal. The officer pulled at his reins and encouraged the horse back to Muwas' lines. No more messages arrived and none were sent. The time for talking had passed. The next morning would be a time for shedding blood in large quantities.

*   *   *

Mokhat placed the fifty Kaska now accompanying him under Palaiyas' command. He was far better at controlling soldiers and had far more experience at such things. They were encamped with the Mešedi under the direct orders of General Zidanta. The general had confided in Mokhat that he wanted them to carry out a dangerous mission directly involved in safeguarding the king. He would tell them what the mission involved just before the battle in the morning. For now they were comfortably ensconced amid the baggage train, stuffing food into their mouths, comforting their bellies.

'I wonder what the old fox wants of us,' Palaiyas put to Mokhat as they relaxed in front of the campfire.

'He'll tell us in his own time. I must say, I'm none too happy at being in the middle of a battle tomorrow. I know this is where Harep's targets are and so we have to be here, but Harep isn't likely to be able to do any mischief, not with them surrounded by so many of his own people.'

'The king's father was surrounded by all those bodyguards and that killer managed to get to him,' Palaiyas reminded.

'You're right,' Mokhat had to agree. 'Still, I wasn't intending to put my life so obviously on the line as to end up in the centre of combat. Even at this late stage I'm trying to figure out a way of standing on the sidelines tomorrow and still look out for their safety. On principle, a Kaska should not have to physically fight for a Hatti. And this is the worst case scenario; both sides are Hatti.' Mokhat was grumbling more out of nerves at the coming conflict, than any sense of cowardice.

'What are you two up to this time?' a familiar voice asked.

'Sire, how quietly you came upon us,' Mokhat quickly answered. 'We were just reflecting on tomorrow's battle. If you overheard...I meant nothing personal.'

'That's all right. We're all full of anxiety for tomorrow. I'm delicately making a tour of the camp...you know...moral,' Tudhaliyas informed them. 'Letting them see the king is with them. A few words of encouragement... calming them. By tomorrow evening it will all be over. We can get back to peace and reconciliation.' The king patted Mokhat reassuringly on the back and moved on through the camp, stopping here and there to talk with the troops.

'Don't worry so, my Kaska friend,' Palaiyas said with a smile. 'I'll look after you. I'm used to this situation. I think in the pre battle manoeuvring, we might be able to find a way of outwitting the fates.'

*   *   *

The next day dawned as cloudy as the day before and both sides were thankful for small mercies. Were the sun high in the sky, their work would be twice as hard in the burning heat. Abandoning his baggage train to the rear, Muwas deployed quickly and early, setting his men to banging their shield trying to intimidate the opposition. The din became ferocious when a little later Zidanta's men were doing the same. It was as if Yarris himself had appeared on the wide plateau. Then the most peculiar message was sent from the gods on high. The ground began to tremble and shake, yet the plateau was one solid flat piece of granite and no breaks or rifts became visible. The banging of the shields ceased abruptly and a grinding and grating of the earth broke into the deathly silence. Horses reared, throwing their riders and the reins of the horses tethered to the chariots had to be held near the horse's mouth so they wouldn't stampede. All the troops sat down on the hard rock surface so as not to be thrown off their feet. The tremor lasted for the time it takes to climb on and off a horse—then it stopped.

Tudhaliyas went out front as soon as the ground stopped shaking and turned to face his men. '*Soldiers, fear not, it is a sign that the Lord Taru is angered by the false Muwas and his Mittani religion.*' As Tudhaliyas spied Tagrama coming through the massed ranks, he pointed, '*Look, our high priest has something to say to you. He will confirm what I've just told you. This tremor was sent as a warning to our enemy over there,*' Tudhaliyas pointed at Muwas' army.

Tagrama managed to shove, push and stagger out to where Tudhaliyas stood. He raised his frame and voice as high as he could, '*I've just heard the king explain to you that the Lord Taru is angered by the false Muwas. This is true! I had a vision in the night when the Lord Taru stood before me and warned me that the ground would shake just before the battle. "Be not afraid," he told me, "for I am angry with Muwas for abandoning me and turning to false gods. Tomorrow he will pay for his sacrilege." That is what I saw in my vision. The shaking of the ground is an omen for our success. Fight hard and we shall be victorious.*'

'*Hurrah!*' the army shouted. '*Hurrah! Hurrah! Hurrah!*'

Tagrama saw the ploy had succeeded and he made his way back through the ranks to the back. Tudhaliyas went back to his position with a smile on his face.

Chapter Fifty-one

Back in Ankuwa, Nikal was in the garden of the villa when the tremor occurred. She and Talarra were making wedding plans, what each would wear and who needed to be invited. Suddenly servants screamed at the top of their voices. A cat tore across the garden terrified. The house rocked and the big walls cracked, the garden walls fell apart revealing the countryside around the house.

'Mistress, we must get further into the open,' Talarra urgently insisted.

'This way, your highness,' one of the gardeners suggested, leading the way through a gap in the partly demolished wall. Another gardener joined them and they hurried out into the road near the villa. They sat down out in the open. The tremor stopped—and Nikal had a rag thrust into her open mouth and a cloth tied quickly round her cheeks. It happened in a flash. Her arms were pinned behind her back and tied tightly. She lost her eyesight as darkness descended when a sack was forced over her head. Talarra screamed but the scream was cut of in mid cry. Rewa had a rope round Talarra's neck and was tightening it. Soon only the limp body of Nikal's maid remained.

'Quick, give me a hand to lift her,' Harep ordered Rewa. 'Better still, you lift her and I'll help her over your shoulder. The donkey should still be where we left it if the tree is standing.'

Harep led Rewa carrying Nikal over his shoulder down the road to where a bucking donkey was straining to get free.

'I'll quieten the animal,' Harep told Rewa.

'*Hee-haw*! *Hee-haw*!' brayed the terrified donkey. 'Long eared lout! Stupid, obstinate animal!' shouted Harep. 'Stay still will ye,' he yelled while pulling at its reins. The struggle to calm the animal went on longer than Harep was comfortable with. He feared that someone would come and inquire what on earth they were doing. Worse, someone might come and give them a hand. Harep wanted to be away from the valley as quickly as he could manage before guards regained their wits and came looking for the princess. The villa had been well guarded, but who could have foreseen the walls tumbling down like that? Harep couldn't believe his luck. It took both Harep and Rewa to calm the kicking donkey.

Nikal lay struggling on the ground with the sack over her head. Then they heaved her face down over the back of the animal and calmly walked along the road as if they were going to market with some produce. They had prepared for this eventuality but the problem was always the same. How to get her out of the house and past the ever watchful guards? Not far away in open country, they had rented a small barn from a farmer, one of the original inhabitants of the valley. They had stabled four horses there. The farmer asked no questions when he saw the twenty golden shekels Harep offered. Now, they made their way to the barn and then left the donkey feeding on the hay inside. They had left Raiysa to live in the barn while they inveigled themselves into the Kizzuwatna royal household.

'We've got to get well away from here,' Harep voiced while he readied his horse. 'I'm taking her across the river, up into the high mountains. We'll pick up more provisions on the way. This may turn out to be a long trip but if what I plan comes off, we'll go back to Hakpis and look for our gold. Are you with me nephew?'

'What about my woman?' Rewa asked.

'What about her? Is she with us?' and he watched his nephew carefully for the right answer.

Rewa knew that look, 'Of course she is. She's with me all the way—come what may. She's sworn as much.'

'Good! Then there's no problem. She can cook for us when we get to where we're going.'

Cautiously avoiding any habitation, Harep led the little band ever northwards from Ankuwa, up towards Kaska country. He held Nikal's reins tightly, leading her horse and Rewa rode side by side with Raiysa, whispering soft reassuring words to her. They had been travelling for two days and were nearing Gaziura, the town prior to Hakpis. 'I'm tempted to stop off here,' he threw over his shoulder to Rewa. 'It's supposed to be for Muwas, you know, like Hakpis was. But we'd better go round just in case.'

'Right'o Unc!' Rewa replied. Rewa had been cooperative ever since he had met this girl of his. For Harep it was most congenial, not having a sullen nephew anymore. Rewa had done as he was told and done it well. The sullen Rewa, Harep promised himself, he would do away with when his usefulness was at an end. This new Rewa was agreeable and he changed his mind. This one he would let live.

While Harep was mulling this over in his mind, the gates of the town were thrown open and a large body of riders came out, heading directly for them. 'Quick, into the woods!' Harep ordered, jerking Nikal's reins in that direction.

Rewa and Raiysa followed into the thick broad-leafed trees close behind Harep. They waited until the soldiers drew near and Harep saw someone dressed in white Hittite priestly robes stare deeply at where they hid, then they rode past and disappeared into the distance. Only then did they emerge from the forest.

'That was close. Did you see who it was? That bloody king of theirs—and he had a bunch of Kaska warriors with him. He can't be looking for his wench already, can he?' Harep mused.

'Maybe he was, but then how did he know we were up here?' Rewa asked.

'He doesn't. We haven't left a trail—and I haven't left the message yet. I thought of doing it here in Gaziura—but now I'm not so sure. Got to think this over. Let's get out of here,' and Harep cantered in a wide circle round Gaziura, in an effort to avoid being seen from the walls of the town. They continued on the road to Hakpis and eventually arrived there in the evening. The town was still a mess. Some people had returned but they were forced to camp outside the walls because of the chaos inside the ruined town. 'We'll camp out here too,' Harep told the group. 'Get your woman to start the fire and food.' Harep dismounted and pulled Nikal from her horse. She struggled half heartedly but was too frightened to put up much of a fight. 'Watch her,' he ordered Rewa, pointing at Nikal. 'I'm going to have a look around—see what the situation is.' Harep went through the burnt-out gate and into the town. The light was fading and he walked with his entire senses alert for any sign of aggression. A few scattered people searched through the rubble. Rats scurried everywhere, the town seemed to have been taken over by them. Some wild dogs and feral cats roamed about wearily eyeing each other. Decay had entrenched itself in the burnt out buildings. Scattered lights came from some, as if someone was intent on reoccupying the abandoned town, but in general, the town had been temporarily forsaken.

Unburied bodies still littered the streets and alleyways, twisted into the positions they had fallen, rat gnawed half eaten faces making for a nightmare scenario. Harep tiptoed around them, careful where he put his feet. He made his way to where the treasury building had stood. The top wooden floor had burnt and the inside was gutted. Hardened as he was he had seen enough, the stench was overpowering. He made his way quickly as he could back the way he had come, back to where Raiysa was preparing the evening meal of porridge and whatever else was left of their provisions. The welcoming glow of the fire couldn't entirely erase the horror of what he had witnessed.

Chapter Fifty-two

Muwas had made a similar declaration to his troops after the tremor, claiming, 'Even the gods are angry with those upstarts for daring to oppose the rightful king of the Hittites. This shaking of the earth is a warning that they upset the natural order of life by murdering the rightful king and demanding the throne be given to them.' His troops needed to hear such words of comfort and they cheered just as loudly as when Tagrama had told the similar tale to his side. Both armies again took up the shield bashing with a gusto seeming to want to imitate the god of thunder. Then when they had had their fill and were satisfied with the loud statement, a lull descended—as deathly as though they had been transported to the netherworld. The lull before the battle.

Both sides eyed each other from a distance of three hundred cubits that being the closest the front line archers stood to each other. A mass of yellow flanked by scarlet confronted massed lines of dark blue and green. Behind the archers stood the sling throwers, who on a good day could lob their pebbly projectiles almost as far as an archer could shoot an arrow. Spearmen were placed behind the infantry line so they could hurl their spears when the lines had closed to around seventy cubits. The silence lasted for an eternity and then the battle was precipitated by both commanding generals, Zidanta and Ammuna, both finally ordering their archers to fire their first volleys. Almost simultaneously the sling throwers hurled their rounded stones into the enemy frontline infantry. Yellow and dark blue tunics fell. Archers reloaded and fired volley after volley as did the sling throwers. More casualties fell on both sides when arrows and stones missed the raised protective shields. That accomplished, the archers and sling throwers of both sides retired to the back of the infantry for the next phase of battle.

Ammuna led the Ininas Chariot Regiment in a charge against the enemy front row, gathering speed all the time as he approached their lines.

Tudhaliyas stood a few paces out front and yelled to the front line, '*Wait!... Wait!.. .Wait!... Wait!...... Wait!...*' and all the time the chariots hurtled closer. Then at the last possible moment, he shouted, '*Now!*' and long thick sharpened logs were lifted by four infantry men in yellow tunics so the pointed end faced the oncoming chariots while the back end was jabbed into a slanted hole to absorb the shock of impact. As the poles came up, the archers loosed a volley at the charging enemy chariots. Horses and chariots were impaled on the long projecting logs in the most gruesome fashion. Tangled and speared green clad bodies mingled with wood in a nightmare scenario. Arrows hit their mark embedding in human and horse flesh. Although the sky was cloudy, the ground was dry and the chariot charge threw up a massive dust cloud, obscuring the horrendous carnage from their Muwas' front lines. To add to the mayhem, archers, sling throwers and spearmen hurled more volleys at any remaining chariots, for the rear chariots actually managed to avoid the logs by veering wide and heading back to their lines.

While Ammuna was snared by Zidanta's new invention, the eight Mittani chariot regiments on the left flank, led by General Shurra, began their attack as agreed, unable to see clearly the outcome of the first charge. This chariot tactic was well practiced and rarely failed, so there was no reason to think the first charge hadn't succeeded in mowing down the frontline infantry. Only when they reached the protruding sharpened logs did they find themselves in the same horrifying predicament. Again the spearmen, archers and sling throwers fired into this blue clad assault by the second column of oncoming chariots, causing considerable casualties. Ammuna in a fit of prescience, had ordered his driver to veer sharply to the left, wishing to observe the damage his chariots would do and so avoided being snagged on the logs himself. Being so close, he watched in astonishment and utter rage at the effect the logs were having on his chariots and turned to try and stop his Mittani counterpart making his charge.

Unfortunately the cloud of dust obscured the fact that General Shurra was already in full sprint and hurtling towards his unseen doom. Ammuna's chariot missed the oncoming chariots of General Shurra and ended passing them in mid field arriving back at his own lines shocked and furious that his opponent had outwitted him. He ordered the driver to swing the chariot towards his frontline. As he did so, Zidanta's Taru regiment came out of the dust to sweep along the Mittani frontline. They caused the classical expected carnage and in return received the arrows and projectiles from Muwas archers and sling throwers, leaving many more bodies behind on the battlefield. Zidanta himself received an arrow through his upper arm while the shield man was busily protecting the driver, which now lodged in his left bicep.

Ammuna sped along the deep blue of the Mittani front line shaking his fist—and as he approached the Mittani commander he yelled, '*General Satukani*! *Forward... forward...get your men moving.*'

The Mittani infantry gave a chilling battle cry of "*Teshub*!" and rushed forward, charging towards their opponents. Ammuna then sent his chariot driver chasing after what was left of the shattered Hatti chariot regiments and ordered them to regroup round at the back of Muwas. He intended to use them as a reserve to plug any weaknesses which might occur.

Chapter Fifty-three

Zidanta's well-trained yellow tunics faced Artatama's deep blue battle line, ready to receive the Mittani attack. Mokhat peered into the distance and just managed to glimpse the sea of deep blue Mittani infantry rushing towards him through the settling dust. He turned to Palaiyas and gave a prearranged signal. It was at this point they were to carry out the secret order from Kantuzzili and General Zidanta to bustle the king away from the front line. The Mešedi had specific orders not to interfere but instead to help in the manoeuvre to protect the king from his own recklessness. Mokhat moved closer to the king. '*Sire, sire, a crucial message from Prince Kantuzzili.*' Mokhat had to shout into the king's ear above the din. '*He insists you come to see him now. He says it's a matter of extreme urgency and will have a catastrophic effect on the outcome of the battle. Please sire, we are to escort you.*'

Tudhaliyas had probably expected some kind of ruse to pull him out of the front line. On the other hand this just could be genuine. He could not tell. He shrugged his shoulders and followed Mokhat—his Mešedi held drawn iron scimitars right behind him, pushing infantry aside. At that moment the front line began to surge forward to meet the Mittani charge and only due to the hefty wedge of two hundred and fifty soldiers allocated to this particular task were they able to make headway towards the side of the infantry formation, out to the right flank. The fifty Kaska and the two hundred Mešedi led by Mokhat and Palaiyas pushed their way steadily sideways until they came out near the scarlet clad Kizzuwatna infantry on the right flank. Then they made their way up the alley in between the yellow and the scarlet to where Kantuzzili sat proudly on his horse at the back of the huge deployment. 'Well uncle, what's so urgent that you had to drag me out of the middle of the battle?' Tudhaliyas demanded as he strode up.

'When a soldier falls in battle it is a regrettable casualty,' Kantuzzili told him looking down from his horse. 'When the king falls, it is the end of the reason for the battle. I'm in charge of strategy and I cannot allow you to throw this battle away by getting yourself killed at the outset. If you insist on acting like a young fool, then as the senior member of your family, I have little choice but to step in and safeguard you.'

As Kantuzzili had begun saying this, the king's face turned into a scowl and a furious look took hold—but near the end of the admonishing speech, Tudhaliyas began to look sheepish. 'I suppose you're right. Only I so wanted to be with my men—to suffer as *they* do on my behalf. But I do see the sense of what you say. If I fell, that *would* be the end of the reason for the battle...all right, uncle...you win. I'll stay here safe and sound and watch my men get killed.' True to his word, Tudhaliyas did watch. He watched the infantry of both sides close to seventy cubits and spears being hurled by either side inflicting more carnage. When the two sides clashed it was simply slaughter at an unprecedented rate. Yellow clad Hatti and blue clad Mittani infantry hacked at each other with axes, scimitar swords, until blood soaked the ground making it slippery and bodies piled up, becoming obstacles under foot. Slowly but surly the yellow bow shaped formation of the Hatti frontline began to give way and straighten out amid increased butchery.

The overwhelming weight of the Mittani infantry, pushed forward by Muwas Hatti infantry behind them, began to compel the bow shape to buckle inwards and still the carnage continued. Then a resurgence of the bow formation threatened to disrupt Kantuzzili's and Zidanta's plans. They had relied on the bow buckling inwards but the ferociousness of the fighting coming from Tudhaliyas' Hittite line began to push the Mittani back onto Muwas' infantry. They in turn pushed the Mittani forward and the bow began again to buckle as intended by Zidanta. Watching from the back, Kantuzzili sighed with relief as he saw the plan reinstated. When the battle had been well and truly joined by the centre, cavalry units on either flanks stormed forward trying to engage their counterparts. If they could defeat the unit in front of them, they might be able to swing inwards on the exposed centre and act as a hammer to the infantry's anvil. Unfortunately for each side both flanks held. General Zidanta had a superiority in cavalry on either flank and that held Muwas' cavalry in check.

On Zidanta's left flank the Wurusemu mounted archers fired volley upon volley into the midst of the Mittani cavalry facing them. The Wurusemu were supported by Prince Talshura and Commander Anuwu with fifteen regiments of scarlet Kizzuwatna cavalry. It was an unequal struggle and Zidanta's left flank began to turn inwards demolishing the Mittani horse. Only the timely intervention of General Ammuna with the remnants of the chariot regiments prevented a Mittani cavalry rout. General Shurra took command of the flagging Mittani cavalry and fought out in front like a man possessed. His example gave new heart to his men and they revived to make greater efforts. The twelve cavalry regiments under General Labamulis on Zidanta's right flank were creating havoc with the five defending Hatti cavalry regiments who were desperately attempting to hold the line. General Ammuna held the archers and sling throwers as a reserve and threw them in to help hold that flank. Again without his timely intervention his left flank would have crumbled. Ammuna was busy at the back propping and plugging up any weaknesses he found. Muwas was shouting from where he sat with Artatama, encouraging and urging him to do better, to do this and to do that, but Ammuna was too busy to listen to such advice. And still in the centre, the slaughter continued well into the middle of the afternoon. By then the bow had well and truly buckled inwards and General Kirruwaiya with his Kizzuwatna infantry on Zidanta's right flank began turning in on Muwas' exposed left flank hemming them in and enveloping them. The Kizzuwatna were engaged in fighting the Hatti infantry at the rear of the Mittani front line.

On the other flank the same was happening. General Tapalass' Kizzuwatna infantry were enveloping Muwas' right flank facing Muwas' Hittite infantry units. The central units were unable to get to grips with the enemy and were useless while the sides were now under heavy assault. They were severely weakened and being taken to pieces bit by strenuous bit. The envelopment envisaged by General Zidanta was in full flow and the ultimate outcome of the battle was clearing in Tudhaliyas' favour. The scarlet Kizzuwatna were seen by Kantuzzili to envelop the green rear of Muwas' infantry. The defenders had to face backwards to resist the assault.

Muwas was horrified when he saw this and he sat stunned into silence on his black horse. Artatama joined General Shurra's cavalry in an effort to stem the tide, but to no avail. In truth, Artatama wanted to be among his own cavalry so that if the worst came to the worst, he could use them to shield and protect his getaway. The separate cavalry battles on each flank were going against Muwas, both flanks were being overwhelmed. The sheer weight of numbers were pushing Muwas' cavalry back and the losses were piling up on the ground. Eventually General Labamulis pushed the remnants of the five enemy Hatti cavalry regiments to where Muwas sat and only then did Muwas draw his iron scimitar sword and join in the fight—but of course, by then, it was far too late. He kept on shouting at his men, '*Fight, damn you, fight!*'

It was all a final desperation—a refusal to admit the inevitable. That the battle had gone against him. Large bodies of his infantry were stuck in the middle of the envelopment unable to use their scimitars, while the edges were being butchered as Zidanta's attackers dug ever deeper into Muwas' packed troops. Some of Zidanta's men began drifting off towards Muwas' baggage train, standing on the northern edge of the wide plateau. A core incentive for any common soldier to fight, whichever side he was on, was not the rights or wrongs of the cause of the conflict, but the possibility of booty at the close of the battle. The wagons were lightly guarded by some sling throwers and archers, the latter picking off the early arrivals with well aimed shots.

Artatama finally gave the command, '*Retreat!*' and his cavalry made great efforts to disengage. Artatama wheeled his horse away and rode off at high speed; followed by around two hundred blue clad, which was all that was left of the five Mittani cavalry regiments of a thousand horse. In hot pursuit were the scarlet of the Kizzuwatna cavalry led by Prince Talshura, General Tapalass and Commander Anuwu, whooping and yelling like a pack of hounds after a boar. At seeing his ally flee, Muwas took flight as well and panic spread through what was left of his entire army, which began to fight desperately to break out of the encirclement. Those that did made a headlong dash after Muwas, were cut down by Zidanta's pursuing troops. The subsequent massacre was directly due to the heat of battle. The slaughter was terrible.

Once the drift towards loot had gathered pace, large groups of infantry and horse began making their way in that direction. They needed to get there quickly as little would come their way if they left it too late. Battles had been lost when what would have been victorious troops, took to looting too early. Their enemy had taken advantage of the looters absence, regrouped and turned the tide. It was always a precarious time near the closing moments of any battle. Muwas' Hittite infantry, when they realised all was lost, threw down their weapons and pleaded to surrender and in most cases the surrender was accepted, but that was not the case with the Mittani. These were foreign invaders. They were butchered to the last man, including General Satukani, who had managed to survive the main carnage in the frontline of fighting by sheer skill of arms. Finally he succumbed and his head was severed, stuck on a spear and brought to Tudhaliyas and Kantuzzili—who were both disgusted but knew that the men's blood lust was of their making and so they accepted the gift with cries of praise and encouragement.

Any of the mounted enemy, or those in chariots, seeing their leaders flee the field, tried to escape as soon as they grasped the situation was hopeless, following in blind panic either Muwas or Artatama. General Zidanta was determined to capture Muwas, seeing him as the cause of all their troubles. The chase divided into a peculiar split, the Kizzuwatna went after the Mittani and the victorious Hittites after Muwas' Hittites who had refused to surrender. Ammuna had fled close behind Muwas taking what was left of the defeated Hittite chariot regiments—which amounted to around three hundred out of the initial eighteen hundred. Prince Talshura had a burning desire to prove himself to his own father, King Shunashura and saw Artatama as a valuable trophy, maybe to be ransomed from King Saustatar, his father, to help fill the depleted coffers. He had seen him leave the field with about two hundred horse and was now in close pursuit. The only possible obstacle might be the coming twilight as the terrible day of battle came to an end.

Zidanta hot on their heels, chased Muwas and Ammuna into the north. Tudhaliyas gathered General Labamulis' cavalry and followed, while Talshura pursued Artatama far into the east heading towards Nesas. Back on the battlefield the surviving combatants were being cleared and the surrendered Hatti prisoners were rounded up and escorted to an area in the western side for processing. Thus the civil war was brought to an end and even with the delay in coming to battle, the losses were atrocious.

Chapter Fifty-Four

Nikal rode hands tied in front and a rope looped through the tie was round the horse's neck so she couldn't lift her hands to her face. She was gagged and a shawl covered her head and mouth, giving the impression from a distance all seemed relatively normal. In this manner Harep and Rewa left the valley, bypassing the normal exit road, heading north uphill along tortuous paths high into the mountains. Raiysa was indifferent to Nikal's fate and made no comment at her treatment, although she could see the young woman was in great distress. They climbed hard. When it became too steep, they dismounted, leading their horses on foot all the rest of the day until they came to the ridge, then followed the crest just below the skyline until they were well away from any pursuit.

'Now I'll tell you what I propose,' Harep told Rewa when they stopped for a short rest, pointedly ignoring Raiysa. 'We're going to Hakpis, or what's left of it and find our money. What d'you say to that?'

What could Rewa say? He wanted the gold just as much as Harep. 'Whatever you say Unc. You're the boss!'

'That's settled then! We're gonna swing round the place they're holding their stupid battle and then head north. I'll be happier when we're home, back in Kaska country. Then we'll send a message to that king of theirs to come and collect his sweetheart—alone. Any tricks and she gets it,' he jerked his thumb at Nikal, sobbing quietly through her gag.

Nikal heard all the conversation but was totally bewildered by her predicament. One minute she had been sitting quietly in her shaking garden, walls collapsing all around her, the next captured by her gardeners and taken prisoner. For a long period she was simply outraged. How dare they lay hands on her, on her royal body? But as the captivity persisted, bewilderment turned to fear and then to self pity. She missed Talarra. She had no idea what had happened to her maid—no idea she had been strangled. Now she lay, cold, hungry and miserable, simply afraid these "gardeners" would kill her.

'Kind of them to have a battle right now,' Harep joked. 'Who knows, Tudhaliyas and his uncle might just be killed! Save me all the trouble.' At the mention of Tudhaliyas' name, Nikal stopped sobbing and her ears pricked up. 'Well looky here, she's listening to us,' Harep looked at the silent princess.

'What if Muwas loses?' Rewa broke into the silence.

'So! Let him lose. What do I care! We have a contract. I intend to fill my part of the bargain and collect the agreed price. What they do to each other is no concern of ours! The contract stands.'

'Hmm! I'll go along with that. What if we can't find the gold?'

Nikal only now understood, listening to the conversation, that she had been kidnapped by those "assassins" she had heard of who were after the Hatti royal family—the one's who had killed Tudhaliyas' father—and she was more afraid than before.

'What if, what if…leave the "ifing" to me. We'll find it. I know that treasurer. *If* the looters didn't find it, then my dear nephew, I will. Now there's an "if" you can think on while we're trudging across these mountains,' Harep almost snarled the last phrase. 'Come on, let's get moving. We can't stay here all night. We're still too close to Ankuwa.'

Chapter Fifty-Five

Fleeing north on Muwas' heels, Ammuna suddenly asked himself, *what the Yarris am I fleeing for? The war's over and the fool I followed lost,* meaning Muwas. He allowed Muwas and his cavalry remnant to forge ahead, increasing the distance between them. All the time Ammuna made hand signals to the other chariots to slow down. Finally he signalled for them to stop. He climbed down and sat by the road side, puzzling those with him.

'Shouldn't we be moving?' the senior of them asked.

'What for? Why are we following that loser? Let's wait for Zidanta, or do you want to be fugitives from now on?' Ammuna lay back on the grass and shouted to his driver, 'Let the horses feed—and put something white on the top of your spear,' he ordered the chariot spear thrower. As he left the battlefield, he had been joined by his personal bodyguard of the select fifty and they stayed near their general for his protection.

General Zidanta wasn't far behind and when he saw the stationary fugitive chariots he wearily pulled up expecting a trick. He noticed the white rag, leapt down from his chariot and strode up to Ammuna, who jumped smartly to his feet. Ammuna ordered his men, 'Drop your weapons. The fighting is over.' To Zidanta he said, 'Congratulations, general. We fellow Hittites ask for your mercy and compassion. We surrender unconditionally,' then he handed Zidanta his sword, hilt first.

General Zidanta looked closely into the eyes of his vanquished opposite number and saw only defeat there—no subterfuge. He took the proffered sword. 'In that case General Ammuna...I accept. Your men must go back to the wide plateau for processing and then we'll see about forming them into another regiment.' Zidanta still looked closely at Ammuna, trying to decide what to do with him. He rubbed his bandaged left bicep where the arrow had lodged. After what seemed like a long time to those nearby, he said, 'Subject to his majesties approval, I'm going to offer you a job—interested?'

Ammuna was taken aback by such an idea. They had been trying their damnedest to kill each other not so long ago —and now here he was being offered a job by his enemy. 'May I ask what kind of job?' he asked cautiously.

'I want you to be my second in command, my deputy. You've proven you can command an army, even though you're not too inventive—but I'll soon straighten you out there.'

That really astonished Ammuna. 'I...I...I don't know what to say...' he stuttered.

'What is there to say...just say yes!'

'But of course...I mean...yes.' He still couldn't believe it. Then he looked quizzically at his new boss. 'If you don't mind—I have a question that's been nagging at me.'

Zidanta frowned, 'What is it?'

'Whose idea was it to defend the frontline infantry with sharpened logs?'

'Hmm! Caught you off guard there, did I?' Zidanta allowed himself a chuckle. 'As a matter of fact, it was mine. I've been thinking of that one for a long time—how to stop one of my chariot charges—wondering if an enemy might come up with a countermove. So I finally came up with that. Impressed?'

'Yes, general, I am.' Ammuna meant that. 'It totally destroyed my chariots. It broke the moral of my troops, seeing their chariots wiped out like that. They kept wondering what other tricks you had up your sleeve...I will serve you well general, I promise that.' And he saluted his victor and commanding officer, as did all those present, a form of respect for the victor of the Battle of the Wide Plateau.

'Now my dear deputy, we must return to the battlefield and sort out the casualties. Although I dare say Kantuzzili's been busy in that respect.' General Zidanta offered General Ammuna his sword back, by the hilt.

*   *   *

Mokhat and Palaiyas were pushing their horses to the limit, riding with Tudhaliyas, when in the distance they spied General Zidanta's large group of stationary chariots. The king came abreast and pulled up. 'How far ahead is Muwas?' he demanded, but then was astonished to see the enemy commander standing next to Zidanta.

Ammuna responded, 'Not far your majesty. You should soon catch him if you ride hard.'

'Right! Everything in order here, general?' Tudhaliyas asked Zidanta.

'Yes, sire,' snapped Zidanta. 'I've just made General Ammuna here, my deputy, if that meets with your approval?'

'As you see fit, general, as you see fit. Congratulations on our victory. See you later. Must dash.' And he was off. Mokhat, Palaiyas and the fifty Kaska had little choice but to hasten after the king. The three hundred Mešedi followed their fast disappearing king with General Labamulis and his cavalry in tow. Tudhaliyas was not about to lose Muwas, not at this late stage. Mokhat had no idea where Harep and his nephews were and they could easily have laid a trap in the aftermath of the battle. In fact it might be just another of those underhand stunts he would pull. The only way to safeguard this king was to stick to him like sap-glue. Never let him out of his sight. They travelled doggedly late into the night until sense finally prevailed and they halted. 'I'm glad your majesty saw fit to stop,' Mokhat almost admonished. 'More of this and the horses would have been useless.'

Palaiyas whispered something to Mokhat.

'Sire, my friend here has an idea. Maybe you could order one of your soldiers to ride to the capital and procure some fresh mounts. While he's there he could proclaim the outcome of the battle—that would give him authority. Get someone else to bring the fresh horses to us. If he heads directly west he should intersect us—wait until we arrive. Our mounts will be done in by then.'

'It's so frustrating,' Tudhaliyas mumbled. 'I should have cut him off before he managed to escape.' He still thought of his own quest to capture Muwas. Then he found a boulder and sat down. 'I was so absorbed by the struggle in the centre of the battle that I passed up the opportunity to get Muwas. I did hear what you just said. I'll send someone to the capital in a bit when the horses have rested. It's a good suggestion. By the way, any idea where Muwas was bound for?'

'No sire. Not to Hattusas, that much is clear. He's swerved directly north and the capital is north-west. Can't be going to Hakpis—although the town supported him—place is a ruin. What about Gaziura? That's where they were taking the statue of the bull.'

'By the storm god, you've got it,' Tudhaliyas exclaimed. 'Gaziura must be his destination—it also supported him. But no matter where he goes in Hatti, he's a marked man. I'm surprised he didn't go with Artatama. I would of in his place.'

'Maybe he's still harbouring hopes,' Mokhat suggested. 'He must be desperate. From king to fugitive in one day. I almost feel sorry for him—mind you—only almost.'

*   *   *

The chase after Artatama was just as bothersome. Prince Talshura had made a mad dash after the departing

Mittani prince and kept him in sight for a long time, but as night fell, he lost him in the darkness. They had no choice but to halt and rest their exhausted mounts on the banks of the minor branch of the Marassantiya River. Six hundred scarlet shirts after two hundred dark blue shirts. They threw caution to the wind and lit a fire despite it probably giving their position away. 'If I were him, your highness, I'd muffle the horse's hooves and walk slowly through the night. Alternately, for all we know they may be watching us right now,' General Tapalass suggested to Talshura.

'Can't be helped,' the prince responded. 'We'll get an early start in the morning. Make sure the men and horses eat and rest. It'll be a long day tomorrow.'

'Yes highness.'

'General! Do you know where we are?'

'I have a map on deer skin. A few were given out by General Zidanta just in case something like this happened.' Tapalass pulled it out of his side pouch and unrolled it. He grabbed a burning branch from the fire and held it so the prince could see. 'If I understand it, Artatama is going back to Mittani through Nesas and that's there,' Tapalass pointed. 'We have to cross two rivers before Nesas, that's assuming we don't catch him before then. We're currently camped on the banks of the first river, here.'

'What do you think our chances are of catching him?' Talshura looked tired. 'It looks like a straight line from here to the Taurus, then on to Mittani. We've got to overtake him somehow.'

'Yes highness, we have to overtake. May I suggest we sleep on it. I'll see if I can come up with something in the morning.' But in the morning the general had little to offer the prince in terms of a plan to overtake Artatama. 'I'm sorry highness, but other than growing wings, there's nothing faster than our horses. I've racked my brains and the only plan of action I can offer is to ride hard and hope something else interrupts their flight to the Taurus Mountains, or they are slowed by events we have no control over.' Tapalass hung his head as if he were stupid for not managing the impossible for his prince.

Talshura commiserated, 'You tried your best, general. Don't feel so downcast. Let's finish eating and then we'll move off. See what the day brings.'

The next morning he insisted on doggedly continuing the chase after crossing the minor branch of the Marassantiya River. Talshura was fuming at not having caught sight of Artatama all day. Since going after him immediately following the battle, he hadn't laid eyes on the fleeing prince. Only his trackers reported they were on the right trail not far behind the Mittani. All through the next day they rode hard hoping to catch sight of the enemy and although they spied a dust cloud a number of times which might have been them, they did not actually lay eyes on them. On reaching the Marassantiya River in late afternoon, the horses were near to dropping and he was forced to call a halt. Not far on the other side of the river lay Nesas. A solid wooden bridge crossed the river to the town but Talshura thought it prudent to wait for daylight before crossing and ordered the troops to camp a little to the side of the bridge. Whatever the rights of his current pursuit, his soldiers were still Kizzuwatna cavalry, while the escapees were Mittani cavalry but both were on Hatti soil. The town might not take too kindly with foreigners settling their scores on their territory.

At the forefront of his mind, Talshura had all the intention of catching Artatama no matter what it took, but at the back of his mind, he had made Nesas a decisive spot. He would review the situation if and when he got there. Now he was only a short distance from it, he was being forced to admit he might not catch the Mittani prince. The thought of him escaping galled. 'I'm going to share with you what are in my thoughts,' Talshura told General Tapalass.

'Highness?'

Both sat cross-legged comfortably round a fire watching the river flow by. A glorious clear evening came on the heels of the setting fiery sun, red as the fire they sat by. A newly caught deer roasted on a spit over the fire and the smell made their stomachs grumble.

'If we don't catch sight of Artatama tomorrow, I'm calling off the chase.' Talshura did not look happy at the prospect. 'We'll head back to Ankuwa and pick up my sister. Then go up to Hattusas. How will that go down with you and the men?'

'Highness, we would follow you all the way to Mittani if you so wished. If you've decided to go to Ankuwa, it will be fine with us. We are at your command.' The general was indifferent where he served his young prince.

The next morning they crossed the wooden bridge and shortly came upon an ancient walled town with open gates, but a town that was in commotion. The sentries were weary of the large group of alien soldiers dressed in scarlet. Talshura hailed one of them, 'We're looking for a bunch of Mittani who might have come through here. Have you any news?'

'*That* bunch of thieves, may Yarris curse them all the way,' the man replied.

'Why? What happened?' General Tapalass added his inquiry.

'They've stolen all our horses. There were too many of them. Took us by surprise—last night,' the man complained.

'Who's in charge here?' Talshura demanded.

'The Watch Officer, through the gate on the right.'

'Thanks,' shouted the general and the troop continued in. They came across someone who was yelling orders at a small group of soldiers. 'Ho there, you in charge here?' the general shouted.

'Who wants to know?' the officer shouted back.

'Prince Talshura of Kizzuwatna, ally of the king of Hatti,' General Tapalass responded.

'Which king might that be?' he said cautiously.

'King Tudhaliyas, sovereign by right of battle,' Talshura told the man.

'Then you're welcome. We've just had a run in with a Muwas ally and we didn't take too kindly to it.'

'We heard on the other side of this gate from one of your sentries. What happened?'

'Bunch of Mittani claiming to be allies came in last night and when we let them in, they ran off with all our good horses. Left a lot of half dead steeds in exchange. Crept out in the middle of the night like thieves. One of them called himself a prince and gave himself airs. Nothing but a brigand, in my opinion.'

'We won't argue with that. We want them as much as you do,' Talshura reassured the gate officer. Then to Tapalass, 'That's it. We're going back to Ankuwa. I hate to let him go like this but with fresh horses we'll never catch him.'

Chapter Fifty-Six

General Zidanta was back on the battlefield, glaring gloomily at the carnage. His soldiers were stripping the dead, piling the bodies on the uprooted sharpened logs used in the battle with the chariots, making use of them for funeral pyres. Most of them were Ammuna's green clad troops and he was just as glum at so many corpses. 'This is what it ends up as—their bloody arguments,' Zidanta spat out. 'They fight over the throne—we die. What a waste! In the coming days there's going to be the sound of much wailing and lamentation in thousands of our homes in this mournful land of Hatti. It's a disaster of considerable proportions to lose so many.'

What could Ammuna say? He felt it even more than Zidanta. 'A total disaster, I agree. But in life we soldiers are hostage to fortune and our lot is that of sorrow when we lose.'

Zidanta stared closely at Ammuna. 'There's a lot more to you than meets the eye at first glance, general.' Zidanta called over one of his officers who seemed to be of Ammuna's size and asked him to get him a yellow tunic for Ammuna to wear. Some of Zidanta's senior officers knew Ammuna by sight and as they toured the battlefield, were astonished to see the enemy commander with their commanding general and even more dumbfounded to see him wearing a yellow tunic. But they obeyed orders and adapted. When Zidanta was satisfied he had seen what he needed to, they went to find Kantuzzili. They found him in a pavilion tent set up amidst his baggage train on the south side of the field. He sat listening to the reports from various yellow and scarlet clad officers. Zidanta strode in followed by Ammuna.

'My dear general, I'm extremely delighted to see you. We're just making a tally of the casualties.' He stopped and stared at Ammuna, frowning at the yellow tunic, then looked to Zidanta for an explanation.

'I've made him my deputy. The king's been informed. We met him in hot pursuit of Muwas. Have you any objections?'

'On the contrary; I approve wholeheartedly. Excuse me, I was just surprised. I was hoping we would begin to heal the rift of this civil war and I can think of no better start to the healing process than this.' Kantuzzili turned again to Ammuna, 'Welcome aboard General Ammuna.' He approached him and held out his hand—they clasped each others forearm.

'Thank you, your highness. I will do my best to serve your family.'

At that moment King Shunashura entered followed by General Kirruwaiya. All in the tent bowed their heads towards Shunashura in respect to the presence of senior royalty. 'Please continue. Don't let me disturb you. I've just come to contribute our casualty figures as requested.' He handed Kantuzzili a clay tablet and sat on a couch while his general stood behind him.

'The final count,' Kantuzzili informed the gathering when he had studied the data given him, 'of the casualties is this. Of the twenty thousand Mittani infantry who took to the field at the outset, not one was left alive. That will teach Saustatar to stick his Mittani nose into Hatti affairs. Five thousand of Muwas' infantry survived out of fifteen thousand. That's ten thousand brave Hittite soldiers dead. The death toll caused to our side was a horrendous seven thousand, not counting the wounded. As Hittites we lost a combined seventeen thousand infantry alone. The army's lost three whole infantry regiments.' He stood silently shaking his head. 'What a shambles—what a waste! Only our enemies can be happy with the outcome.'

'I was never happy with the Mittani being here,' Ammuna said quietly, almost to himself. 'I told Muwas this many times. He answered he had no choice.'

Kantuzzili frowned at the interruption. 'The Kizzuwatna lost three thousand infantry in their ferocious envelopment, according to the clay tablet handed to me.' He paused, then continued. 'They fought well and died... bravely. Of the thousand Mittani cavalry, only the two hundred with Artatama survived. Muwas has around the same number with him and so eight hundred went down—and we lost four hundred plus.'

'This is a day that will go down in infamy in Hittite history. Around forty-four thousand dead in total—not something we would want to put on the wall of the Great Audience Hall in Hattusas,' General Zidanta declared. 'Something needs to be done in the event of a similar dispute. We can't go through this again.'

'Yes general! I know you're right.' Kantuzzili felt the implied blame. 'Tagrama had the solution and I wish we were able to listen to him, but it would only have worked if both sides were receptive. A vote of the nobles. By the way, where is Tagrama?'

Kirruwaiya volunteered, 'I saw him a while ago, ministering to the wounded with some of his priests.'

'Right! We'll have to find a way of building that idea into our succession in the event of the throne ever being in dispute again,' Kantuzzili declared.

'Yes, it seems a long time ago but I remember that idea. At the beginning when all this started,' Zidanta agreed. 'But Muwas would have none of it. He wanted revenge, or so he claimed. Isn't that right general?' Zidanta looked at Ammuna.

'Personally, I always thought that an excuse,' Ammuna replied. 'What Muwas really wanted was the throne, no matter what it cost.'

'That's why its called the "big game,"' King Shunashura chipped in.

*   *   *

Tudhaliyas rode like someone possessed and his animal suffered at being pushed so hard, as indeed did all the mounts. The next day around noon, they came across soldiers from Hattusas, waiting for them with fresh horses.

'When your friend suggested this, I thought he was mad,' General Labamulis told Mokhat. 'Up to the capital, collect the horses, then back down here. I was sure we'd pass this point before the horses arrived. But I see why you did that. Our horses are so exhausted that the fresh mounts easily outdistanced them.'

'You should trust me by now,' Palaiyas retorted, having heard the interchange.

'Well done!' Tudhaliyas added his appreciation of Palaiyas. He then went and had a word with the officer in charge of the five hundred fresh mounts. 'How has the capital reacted to the outcome of the battle?'

'Especially well, sire. You must have noticed when you were there, the majority were for you,' the captain answered.

'Yes, I did. Still, I'm pleased.' The king was more than simply pleased. 'I'm sending General Labamulis here, back with you so he can tell them in the capital that I will be in Hattusas shortly—after I've taken Muwas into custody.'

'Yes your majesty,' and both remounted.

The two columns split. General Labamulis and his cavalry joined the soldiers from the capital and led them back up there taking the exhausted mounts with them. Palaiyas took point and led the king's group towards Gaziura. The fresh mounts made a big difference making for more comfortable riding and the distance to Gaziura was eaten up in no time. The road up to the gates of Gaziura went between a large forest of broad leaf trees like some majestic thoroughfare. The pursuing party just managed to catch sight of Muwas and the cavalry following him, as ahead they entered through the gate of the town.

'*Open up*!' shouted Tudhaliyas when they came to the closed gates. '*You—up there*,' the king yelled to a sentry atop the wall, '*do you know who I am*?'

'*A pox on the lot of you, why should I care*?' the sentry shouted back.

'*I am your lawful king, victor of the battle and you have my defeated enemy inside your town. I demand you open the gate and hand him over on penalty of destruction. Call the officer in charge.*'

The sentry stared hard at the unfamiliar yellow tunics, but then decided on a course of caution. 'I'll fetch the Watch Officer.'

A short period went by and another soldier appeared. 'Who did you say you are?' he inquired.

'King Tudhaliyas, rightful sovereign of the land of Hatti. These are my men. I demand you give up the fugitive Muwas who's just taken refuge in your town. If you refuse, I shall take this town by storm and make you pay a heavy price. You have but a short time to surrender Muwas to me.'

Even from that distance, Palaiyas noticed the officer looked afraid. The officer knew this was no idle threat. If Muwas was running from these pursuers, it could mean only one thing. The fleeing king was no longer who he claimed to be.

'Sire, beg you to pardon me. I cannot make this decision on my own. I will fetch the town governor. Let him talk to you.' With that he was gone.

'What do you think? Will we have to storm the town?' Tudhaliyas asked Mokhat.

'Let me lead my Kaska off to the side, so they can see a separate group. If you point us out to the governor and mention Hakpis, I think he might find it more urgent to make the right decision.'

'Think so? Right! We'll give it a try.'

A longer time went by until the governor appeared in place of the officer. He looked closely down at the riders and said, 'How do I know you are who you say you are?'

'I could ask you the same question. But I think you *know* I am, who I say I am. The real question you should ask yourself is, are you willing to risk your town with this insolent delay. If you notice, I have some Kaska warriors waiting over there. The larger force is waiting to the north. On my word, they will surround your town tonight and we will take it by force in the morning. Remember Hakpis! They sided with Muwas and paid the penalty. Are you going to hand over Muwas or die in defending a lost cause. Why is Muwas hiding in your town? Because he's just lost the battle to me for the throne. Choose or be destroyed. You have but a short time.' Tudhaliyas raised his hand and a Kaska war horn sounded.

Believing what he had just heard, the governor retreated from the battlements clearly a convert. The Kaska warriors with the new king could not be ignored. After Hakpis was destroyed, the town had taken in many refugees from that devastated town. They had horrendous stories to tell. Only a short time later, the gates were thrown open and the governor himself stood there, inviting the king's party inside. 'Your majesty, forgive our caution. We'd no idea Muwas was a fugitive when he arrived. We see our error now and apologise for our previous behaviour. I hope you will not hold this against us.' The governor seemed properly contrite.

Tudhaliyas stared at the governor frostily. 'Whether I hold it against you will depend on what happens next. Where is Muwas?'

'The townspeople will have disarmed his followers by now,' the governor informed. 'As for Muwas; I have sent instructions to have him bound and put under guard in a room of the citadel. If you will allow me to show you.' The governor led the way and Mokhat followed the king. Palaiyas headed the Kaska warriors and the Mešedi. As with most citadels, it stood on an artificial mound and was the most substantial building in the town. It was the governor's official residence. They walked the narrow streets of the town and right through the citadel gates. Up the flight of stairs and down a short corridor, they found a room guarded by two of the town's soldiers. The governor opened the door for the king and there, tied to a chair, sat Muwas, looking extremely angry. When he saw Tudhaliyas, he scowled, struggled and tried to bust free.

The chair Muwas was tied to wobbled—then toppled over with a crash, watched by Tudhaliyas, Mokhat, Palaiyas and the astonished governor. Muwas' bonds were either sloppily tied, or deliberately tied so he was able to struggle free of them. Mokhat shouted a command in Kaska and his warriors rushed forward to surround the usurper, blocking the escape window holes. Muwas jumped to his feet, shook off the last of the rope and picked up the chair as a weapon.

'Leave him to me,' Tudhaliyas shouted. 'I've been looking forward to this.'

'I cannot stand by and allow you to put your life in danger,' Mokhat insisted.

'May I?' Palaiyas moved forward into the ring created by the Kaska warriors.

Tudhaliyas looked angrily at Mokhat, exasperated at being denied the chance of directly challenge his enemy. He knew the Kaska priest was only doing his job of protecting him. For an instant he had been ready to order his Mešedi to intervene so he could fight Muwas, but then he realised that would be foolish. The priest might even order his warriors to use force. Fighting between Kaska and Mešedi was unthinkable, not now. He shrugged and gave in, nodding his assent to Palaiyas.

Muwas glared at them all as though gone mad. His face showed like a wild beast and he prodded the air with the legs of the chair. Palaiyas removed his sword and dagger, throwing them aside towards Mokhat while Muwas watched. Then square on, the son of the prince of Tiryns faced the ex Gal Mešedi and would-be king, indicating he was offering bare-handed combat. Neither had weapons and the match ought to be fair and equal on terms. Muwas looked round the room and saw no option. He threw the chair aside and faced Palaiyas, arms outstretched in a wrestler's stance. Palaiyas did the same and they began circling each other. Muwas lunged for a grab at Palaiyas and Palaiyas nimbly stepped back, forcefully brushing Muwas' arm away. They circled looking for a weakness, sizing each other up, looking where they could get a hold. Both observed how the other crouched, what force would be needed to off balance their opponent. Muwas lunged again and caught Palaiyas' belt, pulling him forward, their heads cracked on one another. Neither flinched.

Palaiyas held Muwas' belt and they were now locked in each others holds ever circling. Muwas tried to lift Palaiyas and thrust his leg forward for a trip. Palaiyas countered by pushing back and jumping over the trip leg. They tugged at each others belts in rough frustration, continually circling. Palaiyas let go of Muwas belt with his right hand and hit Muwas in the face with his fist. Muwas grimly held on, blood running down from a cut high on his cheek. Quickly Palaiyas regained the belt hold.

Muwas made a kick for Palaiyas' groin and Palaiyas avoided it by swivelling aside, but in going for the kick Muwas had unbalanced himself and Palaiyas lifted Muwas right leg upwards as hard as he could, throwing Muwas head over heels. Muwas landed hard on his back, the breath knocked out of him. Mokhat almost cheered but checked himself. The watchers all had smiles on their faces seeing Muwas' predicament. Muwas jumped to his feet and again began circling with Palaiyas, looking for an opening. Both were experienced fighters and neither gave an easy opening to the other. Muwas lunged for the belt hold but Palaiyas side stepped and swung his right fist connecting with Muwas' left eye. Muwas fell on his hands and knees, stayed there to get a breath, but then jumped up fast and tried to kick Palaiyas in the side—missing—while Palaiyas swiped Muwas' raised leg with his leg landing Muwas on his backside.

When Muwas rose, Palaiyas jumped at Muwas' chest with both feet landing there with a thud, knocking Muwas back on his posterior again. On his back three times in a row, Muwas seemed to foam at the mouth in rage and leapt at Palaiyas both arms raised. Palaiyas dodged aside, Muwas brushed by and Palaiyas hit him on the nape of the neck, sending him to the floor again.

Muwas got to his feet and if looks could kill, Palaiyas would have been struck dead there and then. Muwas seemed to realise his anger was playing him false and he made an effort to calm himself. He offered the belt holds again by circling with arms raised to that height. Palaiyas accepted. Both men regained their belt holds. Palaiyas pulled Muwas to the left while Muwas countered by pulling Palaiyas to the right. Palaiyas landed another punch on Muwas, who immediately landed a blow of his own in return.

The fight lasted a long time in this manner, with blows and counter blows, throws and falls made by each combatant until both were badly bloodied and exhausted. Only the watchers were enjoying the bout, seeing the losing contender for the throne of Hatti being mauled by an Ahhiyawan mercenary. The final insult. Palaiyas made an extra effort to finish his opponent by rolling on his back and propelling Muwas over him, helped by a foot in the stomach. Muwas landed on his right shoulder, dislocating it. He howled with pain and the room burst out laughing. He saw no point in continuing—Muwas' right arm was limp and he lay injured, exhausted, glaring defiantly around the room.

The nearby Kaska warriors came and brutally laid hands on the bloodied and defeated Muwas. They dragged him roughly across the floor and out of the room, Muwas all the time yelling in pain. In the corridor, Mokhat told his warriors to hold Muwas still while he grabbed Muwas' limp arm and pulled the joint straight, then pushed, snapping the bone back in its shoulder socket. Throughout the procedure, Muwas yelled as though they were skinning him alive.

'My goodness, I did enjoy doing that,' Mokhat declared to all in earshot. 'Take this prisoner outside,' he told his Kaska, 'and make sure you bind him properly.'

Palaiyas smiled, blood and sweat running down his face. 'I did enjoy kicking the shit out of him. It's what he deserved!'

Tudhaliyas came to Palaiyas and patted him on the shoulder. 'Good work! I would've felt a lot better if I had done it—but you did a good job. I shall have to find a way of rewarding you. Think on that!'

The governor of Gaziura beamed happily. 'Your majesty,' he interjected, 'we are your loyal subjects and again I apologise on behalf of the town for our initial mistake. I hope you will see fit to forgive us.'

Tudhaliyas looked sternly on the governor. 'Keep Muwas' soldiers in your dungeons, the ones that arrived with him. We will collect them later. Make haste and provide us with fresh horses and provisions—I'm taking Muwas back to Hattusas. If all is done as I command, you will have my forgiveness.'

The governor looked relieved and hurried away to obey the king's commands.

Mokhat helped his bloodied friend out to the citadel entrance and sat with him on the top steps. The governor's servants brought refreshments, fruit, drinks and meat. They sat in a relaxed mood as women servants came with water to clean up Palaiyas—and he winked at Mokhat, while enjoying their enthusiastic ministrations. 'I told you they can't keep their hands off of me,' he laughed.

Chapter Fifty-seven

Leaving Gaziura, Tudhaliyas led his party out in a manner befitting a king, with the townspeople cheering him through the open gate. The town governor had explained to them the outcome of the battle on the wide plateau which necessitated they make a quick change of allegiance. The departing party came out of the gate without looking back and travelled down the majestic thoroughfare in between the forest. In the distance Mokhat noticed a small group of riders veering off hard into the dark forest.

'Did you see those four riders? They're up to no good —look at them—how they're trying to hide from us. Riding into those woods,' Mokhat threw at Palaiyas as they rode past.

'It's the times we live in. Remember we've just finished with a civil war,' Palaiyas reminded Mokhat.

'I know that, its just...I wondered who they were. Probably more of Muwas' lot.'

They rode passed the spot where the suspicious riders had gone into the wood. Most thought no more on the matter, but Mokhat stared hard into the dark forest trying to spot the riders. From inside the wood, Harep in his turn watched them go by. The royal party trotted past and headed south-west towards the capital. It was a long two day journey in the heat of near summer, even though they rode through a landscape filled with splendid greenery. Tudhaliyas was looking forward to a renewed peace and promised himself he would do his utmost to help the healing process after the fractious fighting. Three long months had passed since the old king had been assassinated—and the new king was now on his way to his capital to be officially installed. On the afternoon of the second day after leaving Gaziura, they crossed over rolling hills and into the rich fertile plain which supplied much of the capital's corn. While riding through the plain, Mokhat suggested they send a messenger ahead to announce the imminent arrival of the rightful claimant to the Hatti throne. This done, the royal party finally rode upwards onto the granite grey promontory upon which Hattusas stood. They passed by the sacred rock-sanctuary, revered by both Hatti and Kaska alike and all were shocked to see the area in front of the wall littered with broken debris. The only person smirking at the sacrilegious sight was the prisoner Muwas.

Nearing the capital they crossed the north stream and suddenly heard long horns sounding from the northern ramparts of the city wall, heralding a fanfare to welcome the new king back to Hattusas. The north gate was wide open, sentries in yellow tunics stood at attention on either side of the arched gateway. Everyone in the royal party was smiling happily at the reception they were receiving. Tudhaliyas beamed at his companions and at anyone he caught sight of, then they rode through the tunnel and emerged facing the northern part of the Great Temple. Crowds had gathered as the news spread. They were pushing forward to see their new king, cheering wildly as the royal party rounded the temple towards the main entrance. When they spied the bound Muwas hemmed in by the Kaska warriors, the crowd hissed and booed. Tudhaliyas dismounted and was met by Tagrama, high priest of the land of Hatti. 'Sire, may I be one of many to congratulate you on your great victory and your safe journey to your capital.'

'Your eminence, I humbly thank you on behalf of my family for your staunch support throughout these difficult times.'

Tagrama saw Muwas sitting on his horse and glared his hostility towards the pretender. Muwas wasn't gagged and spat in the high priest's direction. That prompted the nearest Kaska to slam the back of his hand into Muwas' face, drawing blood from a split lip. 'Mind your manners, you damned *hoodlum*,' the Kaska told his sullen prisoner.

'I stopped to pay my respects and give my thanks to the Storm God of Hatti, Lord Taru,' the king told the high priest.

'Sire, we just arrived this morning from the battlefield and the temple is full of wounded...but that shouldn't stop you paying your respects. Just thought I'd advise you of their presence.' Tagrama led the way inside while the royal party waited outside in the heat and the noise coming from the bustling crowd. He ordered a nearby priest, 'Get someone to gather a group together to go and collect the valuables from the holy caverns.'

The priest rushed to obey and the royal party continued towards the naos.

Outside, a soft rotten medlar came flying from the crowd and hit Muwas on the back of the head. He turned like an animal and glared in the direction of who might have thrown it. Rather than being cowed by the accusatory stare, bold as brass, more medlars came flying in Muwas direction and hit him in the face, chest and upper parts of his body.

Mokhat jumped up on the horse's back and stood there balancing, holding his arms up, trying to calm the crowd, 'Please...no more...we know how you feel. He will be put on trial.' Then he used guile on the onlookers, '*Do you trust your new king*?' he yelled. He stopped talking and waited for the crowd to settle down. 'That's better...well? I asked you a question...do you trust your king?' Mokhat was dressed as a Hatti priest and they listened out of respect.

Finally a voice came from the crowd, 'Yes, we trust him!'

Another voice added, 'We'd trust Yarris over that one there.' The wit pointed at Muwas.

Muwas stank with the rotten medlars he now wore and looked more cautiously at the sea of hostile faces surrounding him as it sank in that the crowd was in a position to pull him off his horse and deal with him in their own way.

The horse moved and Mokhat almost fell off. Then he shouted again, 'Then trust him to deal with this prisoner with the justice he deserves. Will you do that?' Mokhat sat quickly back on the horse.

'Nice trick,' Palaiyas complimented.

He referred to Mokhat's ability to stand on the horse's back. Mokhat assumed he was being complimented on subduing the crowd.

'Thanks, I had no choice. When a crowd gets nasty, our few numbers would be no protection.'

Palaiyas did not understand the reference to the crowd and shrugged his shoulders. At that point, Tudhaliyas emerged from the temple and the crowd forgot Muwas and renewed their cheering for their king.

The royal party led by Tudhaliyas made its way through the streets of Hattusas from the Great Temple to the Great Palace on the other side of town. Crowds packed the streets, held back with immense difficulty only by a few soldiers. The townsfolk cheered themselves hoarse all along the long road flanked by flat topped houses. Muwas got booed and more rotten medlars. By now, he was less defiant. In truth, they cheered not only the king but the end of the civil war. Now the food supply would be restored and the soldiers installed back to their normal numbers. On reaching the Great Palace, Mokhat like so many before him, glanced at the narrow corbelled arches of its citadel gates flanked by portal sculptures, opening up into the lower paved courtyard holding stables and an armoury. They passed various guardrooms and went through the official access to the upper palace proper. A guard of honour dressed in yellow was at attention in the lower courtyard of the citadel, welcoming their king to his royal residence. Hatti soldiers stood at attention on either side up the entrance stairs.

'Take this prisoner to the dungeons,' Tudhaliyas ordered a senior officer.

Soldiers pulled the weary Muwas roughly from his horse and marched him away to the innards of the palace. Other soldiers lined the passages up the stairwell all the way to the Audience Hall, snapping to attention as the king went by. Just inside the hall stood Prince Kantuzzili flanked by King Shunashura on his left and General Zidanta on his right. Proudly, with a bearing befitting the true heir to the throne of Hatti, Tudhaliyas marched into the vast Audience Hall towards the throne. On either side of the hall, on the walls were enormous murals depicting the great events from Hittite history all the way back to Labarnas. Tudhaliyas halted before the black bull throne and turned to face his audience.

His audience waited for him to mount the rostrum and take his place on the throne—but Tudhaliyas faltered. Kantuzzili came to his nephew, 'What's the matter? Why hesitate?'

'I want it all to be just right. I want to be officially anointed by Tagrama in the Great Temple. That's when I'll feel the full weight of the crown, the right to sit on the throne with no one questioning that right.'

'No one questions it now. Shall I tell you when you *won* the right to sit on that throne? The moment the battle *turned* in our favour. That *right* has always come about by the might of the sword. All else is trimmings.' Kantuzzili took his nephew's arm and led him up the steps, to the throne.

Tudhaliyas felt the faultlessness of what his uncle had just told him and knew it to be right. When all was said and done, the might of the sword silenced all opposition. The frills would come but only because he had won the recent battle. He took his place on the throne and looked to his left —to where Nikal would sit. He beckoned all those waiting to approach. 'King Shunashura,' the king asked quietly, 'where is your daughter, my fiancée?'

'Sire, she is where we left her. In Ankuwa. Waiting patiently for us to finish our battle and then to come and collect her.'

'We've finished with battles! Has someone gone to bring her to the capital?' Tudhaliyas seemed almost aggressive in his questioning, but all he wanted was to see Nikal and couldn't understand why she wasn't here to greet him.

Kantuzzili answered, 'We've sent General Labamulis with a squadron down there to fetch her. He knows the route —and the princess. He'll soon have her here.'

Chapter Fifty-eight

Harep rose early the next morning, eager to get started on the search for his gold. Raiysa was already stirring something over a rekindled fire. Over what passed for breakfast he told Rewa, 'I want you to stay here and guard her,' he nodded at Nikal. 'The place is chaotic and full of undesirables. Two women alone won't stand a chance.'

'Right'o Unc. I'll watch her, don't worry.' He winked at Raiysa who was watching the pair of them.

'Stay here, where I can see you; no wandering off. Make sure your sword is ready.'

'I'm all right. I can handle myself.' He said that in a meaningful way, with an undertone. He talked to Harep with a double message, but Harep wasn't listening.

Harep was already thinking of how to find his gold. Harep grabbed his own belt with sword and dagger and hurried on his way back into the stinking town. He made straight for the burnt out treasury again and began searching for some sign. He found what he thought was the treasurer in one of the alleys leading from the building. The clothes were familiar but the face was gnawed away as was all the exposed flesh. He stared for a long time at the corpse trying to work out what he was doing when he died. The body had an arrow through the back, but that wasn't what killed him, although it was fatal. What killed him was a sword thrust to the stomach. Harep kicked aside the outstretched hand and peered closely at a scratch mark he had uncovered. 'Well I'll be,' he mouthed silently to himself.

The dying treasurer had scratched a crude drawing of a dragon as his last act on this earth, before giving himself up to the long journey to the netherworld.

'Illuyankas!' Harep rubbed the tattoo on his chest. 'Let's see…he seems to be heading back to the treasury when someone caught him,' Harep mouthed. He stood back and looked at the position of the body. 'I wonder where this alley leads?' He sheathed his sword and drew his dagger instead. For close encounters it was more efficient. One last look at the treasurer and he made his way up the alley to where the former treasurer might have come from. He came out in the direction of the citadel. 'Thought so!' he mouthed.

Rats scurried everywhere, looking for more food. Above him on the roof a cat looked down on him inquisitively. Harep hurried through the arch leading to the courtyard and across to the citadel entrance, now blackened with smoke. On either side of the entrance he searched for more scratches—and found one on the left, near the door hinge. Another dragon. 'Heh! The wily old bugger,' he mouthed quietly. Through the charred entrance, the place inside was solid enough but everywhere he looked, bodies lay amidst the signs of ferocious fighting. This is where the few soldiers of the town had made their last stand—and died in a hopeless fight. Rats had taken over the whole building and scurried about underfoot. Harep drew his sword and swiped at the floor, making them dart out of the way. One big one tried to jump for his face but Harep knocked it aside.

He wondered where to next. On the left was the great hall—nothing there. Where was the next scratching? Couldn't be upstairs—it did not make sense going that way. He looked for the way to the dungeons. Right at the back of the citadel he found what he was looking for. The stone staircase leading down to the bowels of the building. By the wall on the side of the stairwell, he saw it—another scratched dragon. The stench coming from the bottom was overpowering. Harep pulled a torch from the side of the stairwell and began trying to light it. Lighting the torch took an effort. He vigorously struck the two flint-stones together until a spark jumped onto a little tinder he had taken from his pocket. The tinder caught and he lit the oil on the torch. From the glow he saw a mass of rats running from the light. The thought of the gold enabled him to put the rats out of his mind. He placed a kerchief over his nose, held the torch high and gingerly made his way down the stairs.

*   *   *

On the way down the stairwell, Harep brushed aside many a rodent with his foot—and pushed aside a few bodies of decomposing soldier blocking his path. The light from the torch was his only comfort. When he reached the bottom he wondered where he was to look next. He found more torches stuck on the wall and lit them. The place was enormous. Corridors branched off in four directions. He examined the corner of each corridor for a scratched figurine—and found one on the opposite side. The corridor leading straight in front had been indicated by the departed treasurer. As for the overwhelming stench, he concluded it came from the murky atmosphere mingling with the many decomposing bodies. Harep went down the corridor indicated, lighting any torches he could find. Before him were a series of dungeons on either side, cell doors open. *He wouldn't of put the gold in a dungeon, surely*, he thought. He crept further down to where an area opened up into a large working space. He found more torches and set them alight. He had a strong stomach but some of the torture implements made him shudder with what they were intended for.

He walked round the room from left to right searching for the dragon clue. Various racks hung on the walls holding strange bronze instruments of torture. Other weird contraptions stood or leaned against the wall. On reaching the far side of the room, he found a number of barrels, one with oil, another two were filled with water. Next to them was a large sandbox. Nearby was an oblong brick tank that held foul looking water. He peered everywhere, looking for a

scratch mark. Then he found it, the mark of Illuyankas, very
faint and smudged, barely visible. It was scratched on the
wall opposite the sandbox. If he wasn't looking for it, he
would never have found it. He stood back and gaped at the
open container. *The sly old money bags! What a place to
stash the gold!* It was a permanent fixture too heavy to shift.
He stuck his hands in the sand—and found only sand. *Bloody
thing better be here,* he half mouthed. He began digging and
scooping but the sand couldn't be moved without sliding
back in on itself. After a few more tries he gave up, sweat
pouring down his face. *It's no good, I'll have to get Rewa to
help, sodding thing.* He hoped not to involve Rewa because
of the discrepancy. At the outset, he had told his nephew
there was only thirty thousand but he was expecting to find
forty-five thousand.

He looked at the round fire in the middle of the room
and found a shovel nearby for clearing the ashes. He began
emptying the sand from the sandbox, still trying to avoid
involving Rewa. After half of the sand had been piled on the
floor, he hit something solid. He dropped the shovel and dug
in with his bear hands. Just then, the light from the nearest
torch began to fade and he had to go light another torch and
brought it to the container. He stuck it in a holder above the
sandbox—and saw a yellow glint from inside. He had torn
one of the leather pouches with his shovel and gold shekels
had slid out—now exposed, glinting in the torchlight. He
stared greedily at the gold. The sandbox couldn't be that full
of gold; it would mean far more than the forty-five thousand
promised. Carefully he lifted out the torn pouch and placed it
on the floor to the side putting the few spilled coins in his
side purse. Then he began extracting bag after bag of golden
shekels, lifting each pouch out as if they were full of eggs.
After some time the box was empty and the bags piled up
behind him. He counted them. From experience he knew each
bag contained the value of a thousand shekels and he had
counted out a hundred and twenty seven bags—a hundred

and twenty-eight counting the torn one. *A hundred and twenty-eight thousand golden shekels. A hundred and twenty-eight thousand golden shekels,* he repeated to himself, not able to believe his luck. *Must be the whole town's treasury.*

He couldn't hide this from Rewa, nor did he need to. More than enough for them both—and much more. Because of the amount on the floor, he could be generous. He would give Rewa forty thousand—far more than he had promised. He felt light headed and skipped round the room like a little boy. Finally, he calmed, found a rag, and dipped it in the water barrel, going round dousing all the torches except one. Retracing his way back up the stairwell, careful where he stepped, he made his way out of the citadel front entrance to the courtyard. Through the gates, down the narrow alleyways and back out of the town to where he had left Rewa. He found Rewa worried and almost pleased to see him. 'What's the matter nephew?' Harep inquired cheerily.

Nikal was concealed inside the makeshift tent they had erected the night previous. Raiysa was tending the fire, a hare roasting over it. 'Had some rough types looking us over,' Rewa told him. 'Managed to get a couple of hares from them but I got the impression they were after the women and horses. I'm relieved you're back—did you find what we're after?'

'Slow down nephew…how many were there?'

'Only three…but they had friends who kept out of sight.' Rewa was a bit ruffled. 'I think we're going to have trouble with them.'

'Get your stuff together, we're moving. It's a bit messy inside there—better stick close to your woman,' Harep threw his thumb at the walls of the town.

'Can't we stay out here? Those three said there were lots of rotting bodies in there,' Rewa complained.

'If you want your throat cut…stay here. Me—I'm moving inside. Safer in there. By the way—yes—I've found it.' Harep began collecting his things—took Nikal from the shelter and dismantled it.

'All of it?' Rewa asked.

'And more. How much did I promise you?'

'Fifteen thousand, Unc.' Rewa replied.

'Well, I'll double that if you hurry.'

Rewa's eyes glazed for a fraction as he thought of it. 'What? Thirty thousand?' He couldn't believe his ears.

'That's what "doubling" means, don't it?'

Back on the streets, 'I want to find someplace we can defend,' Harep told Rewa as they made their way through the corpse littered alleyways leading their horses on foot. 'We'll need to find some mules to carry the stuff—and I have to send a message to Tudhaliyas. I've not yet finished with him.'

'But Unc, it stinks in here. Why can't we just take the money and leave?' Rewa whined.

'Nephew!' Harep stopped, pushed his and Nikal's horses aside, and turned to face Rewa. 'Call it professional pride. When I'm contracted to do a job, I *always* do it—no matter what. Just cos we got our hands on the money, it don't make no difference. I wouldn't enjoy it if I didn't fulfil the contract. I'd be lying in the lap of luxury always niggled by not having done what I said I'd do. No, nephew! I wish I could, but I can't. We've got to finish what we started.'

Rewa looked exasperated. Raiysa cringed behind Rewa. Still, thirty thousand. More money than he had ever thought he would have in his wildest dreams. 'How're we gonna send the message?'

'I don't want to go myself to Gaziura and I need you here, but we might be able to get one of these people to go... if we pay them enough.' The party continued until they reached the courtyard of the citadel and then the entrance.

Raiysa had put a cloth to her nose and Nikal couldn't smell anything through her gag. Harep felt safer this far inside town—except for the rats. He assumed most brigands would be too busy fending off others of the same ilk to take much notice of them...at least that's what he hoped. The horses were led inside to the big hall to the left of the entrance and stabled there. They couldn't be left outside because of the wild dogs. A few rats scurried about the floor. They would have to find hay and water for the horses. Nikal was bound to an upright chair and Raiysa set herself to finding wood for the enormous fireplace.

When Harep was sure Raiysa was busy, he took Rewa's arm and led him to the back of the building to where the stairwell was. That's where the rats were more abundant. Again he lit a torch and gave it to Rewa, lighting another for himself from his. Slowly they descended the stairs to the dungeons. At the bottom, Harep led the way down the facing corridor and out to the open area where he had left the sacks of gold.

When Harep pointed to the pile, Rewa simply burst out giggling—he couldn't help himself. The idea of all that gold just lying there was too much for him. Rewa went to one sack and opened it while Harep watched. He giggled some more, jingling the shekels inside the sack. 'Thirty thousand...how much is there here, Unc?'

'More than enough for the both of us,' Harep said cautiously.

'I know that, but how much?' Rewa insisted.

'Tell you what...if you don't ask me again, you get forty thousand...deal?' Harep thought he knew his nephew.

Rewa stopped giggling and looked slyly at Harep. 'Ugh! All right. But I get forty thousand then?'

'Forty thousand! As long as there's no more asking. Do as you're told and I promise you get forty thousand.'

'All right Unc,' Rewa agreed.

'Help me carry the lot to the bottom of the stairwell. Then we'll lug them upstairs and stack them there till we get the mules. Sometime today, we've got to find someone to send to Gaziura with the wax tablet for the Hatti king. Better still, I'll get that princess of his to write the message. That'll make him more agitated.' Over a period of a couple of hours, Harep and Rewa moved the sacks of gold to the bottom of the stairwell and then hauled them slowly up the stairs, stacking them against the back wall. Rewa counted the bags and thought he knew how much money there was, but he kept his mouth shut. He knew there was far more than they were owed and he had worked out for himself that Harep was keeping seventy-eight thousand. Still just a little envious but then he accepted his share was enough for him. Forty thousand he kept reminding himself. He and Raiysa would be set for life.

Chapter Fifty-Nine

On a hot afternoon Talshura led his cavalry into the Ankuwa valley and noted there were no sentries at the entrance. In the aftermath of the battle there was an assumption that there were no need of them. The place was as tranquil as when he had left for the battle—so long ago—almost another lifetime. Ankuwa lay to the right inside the valley, but the first the riders saw were the damaged houses. Almost every house they passed had some kind of devastation and many were a crumbling ruin. 'Must have been that earth tremor we experienced just before the battle, remember?' Talshura shared with Tapalass.

'I fear you're right, highness,' the general agreed.

'It seems to have been more severe here,' Talshura ventured. When they arrived at the villa where they had left Nikal, they could find no one at home. The garden walls were down and the building itself was badly damaged—large cracks split the villa apart. The roof was at a slant and the portico had rubble blocking the entrance. Talshura stood in what was once the front garden and looked around, all the time shaking his head. 'This is terrible. Where's my sister?'

'We'll find her, highness,' Tapalass assured. 'She's probably staying in another house—one that isn't damaged. We just need to go round the villas and inquire for her.'

'Get the men to make camp in that field over there,' Talshura pointed to a nearby field. 'She might be staying in the house Kantuzzili stayed in—we'll look there first.' Talshura led some of the men to the Assyrian merchant's house that had been the royal Hatti residence. The house was in a better state of repair. They shouted and knocked on the gate and it was opened cautiously by an old servant.

'Is your master at home,' Tapalass inquired.

The servant recognised the scarlet Kizzuwatna uniform and opened the gate wide. 'Please come in. I will fetch my master.' The servant, bent with old age, ambled off up the garden path to summon the owner of the house.

Shortly, a man dressed in finely embroidered linen came to ask them, 'Can I help you?'

'Yes, I'm Prince Talshura and I'm looking for my sister. We've just come from the villa we were staying in before the battle and the place is empty. I was wondering if you could enlighten us as to her whereabouts.'

The Assyrian merchant looked uncomfortable and hesitated to answer. 'I...I...I don't know...what to say.'

The stuttering alarmed Talshura and he lost his temper. '*What's happened to my sister*?' Talshura loudly demanded. '*Where is she*?'

'We can't find her...I mean... after the earthquake... she... she disappeared. We haven't seen her since.' The man stood squirming, awkward with having to give the princess's brother this type of news.

'But how can that be? What do you mean you can't find her? She can't just disappear. Have you looked for her... I mean properly?' Talshura was beside himself with exasperation.

'Your highness, we've looked all over the valley. We've questioned everybody... those that last saw her. They have no answers. She can't be dead because there is no body, yet nobody can find her anywhere.' The merchant was apologetic and knew this would mean big trouble for the whole valley. A princess of the royal Kizzuwatna family and a staunch ally of the new Hittite king could not just disappear without serious consequences.

After questioning the surviving servants, Talshura understood what the Assyrian merchant meant. They were frightened and really had little idea what had happened. After the quake the building was unsafe and all the garden walls had fallen to rubble. The only little snippet they could add was that two of the gardeners were missing as well. They were strangers who had been sent from the king to give a hand in helping make the garden blossom. That's all Talshura could get out of them. After the tremor, the servants had come here or gone home in the confusion. That's all they knew. In desperation Talshura went through the whole valley searching, but without success. No one had seen his sister. The original inhabitants of the valley were morose and sullen and did not want to answer anymore Kizzuwatna questions— and made it plain they had wished he would disappear as well. No point in threatening them with his soldiers. It wouldn't help. 'I'm afraid all I can think of is we return to the capital,' he told General Tapalass sadly.

The general saw his prince was distraught and called in the troops from the search. He asked the Assyrian for more provisions and then led the three regiments north out of the valley. 'We'll find her, highness,' the general tried to reassure his prince as they rode side by side. 'She must be somewhere. She can't have vanished.'

'But she has—that's the point—just vanished I mean,' he declared angrily. 'I can't sense her anywhere near. I can usually sense where she is—most of the time. Not this time. I know she's not dead, that's all I know.'

'The quicker we get to the capital the quicker the Hittites can begin the search,' Tapalass advised.

Talshura shrugged, grief etched on his face. The large body of Kizzuwatna cavalry settled down to a long ride to the capital. By the evening both horses and men were tired and the general ordered they make camp for the night. Sentries were posted and after a meal they turned in. Half way through the night, sentries reported they heard riders in the distance and the camp was woken as a precaution. The sentries challenged the riders and discovered they were part of a squadron of Hatti cavalry coming down to Ankuwa. The main body drew abreast and General Labamulis hailed the sentries.

'We are with King Tudhaliyas—we come in peace.' Had it been daytime, the precautions would have been unnecessary but at night in the aftermath of a war, soldiers were still wary.

General Tapalass was with the sentries and Talshura was just arriving. 'Come forward and be identified,' Tapalass demanded.

General Labamulis rode up and jumped off his horse. He saw Talshura and exclaimed, 'Highness, I'm thankful we came across you. It'll save me going all the way to the valley.'

'You're welcome to join us. You there, build up the fires,' he ordered one of his officers. The officer went to order his soldiers to stoke the fires up. 'What brings you down here, general?' Talshura asked.

The Kizzuwatna mingled with the newly arrived Hatti and food was made for the newly arrived cavalrymen.

'Why are you travelling at night, general?' Tapalass asked him.

'I was ordered to the valley by the king to bring his fiancée, your sister, the princess. I can't see her with you. Is she still asleep?' Labamulis asked.

A pain crossed Talshura's face, then he had a thoughtful hope. 'What do you know about the princess? Have you seen her?' confusedly Talshura's interest awakened.

General Labamulis frowned at being asked this. 'Highness, I assumed you had her here with you. I've been sent by the king to fetch her to the capital.'

'You won't find her in the valley and she's not with us,' Tapalass informed Labamulis. 'She's gone missing. We've been looking all over for her without success. We were just going up to Hattusas to tell the king. We've no idea where she is.'

Labamulis was shocked to hear this. 'But...but that's not possible. This is terrible! What am I to tell the king?'

'Leave that to me. I'll tell King Tudhaliyas. My big worry is—what am I to say to my father?' Talshura shook his head in sorrow. 'How am I to explain to him his daughter is missing?'

'What's been happening up there?' Tapalass asked Labamulis.

'What? You mean in Hattusas? Six days after we won the battle, things are returning to normal...apart from this...' He meant Nikal. 'I can't get over this. How can she be missing?'

'Believe me general, we've been all over this problem. We haven't an answer. We were hoping someone up in the capital might have a solution.'

Chapter Sixty

'**S**top putting it off. The sooner you deal with him the quicker we can put this whole matter behind us,' Kantuzzili advised his nephew. 'Send for him and get it over with.'

Tudhaliyas had to agree. Muwas was sent for and brought up from the dungeon. He had had time to think and compose himself and now reasserted some of his old arrogant self, strutting between the guards who finally pushed him into the anteroom behind the Audience Hall. Muwas looked around—he had welcomed Artatama in this same room when he first arrived with his army. 'Well my erstwhile adversary, how are you taking to your new surroundings down there? Comfortable?' Tudhaliyas asked unenthusiastically. 'I can promise your stay there will be short.'

Muwas looked daggers at the king—and then spat on the floor near where Kantuzzili stood.

'Tut, tut. That's no way for a pretender to the throne to behave,' Kantuzzili told him.

Muwas set his face grimly and lapsed into a sullen silence.

'Look—there's nothing personal in this,' Tudhaliyas explained to Muwas, 'it's just that we're in each others way and one of us has to go—permanently. For myself, I'd be quite happy to send you into exile—say to Mittani, but knowing what you're like, I can't afford to store up trouble for the future…watch you stir up problems for us down there. So my dear beaten contender for the throne, I have no choice but to have you put to death. That should put an end to your faction. If the situations were reversed, I would expect no less from you.'

'Of that you can be *certain*,' came the caustic growl.

'I'm gratified you understand. After all, you brought it upon yourself. The son of the man who murdered my grandfather. This could only have turned out this way once you insisted on going after a throne that never belonged to you. Muwatallis broke Hittite Law by having Huzziyas assassinated—and then grabbing the throne. Muwatallis, your father, should have dealt with Huzziyas' sons as well,' the king nodded in his uncle's direction, 'that was his mistake—a mistake I have no intention of repeating. As a last gesture I can let you choose the manner of your death.'

'Huh! Death is death. What do I care how I die!' Muwas contemptuously ejected.

The king flicked his hand at Muwas in dismissal, 'Suit yourself. Makes no difference to me. Guards...'

Muwas interrupted, '*Wait*...if I choose the way I die... will you promise to carry it out exactly as I wish?'

Sensing a trap, Tudhaliyas paused and looked deeply at Muwas...then gave in. What could he possibly think up that might threaten him? 'I promise...how is it to be?'

'Remember...you promised...I want you to do it. You personally. I want you to strangle me with your bear hands,' he smirked as he said it.

Kantuzzili looked astonished at the idea, his mouth dropped open. 'You can't ask a king to do that!' he exploded.

'He promised!' Muwas sneered. 'The promise of a king—does it mean so little to you.' The latter was another jibe.

Tudhaliyas looked equally shocked as had Kantuzzili. Muwas stood there gloating, but then he noticed a slight glint creep into Tudhaliyas' eyes and it alarmed him. It was a glint of satisfaction and Muwas knew he had made a mistake. This son of Himuili might actually enjoy killing him with his bare hands—thus settling a deeply personal score. Before he could change his mind, Tudhaliyas agreed. 'Yes, you're right. A promise is a promise. Distasteful as it may be, I will strangle you—as you request.'

Muwas saw no sign that it would be distasteful in the king's voice. Now he knew for certain. Maybe he had been goaded into asking for Tudhaliyas to kill him—is that why he gave him a choice? It broke his arrogance. He hung his head and Tudhaliyas now smiled.

Muwas realised he had underestimated the hate Tudhaliyas felt for him and now backed away as Tudhaliyas approached the bound Muwas, arms outstretched. Muwas backed into the hands of the two burly Mešedi standing behind him. They grabbed his shoulders and held him as Tudhaliyas reached for Muwas' throat. 'I...I...I didn't...' Muwas tried to say.

Those were the last coherent utterances heard from the defeated pretender to the throne. There followed chocking sounds as Tudhaliyas tightened his grip around Muwas' projecting larynx, all the time smiling and thinking of his father. It did not take long for Muwas' body to slump—but it was held upright by the two yellow clad Mešedi. Tudhaliyas turned and smiled at Kantuzzili. 'That was for my farther... may he now rest in peace knowing I've dealt with his murderer.' Tudhaliyas was satisfied.

'I know!' was all Kantuzzili could say. Kantuzzili did not like what had just occurred, fearing the effect on his nephew's sanity later on, which was precisely why Muwas had chosen this manner of his own death. He had hoped his opponent would have nightmares having to choke him to death, but seeing the smile on Tudhaliyas' face—made him doubt this would be the case.

Tudhaliyas told the two Mešedi, 'Take it out and burn it with the rubbish. No priests or anything of the sort. Put a hood over his head so nobody knows who you're disposing. I want no sign he was here—is that understood?'

'Yes your majesty,' the older one answered.

Tudhaliyas waved for them to take him away and they dragged the dead Muwas out to the corridor—and into nothingness. Thus the promise made at the outset by Muwas of, "crushing the two sons of Huzziyas beneath his feet and their names being erased from all records—to be as *non-people*. Never born—never lived," came about, but in reverse. It was Muwas who was crushed and sent into oblivion.

Chapter Sixty-one

Tagrama was getting everything ready for the New Year celebrations and the coronation. The temple was being cleaned, all the statues scrubbed. The gold-leaf was being retouched where it had peeled. A continual series of sacrifices were being performed to cleanse the building of the dreadful Mittani sacrilege. As it was midsummer, the king would celebrate the New Year by offering the first fruits to the gods in expectation of their blessings for a bountiful year and a good barley harvest.

Mokhat sat on the steps outside the temple with Palaiyas wondering where in Hatti Harep and his nephews had vanished. That Harep was still a threat, Mokhat had no doubt, but since the death of Himuili there had been no evidence of his activity. Mokhat put the death of the king's father down to Harep and now needed to try and anticipate Harep's next move. 'I knew he was good, because that's how they train them, but I've not set eyes on him since that day in Nerik Market. That worries me more than anything,' Mokhat confided to Palaiyas.

'In this case, I leave the thinking to you, you know that,' Palaiyas replied. 'I'm good in a fight, but this Harep I don't know...and I have no idea what he might do next... especially someone who's an assassin. Give me good old fashioned tactics any day.'

'I know. I'm just thinking out loud. The war's over... Muwas is in custody...how's he going to get paid? Looking at it like that...I'd say he'd abandon the job...but I know Harep. He's a determined type...even tenacious...like a dog...once he gets his teeth onto something, he won't let go. But what can he do?' A period of silence followed as Mokhat tried to work it through. From down the main thoroughfare

Palaiyas watched a number of rider approach the temple and as they neared, Mokhat made out scarlet tunics. 'Now what do the Kizzuwatna want up here?' he voiced out loud.

The lead rider turned out to be the young Kizzuwatna prince. He had a number of bodyguards with him, about twenty men. Talshura rode up and waved at Mokhat, jumping off his horse and giving the reins to once of his men. 'I'm relieved that I found you here,' the prince said as he walked up to the sitting pair. He looked tired and dusty, almost close to collapse. He sat near Mokhat and put his head in his hands. Then he lifted his head and looked straight in front, 'I came looking for you. I'm at my wits end…don't know what to do next. Don't know how to tell my father.' He fell silent.

Mokhat could see something was troubling the young prince. 'Better start at the beginning. What's happened?' he encouraged.

'I've been chasing Artatama…and he's got away. We chased him as far as Nesas—then gave up. He got fresh horses and there was no hope of catching him. So I ordered us back to Ankuwa. I wanted to pick up my sister—take her back to Hattusas with me…only I couldn't find her…still can't find her. She's gone missing. No one's seen her since the earth tremor. General Labamulis has just now gone to tell the king.' Talshura was close to tears and he propped his head back on his hands.

'How do you mean missing? Do you know where she's gone?' Mokhat was startled with the story.

'I've absolutely no idea where she is. It's as if she's been swallowed by the earth. All I know is…she's still alive. I can feel that…otherwise I've no idea where she is. We searched the whole valley…questioned the servants. They were no help. All they said was that a couple of strange gardeners were also missing.'

At that last bit of information—Mokhat had a nasty feeling in the pit of his stomach. He did not interrupt but a premonition came upon him—that he had just got his answer on the question he had been pondering scarcely a minute ago, sitting there on the steps. Cautiously he asked, 'What strange gardeners?'

Talshura composed himself, 'The servants told me a couple of strange gardeners, foreigners, had joined them a few days before the tremor. Sent by Tudhaliyas to help with the flowers. Why?'

'I have this horrible suspicion those gardeners might have had something to do with your missing sister,' Mokhat told him.

'What? What do you mean? How?' There was hope and alarm in Talshura's voice.

'I'm only guessing mind you, but it might have been those hard-to-trap assassins we're trying to track down. Harep and his nephews. It sounds like their work...but why? How does your sister fit into this?'

Talshura couldn't believe what he had just heard. He sat staring at the Kaska priest.

Mokhat sat trying to work out what the Yarris would Harep want with the Kizzuwatna princess. '*I think I've got it.*' He startled his listeners with the outburst. 'He's setting a trap for the king—using her as a lure. Once the king finds out, there'll be no stopping him. We've got to go and warn him.' Mokhat jumped up. 'What did you say about General Labamulis going to tell the king?'

'He's gone to tell Tudhaliyas that Nikal's missing. What are you talking about? What trap?' Talshura hadn't understood.

Palaiyas grasped the scheme immediately, only because he had been listening to Mokhat all this while— about Harep and what he might do next.

'I'll explain on the way. Your highness, you might want to go and get your father and bring him to the Great Castle. Anyway...this is what I think...' and Mokhat explained Harep's devious stratagem again to the young prince, making sure he understood this time.

Chapter Sixty-two

Harep had his dagger out and was holding it near Nikal's throat. 'Write this,' he snarled at her. They were at a desk in a room on the ground floor of the citadel with a wax tablet in front of her. Harep had stuck a wedge making pen in her hand and now threatened her with the dagger. 'Write or I'll mark your pretty neck with this,' he stuck it in the skin of her throat.

At first, she had refused, but the waving of the dagger had got her so frightened that she had finally agreed. 'What... d'you want...me to say...?' she stuttered in a frightened voice.

'Write, "I'm being held by my kidnapper. He wants you to come alone—no soldiers—if you want to see me alive. My captive wants to talk to the Hittite king." Sign it with your name.'

Nikal did as she was told. The rats scurried around on the floor and she hated the little monsters. Everything about the place they were in was horrible.

'Good girl! Who knows? Do as you're told and you might come out of this alive.' Harep wanted her to hope. It made her more pliable. He retied her to the chair and went to find Rewa. He found him with Raiysa, arm round her waist. They were staring at the piled-up sacks of gold. 'Now, now. The more you stare at that, the sillier the ideas that pop in your mind. Believe me, I know,' Harep chided them both.

'No, Unc. I'm not after any more than you promised. I just wanted her to see what's waiting for her if she sticks with me,' Rewa explained.

'Look, I've got that silly trollop of his to write this,' Harep held out the wax tablet. He had called Nikal a "trollop" not because he thought she was one, but to denigrate her so it would be easier to dispose of her afterwards. 'Now we've got to find a way of getting this to him.' Then Harep had a thought, 'Those three ruffians, the ones who were looking you over—you think you could find them?'

'Might be able to—why? What you got in mind, Unc?'

'If we paid them enough—carefully—we could get them to deliver this message. What d'you think?'

Rewa screwed up his face in alarm. 'They mustn't see the gold. We'd have the whole town on our backs if they knew what we had back here.'

'*Obviously*! We'll go out to them. Take a hundred shekels with us. That's more than they'll see in a lifetime. We could get them to get us four mules at the same time. Four should be enough to carry this lot. Thirty-two sacks to a mule,' Harep glanced at the gold.

'You said I could have forty,' Rewa was quick to point out.

'Well, one of them can carry forty. It'll be your special mule, *all right*?' Harep said irritably.

Rewa kept his mouth closed. Last thing he wanted was to pick a fight with his uncle. All thoughts of revenge for the death of his little brother had vanished with the arrival of Raiysa. He simply wanted to finish with this business, take his gold and get as far away as he could from this unpleasant relation of his.

'Now your woman knows what's at stake, do you think you can trust her to guard the prisoner while we go see those scruffs?' Harep peered at Rewa.

'She'll guard her, don't you worry. See how she looks at the sacks.'

'Tell her to cut that whimpering woman's hair short. I was near her just now and it's infested.'

'Right-ho, Unc.'

And indeed, Raiysa couldn't take her eyes off of the gold. Her mind couldn't take so much wealth in—and some of it might be hers—if she played this Rewa like she might a fish. Right from the outset, she had been after the gold in his purse—that and getting away from her violent mother—and now she was close to more gold than she thought existed in the whole world. Some of it *had* to come her way—it just had to.

Harep and Rewa left clear instructions for Raiysa. Stay quiet; don't untie Nikal whatever she says or promises; cut her hair; keep the horses quiet and stay hidden. They had be back by evening. Harep gave Rewa a small sack to carry. Both men made their way back through the main town gate and past the place they had camped at. Half way further round the town wall they came on another camp, better built shacks, four huddled against the wall. Men stood around a fire, waiting for hares to roast.

As Harep and Rewa walked near, both of them could feel the hostility coming from the group around the fire. Harep put on his best smile and looked for the natural leader —either physically superior or a weaselly runt with an intelligent face. The burly physique he was looking for stood head and shoulders above the rest at the back trying unsuccessfully to blend in. 'Hi there!' Harep hollered. 'We've come to buy some more hares from you. Maybe do some other trade if you've a mind to. Got any hay? What d'you say? Want to do business?'

'What have *you* got?' responded another from around the fire—not the burly one though.

'We've a few shekels to add to your purses if the price is right,' Harep hedged.

At the mention of money, the burly one came forward. 'What d'you want from us? Only hares?' he said loudly, taking over the negotiations.

'Hares, hay, mules if you can get them.'

'Mules? What d'you want with mules?' the big man asked.

'I'll pay extra if you don't ask any questions,' Harep replied. 'I don't want to know what you're doing here and I don't want to answer any questions.'

The big man pondered this a while in a silent standoff, than seemed to make his mind up. 'How many mules d'you want?' the man asked.

'Four. And as many hares as you can spare.'

'You sure you can pay?'

Harep took out a gold shekel from his purse and threw it at the big man, who caught it dexterously. He put it in his teeth and tested the malleability of the metal.

'Gold huh! Got much more of this?'

'I did say, no questions. But, yes. Enough to pay you. Can we go over there and talk,' Harep pointed to a spot well away from the rest of the group.

Cautiously, the big man ambled over to where Harep had indicated and then waited for Harep to join him.

*   *   *

As soon as Harep and his nephew had left the building, Nikal began to plead with Raiysa. 'Let me go. I can't take much more of this. You're a woman—how can you stand by and let them do this to me? I'm a princess. My father, the king, will reward you handsomely if you'll let me go.'

Raiysa smiled to herself at hearing the promise of a reward, but said nothing—just thought of the gold at the top of the stairs.

'Please!' Nikal continued. 'Have some compassion. Untie me. I won't say a word. Please let me go. I'll go mad if I stay any longer.'

'*Be quiet*!' Raiysa yelled at the distraught Nikal.

'*I won't*—I have to get out of here. Why's he doing this to me? What have I done to him that he should abduct me? I'm not an animal to be tied up like this...' She kept ranting on in this vein until Raiysa could bare it no longer and placed a gag in her mouth. She found a knife and hacked at Nikal's long brown hair. This made Nikal struggle wildly trying to somehow protect her beautiful hair. In response, Raiysa hacked with more relish. When she had shorn her, she then stuck a hood over the wriggling, struggling Nikal. She kicked the hair aside with contempt and went about her chores as if she were at home—all the while thinking of the gold she would have. All she had to do was be patient—stay out of Harep's way, do as Rewa wanted and keep quiet. She would cook and clean—and later—reap the rewards.

*   *   *

Harep faced the burly leader of the small band of brigands. They were out of earshot of the rest of his band. 'I'm sorry for what's happened to your town—I suppose you lived here before it was destroyed?'

'I had a good livelihood four weeks ago; I was the foremost blacksmith here before the Kaska destroyed it,' he conceded. 'Why d'you ask?'

'My nephew says you took a fancy to our women and horses when you sold him those hares. Listen, I'll make a deal with you. I'll get you more money than you've ever seen —if—but only if...you deal with us fairly. I dare say you could kill us, but then you won't see any money...I'll make sure of that. If you decide to try and take us, some of you will die...and frankly, there's no need for it. You were in business recently. Was it better to rob your customers, or make them pay for your work?' It was a long speech and Harep did not know if it would work, but it was worth a try. He might still have to fight—but at least this way, reason might prevail, and he might not. The big man stood for a long time staring at Harep. He turned and looked at Rewa clutching his little sack, facing the rest of the band round the fire.

'You say you can pay?' the big man looked again at the gold shekel Harep had thrown him.

'A lot more than you would get if you tried to take it from us,' and Harep bluntly returned the man's stare.

'How much—and what d'you want?'

'This is between you and me only—you get five hundred shekels, in gold. How you split it with your friends is your business. Do we have a deal?'

A smile broke out on the blacksmith's face. 'Come, have a roast hare.' He led the way to the fire and held his hands up. 'We're going to do business with them,' he indicated to Harep. 'He says he's got shekels to pay us with. We've got to start trying to get back to normal—so I've agreed we'll do business. That means leaving their women alone—and their horses. Am I making myself clear? Only if they don't pay do we get nasty.' He looked at Harep with the implied threat.

Harep smiled. 'Don't worry—we'll pay. It's easier.' The air of uncertainty persisted round the fire as they were each offered a piece of roast hare. The brigands had expected to kill these foreigners and it would take a little time for them to adjust to doing business with them instead. 'Can you pick someone,' Harep asked the leader, 'to take a message to the governor of Gaziura for us. It's urgent.'

'That'll be the miller; he's got no flour to mill right now,' the big man nodded at one of his group.

'Another thing. We need the four mules now—can that be got?' Harep asked.

'They're scattered all over the place but we'll round some up for you. Four you say. Where are you staying? We noticed you'd packed your bags and moved into town.'

'That's right. I thought it might be wise until we knew how this was gonna go. We moved into the citadel. When you get the mules, leave them tied outside.' Harep bit into the succulent roast hare. 'Good stuff, this,' he meant the hare.

'It stinks inside there,' the big man nodded at the town wall, 'with all the dead. As people return, we'll have to start cleaning the place up—burn the corpses. By the way—I can't place your accent—where're you from?'

Harep knew they would ask him so he had prepared a story. 'We're from Kizzuwatna, from the capital, Adaniya. This war is moving people about. We've been sent up here to do some business—when we finish here we're going back down.'

The big man raised his eyebrows, 'Never met any Kizzuwatna. Hmm! My name's Melu. What's yours?'

'Harep. Come, I'll give you the message I want delivered to Gaziura—and a little something as an advance— to show good faith.' The two peeled off from the fire and sauntered along the side of the town wall, followed by Rewa. Harep took the small sack Rewa carried and poked around inside. 'Melu, here's three wax tablets. I want the miller to deliver all three to the governor of Gaziura.' Then Harep pulled a small pouch with a hundred shekels inside from his shirt he had prepared for the purpose. 'That's a hundred in gold as down payment. Don't get greedy, Melu, stick to our agreement and I'll make you a rich man. Get greedy and you can say goodbye to any more.' He slipped the small pouch to the blacksmith so the others of his band wouldn't notice.

The man opened the neck and looked inside, then took in a sharp breath. 'Sod this—I thought you were pulling my leg. It's for real—well I'll be…' he beamed at Harep and Harep saw he had bought the man.

'Good! Then we understand each other.'

'You bet we do…Harep!'

Chapter Sixty-three

General Labamulis hurried up the steps of the Great Citadel to tell the king about Nikal. He dreaded the task. He rehearsed what he was going to say in his head, over and over, but it still sounded like a blow to the head with a blunt instrument. He had prevaricated in the corridors for over an hour, putting off the awful task, but now took himself in hand and was determined to give the king the news.

As he approached the Audience Hall the chamberlain told him, 'His majesty is in the small room at the back, if you're looking for him.'

'You know he sent me down to Ankuwa to find his fiancée?' he told the chamberlain.

'So!' the chamberlain responded offhandedly.

'We couldn't find her,' Labamulis told him. 'She's gone missing. I wonder…could you tell the king. I have to go and look after my men.'

'Oh no you don't! Tell him yourself. Do I look that stupid?' the chamberlain inquired.

Labamulis looked daggers at the man and pushed past him heading for the anteroom behind the throne room. He found Tudhaliyas sitting at a desk reading a dispatch. 'Sire,' he began. 'I don't know how to…' and he broke off there.

'My dear general. Good to have you back. You left the princess with her father, did you?'

'Not exactly, sire. We couldn't find her…'

Tudhaliyas looked up at the general, standing smartly at attention. 'What d'you mean by that last remark? Explain yourself.'

'Sire, we were half way to Ankuwa when we met Prince Talshura. He was coming up to Hattusas to report to you and his father that the princess has gone missing. We returned with him. I came here as quickly as I could—and the prince is down at the Yellow Castle telling his father as we speak.'

'Now wait...you mean to tell me you've lost my fiancée? How could you?'

'No sire, I haven't *lost* her...I never *found* her. The way her brother told it to me was...' he never finished.

'Where is her brother?'

'Down in the Yellow Castle...telling his father...'

Tudhaliyas threw the dispatch down and jumped up, striding quickly out of the room, followed by the general. Coming along the corridor he spied the Kaska priest with others behind him.

'Your majesty,' Mokhat called out. 'I...' he wasn't allowed to finish.

'*Just the man I'm looking for*,' the king shouted back. 'I'm hearing some ridiculous story....' Tudhaliyas saw Mokhat's grim features and knew what the general had said was true. Tudhaliyas steadied himself against the nearby wall. 'No...I thought it was some silly mistake...'

'I'm terribly sorry, sire. It's all true. Prince Talshura is down at the Yellow Castle right now, breaking the news to his father.'

The king raised a pleading stare at Mokhat, willing him to deny the story he had just heard—but the face only confirmed it. 'What happened? Someone explain...' Tudhaliyas said feebly.

Mokhat began, 'Well—you know the princess is missing. Apparently it happened during the earth tremor... you know...the one before the battle,' and Mokhat continued to tell the king his suspicions. 'I think it's our old friend Harep who's behind all this. I think he was one of the "strange gardeners." The other one would have been one of the nephews.'

'You must be right. I sent no gardeners to the Kizzuwatna garden. I'm sure of that,' Tudhaliyas insisted.

'I didn't think you had. The story sounded like it had been concocted to gain access to the household. The assassins are a devious lot.'

'What now? Why take Nikal...what has she to do with killing me? You know them. What do they want and what do we do next?' Tudhaliyas was desperate.

'My guess is we'll hear from him soon. He'll send a message asking for you to come alone to some out of the way meeting place...where he'll try to kill you. This is what I was coming to tell you...to warn you.'

'If I ever manage to get my hands on that assassin, he'll wish he'd chosen another profession. You don't happen to know where their hideout is?' Tudhaliyas asked with venom.

'Yes...the old one; but it's deserted. They all made a run for it when someone began to kill them off one by one,' Mokhat informed with a half grin.

Surprise crossed the king's face. 'What? There's someone out to get *them*? Don't tell me the assassins were being assassinated. That would be *too* good.'

'Well it's true,' Mokhat said, his smile broadening. 'Every time they elected a new leader, someone managed to get to him and do away with him. They got obsessed with the killer being one of them and deserted the castle that used to be their base. That was just after the murder of Muwatallis.'

'How is it you know all this?' Tudhaliyas asked.

'I was their priest—their spiritual guide—to my unreserved shame.' Mokhat looked apologetic. 'Me trying to help you is my way of making amends. I feel if we could just deal with this last head of the order, Harep, we might be able to close down the assassins once and for all.'

At first, Tudhaliyas looked startled and horrified at this confession, then he saw the sincerity in what Mokhat had said and felt a returning compassion for him. He would definitely need the services of this Kaska priest if he was to save his beloved Nikal.

*   *   *

Talshura was still trying to calm himself as he timidly came into the great hall where his father was talking to General Kirruwaiya.

'Ahh! There he is,' Shunashura exclaimed. 'My son! We had news from your soldiers that you'd returned. I'm just sending the general back to Adaniya with most of the army. We'll keep ten cavalry regiments with us to escort us back when we go….what's the matter? You look like you've lost a shekel and found a mina.'

'I…I'm sorry…this is difficult.' Talshura looked at the floor, took a deep breath and blurted out, 'Nikal is missing!'

'What do you mean "missing?" She always goes "missing." What's so different about this?'

'It's different this time, father. This time the Kaska priest thinks she's been deliberately abducted…by the assassin who's out to get Tudhaliyas.'

'But she always disappears—that's what she's like. Then she turns up—all apologetic.' The king couldn't take it in. 'Why does he think this is different?' The king wouldn't let himself believe anything else.

'I know father. Not this time. I looked all over for her. Every nook and cranny in the valley down there. There's no sign of her.' He told his father of the "strange gardeners," of Mokhat's suspicions. The more he talked, the longer the king's face dropped. When he had finished, both stood dejected.

The old man came and put his arms round his son's shoulders. 'I know son how close you are to her. If you feel she's still alive then I trust that. We'll find her…I'm sure we will. We must go and talk with Tudhaliyas. See what his thoughts are—console him—he's part of our family now.'

344

'That's what the priest said. He sent me down here and said I should bring you up to the main palace. I'm hoping that the priest has a plan—for Nikal's sake.'

Kirruwaiya stood listening to the conversation, shocked at the news he had just heard.

'This doesn't change your orders, general,' the king told him. 'Prepare to take the troops back to the capital. With Lukka pirates on the prowl, you're needed there more than here. Dismissed!'

The general bowed and retreated to carry out his orders. Shunashura took his son's arm and they went to the stables to get mounts for the short journey to the main castle.

Chapter Sixty-Four

Saustatar was informed on the morning of the previous day by pigeon-post from Karkamish, that Artatama had crossed the border into Mittani. His son was riding hard to the capital, leading a cavalry regiment. The horses were exhausted. It did not take a genius to work out why. The expedition had ended in disaster. What other explanation could there be? He hoped he was wrong but deep down he knew.

When that afternoon Artatama finally rode through the gates of Wassukkani and on to the citadel, walking up the palace steps, his father was waiting—in the throne room. Artatama walked the corridor and into the Audience Chamber sounding out the drum of defeat with his every step and it carried on the air all the way to the throne itself. 'Father......I....' he began in a tired voice.

'*Where is my army*?' Saustatar shouted. '*What have you done with it*?'

'But father.....'

'I gave you twenty-five thousand troops and all you've brought back with you is one regiment of cavalry. How dare you come back? Why aren't you dead?'

'Father...let me explain...'

'Explain...explain...you good for nothing! What is there to explain? I sent you up there with an army...and...and you lost me the lot.' His rage faltered for a moment as he dwelt on the enormity of the calamity.

'I've been riding flat out for nine days, father....I'm exhausted. Please...just let me tell you...'

'I ought to have you thrown in the dungeon for what you've done. How could you?' Saustatar interrupted. 'Don't you understand what you've done...we're almost defenceless now. Any of our neighbours could invade. When Egypt hears about this...what d'you think they'll do?'

Artatama gave up and sat on the floor—while the king ranted on. He listened for a while, but then lay down and placed his head on his hands and was asleep in no time. As his father seethed on.

Saustatar was also genuinely worried. What would Amenhotep do? Would he send Tuthmosis with more troops? A mere four divisions would be enough this time. As soon as he had heard news of Artatama he had ordered a general mobilisation. Recruiters were sent out to grab every able-bodied male who could wield a sword, throw a spear. Smithies were forging more weapons, uniforms were being manufactured, more horses gathered. Saustatar had to convince his neighbours and those more distant predators like Egypt that they would pay a high price if they were to think of invading Mittani. Then he noticed Artatama asleep on the floor. He jumped up angrily from the throne and was about to go and kick his son awake, when he stopped. The thoughtful moments had calmed him a little and he took pity on his only son and heir. He knew he had had a hard time of it—and suddenly he was gratified he had arrived back in one piece. He called over some guards and got them to lift the sleeping Artatama onto a palanquin and take him to his bed. His rage had left him and was replaced by a deep tenderness for his flesh and blood. Amenhotep could wait.

Chapter Sixty-Five

Riding through the night, the messenger from the governor of Gaziura reached the capital in one and a half days. Fatigued, he rode through the narrow corbelled arches of the citadel gates flanked by portal sculptures. Then into the lower paved courtyard where the stables were located. Dismounting, he gave his horse to a groom before reporting to an officer. 'I have an urgent dispatch from Gaziura for the king,' he told the officer.

The officer had been warned to expect a dispatch—but Mokhat did not know where it would come from. 'Who's it from?' the officer inquired.

'From the governor.'

'Come with me.' The officer led the courier up the stairs to the first floor where Mokhat waited with Palaiyas.

They were playing a board game as he came in. Mokhat had requested he be allowed to screen every incoming message just in case. 'Let's have a look,' he took the wax board from the courier and read the contents, anger spreading on his face as he read.

Palaiyas knew this was the message and said to the officer, 'This is it. This is what the king's waiting for. Thanks, you can go.'

The officer nodded for the courier to follow him back down the stairs.

Mokhat spat out, 'This is Harep's work. Poor thing must have been half frightened to death when she wrote this. Addressed to the King of the Hatti. Look at it,' he pushed it at Palaiyas.

Palaiyas read out loud, '"I'm being held by my kidnapper. He wants you to come alone—no soldiers—if you want to see me alive. My captive wants to talk to the Hittite king." Signed Princess Nikal of Kizzuwatna. Short and to the point.' Palaiyas scowled, 'We can't let him go like that. Someone else must go. He knows you—so it can't be you,' Palaiyas told Mokhat.

'Come, we must take this to the king.' Mokhat rose and took the wax tablet from Palaiyas and left the room. They found Tudhaliyas, Kantuzzili, Shunashura and Talshura animatingly talking in the large dining hall, sitting, drinking. 'Majesty, it's just arrived from Gaziura,' Mokhat walked up and handed the wax tablet to the Hatti king.

The message Tudhaliyas had so dreaded was finally being delivered.

*   *   *

'So it's all true,' King Shunashura said sadly. 'They have my daughter.'

'I'm afraid so,' Tudhaliyas confirmed. 'Read this for yourself.' He passed the newly delivered wax tablet to the Kizzuwatna king.

Mokhat and Palaiyas sat with Talshura round the long table each slowly sipping a goblet of wine.

Shunashura read the note from Nikal and his face dropped even further. 'It's in her hand—I recognise her wedge marks. Heartless monster!' he exclaimed, passing the note to his son.

'The way my Kaska friend here sees it,' Tudhaliyas indicated Mokhat, 'is that they're trying to lure me into single-handedly rescuing Nikal. This assassin thinks I'm stupid enough to go alone so he can kill me. On the others hand, if I turn up with a lot of soldiers, he threatens to kill her. We've got to come up with a rescue plan—one that outwits the assassin. Any ideas?' and Tudhaliyas pointedly looked at Mokhat.

Mokhat cleared his throat for everyone's attention. 'First, where are we to look? Since the message came from the governor of Gaziura, we'll start there. I suspect another clue will be waiting for us up there. Will he have spies watching us? I would. But I'm going to take a chance—and assume he hasn't enough people. So, I advise your majesty to send four cavalry regiments ahead to Gaziura. We'll travel with one regiment as escort. Once we find out where he wants us to go, only three of us will go on ahead, but…the cavalry will be close by. Sire, we need someone to lead the cavalry who's got his wits about him.'

'This is so serious,' Tudhaliyas interrupted, 'that I'm putting General Zidanta in charge of the forward expedition. He's proved himself so resourceful that I can't think of anyone more suited. For me, this is as important as the battle was.'

'Good! I approve of the choice,' Kantuzzili chipped in.

'And I,' added Shunashura. 'He's an outstanding tactician.'

Tudhaliyas' face was set in a determined scowl, 'That's settled. I suggest *we* leave tomorrow and the four cavalry regiments leave *now*, immediately.'

'I'll get Zidanta organised,' Kantuzzili offered and went to find the general.

'Thanks uncle, I appreciate it,' Tudhaliyas called after him, then turned to Shunashura sitting next to him. 'I'm truly sorry I'm the cause of so much distress to yourself and your son. I would not wish this on anybody.'

'I know—and I want you to be assured, I don't blame you. I put the blame squarely where it belongs—on that murdering thug—and the person who hired him.'

'At least I have some good news there. Muwas was executed yesterday by my command. He won't be ordering anymore assassinations.' He did not go into details.

At hearing this news, the five people sitting round the table banged the palm of their hands on the table in praise and acknowledgment of a deed well done. The mood lifted to one of satisfaction and the goblets were raised when

Shunashura proposed a toast. 'To Tudhaliyas the First—and with the help of heaven, to my future son-in-law.'

*   *   *

Two hundred cavalry escort followed Tudhaliyas, Mokhat and Palaiyas past the restored rock sanctuary and down into the plain outside the capital, heading for Gaziura. The emmer wheat was ripening in the scorching sun drenched fields. All seemed at peace with the world but Mokhat was on edge, wondering how they were to rescue Nikal from the clutches of an obsessive murderer. Assassin seemed far too polite for what Harep did. It took them a day and a night of hard riding to reach Gaziura and this time the gates were immediately thrown open to them. Having some of General Zidanta's troops inside may have helped.

When they had reached the citadel courtyard and dismounted, an officer in a yellow tunic ran up to them, 'Sire, General Zidanta's orders, I was to give you this as soon as you arrived,' and he handed Tudhaliyas a wax tablet.

The king strode up the steps to where the governor waited.

'Majesty, *I* was supposed to give you that tablet. It was left in *my* care,' the governor complained.

Tudhaliyas brushed the fat governor aside and strode through the entrance and into the great hall in front of him.

'Bring wine and some food,' Palaiyas ordered the governor who had stopped in the doorway. The fat governor wasn't used to being ignored like that—and now wasn't sure of his position. He hurried to order servants to bring the food and wine asked for, but stayed out of the king's way.

Tudhaliyas sat down and undid the ribbon on the wax tablet. He noted the seal had been broken, probably by Zidanta, then he began reading. At the end, he sat there shaking his head. 'When I get my hands on this Harep, I'll make him pay for his insolence.' He threw the tablet at Mokhat.

Mokhat read, "I'm waiting for you in a cave up the Kittes Mountains. Coming from the south there's three peaks —I'm up the one in the middle. Come alone or you won't see your precious princess alive."

'Well—what now?' the king was worried by what he had just read. 'And why wasn't this sent with the first tablet?' he demanded in the direction of the hovering governor.

The governor hurried over. 'I was ordered...by the tablet addressed to me personally, to wait till you came... before giving it to you,' he replied hesitantly.

'You might as well accept it, you're no longer the governor. I'm replacing you. Where does your allegiance lie —to me or to some murderer? You don't have any *more* tablets to give to me...later?'

The angry sarcasm wasn't lost on the fat man. 'I'm sorry, your majesty, no, there's no more messages. I thought it important to keep the sequence.'

'The note addressed to you "personally," bring it,' the king commanded.

The governor saw he had made a blunder in not sending everything to the king immediately and called for his secretary to bring the tablet. It arrived shortly and Mokhat put his hand out to receive it. 'It just says what the governor told us—no more,' he announced.

'Ex-governor,' Tudhaliyas said loudly.

Chapter Sixty-six

The next morning, Rewa heard movements outside and peered out the doorway. Despite rats running over them, he had huddled down to sleep with Raiysa near the doorway, brushing the horrid little animals off of them most of the night. Four mules were being tethered to a rail in the courtyard by three rough looking men. Rewa was standing guard, not because Harep told him to, but to safeguard *his* share of the gold.

One of the men saw Rewa and shouted, '*Melu sent this lot. All right?*'

'*Fine,*' Rewa shouted back. '*Tell him thanks.*'

'*There's food in sacks. He thought you might be able to use the provisions.*'

'*Yah! Thank him from us.*'

The men waved and left the way they had come.

Harep heard the shouting and came from the main hall where he slept on a long cedar table, out of the way of the rodents. Nikal at one end, Harep at the other. 'What's happening?' Harep asked as he came out to the doorway holding a bow and arrow at the ready.

Rewa stared at the readied bow and felt uncomfortable. 'Where did that come from?' he asked cautiously.

'What, this?' Harep asked casually. 'Picked it up off the street. Plenty of weapons lying around. You might have noticed only a month ago the town's been overrun.' The latter was sarcasm. 'So what was all that noise out here?'

Rewa pointed, 'Got the mules we wanted.'

'Good! Get your woman started on some food, will you.' Harep still hadn't called Raiysa by her name.

'Melu sent provisions as well—on the mules.' Rewa jerked his head at Raiysa, indicating she should do as Harep suggested. 'I'll bring the mules inside and put them with the horses.'

'Good man,' said Harep.

'You trust that Melu?' Rewa asked.

'About as far as I can throw him. He'll behave as long as there's gold. I've told him if he tries to grab it, there won't be any. I think he believes me.'

'Well anyway—we got the mules. We ought to load them and get on our way.' Rewa was eager to get out of the rat infested town. Raiysa kept complaining to Rewa about the rats. 'You've sent the message to the king,' Rewa continued, 'nothing stopping us moving on. We might as well get to where we're going—or should I say, where you're taking us.' The thought of the gold was making Rewa bolder. 'So, Unc, where *are* you taking us?'

'No harm in telling you now. I've a mountain cave in mind. Somewhere where I can see what's coming from a long way off—wide field of vision. No way to ambush us—and no cover. Any sign of soldiers and we can be off like the wind. Only one way up. If they try to deceive us, we go over the mountain.'

'How far is this cave?'

'Up towards Azzi country—a day or so.'

'How's this king supposed to find us? I mean us hiding in the cave an' all.'

'Look, Rewa, leave the planning to me. I've taken care of that. After we've eaten, you go load the mules and get your woman to help you. I want to be out of here before noon. I've got to see Melu and settle with him. All right?'

It was the first time in a long while Rewa had heard his name coming from Harep's mouth and it took him by surprise. All he said was, 'Right! We'll have the mules loaded by the time you get back.'

*　　*　　*

Harep insisted on seeing the leader of the ruffians, Melu, just one more time. He took him the rest of the promised five hundred shekels. He could afford to. He chose the timing carefully—around noon. Rewa was sent on his way with the bound Nikal and Raiysa. Rewa leading their riding horses and the four packed mules through the narrow alleyways of Hakpis towards the back exit. The main entrance faced Gaziura but the back exit faced north. If Harep distracted Melu, there would be less likelihood of the brigand group trying anything. By the time Melu realised they had left, Harep and his group would be far away. Melu would be rich beyond anything he could conceive, but there was no accounting for greed's insidious scheming. Melu might've insisted Harep stay within the town, hoping to milk him of more of the gold. Harep had other business to attend to.

Harep completed his transaction with Melu and promised to see him the next day. He left the satisfied blacksmith and speeded back through Hakpis, out the back exit and caught up with Rewa. On the fifth day after their arrival, they had finally left the ruined Hakpis behind them. They travelled north-east for the rest of the day in a sweltering heat. Nikal all the time complaining through her gag. By late afternoon, they could see the mountains in the far distance. When they stopped for the night in a clearing in a forest, Rewa removed her gag and straight away, she whimpered like a little child, tears rolling down her cheeks.

Rewa made a fire and Raiysa put together something to eat—mostly cold roast hare. They had been happily eating this ever since they had come to an agreement with the brigand leader. Water was still a problem—all of the town's supply had been contaminated. They had been drinking abandoned wine while they were in Hakpis but that simply made them thirstier. Throughout the day, they hadn't come across any clean drinking water. The heat had dried all the brooks. Tomorrow nearer the mountains, Harep assured his companions, there would be plenty of water coming down the gorges.

*   *   *

The forest through which they were travelling had thinned as they neared open sky and there were many exposed tree roots making it necessary to go slow in case the animals tripped. Harep led Nikal's horse, followed closely by Raiysa. Then Rewa came holding the reins of the mule train. Harep with his group were about to leave the canopy covering when the last mule in the string stumbled over one of the tree roots. Rewa swung round on his horse and saw the mule go down on its knees, then its side, jerking the next mule to a sudden halt with a concatenating effect. Harep halted and looked around at the trouble.

Rewa had jumped down and was rushing over to the struggling mule. It was trying to get up. '*Unc, we got trouble,*' Rewa yelled. What horrified Rewa was that it was *his* mule, the one with his forty sacks of gold. He desperately tried to pull it to its feet but there was something wrong with it.

Harep got off and tied his horse to a tree giving Nikal's reins to Raiysa, saying, 'Keep an eye on her,' meaning Nikal. He walked back to where Rewa was sweating and struggling to raise the mule from the ground. 'Give it up, nephew,' he told the frantic Rewa. 'Can't you see its lame.'

'It can't be—it mustn't be—I won't let it be…' and he continued pulling at the mule's reins. 'Help me Unc,' he pleaded.

'Don't be a fool. Can't you see the animal's finished. Cut its throat and be done with it. *Rewa*!' Harep yelled, '*Stop it*!'

Rewa finally heard and stopped. 'But…but…how…' he was almost in tears and sat down heavily on the ground near the distressed braying mule.

'I'm just as unhappy about this as you are, but you're going to have to transfer the gold to your own mount—and walk,' Harep remonstrated.

At the suggestion, Rewa picked up and his face brightened. 'Why didn't I think of that?' he said in wonder. 'Of course—transfer the gold.' He jumped up and began tugging at the straps.

Harep came over and clipped him sharply round the head, 'First you deal with the mule, you dunderhead. What are you waiting for? Cut its throat!'

Rewa felt the smack and looked round sharply, hand on dagger. Then he realised what Harep had said. 'Sorry Unc. Forgot! I'll do it right away.' He had put his hand on his dagger to use it on Harep, but now pulled it out as if he had always meant to use it on the mule. He went round to where the big vein stuck out on its neck and sliced through it. Harep held it down with his foot and Rewa held its head until it stopped struggling, giving a final death rattle. The legs continued to twitch from the residual nerve impulses firing uncontrollably.

'Now you can unload the gold,' Harep spat out.

'Sorry Unc. Forgot!' Rewa repeated.

Rewa stood looking in the direction Harep had taken. He felt abandoned. For the first time in a long time, he was alone. He had always had his little brother with him, until Harep killed him. Then there was Harep with him all the time and now Raiysa was his constant companion. Always someone to keep him company. Harep had told him where to follow him, but to make sure he did, he insisted on taking Raiysa with him and regardless of Rewa's predicament, on pushing ahead to the mountain cave. Raiysa had been reluctant to go, but Rewa made it clear he wanted her to go along with Harep. It was the way Harep suggested it. "She's coming with me," in a tone of voice that brooked no argument, not without a fight.

He stared at his horse, loaded with all forty sacks of gold, looking overloaded and uncomfortable. *I wonder if I dare,* went through Rewa's befuddled mind. He led the horse to a fallen tree and got on the trunk, holding the reins. Then he climbed on its back. He desperately wanted to catch up with Harep and Raiysa. He couldn't bear to think of her alone with Harep. He nudged the horse forward and it hesitantly took a number of steps—then a few more—before stumbling to the ground on its forelegs. Rewa went over its neck and cracked his head on a tree stump that knocked him out cold. He lay there unconscious with the horse on its side as lame as the mule he had just had to kill.

Chapter Sixty-seven

When Prince Hapu, the Egyptian Ambassador to the Hittite Court, informed pharaoh of Tudhaliyas' great victory, Amenhotep immediately sent his congratulations and a ship to Adaniya loaded with gifts and gold from the famous Nubian goldmines. The goods were to be transported on to Hattusas. He sent another note to his ambassador with instructions to propose a formal treaty of friendship and a way of cementing the alliance. Maybe a Hittite noblewoman, a relative of the king, could come and join his harem. He would leave the arrangements to the ambassador.

Pharaoh sat in his palace in Waset with his Djat and a few of his generals, musing as to how to use the turn of events to his advantage. Dancing girls gyrated on the floor in front of them to the sound of drums, flutes and lyres. 'It might be worthwhile if you suggested to King Ashurbelnisheshu of Assyria that it's a good time for him to free himself of the Mittani chains while the Mittani army is shattered,' pharaoh told his first minister above the music.

'Sire, I will be pleased to forward your insightful idea as soon as I reach my scribes—or would you have me do it now?' his Djat inquired.

'Let's relax for the moment, but do it as soon as you get a chance.'

'As you command, so I obey, beloved of Horus,' the minister responded.

Chapter Sixty-eight

Mokhat and Palaiyas were out front acting as scouts through the forest, while Tudhaliyas led the two cavalry regiments a little distance to their rear. They had picked up the regiment left behind in Gaziura by Zidanta, who had sped off to the north towards Hakpis, so they were told, supposedly chasing after Harep.

'What instructions does Zidanta have?' Palaiyas asked Mokhat, puzzled as to what the general was up to. 'If he's not careful, he'll make more problems than he'll solve.'

'I don't know what his instructions are, but he's a wily fellow. I'm sure he'll go carefully.' Mokhat pulled a face at having to answer the question. 'I only know what that ex-governor of Gaziura told us. He's gone to see if he can prevent the assassins from reaching the mountains. Waste of time if you ask me. Harep's had a good head start and must be up the Kittes by now.'

'You know where these mountains are?'

'We're not far from Hakpis now, when we pass it you'll see them.' From the direction of Hakpis a cloud of dust could be seen as though a lot of riders were approaching. 'My hunch is you can ask the general himself what his instructions were,' Mokhat added with a smile.

Mokhat was right, General Zidanta appeared from the dust cloud and slowed for the scouts. 'We've got something to show you,' he shouted at Mokhat. As the riders passed, Mokhat saw they had a prisoner. Zidanta rode up to the king and saluted.

'Good to see you general,' Tudhaliyas greeted.

'Sire, I have news of the princess,' the general informed.

'Good or bad news?'

'A bit of both.'

'Well? Out with it, man.'

* * *

'Are you sure there were two women with them?' Tudhaliyas pressed the hapless blacksmith.

'Yes, your majesty—two men, two women. The leader, an older man, called himself Harep. There was a younger man with him.'

'What were the women like? Describe them.' Tudhaliyas was anxious to know.

The blacksmith was diffident, 'Both young, but the one they kept hidden looked like she was crying and being kept prisoner.'

'Was she well, not injured?' Tudhaliyas wanted to squeeze every bit of information out of this big man.

'As far as I could tell, sire, neither was injured.'

Mokhat stood to the side listening to the prisoner Zidanta had brought back.

'There should have been three men and one woman—now it seems there's two couples. No wonder we couldn't find them. We didn't even have the right description of them,' Palaiyas complained into Mokhat's ear.

'And when did they leave?' Tudhaliyas was relentless.

'The day before yesterday, around noon. Sneaked out the back way they did—without so much as a bye-your-leave.' The blacksmith was sweating.

The king turned to Zidanta. 'Hang on to this fellow. He might know more than he's telling. Did you hear that? We're two days behind. We've got to get going.'

'How'd you know all this?' Mokhat took over the interrogation while Zidanta calmed the king.

At the sight of the priest, the blacksmith felt a measure of relief, 'I did some business with them, sold them some food, some mules.'

'What were the mules for?'

'How should I know?' the big man began to reassert himself.

'You must have had some idea,' Mokhat persisted.

'They came to find something in Hakpis. That's my guess. Whatever it was—they must've found it—loaded it on the mules and scarpered as quickly as they could.' The blacksmith was still alive and nearly insolent. He was sure he'd be dead by now.

Zidanta managed to convince the king that speed was not the essence, but good intelligence mattered more.

'We have to outfox him. At least that's the general's opinion. What do you think?' Tudhaliyas asked Mokhat.

'I think the general is right. We can't go charging on after him. If we caught up with him, say on the road—what's he likely to do? I think he'd panic, kill the princess and make a run for it. No! I advise caution,' Mokhat counselled.

'Oh well then, we'll go on cautiously.' It was hard on Tudhaliyas, being cautious.

*   *   *

Zidanta's scouts heard a commotion coming from somewhere in the forest and went to investigate. Wolves were howling from that direction.

'What mischievous sprite has stirred them up?' shouted Palaiyas to Mokhat.

'We'll soon know,' Mokhat responded.

Tudhaliyas rode side by side with Zidanta, deep in conversation, oblivious of the furore. When the large party rode abreast of the disorder, scouts were returning with a dishevelled young man among them, obviously relieved at having been rescued.

Mokhat took one look and yelled to the scouts, 'Hold him fast. He's one of them.'

362

The scouts moved to grab the man and he managed to stab one of them with a previously unseen dagger he held up his sleeve. Other soldiers jumped off their horses and raced to help their colleagues. Soon he was disarmed and roughly brought before Mokhat. The king dismounted as did the general. A small group surrounded the dishevelled youth. 'Bind him!' the general ordered. Soldiers brought rope and hurriedly carried out the general's command.

'You were with Harep in Nerik,' Mokhat informed the youth, staring into his face. 'In the market place. I only caught a glimpse, but I remember you. One of Harep's nephews if I'm not mistaken.'

The youth struggled but he hadn't the strength to loosen his captors grip.

Mokhat said menacingly, 'Let me see, now. If I remember rightly, your name is....Rewa.' Mokhat had seen him in the fortress.

Rewa nodded reluctantly and sullenly.

'What were you doing in there?' Mokhat meant the forest.

'Trying not to get eaten.' Rewa answered impudently, beginning to reassert himself.

Mokhat thought Rewa wasn't going to give him anymore information and went to find the lead scout who had first came across him. He found him in a group snatching a quick meal. 'Where'd you find him?' he jerked at Rewa.

'Up a tree with wolves howling round the bottom,' the officer informed Mokhat. 'I'd say he's been up there quite a while. He was overjoyed to see us when we chased off the wolves.'

Mokhat went back to Rewa. 'Where's Harep?' he asked bluntly.

Rewa was no longer afraid and spat on the ground, suggesting that that was his reply.

'I'd like to see you do that when they lop off your head,' Mokhat held the young man's gaze.

Rewa shifted uncomfortably while two soldiers held on to him.

Mokhat said in Kaska, 'Whatever you were up to—it's over for you.' Then he took him by the neck with his right hand. 'Get that through your thick skull. We can execute you here and now, or take you back to Hattusas—but only if you cooperate. Am I getting through to you?'

Rewa was surprised to hear the Kaska tongue. He still had no idea who Mokhat was—no memory of him. He looked closer at Mokhat, only then seeming to recognise the ministering priest to the assassins. He pulled back, shocked at seeing the priest here with the Hatti king. 'What are *you* doing here?' he expelled.

'Never mind that—where's Harep? Where's the princess?'

Rewa's world was falling apart. If he died here, he would lose the gold—and Raiysa. He ought to try and save himself. 'Harep has her. He's taken her to a cave up the Kittes Mountains. It's all in the message he left.'

'Is she all right? And who's this other woman with her?' Mokhat was trying to restrain himself.

'She's safe for now. She won't be for long. He's gonna kill her as soon as he kills the king,' retorted Rewa.

'You stupid boy, you think we'd allow that to happen?' Palaiyas cut in. He had been following Mokhat's interrogation. 'Thousands have just died for this new king of ours, and do you really think we'd allow some lone assassin to just kill him like that? Grow up man!

Chapter Sixty-Nine

Rewa lay where he fell, comatose for a whole day and a night before regaining consciousness. He woke the following morning with the dawn chorus. A blinding headache blurred his vision. He opened his eyes and felt disorientated. Some animal nearby scuttled away. For an instant he had no idea where he was. He gave a dry retch and tried to vomit with overpowering nausea. Worst of all, when he did focus, he found his horse lying dead where he had fallen. He screwed up his face in pain and rubbed the spot where he had hit. Caked blood. It had spread on his scalp in a sizable area. He shook his head to clear his vision but then winced with the overwhelming pain. A growl came from somewhere making his ears prick up. With difficulty he got to his feet and tried to locate where the animal was. Animals. *Why hadn't they attacked?* he wondered. A small pack of wolves milled around in the distant trees. They directed more growling and snarling in his direction. *Maybe they're not that hungry.* He drew his dagger and looked for something to throw at them. He bent and picked up a stone, but almost keeled over with the effort. As he stood, the scene swam hazily in front of him and he rubbed his eyes.

When his vision cleared he threw the stone at the pack and they backed off a few paces. *This won't do*, he told himself. He went over to the horse and gingerly began unloading the sacks of gold. *Damned stupid fool*, he chided himself. *Whatever possessed me?* He dug a pit with his hands in the forest floor and began to bury the sacks. When he had finished he marked the place with a cairn and sat and pondered, *What the Yarris am I to do now?*

* * *

Harep reached the base of the Kittes Mountains, him tugging on the reins of Nikal's mount and Raiysa pulling the reins of the lead mule. They had stopped for water in the clear stream cascading down from upon high. Both humans and animals drank thirstily. Earlier they had gathered lots of wood for the cave fire and loaded it on the mules.

Raiysa was close to a lot of gold but did not feel safe with Harep. She filled a water skin and handed it to him. She thought she could control Rewa, but not Harep. He had murdered her mother with such ease as if he were scratching himself. Brutality she understood, but that went beyond brutality.

Her uncertain predicament made her morose and Harep noticed. He ignored her together with Nikal's whimpering and gazed up at the middle peak. Somewhere up there was his cave. There he hoped to ensnare the lone Hittite king into it and complete his mission. Then he could retire. He had been up there only once before and then he was hiding from Assyrian mercenaries who were after him for murdering their merchant master. That was two years ago. After filling all their water skins, Harep dismounted and went up on foot leading his horse. Nikal was tied with a long rope to the neck of her horse and forced to walk—her horse pulling her along. She made more whimpering sounds but had no choice. Climbing the mountain took the rest of that afternoon. Late in the afternoon Harep spied the mouth of the cave three quarters of the way up. He removed his bow and strung an arrow. The last time he had had to evict a mountain lion—he wasn't taking any chances this time. Guardedly he approached the mouth of the cave, listening for movements from inside. It was occupied. He heard a loud deep growl which could only be another lion. It might even be the same one he had thrown out previously. 'Soon have the bugger out,' he announced to no one in particular.

He went back and gathered a couple of torches he had brought from Hakpis and lit one with tinder kept going in an earthenware pot. He then lit some wood, starting a fire going in the open. With more wood going on the fire he took a couple of short logs, poured a little oil on them and as they flared, lobbed them inside the cave. A flurry of flapping wings was followed by a number of bats flying out of the cave. 'Come on out, you're in my new home!' he joked, more for his own amusement. 'Follow the bats, my beauty…' he added. The growling in the cave got louder as he lobbed more lit wood inside. Smoke began coming from the entrance and without warning a huge bronze coloured lioness came bounding out. 'There you go my beauty! Find some other place to live!'

Harep went into the smoky darkness and gathered the thrown in wood into a neat fire deep inside the cave trying to exorcise the cold and slightly clammy air. Returning, he pulled the reluctant animals inside, Nikal's horse pulling her in. Raiysa had to struggle to get the mules in, they being stubborn animals and did not like the smell of the cave. They could probably still smell the odour of the mountain lion.

*　　*　　*

Harep was watching Raiysa put together some food for the three of them for the evening meal. The cave was large with loose rocks on the floor covered liberally with bat dung. To the right, against the wall, parts were muddy where water had seeped in and settled. Outside the contrast could not be greater, summer was upon them and the sun beat down mercilessly. Nikal was put out of the way, tied up at the back of the cave, hands and feet. She was shivering in the cold.

'If that nephew of mine hadn't overloaded his mule, he'd be here right now,' Harep told her. 'Don't worry, like a bent mina, he'll turn up. He's as stubborn as his uncle.'

In response, Raiysa did not say a word. She just busied herself with stirring the porridge for what was left of their little group. All she could do was hope that this horrid uncle was right—that Rewa would soon arrive. Then everything would be all right again.

'It's a funny old world,' Harep informed her, becoming chattier. 'All this greed! You chasing my nephew for his gold, me chasing the Hittite king for the same reason. It's a bit like going around in circles.'

Raiysa still kept her mouth shut. She felt that if she began to answer back, she would have a hard time stopping. Her nerves were frayed. Her attention was distracted by the roar outside the cave.

'*That damned lion's back*!' shouted Harep. He ran to where he had put the bow and arrows, quickly stringing one and warily going to the cave entrance. He loosed off one arrow, followed by another. 'Missed the bugger. Better sleep right at the back of the cave tonight. We'll have to take turns to keep the fire going.' Harep cleared the loose rocks on cave floor and bedded down a distance from the horses and mules, while Raiysa curled up near Nikal trying to comfort her now *her* gold was somewhere else. She lay thinking of Rewa and earnestly hoped he would arrive sometime the next day.

During the night the mountain lion kept vigil outside the cave deterred only by the fire near the entrance. By dawn all had quietened prior to the onset of another day. A day that passed without incident—without Rewa's arrival, making Raiysa more miserable—without the mountain lion pestering them—a day when Harep prepared to receive and deceive the Hittite king.

Night followed day and the tension rose in the cave. The clammy air inside was depressing and no amount of flames seemed to make a difference. All sat huddled round the dwindling fire. Something about the limestone structure of the cave seemed to keep the hot air outside from entering. Harep was on edge, Nikal cried while Raiysa put her arm round her shoulder and made herself more miserable thinking of the gold slipping out of her grasp. 'Can't you keep her quiet?' Harep threw at Raiysa.

'Not while she's alive,' Raiysa said almost inaudibly.

Harep said, 'Hmm!' surprised she had answered him at all. 'We'll have to see about that.'

Chapter Seventy

Late afternoon on the second day after Harp had entered the cave, the three regiments led by King Tudhaliyas reached the base of the Kittes Mountains. They had ridden long and hard, trying to keep out of sight as they neared the mountains, but with so many it was difficult. Palaiyas had intervened with the king on behalf of Rewa and asked he be given charge of him. Tudhaliyas was of a mind to execute him on the spot back in the forest, but Mokhat persuaded the king to grant Palaiyas' request. He might come in use in prising Harep out of his mountain cave.

Young Rewa was thoroughly dejected, feeling events slithering away out of his control. The gold was buried out of reach but then he did not expect to survive his captivity. They had promised him as much. That meant a sad farewell to Raiysa and any future with her. It had all gone wrong as far as Rewa was concerned and Palaiyas encouraged that belief with various threats.

At the bottom of the middle mountain, Zidanta was instructed to take most of the six hundred troops and surround the entire base. 'I don't want him to escape no matter what happens. Circle the base,' Tudhaliyas ordered the general. 'I'll keep my Mešedi with me. They'll be enough.' They left their mounts at the bottom with some of the bodyguards and began the ascent on an uphill path, keeping low. Mokhat went in front, Palaiyas followed and Tudhaliyas brought up the rear with ten Mešedi. Rewa was gagged and bound, being hauled along by two huge Mešedi. The going was difficult forcing them to travel single file.

A small crevasse ran vertically down the mountain side and Mokhat held his hand up hearing a muffled bleating.

'What's the matter?' Palaiyas whispered.

'There's something in the chasm to the right. See... there!' Mokhat told him in a whisper.

Palaiyas drew his sword and went to have a look. He disappeared down into the earth. A hand came up signalling for them to come and see. When Mokhat reached him, he found a shepherd in the crevasse with about twenty goats, anxiously making an effort to keep the animals subdued.

Mokhat went down to talk with him, in Kaska, to calm him.

'What's he doing hiding in here?' Palaiyas wanted to know.

'Just that! He saw such a large group of soldiers that he thought it safer to hide his flock—just in case they took them for food.' Mokhat was still reassuring the frightened shepherd. 'He says he always brings the flock up to the high pastures this time of year—it's cooler up here and the grass is lush. He says he stays in a cave high up on this mountain. It must be the same cave Harep's in.'

'Why don't we use the goats as cover?' Palaiyas suggested.

'What cover? How can you.....?' he broke off as he saw the possibility. 'You mean use them to get closer to the cave?'

'You have it. As I said before—Harep knows you so it's got to be me.'

'What about your accent? He'll know you're not Kaska.'

'I'll just have to be careful not to talk too much. Can't be the king—so no one's left. Ask the shepherd if we can swap clothes. Then I'll go up and claim the cave. I might be able to get inside.' The shepherd was in no position to say no and handed over the flea infested goat skin garment.

'After you've got him chatting, I'll come up and try to talk him into surrendering,' Mokhat said. 'As his spiritual advisor—I have a right to try. I might be able to distract him while you look after Nikal—if you can get into the cave.'

Chapter Seventy-One

As sunlight breached the mouth of the cave the following morning, Harep came out and stood in the warmth, peering down at the base of the mountain. The trail was clear below but he thought he saw movement far down to the left. It held his attention. He stared at the spot until he saw a goat coming up towards him—followed by more goats. 'What the blazes? Hey! Anybody there?' Harep called out in Kaska. In response, he heard more bleating of goats and the sound of stones falling down the mountain. As the goats neared, Harep made out a torso and a dark human head sticking out of the flock. When Palaiyas became visible and neared the cave, Harep called out in Kaska, 'What d'you want up here? Go away!'

Palaiyas shouted back in his guttural Hatti, 'What are ye shouting at me for? What are ye doing up here? 'Ere, you're in my cave!'

'Your cave, who says so?' Harep asked in Hatti.

'I say so! Each summer I brings my goats up here into the high pastures and every night I spends my nights in that there cave. So you tell me, stranger, who's got more right to it? I live in these parts. I don't recognise you.'

'And I don't know you. *Go away*!' Harep shouted angrily.

'*You* go away!' Palaiyas shouted back just as loudly. 'It's my cave! Go find your own cave. You can't just come and take someone's cave like that.'

Mokhat was further down, lying flat against the loose stones of the mountain, listening, admiring the exchange—and Palaiyas' performance.

Reluctantly Harep said, 'Come up here, let's talk this over.' He thought it best to kill the shepherd. No one would miss him. Palaiyas was aware Harep might try something of the sort and approached watchfully, pushing the flock before him. Harep stood at the mouth of the cave.

Palaiyas came forward to within ten cubits leaning on his shepherd's staff. He stopped where Harep was not able to reach him. The goats wandered inside the cave as if they knew what they were doing.

'All right,' Harep said slyly, kicking a stone carelessly downwards. 'Tell you what, why not both of us use the cave —it's big enough. What d'you say? You go in the back and I'll have the front—I'm expecting visitors.'

'I see you've a dagger in your hand. Is that for me?' Palaiyas asked trying to be innocent.

'Get rid of your staff and I'll put away my dagger.'

Mokhat had crawled in as close as he dare, moving each stone carefully out of his path, in behind the goats, finding cover in a shallow ridge just stopping in hearing distance. He heard the conversation and picked out a largish stone, throwing it over to his left, Harep's right. As Mokhat lobbed the stone so Palaiyas threw his staff inside the cave. Harep heard the stone fall and quickly glared in that direction. This gave Palaiyas the chance he had been looking for and he swiftly forward somersaulted into the cave past Harep in pursuit of his staff.

Harep wheeled about sharply on the gravel facing Palaiyas, who was now on his feet holding his staff again. 'You're no shepherd,' Harep spat out. He had seen the shepherd move like a fighter and his anger rose.

Palaiyas glanced inside the darkness and discerned a frightened young woman with her back against the wall on his right. Animals noises came from somewhere at the back of the cave.

'What d'you want?' Harep demanded. He knew he had been outmanoeuvred, but by whom?

'*Harep*!' came a familiar voice from outside the cave. 'I want to talk with you,' Mokhat spoke in Kaska. Mokhat had decided to make his move.

Palaiyas moved closer to Harep, staff at the ready.

For an instant, Harep screwed up his face trying to place the voice. Then recognition hit him. 'Is that you Mokhat?' he called out.

'Your spiritual advisor come to advise you,' Mokhat said playfully.

Harep turned to look for the priest and Palaiyas moved in with his staff. An expert with the long pole, Palaiyas lifted the staff bottom end first and hit Harep sharply in the groin. Harep yelled in pain, 'Argh, you shite!' and threw the dagger at the so-called shepherd.

Palaiyas was expecting it and moved rapidly aside. In a counter move Palaiyas gave Harep a second swift blow on the side of the head. That put Harep down and he grabbed his skull. Mercilessly Palaiyas thwacked him again to the side of the cranium hoping to knock him out.

Mokhat came running in to see Palaiyas administer the last blow.

'*Arghh-h-h*!' shrieked the young woman with her back to the wall—and then fainted onto the floor of the cave.

Mokhat rushed past Palaiyas looking for Nikal. He found her gagged, bound hand and feet, at the back of the cave. Quickly he removed her gag and undid her bindings. She hadn't even the energy left to say a word; she simply whimpered. She had watched the fight and saw Harep go down, but being emotionally exhausted, she did not feel anything.

Tudhaliyas came running in followed by his Mešedi, including the two dragging Rewa along. The king almost sprinted to where Mokhat held Nikal. 'My poor darling,' he knelt down on the loose stones and took her from Mokhat into his own arms.

At hearing his voice she burst out crying and buried her head in his shoulder. 'Oh Tudhaliyas...it was so horrible,' she sobbed.

'You're safe now....shush there...you're safe.' He soothed.

She wept into his shoulder as a child might when woken from a nightmare. He made soothing noises in return.

'There, there! Hush now, it's all over. We're going home.' Tudhaliyas rocked her in his arms.

Rewa spied Raiysa lying unconscious and struggled with his captors, pleading with his eyes. Palaiyas nodded to the Mešedi and they undid his gag but not his bonds and let him go to her. He knelt on the cave floor and put his mouth near her ear. 'Raiysa...Raiysa...wake up,' frantically he called.

She stirred and sat up. Seeing his face she grabbed him round the shoulders oblivious of the bindings.

Mokhat noticed Harep waking up and nudged Palaiyas to hold him. 'We need to secure him or he'll make trouble,' Mokhat asserted.

Palaiyas undid Rewa and used the rope to tie Harep firmly. Tudhaliyas was leading Nikal from the back of the cave and was oblivious to what was occurring. She was trying to hide her shorn hair with a scarf.

Mokhat interrupted him, 'Sire, may I ask a favour?'

'Anything! I owe you so much.' Tudhaliyas gazed lovingly at Nikal. 'We're going back to the capital to arrange for Tagrama to perform a marriage ceremony. You're invited, of course. Sorry! What favour?'

'I'd like you to pardon this boy,' he motioned at Rewa. Mokhat's sharp eyes had watched Rewa holding Raiysa and felt sorry for him. 'Look at him. I don't think he's going to do anymore killing,' and Mokhat pointedly stared at Rewa, 'are you?'

Rewa heard his name and shook his head, 'I promise I'll behave...honest.'

'We've had so much death in recent weeks, I thought we might give life a small chance.'

Tudhaliyas listened to the entreaty, then looked to Nikal for guidance. She just nodded. 'Very well,' he agreed. 'I give him to you. Do as you see fit with him.'

Rewa lifted Raiysa from the floor and put his arm round her waist to support her and walked slowly out of the cave with her leaning on him.

Tudhaliyas waited an instant, then said, pointing at Harep, 'He's also yours to do as you will. As I understand it, he's one of your flock.' Then the king and Nikal slowly left, him holding her tightly, protectively, she leaning against him for support.

'I love you...but you must know that by now,' Nikal whispered in his ear. Then she looked sad for an instant as a memory flashed into her mind. 'I will miss Talarra, poor dear.'

Tudhaliyas led Nikal out of the cave with the Mešedi following. The bodyguards led out the three horses and mules. The gold had been repacked and was to be returned to the ruined town—to be used for rebuilding it. The goats remained at the back of the cave for the shepherd to pick up when he managed to catch up with them. A generous sack of gold had been left for him as recompense for his help.

Mokhat made a lifting motion with his right hand. Palaiyas understood the signal and pulled Harep to his feet to face Mokhat. The priest gazed pityingly at one of his flock and dug inside his cloak, looking for something. From inside, he pulled out a small bulbous pottery container with a stopper and showed it to Harep.

'Yaah, so what? What are you showing me?' Harep was furious and looked daggers at Mokhat. All his careful planning had come to nought.

Harep struggled but Palaiyas held him tight.

Mokhat said slowly, 'I keep this with me all the time. Remember Molut...and Walhape?'

Harep frowned, but then it suddenly dawned on him what was being said. '*Yo-u-u-u-u...*' he screeched. 'It can't be...it was you...but why....?'

'Yes, Harep,' Mokhat interrupted. 'It *was* me! And now for the last head of the Assassin's Guild.' Mokhat had a grim satisfaction on his face. 'Palaiyas, grip him tight.'

'*W—h—y*......?' Harep repeated, his cry echoing through the clammy air of the cave.

Mokhat had picked up a stick from the cave floor and pushed it in Harep's mouth, forcing him to open his clenched teeth. Then he pulled his hair, forcing his head back and poured the contents of the vessel into his mouth, removing the stick, holding his nose and mouth closed. Harep had little choice but to swallow. He choked, coughed, then tried to spit it out but it was too late. The toxin was on its way to his stomach.

'*Ahhh*......*you*......*you*......' Harep's eyes glazed with those last stammers.

Mokhat spoke softly to the dying assassin. 'Can you hear me? You've the poison of a deadly mushroom inside you. A recipe courtesy of my brother, King Kasalliwa. A purified fluid, tasteless and without smell. The result is deadly. Did you know he was head of the Assassin's Order before he became king of the Kaska?'

Harep slumped at the last words and Palaiyas let him drop to the stony floor.

'I hereby dissolve the Assassin's Guild.' Mokhat dropped the pottery vessel, smashing it on the rock floor of the cave. 'Oh! How clumsy of me!' he smiled sadly at the debris.

Palaiyas looked down at the shards and said, 'Is that it? Have we finished?'

In an overwhelmingly tired voice, Mokhat replied, 'Yes...I think so. With Harep dead, it *ought* to be the end of the Assassin's Guild. Let's go home.'

END

Madduwatta's Rebellion

Sasha Garrydeb

This is the second volume of the Hittite Trilogy and scheduled for publication in February 2011. The 3rd volume is due in 2012.

It has been three years since the Battle of the Plateau put Tudhaliyas on the throne in the Hittite Empire, yet instead of feeling secure, he feels menaced. His chief spy, Satipilli, has vanished, and trouble is brewing in the west, possibly from Ahhiyawa. The Mittani are threatening Ishuwa on the eastern border, seeking revenge for their humiliation in the civil war. All this requires reliable intelligence reports. Tudhaliyas is forced to turn to the unknown faces of Mokhat and Palaiyas and asks them to go to the west, to Millawanda, and discover what has happened to Satipilli, the chief spy of the Hittites.

On their journey, they are followed and someone keeps trying to kill them; with each failure, their attempts become more desperate. The assassins follow Mokhat and Palaiyas but are finally dissuaded; then they suddenly reappear in Khemet (Egypt). Somebody doesn't want them to complete their mission.

At the close of the Old Kingdom in 1417 BC, Madduwatta, the Governor of Lukka, a nominal vassal of Tudhaliyas, has plans of his own. How is he implicated in all this? He has his eyes on Arzawa. He badly needs friends, and will ally himself with anyone prepared to help him achieve his goal. But who has stirred him up? Who has gone to all these lengths to create a rebellion for the Hittites?

Meanwhile, Ahhiyawa is in the grip of a Civil War, with two brothers fighting it out for the throne in Millawanda. The outcome of the conflict will impact on their neighbours, Arzawa, the Hittites, and the Governor of Lukka.

Palaiyas, a Prince of Tiryns, decides to go home to make peace with his father, the king. While in Tiryns, he's abducted by his uncle, Elektryon, the king of Mycenae, and brought to account for his desertion; then forced to complete his tour of duty on Keftiu (Crete). Mokhat follows him and rescues him. After Khemet (Egypt), Ugarit, and Lukka, they finally discover the truth. Mokhat falls in love in this romp through the ancient Med, all in a search for Satipilli.

The Wizard of Kalar

Sasha Garrydeb

On the distant planet of Kalár the two hundred year old life cycle of the Schánda once again menace the idyllic lives of the Boláni, a small tribal village of forest dwellers living in their hollowed Lándo trees.

The schánda stand half a cubit high, have a two hundred year life-cycle and normally live up on the northern edges of the tundra of the planet of Kálar. They are an insect, something like a cross between a spider and a scorpion. The adult form has no poisonous stinger and isn't carnivorous. Then the mating urge mutates the schánda into a massive swarm of ferocious carnivores. It doubles in size, grows the stinger and large claws in its fourth and final moult, then begins its long march from its home-ground in the North of Kálar, south to its mating grounds on the shores of the Golden Sea.

In its path live the small peaceful Bólani tribe who make their homes in living Lándo trees in the forest. Around the same time as the schánda begin their journey, the Bólani's collective unconscious, an imbedded memory of these carnivorous insects, triggers nightmares. They dream of an unstoppable carnivorous procession intent on eating their way to their mating grounds, heading their way.

The Bólani must gather their possessions and flee ahead of the encroaching swarm. They escape south to the shores of the Golden Sea just ahead of the voracious insects. Their long march to the shores of the Golden Sea takes them through a series of adventures with small blood sucking insects, vicious storms, predatory birds, unfriendly villages, lakes of volcanic lava, and desert worms. Only the skill of their apprentice wizard, Morác, saves them from disaster—transforming his powers in the process. Even when they reach the Golden Sea their problems are not at an end. Imprisoned by a coastal tribe and then buffeted by storms on their flimsy rafts the dynamics of the tribe are changed forever before they finally manage to return to their small forest village back up in the far North.

This is an eco-fantasy tale stretching the imagination beyond the solar system.

Worlds Beyond Ours

Sasha Garrydeb

In the fourth millennium humans finally invent the warp-drive and set out to explore the Galaxy. The first mission is sent to our nearest star, Alpha Centauri, and the starship returns to a stormy acclaim by earth's population. It then comes as a shock to our planet when aliens visit earth and announce that the Galactic Federation intends to lift its quarantine around the Solar System. Since humans now have warp drive capability, would they like to join the Galactic Federation?

This story brings humanity for the first time into contact with a variety of alien life-forms: elfin-like creatures, dinosauroids, insectoids, and many more, when Earth's Embassies are sent to other worlds. As the humans fan out from their home world they encounter a number of adventures which shape humanity's future for generations to come. Wonders like floating cities in the sky, terraforming other planets and genetic advertising.

The story at the end comes full circle when it culminates in another first contact, but this time from our neighbouring galaxy for this Galactic Federation.

Printed in Great Britain
by Amazon